OPERATION DAMOCLES

"Louder, Colonel Brinkmann! Head high! *Whom must we primarily serve?*"

"*Our people, and our Führer Adolf Hitler.*"

"With pride, Colonel Brinkmann! With *conviction!* Now, *why do we obey?*"

"*From inner conviction—*"

"Precisely!" snapped Tempel. "Show your *conviction!* Remember, you are not *pretending* to be an SS officer—you are *learning* to be an SS officer.... *The more successful you are in this role, the more you will help to destroy Hitler!*"

The Damocles Sword

The Damocles Sword

Elleston Trevor

PLAYBOY
PAPERBACKS

To
Jean-Pierre

1

LONDON, JULY 1939

The gates of the palace were opened at 3:15 in the afternoon, a few moments after Big Ben had chimed the quarter, and within twenty minutes the parking area of the forecourt was full, and traffic began flowing into Wellington Barracks. Along the Mall the police were watching for the windscreen stickers and directing the guests into parking lanes. The sunshine was hot and the air sultry and, in their summer dresses and wide floppy hats, the women were more fortunate than the men in their dark formal suits. By a quarter to four the pavements were crowded along the Mall, Birdcage Walk and Buckingham Gate. Ten thousand people had received invitations, and more than eight thousand were expected to attend.

Shortly before four o'clock a retriever was caught in the traffic jam and run over, and its squealing pierced the nerves of the people nearby until a policeman put the animal out of its misery. One woman fainted and had to be given first aid. The crowds moved on toward the palace, now hurrying.

The band of the Coldstream Guards struck up the National Anthem as the royal family appeared from the Garden Entrance promptly at four o'clock, and within a few minutes the king moved off, escorted by the Lord

7

Chamberlain, leaving the two princesses with their mother as the presentations began. Not long afterward, the guests began converging slowly on the refreshment areas, some of them to await the arrival of the king at His Majesty's tea tent. Everyone complained of the heat, and, of course, of the international situation, though voices were lowered in the vicinity of the Diplomatic Tent. It was noticed that the German Ambassador had few people around him, and in any case seemed in no mood for light conversation.

The civil band had now taken over from the military for a while, and many of the guests found the music cheerful.

"It's up to Mr. Chamberlain," a lady in mauve was saying. "He'll do it again, of course—he's more clever than some people give him credit for." She patted gently at the perspiration below the brim of her muslin hat, and noticed that Lady Barbara had brought that *awful* child again this year, the one with the whining voice. The girl wasn't *ready* yet for royal occasions.

Conversation drifted across the crowded lawns, most of it desultory as the guests moved ceaselessly, trying to catch a glimpse of the royal family.

"Absolutely pathetic," a young chargé d'affaires was saying quietly near the Diplomatic Tent. "Every bomber was obsolete and they're still using biplanes for fighters, except for half a dozen new ones. My host kept on apologizing to me, for some reason. The thing is, if Hitler decides to go into Poland, their air force won't stop him."

"Then I suppose we'll have to."

"We'll have to try."

King George moved quietly among his guests, the Lord Chamberlain introducing him to those he had not met before. He smiled for them punctiliously, though it was noticed that he looked tired, and sometimes glanced across the lawns to where the queen's party was moving, as if he missed the comfort of her presence.

This afternoon, however, his stutter was hardly noticeable, thanks to his constant efforts to overcome it.

Over by the general tea tent a small throng had gathered, attracted by raised voices. Lady ffoulks-Barrington had fallen, valiantly trying to curtsy at the age of eighty-three. A first-aid unit of the Navy was quickly called to the spot, and the queen was seen to be upset, feeling she was herself the cause of the accident. A stretcher was brought for the fallen guest, who seemed to be in some pain, and it was a few minutes before the queen could continue to greet people with her customary charm.

The talking had more energy around the Diplomatic Tent, where the foreign contingent was dutifully awaiting the arrival of the king.

"Labour's shouting its head off about conscription, while the Tories are all out for further appeasement to calm Hitler down. God help the Poles, that's all I can say."

"I think it was an act of absolute lunacy."

"What was?"

"That pact we signed with them."

"Oh. You may be right."

Two men were standing alone beneath one of the trees, a colonel in uniform with Intelligence Corps insignia, and a slightly younger man in morning dress. Their heads were down as they talked quietly, and the civilian —Sir Thomas Benedict, a newly elected Member— poked at the grass with the toe of his polished black shoe. "Made an awful gaffe just now," he said, half to himself.

"What?" Colonel Fenshaw turned his head abstractedly. He had been gazing somberly at Herr von Ribbentrop, thinking what a clown he looked in that big top hat.

"I said I made an awful gaffe," Sir Thomas told him again. "Bumped into Harris just now—you remember his boy was killed on a motorbike a few months ago?

By way of condolence I said well, at least the boy wouldn't be sacrificed in this senseless war that's coming. Then I remembered he's got another son, of military age. Damned stupid of me." He jabbed rather hard at the grass with his toe.

"He knew you meant well," the Colonel told him.

"Think so?" Sir Thomas felt slightly better; he'd been depressed all day as it was, with the news coming in, and Vanessa over there in Berlin making eyes at that bloody Jack-in-a-box. He hesitated for a moment before speaking again. "Something you might do for me, Brian, if you will."

"Anything you say."

"The king telephoned me yesterday, about my daughter."

"Vanessa?"

"Yes. What he *said* was that I ought to persuade her to come home as soon as possible, in case she gets stranded over there if 'the situation worsens'—which is the phrase he used. What he *meant,* of course, was that when the daughter of someone in my position spends most of her time in Hitler's entourage, it looks as if we're unofficially endorsing his policies."

"Quite so." Colonel Fenshaw gazed across the lawns to where the king's party was moving. His commanding officer, General Westerby, had brought up the matter of "the Benedict girl" a couple of days ago at the club, saying that more than a few people in high places were becoming embarrassed. The Benedicts were close friends of the royal family and Sir Thomas had become an important figure in the House, and it was common knowledge that his daughter had been following Hitler about for months, and that the astute Reichschancellor had taken pains to encourage her attentions. He didn't want a war with England, and Vanessa Benedict might prove useful as an intermediary behind the scenes.

"You want me to send Martin over there?" Fenshaw asked after a moment.

Sir Thomas looked up quickly, relieved. "Yes. Of course, I've asked him to go and bring his sister back, more than once, but as he says himself, she's pretty strong-willed. But if you sent him to Berlin officially, with *orders* to bring her back, it might do the trick."

The Colonel thought about it, watching the colors of the uniforms and the women's dresses flowing across the lawns. "Orders are one thing," he said doubtfully. "She's a free woman, after all."

"Martin would do his level best to persuade her, if you gave him official sanction. I'm his father, but you're his commanding officer. There's a difference."

They began strolling across to His Majesty's tea tent, so as to be there when the king arrived. "I'll have to talk to General Westerby first," Fenshaw said. "This isn't really an Intelligence matter."

"But you think he might agree?"

Fenshaw reflected. "We'd be doing the Palace a favor. That's going to carry weight, when I put it to him. Give me a few days, and meanwhile we should keep this strictly confidential."

2

BERLIN, AUGUST 1939

Outside the Reichschancellory the massed crimson banners hung limp in the evening air, their colors deepening as the floodlights took over from the dying glow of the sunset. Pigeons dipped and wheeled above the stone frescoes, sometimes swooping past the lower floors of the building, their wings spread wide and seeming motionless, gilded by the lights. The ground-floor windows were radiant, and passers-by could see the brilliance of the chandeliers inside.

The vast Hall of the Ambassadors was already crowded, bedecked with uniforms and the silk and satin gowns of the women, their colors complementing the rich blooms of roses and hydrangeas under the grouped spotlights. Shortly before eight o'clock the great doors at the far end of the hall were swung open, and suddenly the Reichschancellor was among his guests, already shaking hands with those at the head of the lines.

The drone of conversation had dropped to near silence as the doors had opened; now the hall was filled with a low and vibrant murmuring, as if the Chancellor, simply by his presence, had commanded a change of mood in the spirit of the people. The men in uniform had stiffened suddenly, and the women had leaned forward a little toward the single figure, their eyes eager and their lips parting as they waited, their breath coming faster.

"Oh, I can't see! Is he there yet?"

"*Shhh* . . . yes, darling."

"The Führer?"

"Yes. The Führer."

"Oh . . . will he shake hands with me?"

"He's going to shake hands with all of us, but only if we keep very quiet."

In a moment a low booming laugh sounded above the murmuring, and someone said, "That's Field Marshal Göring."

A few of the women laughed lightly, their nervousness allayed; things would be less solemn with Göring here: he was always so jolly.

A girl in a turquoise sequined gown dropped her fan, and it clattered on the marble; heads turned, and her face was crimson when she straightened up from retrieving it, too embarrassed to notice that several of the personal SS guards had lifted their heads sharply at the sound.

A short bearded man in coattails, newly arrived from Geneva, was whispering. "That is Himmler over there, yes?"

"Yes."

"And just behind him—the tall blond man?"

"Heydrich."

"My God, the *power* that is here tonight . . ."

"What? Oh, yes. They are powerful men."

Not far from the head of the lines stood Vanessa Benedict, rather tall, a little gawky in her ivory satin dress, devoid of jewels but with her wide eyes shining as she stared at the Reichschancellor.

"Don't you *see* it?" she asked the man beside her in a low, intense whisper. "Don't you *feel* it in here?" She darted a look around her, but only for an instant before her eyes were drawn irresistibly back to Adolf Hitler. "Can't you sense the excitement in here, the *pride?*"

"Yes," her brother said.

"Doesn't it make you want to yell out *Heil!* at the top of your voice?"

"Frankly, no. I'm more used to 'God Save the King.' "

"Oh, *Martin* . . . you're so *English!*"

"We both are, actually."

She stopped talking now; the Chancellor was only a few yards away. Martin could feel the excitement in her, shaking her like a fever as she watched the short man in the simple uniform greeting the guests. Vanessa had always been a lively girl, buzzing with new ideas and ready to shout their praises from the housetops; but he had never seen her like this, quivering with tension, her hands locked together in their long white gloves, her eyes shimmering as she waited for Hitler to approach, as if she waited for a lover. Martin had noticed this in some of the other women present.

Suddenly she was taking a step forward and saying, "Good evening, my Führer," as the man took her slender gloved hand in his, bowing slightly and offering his thin smile.

"Vanessa, my dear young lady . . . I'm so glad you could come."

"I am always at your command, my Führer. Always." She turned quickly. "Let me present my brother, Martin." With a soft ring of triumph she said, "The Reichschancellor . . ."

Martin noted that they both used the familiar "thou" to each other, but the thought slipped from his mind as he returned the dark penetrating gaze of the man in front of him. As they shook hands he felt a sudden tension in the air, as if all the deep half-muted excitement in this enormous room had become focused here. Unnerved, he heard himself saying in German, "A privilege, Herr Reichschancellor."

"Your sister has talked about you a great deal, Herr Benedict. Welcome to Berlin."

Martin was aware of brief impressions: a faint smell of carbolic soap, or perhaps hair pomade . . . a sense of raw energy, though not in the handshake or in any physical way—it was like a dark force vibrating, its violence held in check.

Vanessa was taking her brother's arm affectionately. "I rather suspect he's here to take me back to London, but of course I'm not going to let him!" She laughed easily, but Hitler looked quite put out.

"I very much hope, Herr Benedict, that you'll let your sister stay with us for as long as she pleases. We're all very fond of her, you know, and she has a brilliant flair for modern politics."

Martin could think of nothing to say. His mind felt strangely numbed.

"Thank you, my Führer," Vanessa was saying quickly. "But it's you who have taught me all I know of politics. And I shall certainly send my brother home without me"—her eyes shining and her head lifted—"my place is here with you."

There was an unholy row, of course, at the hotel. The reception had lasted nearly three hours and everyone had drunk champagne—except for Hitler, who had kept to his *Fachinger*—and Vanessa was still in a glow of complete euphoria because she had written *so* many letters to Martin about the Führer and the New Order and the *dazzling* future of Germany and *everything* that was going on here in Berlin, and now he was *here* and he'd actually *met* Herr Hitler and seen everything for himself.

"Wasn't it simply *marvelous* tonight?" She peeled off her long gloves, glancing into the gilt-framed mirror and shaking back her hair.

"It was quite an experience." Martin's head was throbbing, though he hadn't taken much champagne. "Mind if I open the windows, Vessa?" This was her room, the one she'd booked for the occasion, putting him in a double suite on the same floor. "The first time you meet the Führer," she'd told him earlier, "it's the Adlon or nothing." One of the French windows was jammed, and he gave it a jerk, banging it open, feeling both relieved and surprised by his small show of anger.

"That's Dr. Goebbels's back garden down there," Vanessa told him, coming to stand with him on the balcony. "Behind the American Embassy . . . those little trees there, can you see?"

The heat of the open air merged with that of the room inside; there'd been no relief from it all evening. "Can't we see," Martin asked her, "the bathroom ventilation pipes of the Göring residence from here too?" He suddenly realized they were both speaking in German, and felt angry with himself.

His sister stood back from him, her hands tightening. "You know, Martin, you've been an absolute *pig* the entire evening!"

"Nothing like calling a spade a spade." But his tone was perfectly level: he'd got himself under control. And this time he'd spoken in English.

"You used to *love* Berlin!"

He looked down at the blaze of light along the Wilhelmstrasse, hearing the laughter of the throngs strolling in the late summer heat as they left the restaurants and moved on to their favorite nightclubs. It all looked so carefree and reassuring, but General Westerby had told him a week ago: "From our analysis of reports from informed sources, we believe there'll be a war. Hitler means to go into Poland, and we're committed to protect her." With a touch of irony: "All other considerations apart, your sister would be safer back in London."

He spoke over his shoulder. "Yes, I used to love Berlin. I don't anymore."

He'd first come here when he was only three years

old, when his father had been ambassador, and within two years he'd been prattling away in German, making German friends, going to a German kindergarten. Later, on visits to the University, he'd come to love the city —or perhaps just his new friends, the parties, the girls. . . . But later still, when he and Vanessa were here for the Games three years ago, he'd sensed the hysteria behind the proudly waving flags and banners, an ominous stridency in the massed voices of the Hitler Jugend in the packed arena of the Sportpalast. Something was getting out of hand in Germany, and he didn't want to be a part of it.

He turned to look at Vanessa. "Germany's changed. It's a dictatorship. But let's not row about it—we haven't seen each other for almost a year."

She softened, her slim hands loosening as she watched the lamplight falling across his blond head. "You know, Martin, you really look so wonderfully Aryan. . . ."

"Would you mind very much if we both spoke in English?" he asked curtly.

She opened her mouth in disbelief. "You even hate our language?"

"It may be *your* language, but it's not mine. And as for my looking so Aryan, we've got Danish blood in the family—they're blond and blue-eyed too."

"Martin, why are you so angry?"

"I'm not angry. It's—" He shrugged. "All right, I am angry, yes. It's the way you kept calling him *my* Führer like that, and looking at him as if he was a god or something."

She said, "He is."

"Oh, really? The god of what, precisely? Prison camps?"

She lit a cigarette, her hand shaking. "Those stories are wildly exaggerated—by his political opponents!"

Martin stared. "Are you joking? Don't you know what happens to his political opponents?"

"It depends who you listen to. If—"

"I'm damned sure I don't listen to Doctor Goebbels."

"Propaganda is an essential part of any new progressive regime. It's—" She stopped short, vexed with herself. "This is silly, Martin. I don't want to spend our time together arguing. How long are you here for?"

He said quietly, "I'm leaving tomorrow."

"Oh, not *tomorrow* . . ."

"We both are."

She stiffened, and her tone was crisp. "Sorry, old boy. I like it here."

They heard a sudden crashing of glass in the street below, a bottle falling or perhaps a window breaking. Almost at once there was laughter, and Martin felt a chill. Something had been broken, destroyed; and they'd thought it funny. Had they laughed like that on Kristallnacht?

"Vanessa," he said, dropping her childhood name, "I've been sent here to take you home."

"Oh, really? Who sent you?"

"Father. Indirectly."

She gave a deep sigh. "He's always ringing me up about it. I do wish he'd *understand*. He—"

"Actually it was my CO who sent me, directly. General Westerby."

Her eyes widened. "What on earth for?"

"You're embarrassing people in London. Father, the government, even the king."

"*Embarrassing?* Thank you very much! Well, you can go back and tell them—"

"Listen to me, Vanessa."

And she did, standing there with her bare arms folded and the cigarette forgotten as her brother drove his argument home, politely but firmly; and when he was finished she went over to the writing table and opened a drawer and turned back to face him with a small ivory-paneled gun in her hand.

"If you try to make me leave Berlin I'll shoot myself." Her face was white.

Martin was appalled. "Where did you get that?"

"He gave it to me."

"Who? You mean—"

"The Führer. *My* Führer."

He moved toward her. "Let me have it, Vanessa."

"No."

That was just the beginning.

"Your papers."

The boy stopped.

"Hurry up!"

The eyes of the two Gestapo men were in shadow, below the peaks of their caps. A taxi went past slowly. The boy gave them his papers, looking carefully around him. He was thin, dark, bare-headed; he was seventeen, tall for his age. He held the attaché case close against one leg, slightly behind him.

"Where are you going?"

"Home."

They gave him back his papers. "What's in your case?"

"Work. School work."

"Open it."

The boy swung the attaché case high in an arc, letting it go, and darted past the two men, his thin body angled forward in a fast sprint toward the intersection. One of the men went after him; the other ran toward the case; it had burst open and papers were strewn across the pavement.

The boy gave them a chase but they had him inside the police jail within twenty minutes. The Gestapo man hadn't been able to run as fast, but he had shouted for the boy to be stopped, and some revelers coming out of a nightclub brought him down, laughing uproariously, thinking he must be a Jew.

By midnight, they still hadn't broken him. By then he could barely talk, though he was still conscious. The men moved about in puddles of water: they had revived their prisoner three times with a bucket. His blood had dyed the puddles a pale rust color.

Soon after midnight an inspector came in with some identity papers and threw them on to the small scrubbed table. "These are the real ones."

"Where were they?"

"In his dormitory at the school. We worked on the girl."

"What girl?"

"The one who was with him, just before he was stopped. They picked her up too."

A sound came from the figure sagging on the straight-backed chair, and the head dropped forward.

"Very well, Franz Wilhelm von Gerlach, now we will start all over again. Who were the others?"

The figure was silent.

"Who were the others?"

Silence.

"He's passed out again. Stand clear."

The bucket swung.

As the interrogation continued, a clerk came in and began sorting through the leaflets, mainly to see if they differed in their wording. There were 132 of them, quite well printed on semigloss paper. *What the leaders of the National Socialist party call the "New Order," we call tyranny. What they call progress, we call a reversion to the dark ages. What they call freedom, we call enslavement. We, the youth of Germany, demand of Adolf Hitler that he disbands his secret police forces, and that he leads his country back to the ways of decency, humanity and justice.*

There were twelve paragraphs to each leaflet.

"It should be 'disband,'" the clerk said, "and 'lead.' Subjunctive." He sat with his feet drawn up on the rung of the chair, clear of the puddles.

"Who were the others?"

The heavy man drew back his fist again; he was sweating profusely, and had taken off his black tunic.

The boy moaned all the time now, as if he were singing, very low. It had started when they'd mentioned the girl.

"Von Gerlach," one of them said. "Would he be the general's son?"

"That'd be interesting."

He was sleeping when they came to his cell, and the blinding light woke him before they spoke.

"Sign this."

"What is it?"

"The D.11. Protective Custody Warrant. Come on, sign!"

The man kept waving the red form in front of his face, thrusting the pen at him.

Franz read some of the words, his eyes squeezed to puffy slits against the bright light. *Placed in protective custody due to the risk that he might otherwise misuse his personal freedom to engage in acts detrimental to the National Socialist State.*

He took the pen, but couldn't manage with it in his right hand, because he had raised it to shield his face when the truncheon had come down, and his fingers were blue and swollen. He signed his name with his left hand, as best he could.

"Good boy. Now you're going to tell us who the others are, aren't you?"

Looking down, Franz said through his bruised lips, "No."

They dragged him upright and manhandled him along the dark green corridor and threw him into the room with the wet floor and filled the bucket from the tap near the rear door of the cellars.

"Georg! Give me a hand in here. And get the doctor along to stand by."

Another man brought the bucket, slopping the water a bit because it was almost full.

"Right. *Who were the others?*"

There was no answer.

The shadow of the truncheon swung across the ceiling.

On the wall over the narrow green door the clock was at 5:32, not long before dawn.

3

The call came through a few minutes after six o'clock. They were both in Vanessa's room again. They had argued hotly for nearly an hour, and then telephoned London, finding it difficult because, as the operator told them, the international switchboard was jammed with foreign residents and tourists calling home to reassure their families that they were all right; it had been going on, she told Martin, since the Poles had started their threats of war against the Fatherland.

Vanessa had listened to all Sir Thomas's arguments against her staying on in Berlin, and had at last broken into tears without anything definite being settled.

Martin had finally gone to his own room and telephoned home again, telling his father that Vanessa had a pistol and had said she would kill herself if she had to leave Berlin.

"Do you think she's serious?"

"I don't really know." Martin felt too tired even to think straight. "I'd say she's just being dramatic. Everything's dramatic now, in this bloody place."

They had talked for ten minutes, and then Martin had tried to sleep, but couldn't. His sister had called him on the house phone about an hour ago, saying she felt "lonely and desperate." *More* drama.

Now he was in her room again, standing by the open doors to the balcony, half-listening to the sounds of the traffic below, half-listening to his sister's voice, sometimes emphatic, sometimes pleading, as she talked to Father on the phone.

"But he *loves* England. He's always telling me that. He says England is a brother nation, and that we can both contribute to lasting peace in a new Europe, working together."

The more he listened, the more Martin realized how much his sister had changed—or *been* changed by Hitler's blandishments and Goebbels's lies, repeated and repeated until she'd come to believe them. Yet she'd always been so fiercely independent in her thinking. . . .

"Germany is to have power over the land, while England will retain her power over the seas. It's so beautifully *logical*, Daddy, and if only you could *hear* him for yourself . . ."

Martin looked at the writing desk more than once as the talking continued. He could get to the top drawer easily, while her back was turned. But then she'd miss the gun later, and realize what he'd done; and there'd be another unholy row.

Finally she said, "Yes, he's here. All right. And Daddy, do *try* to understand." She held the phone to Martin, wearily.

"Yes, sir?"

His father spoke quietly and steadily. "All I've managed to do, so far, is to let her get it all out. That will leave her pretty well exhausted. You don't need to talk to her anymore, for a while. Let her rest. What I've suggested is that she comes home for a few weeks, until the international situation blows over—though of course it won't—and then returns to Berlin again, if she wants to. I think she'll let me have my way. It's the thought of leaving the place *forever* that's making her so obstinate. I'll call you again about twelve noon, your time. Please be there, and of course make sure that your sister is there too."

"I will."

Sir Thomas tried to get a little wry humor into his tone. "You must have had a rough night. The distaff side of the Benedicts are known for their strong will."

"Yes, I can confirm that. The problem is, we all love her. Otherwise she could go and fly balloons." He got a weary smile from Vanessa.

"Of course. And she loves us. She'll see the sense of things pretty soon. We'll talk again at twelve o'clock, providing the lines aren't saturated. Keep your chin up."

It was evening, after two more phone calls and hours of wearying argument, before Vanessa stubbed out her umpteenth cigarette and said slowly, "All right, old boy. You win. I'll go home for a few weeks, and then come back. But you'll have to give me a day or two, so that I can say goodbye to all my friends, and pack."

"There's no need—" But he stopped short; he'd been going to say there was no need for a lot of dramatic goodbyes, if she was leaving Berlin only for a week or two; but once she was away from the insidious atmosphere of the city and that dangerous tin-pot little god of hers in the Reichschancellory she might, as Father had said, see sense. In any case, war was coming. "Fair enough," he said. "I'll book a plane for Saturday. For both of us." He was too dog-tired to feel the relief.

"All right, Martin. Saturday."

But something in her voice warned him, and he put his arm around her shoulders. "Meanwhile, I'll look after that little toy you've got in the drawer."

She moved away from him quickly. "No."

"It'd be perfectly safe with me."

"It was a present. I prize it."

"Of course, but—" He opened his hands, defeated. "I don't want you to do anything stupid, Vessa."

In a small voice she said, "I won't."

"Imagine how we'd all feel."

"Of course."

He left her standing there near the open doors, her

arms folded, her slim hands clasping her shoulders as if she were cold, though the warmth of the new day was already entering the room.

"Benedict? Oh, yes, I've met your father quite a few times. A privilege, clever political mind. What are you doing for lunch?"

"I've no actual plans, sir."

"You can join me, then."

"Thank you."

The Major took him to Horcher's, and chose a secluded table on the far side from the doors. Major Brooks, on a routine visit to the Embassy. Affable, talkative and a good listener, Martin decided. He'd been arranging the flight to London for next Saturday when Brooks had run into him at the main desk.

"Thank God for Horcher's. Not many places you can find a decent meal, these days. You know Berlin well?"

"I was here at kindergarten, and I've made a dozen or so visits since then. University, the Games and so on."

"Ah. That's right, your father was at the Embassy, 1909."

"Nineteen-ten, actually."

"Ah. Right. Kindergarten, eh? So you speak fluent German."

"Yes."

Major Brooks forked his cold *Wurst* and said thoughtfully, "And with your looks, I suppose you could actually pass for a German. Right?"

"Probably. Though frankly I'd rather not."

"Ah!" The Major nodded vigorously. "Place has changed a bit since that gang got into power, m'm?" He glanced around him, and Martin thought fleetingly that any German national overheard making a remark like that would be taken straight to a prison camp. "If you want my opinion, Benedict, we're going to have to put these blighters where they belong. You think they care a tuppenny damn about Danzig? Of course they don't. They want war. And they've got to take Poland first, or they can't risk an offensive in the west. Right?"

"That seems to be the general opinion, sir, yes."

As the lunch proceeded, Martin found himself talking more than he normally did, as the Major drew him out on the subject of Berlin, the Chancellor, and the possibility of war. He also threw in one or two personal questions about Martin's background, and listened attentively, toying with his *Apfeltorte* and nodding in all the right places.

"Raced at Brooklands, did you? What kind of car?"

"A Frazer-Nash."

"Ah! One of the chain gang, eh? Beautiful motor car."

"That one was, until I crashed it."

The Major looked up. "Crashed, eh? Came out all right, obviously." He asked casually, "Got any scars to show for it?"

"Only on the legs."

"Ah. Lucky."

It had been another of those personal questions, and Martin noted it as they sipped their coffee.

"Benedict . . . Benedict . . . Now I've got it! You were on the stage, weren't you, in London? Five or six years ago?"

"Just for a while."

"Of course, of course—*Cyrano de Bergerac*. Right?"

Martin laughed briefly. "Don't remind me of the notices."

"You were good in that one—very good! My wife quite lost her head over you, I remember clearly. Well, well—Martin Benedict, the actor, now it all comes back to me. What made you give it up?"

Martin gazed across the dining room, carried back in his thoughts for a moment. "It was too artificial. If

I'd been any better at it, I would probably have discovered the deeper realities of the game."

"Well, I think you were damned good, you know. Damned good."

Later, walking back to the Embassy in the warmth of the afternoon, Major Brooks slipped a final question into their conversation. "Have you any friends in this country? Close friends?"

Martin found himself thinking at once of Hedda. But she wasn't really a close friend. "No, I can't say that. Mostly the kind of friends you make on irregular visits, and then lose touch with."

"Ah. Any of them anti-Nazi?" He glanced around him again, and Martin realized the Major must have been in Berlin for quite a time: he'd developed the well-known "German look," the quick glance over the shoulder.

"I don't know them well enough," Martin told him, "to know what they think about the Nazis."

"They wouldn't shout the odds about it, in any case, would they? Doesn't do, in this place."

They parted company soon afterward, outside the British Embassy, and on his way back to the Adlon Hotel Martin reviewed their two hours of conversation, trying to make some kind of pattern out of it. He was now sure that Major Brooks hadn't run into him at the Embassy by pure chance, and that the impromptu invitation to lunch had not been a gesture of courtesy between fellow officers.

In the evening there was a further telephone call from his father in London, asking after Vanessa. Martin told him:

"She's bearing up well enough. We had tea together, and talked about home, and her friends there. I'd say everything's going to be all right, once I'm on the plane with her."

"You're doing a splendid job, Martin. I have informed General Westerby. And of course your mother's tremendously relieved."

"Good show. Give her my love, will you?" Before he rang off, he remembered the Major. "I had lunch with someone you know, by the way. Major Brooks."

"Brooks?"

"Major Stanley Brooks, Royal Signals."

"Oh? I don't think I've met him. But in case I'm wrong, please give him my best regards."

"Out!"

Feet tramped along the corridors.

"Out!"

Doors banged, slamming back on their hinges.

"Out!"

Franz rolled off the bare wooden bench and got to his feet and stood swaying, wondering what was happening.

Outside in the courtyard of the big building, engines were starting up.

"What time is it?" asked the man with the smashed hand.

"I don't know."

"Come on, you lazy bastards—out!"

The door of the cell slammed back and Reintz stood there, truncheon in hand. Franz got past him through the doorway with only a light blow, but he heard the man with the smashed hand give a grunt of pain as he followed. His name was Clemens, a senior partner of a tailoring firm in Potsdam, established in 1873 and now with four branches, two of them in Berlin and two in Hannover. He had told Franz all this, and other things, during the night. Yesterday afternoon, after the final interrogation, he had been too slow in going through a doorway, and they had slammed the door on his hand. This he had told Franz, too.

"Out! Out!"

The whole building was alive with running men.

"Don't put your shoes on! Who told you to put your shoes on?"

A man was sent reeling against the wall in the bleak lamplight of the corridor.

The building swarmed in the night.

"Come on there, at the double!"

Franz looked around for Clemens, and stopped, waiting for him to catch up. Clemens wasn't a young man, and couldn't get his breath.

"What are you standing there for, you stupid clod? Get on!"

The truncheon swung and hit the wall and Franz went lurching after the other men, untouched, untouched this time and trying to understand this new sensation; normally when they hit out there was nothing you could do, you just waited and held your breath till it came; but not this time; it must mean something, some kind of independence, some kind of freedom, snatched out of the dark.

"Get those shoes off! Hang 'em around your neck, come on, like all the others are doing, are you bastards blind or something?"

Franz ran in his socks. His shoes were in the cell; there hadn't been time to get them. It didn't matter. He looked back again for Clemens, but couldn't see him among the line of running men in the long green-painted corridors. He couldn't catch up. "It's my asthma," he'd told Franz in the night, when they'd talked to each other endlessly to keep their minds on the life they had known before, the one that had been interrupted. "I've been to every spa in Europe, but there's no real cure, you know, not for asthma."

"Form up in lines! Quick, now, come on!"

They were in the big courtyard, shoving one another to make room, dodging the men in uniform, the acrid stink of exhaust gas on the air as the long black vans started moving away, taking the first of them. But the courtyard was almost filled by now with jostling men as the cells emptied, and when the last van swayed through the gates there was still half their number left.

A light clinking sound came into the night, like Christmas sleigh bells.

"Stand still, you bloody clods, stand still!"

They obeyed, standing like patient cattle as the guards went along the lines, looping the chains around their waists and passing on, looping the next, and the next. It took a long time, but the night was warm and the sky cloudless.

Franz looped the thin iron chain around his waist and passed the rest of its length to the next man and stood waiting again, thinking. Had they informed his father yet? Certainly. His father was a general, one of the youngest and most brilliant in the Army; but he had no time for Hitler or his wild policies, and this was known. Certainly he would have been informed of his son's treasonous acts. Yet Franz regretted nothing.

Sigrid had said, two months ago, "They've arrested the Gotthelfs." She had said it angrily, throwing the door open and surprising them at their clandestine reading, so that they had slid their copies of Zweig and H. G. Wells and Freud under their chairs, thinking it might be someone else. *"All* of them," Sigrid had said with a soft fierceness, "even Benni." Benni was three years old, and only yesterday they had given him a ride on Franz's new bicycle, holding him firmly on the saddle.

Franz knew the Gotthelfs had been arrested, but he hadn't yet told anyone. He had felt too sick about it, knowing what the night sounds had meant: the rapping on the door, the voices raised, the scuffling of feet and finally the vehicle starting up and driving away. He'd been expecting it for a long time. They all had.

"We must do something," Sigrid said, shutting the door and sitting cross-legged on the floor among them, throwing back her dark hair.

"Why *us?*" Jakob asked, and she swung to look at him.

"As long as we go on asking that," she told him slowly, "nothing will ever get done. That is 'why us.'"

Standing with the chain around his waist, Franz thought again that by this time Sigrid was probably dead.

"All right," a guard shouted suddenly, *"we're going to move off!"* He waited until there was absolute silence, and then lowered his voice. "You'll run in your socks and you won't talk. You won't make any noise. Any one of you making a noise will be dealt with, and you know what that means: it means you won't ever reach where we're going."

The other guards formed up alongside the prisoners and started swinging their clubs. *"Move! Move, you bastards!"*

They went through the gates at the double, one man stumbling and giving a whimper as a truncheon came down, the rest of them pulling against the chains to make sure the ones behind them didn't lag. *"Move!"* The guards ran alongside them, aiming steady blows at their heads if they seemed to be going too slowly. *"Move, you lazy sods, come on!"*

Franz tripped, regained his footing and ran on, pulling at the chain. She was probably dead by now, he thought, because she had been the ringleader, from the moment she'd come into the room like that and told them about the Gotthelfs. Sigrid had found the small hand printing press at a pawnbrokers, and bargained for it; she and Karl had done most of the composition work. It was easier, already, to think about her as dead, rather than fear for her all the time. It would happen to all of them before long, but she would be first, and in a strange way it was ennobling, and Franz, running steadily in the pack of chained men through the night, thought of Sigrid with veneration.

"Keep moving!"

They were running in their socks, Franz assumed, so as not to wake the populace; it must be very early, for there was no traffic. They were being smuggled out of the city by dark, like something unclean, so that by morning the streets would look orderly again.

But one man, beaten too hard or simply exhausted, had dropped to his knees, and those near him had to lift him and drag him along by the chain with his feet still on the ground; and after a while his socks wore through, and then his skin, and he began leaving two parallel streaks of red on the tarred surface of the street, detracting from the neatness that should be there in the morning.

"Keep moving!"

The black clubs swung and fell, and the sound of the chains grew faster, the incongruous sound of sleigh bells in the summer night.

The train was waiting for them when they reached the station. They had expected that; they'd heard about the long dark trains that left Berlin night after night. It was said that war was coming, and some people spoke against the idea, because they had no enthusiasm for another war; and there were also those who listened to the "black" radio, and told their friends the news from overseas, or at least told the people they believed to be their friends; and these nights the trains were growing longer.

"Halt! Halt, you bastards!"

They stood in their lines along the platform, smelling the coal and the steam as the enormous engine towered over them with its smoke clouding the stars. Franz looked for Clemens, his new friend, and saw that he stood sagging with his bald head down, supported by the men closest to him. Clemens had asthma, and couldn't ever keep up. Franz had been on this particular platform before, many times; from here they'd taken the holiday train to the Black Forest, he and the other students; and from here he had taken the train for home, at the end of the winter term.

The guards moved constantly, keeping their prisoners in order, and the sound of a whip came singing thinly from the far end of the lines.

"Where are they taking us?" a man whispered.

"I heard it was Buchenwald," someone answered. "They've got a camp there."

4

By six-thirty in the evening the restaurants along the
Kurfürstendamm were filling up, and people still crowded the pavement cafés, sitting at the little iron tables
with their ice cream and ersatz coffee. By seven o'clock
the traffic was clogging at the lights, and a taxi was hard
to find.

Martin had been waiting five or six minutes, standing with one foot on the pavement and one in the road,
watching the traffic for an empty cab. People strolled
past him, many of them laughing in the warm late-
summer air; the people of Berlin laughed easily, Martin
had noticed in the last few days, as if they were whistling
in the dark. Newsboys shouted at their stands, but sales
were slow; nobody wanted to hear about the "militant
Polish fanatics" or "Germany's readiness" for war.

When the traffic stream was blocked by the lights
at the crossroads, Martin watched the crowds instead.
Not all of their gaiety was false; a lot of people were
truly enjoying themselves. A party of children were
throwing streamers at one another across a café table,
one of them blowing a horn while the others hunted
the last of the currants from the birthday cake; three
businessmen, still in their formal suits, were linking
arms along the pavement, singing impromptu snatches
of the *Horst Wessel;* two women were dancing to the
raucous rhumba beat from a gramophone.

The people at the café nearest the traffic lights fell silent for a few minutes as two Gestapo men stopped on their rounds, bending over a man sitting alone; for a moment he seemed unable to find his papers, then held them out, waiting. One of them took his arm and he stood up, protesting at first but going with them when he saw it was useless, his short black-coated figure seeming to dangle between the two uniformed men as they took him to the van parked at the curbside. Then talking broke out again, more loudly now, and Martin heard the word *"Juden"* passing among the tables. A woman began laughing and her friends took it up, banging their spoons against their coffee cups; she must have said something especially funny.

A taxi swerved suddenly into the curb and Martin got in, slamming the door; but before it could pull away the door opened and a young SS lieutenant put his head in.

"Will you allow me to share? I'm late for duty."

"Of course. Jump in."

As the taxi swung back into the traffic the lieutenant said with a laugh of recognition, *"Martin!* I didn't know you were back in Berlin!"

"I'm afraid I—" He searched the young officer's face. "Good Lord, it's Rudi!" They shook hands warmly. "I didn't recognize you in the uniform!"

"But what a pleasing surprise!" Rudi said in English.

Martin laughed again. "Your English is still terrible." They went back to German, asking each other about their friends and families.

"And the beautiful Vanessa?" the young lieutenant asked.

"Still beautiful," Martin told him, remembering that Rudi had been rather keen on her when they'd last met at the Olympic Games. "We're flying back to London together in a few days' time."

Rudi's dark face became serious, and he glanced down. "I suppose that's wise, yes. It's a shame, isn't it?"

In a moment Martin said, "So you think it's certain?"

"War? Yes. Have you read the *Völkische Beobachter* today?"

"I saw the headlines," Martin lied. The *Völkische Beobachter* was Hitler's organ for propaganda.

"Germany is ready." Rudi swung his young intense face to look into Martin's eyes. "We hope to remain good friends with England, of course. The Führer wishes it. But we are ready, for whatever we have to do."

Martin was trying to recall the eighteen-year-old boy in the tennis flannels only three years ago, cheering the British teams lustily, his arm around Vanessa whenever he found the excuse as they sat together watching the arena; but Rudi had changed, almost unrecognizably, and not just because of the smart gray uniform. He had become very intense, jerking his hands in sharp gestures as he talked, a note of reverence coming into his voice whenever he mentioned Germany or the Führer.

"I'm in the Germania Regiment, you know. It's one of the elite: our particular duty is the protection of the Führer himself. You can imagine the *pride* I feel, the *responsibility!*"

"I congratulate you," Martin said, and then let Rudi go on talking as he watched the glittering avenue for a moment, seeing it blacked out suddenly in his mind's eye, the crowds melting away to leave the buildings silent under a droning sky.

"Peter is in the same unit with me—you remember Peter?"

"Of course." Martin looked away from the window. "Did he marry Hedda?"

Rudi hesitated. "No. They broke it off." His dark eyes became shadowed again under the peak of his cap.

"Oh? Why?"

"Actually, *she* broke it off. She said it was because Peter had joined the SS. But of course there must have been some other reason—it couldn't have been that."

"Why not?"

Rudi looked surprised. "Because we are the elite. Especially the Germania Regiment—one of the closest to the person of the Führer!" He waited, but Martin said nothing. "It was just an extraordinary reason for her to give—just a stupid excuse."

In a moment Martin said slowly, "Hedda wasn't given to making stupid excuses for anything. I remember her very well."

Rudi looked away. "She'll have to get over that attitude of hers. It could get her into serious trouble."

Martin kept his tone light. "When did they break it off?"

"What? About a year ago."

The taxi was slowing. Rudi had asked to be put down in the Leipzigerplatz.

"What's Hedda doing now?" Martin asked him.

"She's a nurse, at the University Hospital." His smile was cynical. "I think she went into nursing to avoid her National Labor Service."

"Oh, I don't know about that. It's a fine profession. Think of the *pride,* the *responsibility.*"

Rudi's eyes flickered, but he said nothing. When the taxi drew in to the curb he got out at once, without offering his hand. "It was a pleasure to see you again," he said with cool formality. "You must try to keep your country out of the war. We should remain friends, don't you agree?" His heels came together smartly. *"Heil Hitler!"*

LONDON, 15 AUGUST 1939

The three men had come together in the small stuffy room at the top of the house in St. James's Street: a king's equerry, a military officer and an American. They were a few minutes early, and the fourth man had not yet arrived. It was evening, and the sunset cast a ruddy glow across the rooftops, so that the whole city looked as if it were on fire.

"Just how important is this operation?" the American asked. This time last evening he had been in Washington.

"It's hard to say," the officer told him, "specifically." He stood at the lattice window, watching the silent conflagration of the sunset. "But it goes right up through the hierarchy of British Security Coordination and the man we call Intrepid. And ultimately, of course, to the king."

"I don't see how this whole thing works," the American said in slight exasperation. "I mean, where does Chamberlain come into it? And what about Kennedy?"

The equerry swung around to look at him, speaking before the officer. "It isn't a question," he said with careful articulation, "of whether England is prepared to go to war with Hitler. It's a question of whether a few key people—Churchill, Intrepid, yourself and certain others—are prepared to outmaneuver Chamberlain and his appeasers, and indirectly your own ambassador, and try to stop the Nazis from invading and overrunning this island." His voice was quiet with worry and fatigue; in the past few weeks he had slept only a few hours each night. "So Chamberlain doesn't come into it at all, and neither does your ambassador. They are being kept totally uninformed of our plans, and we are working, in fact, against them. We have to. We want England to survive. Without the ultimate authority of the king, of course, our acts would be treasonable."

The American lit a cigar, throwing the match into the ashtray with a jerk of frustration. "But Jesus, how can a democracy with a parliament do things like this? I mean, I'm delighted—it wouldn't work otherwise, but . . ."

"We are also a monarchy," the equerry said, "and

by ancient charter the directors of British secret intelligence are confirmed in their appointments by the monarch. And thank God for it, because otherwise we could do nothing except stand by and watch the Prime Minister and his appeasers scuttle the kingdom—and the rest of the free world with it." He looked reflectively at the American. "In just the same way, you are directly responsible to Roosevelt, and in the utmost secrecy, leaving the State Department totally uninformed. So you shouldn't really find our methods so surprising. These are desperate times, and we must choose desperate measures."

"Churchill," added the officer, "has very limited powers without the king's authority, even as First Lord of the Admiralty. Of course, if he ever becomes Prime Minister he can take over the whole thing himself, quite legitimately." He said slowly as an afterthought, "As a matter of fact I think it's the only hope we've got."

They turned suddenly as the door opened and a civilian in a gray alpaca suit came in. "Am I late?" he asked, and moved energetically to the end of the table, the carnation in his buttonhole glowing as he switched on the lamp.

"No, sir," the equerry told him. "We arrived a little early."

"Splendid." He dropped his black briefcase on the chair next to him and took out some papers. "Then let's get on."

The meeting lasted over three hours, and it was past ten o'clock when the American and the king's equerry left together, going down the rickety stairs and out through the narrow door by the tailor's shop. In the room at the top of the house, now full of tobacco smoke and littered with papers, the officer said to the civilian:

"There's one last matter, sir, if you have a moment."

"Very well. But for heaven's sake let's open a window. Not a cigar man, myself."

"Quite so, sir. But fortunately, it's the worst thing we can say about him."

"Oh, absolutely. Stout fellow, yes. So Roosevelt's in with us, providing they reelect him." He banged one of the windows open, disturbing a pigeon outside. "You know, there *is* just a chance for us all. One in a thousand, but a chance." He came back to his chair and began putting the papers into his briefcase. "But you were saying—?"

"We've had a signal from Brooks, sir, at the Embassy in Berlin. He's got a man for us."

"A man?"

"For 'Damocles.' "

"Oh." The man in the gray suit looked up quickly. "I'm listening."

"Educated Tonbridge and Oxford. He left—"

"Is he any relation to Sir Thomas Benedict, by the way?"

"Yes, sir. His son."

"Thank you. Please go on."

"Well, these are the salient points of the information we've gathered so far. I'll run through it briefly. He speaks faultless German, according to Major Brooks. He was in Berlin from a very early age and has made nine later visits in all, perfecting the language at the University in 1934. He is now thirty-two years old." The officer swiveled his chair to get more light on the papers. "He was on the London stage for two years, mainly feature parts but playing the lead in *Cyrano de Bergerac* for six weeks—a success with good reviews. Before he applied for a commission in the Intelligence Corps he took a group of people on safari in Africa, and another group along the Amazon for research in tropical diseases. He then—"

"Is he medically qualified in any way?"

"There's nothing mentioned, sir, no."

"Go on."

"He then started racing at Brooklands, but crashed and gave it up at his parents' request—he was nearly killed when the car rolled over, flinging him clear. Among his other exploits was a tussle with a burglar at his father's country house in Surrey—he came close to injuring the man fatally, because the burglar was disturbed in his mother's bedroom and Benedict thought she was in some danger—he had a knife. Benedict threw him against a wall and broke his back."

"He's a big chap?" asked the civilian.

"No, sir. Six feet tall, but rather thin. It was just that he was afraid his mother might get hurt."

"He's not normally irascible?"

"Apparently not, though he once challenged another actor to a duel in Richmond Park, during the time when *Cyrano* was running. Something about a girl. The police broke up the duel before anybody got hurt."

The civilian fingered his iron-gray moustache contemplatively. "Sounds rather a fidget. What about actual brains?"

"The official and confidential intelligence ratings are very high. The psychologist's report describes him as reflective, observant and intuitive. Self-confident, slow to take offense."

"Girls?"

"Oh, yes, he's perfectly—er—conventional."

"He's not engaged?"

"No, sir. He saw rather a lot of a girl named Hedda in Berlin, but when he returned to England the relationship faded out. She was herself engaged to be married."

The civilian got up and stretched his legs a little. "What about the other four candidates?"

"Only one of them speaks perfect German, and he's only twenty-five years old. Too young for the particular mission we're thinking of."

"Too young for the rank."

"Quite so."

The man in the gray alpaca suit stopped his pacing

in front of the open window, feeling the cool air on his face and listening to the quiet murmur of the city, thinking how peaceful it was, and doubting that it would long remain so. "The reports from Danzig are not reassuring. The roads are blocked with barriers and tank traps. Light artillery and machine guns are being brought across the Nogat from East Prussia, by night. The city itself is jammed with German lorries and troop transports. In other words, Danzig is under intensive militarization." He turned away from the window. "So there may not be much time left to us, to establish our man in Berlin. Please get hold of this chap Benedict as soon as possible and ask him if he's willing."

BERLIN, 16 AUGUST 1939

"Give me a number 5."

The circulating nurse selected the catheter from the unit.

"That's a 5?"

"Yes, Doktor."

"It's bigger than I want."

She handed him a number 6. The new line of catheters was numbered in reverse proportion to their size.

"A 6?"

"Yes," she nodded.

He cut into the artery wall and made the insertion, feeling the pulse after pressurizing. "Better. Much better."

The ulnar artery had been partially severed: it was a crushed forearm case, a munitions worker. The surgeon began making fine sutures. The time was now 10:31 at night; they had begun operating just before 5:00 p.m. Two of the scrub nurses had changed places and an hour ago the team had started glancing up at the big wall clock, one of the signs of fatigue.

The surgeon next began suturing the tendons.

"The grafting will have to wait for a few days. The tissues are too swollen. My main concern at the moment is infection." He was speaking chiefly to the trainee nurse standing next to the anaesthesiologist. She had been very good, except once when an instrument had fallen and she'd stooped to pick it up. "Kick it aside," the senior scrub nurse had told her sharply.

"All right," the surgeon said now. "We're going to begin closing."

At 11:47 he dropped the last needle on to the bloodied tray and walked away from the operating table, standing for a moment near the basins and lifting his shoulders and head as high as they would go, his eyes clenched tightly; then he slumped suddenly, relaxing.

"Very good, Fräulein. You were very good."

"Thank you, Doktor."

The smell of the antiseptic was making her sick, but it would be another fifteen minutes before she could leave here. The surgeon was speaking again.

"Take him to Recovery. And watch for signs of infection. Watch like hawks. Like eagles." He bent over the basins and knocked a tap on with his elbow, moving his feet slowly up and down like a tame bear, to get the circulation back. It was 11:51.

"Who?"

"A Herr Benedict," the desk nurse said.

"I don't know any Herr Benedict." She didn't want to know anyone at all; she wanted to get home and drop onto the bed and sleep, and sleep. It had been her first operation.

"An Englishman," the desk nurse told her.

"What?" She looked along the corridor to the waiting room and saw a man with fair hair, pacing. Then she remembered, and went toward him, thinking she should hurry, and try to look more pleased to see him.

"Martin!" she said, but it sounded false, too bright. It was just because she was tired.

He stood holding both her hands, watching her eyes.

"I came at a bad time," he said quietly.

Other things came back to her: his quick understanding, his quietness. They had been singing together, the last time she had seen him, arm in arm with Peter and Rudi and Liese and the others, marching away from the Sportpalast with the crowds, singing *Deutschland, Deutschland über Alles* until they grew tired of it. At least, she remembered now, Martin hadn't been singing. He and Peter had been arguing about the anti-Jewish posters along the railway embankment, and the way the Führer had left his box early to avoid having to shake hands with Jesse Owens, the American Negro. Peter had said it was nothing to do with that.

"No," she told Martin, "it's not a bad time at all. Not to see you." She managed a laugh of pleasure. "It's been three years!"

"Yes." He kept her hands in his, watching her quietly. She looked tired, he could see, but more than that. There was a reticence, a withdrawal; he felt he was looking at her from a long way off. "Let me take you home. Is that where you're going?"

"Yes. It's been a long day."

They began walking together to the revolving doors. "Do you still live in the Grünewald?" he asked her.

"Yes. But a different place. A flat of my own." He took her arm as they went down the steps to the street. "How long have you been waiting for me?" she thought to ask.

"I came here at about seven o'clock." He began looking for a taxi.

"Since *seven?*" She looked at her watch, then up at his face, "But *Martin* . . ."

"After three years," he smiled gently, "a few hours didn't make much difference."

*   *   *

They swam in the Havel, all morning, and had lunch at the little café near the bridge.

"Do you see Peter these days?" Martin asked her.

"No. He is an SS officer." She glanced around her.

"I ran into Rudi yesterday. Rudi Mahler."

"He is in the same unit." Her tone was curt.

All the morning they'd talked about the times they'd shared before, and the people they'd known here in Berlin; and she'd told him something of her childhood, asking him about England and his family. They had unconsciously avoided discussing the new Germany, or the National Socialists; but this couldn't be kept up forever, and they both knew it. So much had happened in Germany since they'd last seen each other.

"It's strange," Hedda told him as they drank their coffee, "about your sister."

"Yes. Well, not entirely. She was always rallying to some romantic cause or other, head high and banners flying."

Hedda was silent for a moment, looking down. "The Nazi cause is romantic?"

"She thinks so."

"Do you think so?" She didn't look up.

"No. They're a pack of gangsters."

Now she raised her eyes, quickly. "You knew it was safe for you to say that, didn't you?"

He smiled. "Otherwise I wouldn't have said it." They were both speaking softly. The nearest people were a few tables away and they were in the open air, with the river drifting past toward the bridge. Watching her, he didn't want to talk about the Nazis, or Vanessa's stupid idolatry, or anything except the young woman who sat opposite him with her quiet eyes and her dark hair still wet from swimming, and the soft laugh that had sometimes come when they'd been splashing about in the water and he'd managed to make her forget whatever it was on her mind. It was something serious, he knew that now; but he wasn't going to ask.

"I think," he said slowly, still watching her, "you're the most beautiful woman I've ever seen."

She smiled briefly. "Thank you." Then she withdrew into herself again, and so deeply that he felt she was hardly with him. "I've got to go soon. I'm on duty again at three."

"All right." He had to control the urge to ask her what had happened in her life since they'd last met, so that he could know her a little better before he had to get on the plane for London, the day after tomorrow.

"You're always so gentle, Martin. I remember it so well. You never question, or insist." She put her hands on the table, palm upward, so that he could hold them. "That was why I liked you so much. Why I like you." Her eyes were wet, and she closed them, and said with her hands in his and her voice faltering, "Last week they arrested my brother, and I'm terribly frightened for him."

Martin drew a long breath. "Franz?"

"Yes."

"What for?"

"He was distributing leaflets, and putting posters up, and that sort of thing." Her voice was shaking now and he strengthened his fingers around hers, waiting for her to go on, giving her time to control herself. She wanted to break down and cry but he knew she wasn't going to; he was remembering things about her that he thought he'd forgotten. "He's only seventeen years old," she said after a little while. "That's so young."

Martin paid the bill and they left the table, walking slowly down the sloping grass to the river; it was difficult to talk with people around.

"Where is Franz now?" he asked Hedda.

"In one of the KZs."

His mouth tightened. "Are you sure?"

"Yes."

They walked through wild flowers, reached the bank

and sat there, watching the water. "Which one, do you know?"

"Someone said it was Buchenwald." She still spoke in almost a whisper, though they were alone now; it was because she was talking about something that couldn't be true, that mustn't be put into words. "They took me along for interrogation, for three hours. But I didn't know anything about it." With sudden soft impatience —"I couldn't even have imagined how incredibly stupid he was being."

Martin had his arm around her shoulders, but couldn't make her stop trembling. "Can't your father do anything?"

She shook her dark head. "No. He's in disfavor already. He spoke his mind recently at a military briefing, and Hitler was there. Hitler doesn't trust any of his generals. He's afraid of their intelligence."

"And power."

"They haven't got any power left," Hedda said. "They simply have to obey orders."

A water bird sped from the bridge and skimmed the surface of the water, scooping up an insect and leaving ripples.

"At his age," Martin said, "they'll be lenient with him. A sharp warning, then they'll let him go."

She said slowly, "They are murdering infants in arms, out there in the camps. In front of their mothers. It's absolutely imperative, you see, that I don't console myself with illusions, because it won't help him."

"You've appealed, of course?"

She gave a kind of laugh. "You think there was a trial? This isn't England, Martin. This is the New Germany." She freed herself gently and stood up, finding her swimming costume and rolling it into the towel. "When did you say you were going back?"

He got to his feet. "On Saturday. The day after tomorrow."

"So soon." She gazed across the river, her eyes nar-

rowed against its reflected light and glinting with the
tears she refused to shed. She was absent again, miles
away, and Martin felt angry with himself for not knowing how to bring her back and keep her close, so that
in some way he could help. But there was no way;
he knew that.

"There's still tomorrow," he said.

She moved her dark head and looked at him. "No."

"Aren't you free tomorrow?"

She laughed again, mockingly. "I shall never be free
again. There's a war coming, Martin, and you're going
home. This is the last time we'll see each other, and
. . . it'll be easier if we say goodbye now."

Suddenly it was over, he thought. Hedda, freedom,
peace. They were all caught up in the dark wind that
had started rising.

"Are you sure?" he asked her.

"Yes."

He came close to her and she held on to him tightly,
shutting her eyes and listening to the river and trying
to forget, just for these few moments, the hideous dark
of the future. Then she kissed him and they walked hand
in hand along the bank toward the bridge.

The next morning Martin called at the British Embassy
for any messages and found a cable for him, with orders
to rejoin his unit immediately in London. He went to
the telephone and rang up Vanessa at the hotel, asking
her to pack right away and be ready for the next flight
out of Berlin.

LONDON, 17 AUGUST

Just before noon Sir Thomas Benedict drove into
Queen's Gate, left his car at the curb and climbed
the steps to the flat his family maintained for their
visits to town. He noticed a work crew had started

piling sandbags along the railings, opposite the basement windows. In the far distance, through the trees, he could see the anti-aircraft unit digging in with its five-inch gun beside a pile of camouflage nets. The papers had spoken of "maneuvers."

The telephone was ringing when he opened the front door, and he went inside and picked up the receiver.

"Hello?"

"Is this Sir Thomas Benedict?" The voice had a German accent.

"Speaking."

"One moment, please. There is a call for you."

He waited, dropping the copy of the *Times* on to the Louis Quinze side table and watching the sunshine glowing in the stained glass panels of the front door.

There was a click on the line and he thought he heard a man's voice, rather faintly.

"Hello?" he said.

There was another long silence, and then the man's voice again, a little louder.

"Father?"

"Oh, hello, Martin! How are things over there?"

Silence came again, and Martin's voice sounded quite odd when he spoke now, completely toneless.

"Father . . . I'm sorry. Vanessa . . . Vanessa has killed herself. I'm sorry. . . ."

5

Martin stared at the wreath of blood-red roses and felt the hatred burning inside him.

". . . And now do we bring her body here, to lie beside those of her beloved forebears in the presence of the loved ones she has been chosen, by the will of Almighty God, to precede to this hallowed place . . ."

By tradition it was a private ceremony, confined to the members of the family and their closest friends; but the village high street had become jammed with traffic early in the day, and people lined the ancient stone wall that ran from the church to the rectory, some with children on their shoulders. "There must be a hundred of them," Constable Brewster had told one of the churchwardens in disgust. "You'd think they'd have the decency to stay away."

Nothing had been revealed to the press, but a reporter had been nosing about last night, plying half the patrons of the Blue Boar with beer to loosen their tongues. He hadn't got much from them, but enough to run a small headline in the late-night final in London: *Private Funeral for Hitler's Mistress in Surrey Village.*

". . . And to cherish her memory as if she were with us still, so that she shall remain with us in our hearts forever more . . ."

51

Martin stared at the roses, wanting to go across to the wreath and tear it apart and trample it under his feet. He'd been shocked when he'd seen it there on the coffin and read the inscription, swinging around to face his father.

"Did you know about this?"

"Yes, Martin. It was discussed in the highest quarters, believe me, and the final decision was to let it remain. But I know how you feel."

"I doubt it."

Martin had not been easy for them to deal with, since he had landed at Croydon Airport last night with the coffin. *"I should have taken the gun away from her,"* he'd kept on saying, feverish with guilt.

A breeze blew across the heads of the mourners, bringing the first dead leaves of the autumn drifting down, one of them coming to rest near the simple inscription borne by the blood-red wreath: *In Memory of a True Friend, from Adolf Hitler.*

On the far side of the coffin the man with the thinning hair and the small foreign lapel badge stood with his head bowed as the last prayers were spoken. He was the chargé d'affaires from the German Embassy in London, and Sir Thomas had told Martin privately, "There were discussions about him, too, but again, we had no valid excuse for refusing his official request to attend. It would have amounted to a diplomatic insult, and our relationship with Germany is extremely sensitive, as you know."

Martin stood with the hatred consuming him. Until she had gone to Berlin two years ago, Vanessa had been so very English—fair-minded, kicking against every kind of authority, contemptuous of the politics of mass-persuasion and ready to fight to the death for liberty—her own or anyone else's. Then she'd somehow come under the spell of a power-hungry brute who was the incarnation of authority itself and whose genius for mass-persuasion was threatening the liberty of the whole civilized world.

In Memory of a True Friend . . .

God knew how it could have happened.

We now have to ask you to identify the body, Herr Benedict. A formality, you understand. The door still open, with the hotel staff crowding into the passage outside and the three policemen standing to attention, watching him. And on the floor, Vanessa, his sister, the cloth drawn back so that he could see her face with its hideous wound and the caked blood and the powder marks. Not far away, on the rose-patterned carpet, the framed photograph of Hitler. She had taken out the glass and written across the print, using her lipstick: *Auf Wiedersehen, mein Führer!*

And nearby, on her other side, the small ivory-paneled gun.

He gave it to me.

People had begun moving around him. In a little while he realized he'd been standing alone, but didn't know for how long. Then his father's hand was on his arm. He said to his father, *"I should have taken it away from her."*

"You must get over that, Martin." Gently he moved his son away from the graveside, to where his mother and the rest of the family were waiting. "If you'd taken it away from her, she would have done something else. If it was anyone's fault, it was mine, for sending you out there to bring her home."

"I didn't let you down," Martin told him, his voice a strange soft singsong just this side of breaking. "I brought her home."

His father gripped his arm. "What we have to do," he said quietly, "is to comfort your mother, in any way we can."

Room 15 was right at the end of the passage on the top floor of the building. The lift reached no higher than the floor below, and a civilian had escorted Martin to a short flight of stairs with its own separate door. The civilian had said nothing at all on their way to Room 15.

General Westerby himself opened the door, and the civilian went back the way he had come, without a word being exchanged.

"Come along in, Benedict." The General stood aside for him and closed the door firmly. Another man was in the room, short and disheveled, in a crumpled old green sports jacket and cracked suede shoes. "Captain Benedict," Westerby told him, and said to Martin, "This gentleman is a member of His Majesty's Government."

"How do you do, sir."

"Ah, yes, Benedict," the short man said, eyeing him obliquely as ash fell from his cigarette onto the sports jacket. "Happy to know you, yes."

The General told Martin in low tones, "My sincere condolences. A shock for us all, of course."

"Thank you, sir."

"If you don't feel up to this interview, just say so. But it's of vital importance and I'd like you to do your best. Now I'm going to leave you with this gentleman, and you should know that you can speak with absolute confidence, just as if you were speaking to me. Understood?"

"Yes, sir."

When the door closed behind the General, Martin noticed that the scruffy-looking civilian was still observing him, standing perfectly still with his hands buried in his pockets and the cigarette dangling from his lips.

"Relax," he told Martin in a rather high, weary tone. "Stand at ease, and all that. Sit down if you like. Rotten show," he said with a certain kindness, "about your young sister, yes, condolences. Got herself into the wrong set, could happen to anyone. You must be rather cut up. You want to come back some other time, for this little powwow?"

Martin stood at ease, but no more than that. There was something about this little man, despite his appearance, that suggested discreet authority of a high order. "No, sir. I'm ready now."

The man nodded, letting more ash fall. "Good show." He began pacing now, his crêpe-soled shoes rucking the loose Indian rug as they shuffled from the window to the desk. "You've met Hitler, I understand. Only once?"

"That's correct. For a minute or two."

"That's all?"

"Yes."

"D'you know any of the other people? Göring? Goebbels? Himmler? Any of the hierarchy?"

"No, sir. I was introduced to Göring and Himmler, the same evening, but that was all it was—an introduction." His mind slipped strangely, and he saw Vanessa's brilliant smile, heard the clicking of heels and the murmur of voices in the background. It had happened before, in the last three days: Vanessa kept flashing vividly into his mind.

"Are you all right?"

"Sir? Yes, perfectly all right."

The man was staring at him, his round blue eyes contemplative. "M'm. Do you feel you could—shall we say—insinuate yourself into the Nazi hierarchy, I mean as the brother of someone whom Hitler appeared to"— he waved a vague hand—"to admire."

"No," said Martin. "I don't."

The civilian cocked an eyebrow. "Not much love for them, of course. Their fault, for the most part, I suppose. Took her in, as they've taken in the entire German population, yes, see your point."

"It's simply that I've no real influence in Berlin. A mere introduction, plus my relationship to—to someone who no longer—"

"We'll drop the matter," the short man said firmly. "It's of no importance. I just wanted to cover every aspect of the situation." He wandered to the desk and dropped the cigarette end into a heaped ashtray. "And the situation is this. An operation is to be mounted by a certain unit of the Z organization of the SIS, at present based in The Hague. We are seeking an agent, who will operate alone but who will have close support in terms of shelter on enemy territory, wireless communication, code and cipher facilities and so on. Of several people we've investigated, you seem to be the best hope. The SIS first got on to you because of your slight connection with the Nazi hierarchy, but you've got other qualifications—which this fellow Brooks got out of you in Berlin." He stopped shuffling and stood directly in front of Martin, his pale blue eyes brooding. "The only thing we haven't done to you is put you under an X-ray machine."

Martin watched him attentively. The man's voice was still quiet, but it had lost its vague, meandering tone; he was now choosing his words carefully and his gaze was direct and unblinking. "If you were to take this job on, you'd have to transfer from the Intelligence Corps to the SIS, keeping your rank and pay but losing everything else in the way of privileges, leave and so on. You'd be working under civilian cover in Germany, and you would remain there after the outbreak of hostilities—which will occur very shortly. You would work alone, as I've said, but with every possible support."

He turned away and shuffled back to the window, peering out at the first of the streetlights coming on along Whitehall. Big Ben was sounding the quarter, and he seemed distracted by it, as if the passing of time was important. In a moment he turned back to face Martin. "Your work would be difficult, exacting, and hazardous in the extreme. You would stand as much chance of coming out of this operation alive as an infantryman would standing in the front-line trenches of a war. There's one consolation: your life would depend a great deal on your own initiative, your own wits and your own guts. That gives you a slight advantage." He shuffled a few steps closer. "If you decide to do it, you'd leave for Berlin before noon tomorrow, which would give you the morning to pack up and say goodbye to your family and friends. It's impossible for me to give you any more information at this point, in case you decide against it; even as it is, I'll remind you of the oath of secrecy you took when you joined the Intelligence Corps. The thing is, you've been warned. This isn't a suicide mission, but it's damned close, and in all fairness you should know that. Is everything clear?"

"I think so."

"M'm. Plenty of missing pieces, but you get the drift. I'm giving you till midnight to make a decision. Not long, I know. Best I can do."

Martin said at once, "I don't need till midnight, sir. I'd like the job."

The civilian let his wide blue-eyed stare range over Martin's face. "There's nothing in the reports on you that suggests you're impulsive by nature."

"This isn't an impulse."

"You're upset by the loss you and your family have just sustained, I can quite—"

"If I stay with the Intelligence Corps I shall probably spend the entire war in England, or at least on Allied territory. Working for you, I can get close to the enemy. I want to do that. Very much."

"Now look here, Benedict, we're not interested in heroics, or in personal vendettas. You'll be working for England, not for your own sense of outrage. Understand that."

Martin gave himself a moment to think. He wanted this job and he wanted it urgently, but a wrong word now could lose it for him. With great care he said, "I take it, sir, that if I succeed in the mission, I shall be damaging the enemy substantially. It sounds like that sort of job. And that's all I want to do. I'm asking you to count on me."

The civilian went on staring at him, his hands deep in his pockets and his shoulders slightly hunched inside the faded sports jacket. His eyes gave away nothing whatsoever. Then he turned and shambled across to the desk and sat behind it, crossing his short legs and putting his feet on the desk top.

"This isn't going to be a game, Benedict. It won't be like racing a car around the track or playing the fool with sabers in Richmond Park. We shall require your total dedication. Total discipline. Total obedience to orders. And if you should get caught, as an agent on enemy territory in time of war, we shall require you to take your own life, and immediately, to avoid interrogation. Are you prepared to do that?"

"Without hesitation."

The man watched him for a moment. "I can still give you till midnight."

"We'd be wasting valuable time."

"Very well. You've got the job. I can now tell you quite a lot more about it, so you'd better sit down."

6

BUCHENWALD FOREST, 26 AUGUST 1939

The man with the beard fell slowly, his knees folding but his body still upright, so that as he went down he seemed to be praying, for his eyes were closed. The brown leather suitcase hit the road alongside the file of marching men, bursting open to reveal shirts, a shaving kit and three bundles of money. As his body keeled over, he fell forward on his face, and two or three of the men behind him were walking over him before they realized it.

"*Drag that man clear, you scum!*"

Corporal Trot was hurrying up from the rear, his club swinging on a thong at his wrist. He was stocky, fair-haired, twenty-three years old, and had been at school in his native town of Sonderhausen, near the foot of the Harz Mountains. He had learned the flute there, and was quite good on it.

"*Drag him clear, are you fucking well deaf?*"

The file broke up and several prisoners made haste to pull the fallen man to the side of the road, where autumn flowers were blooming, the dust silting on their leaves and petals as the men marched by. Corporal Trot kicked the man twice, once in the face and once in the groin; it was a method he'd worked out for himself: if they didn't wake up when he kicked their faces, they'd wake up when he kicked them in the groin, if they were going to wake up at all.

This one didn't move, and Corporal Trot was disappointed; he liked hearing them whimper and ask for mercy. But he'd seen the stuff spilling out of the suitcase, and would have to buck up and stake his claim before the other guards reached him. So he pulled his revolver and held it two feet from the man's head and fired once, feeling that sudden kind of liquid heat in his groin that he always felt. Some of the blood came up onto his boots and he cursed the man and fired again, not liking to be got the better of. Then he went to the opened suitcase. He pushed the bundles of money inside his tunic, kicked the rest of the stuff across the grass and searched for anything that might be interesting. But there was nothing worthwhile. The shirts looked like silk and the shaving kit was leather and he could make out a silver schnapps flask, but he couldn't take everything he saw—he'd need a whole bloody truck and a warehouse. Money was the best thing, and he always went for that.

"Come on, you scummy bastards, stop dawdling!"

The file of prisoners began moving, but it took the last of the strength of some of them and they began toppling over and dropping their belongings, and Corporal Trot yelled at the others to drag them clear, and the whole process started again.

Two thousand prisoners, in the last two weeks alone, had been marched from the railway station in Weimar to the camp, and it was filling up satisfactorily.

Franz von Gerlach was marching with his eyes shut. Over the last nine days he had learned several ways of keeping his sanity and staying alive, and this was one of them: to shut your eyes whenever there was a chance, so that the world going on outside was less real—you could only hear it and feel it and smell it. That was bad enough, of course, but you still had a slight advantage. You couldn't shut your eyes whenever

you liked, naturally; he had shut them when the
prisoners had been lined up alongside the train at
Aschersleben, about halfway from Berlin, and a guard
had seen him and dragged him out of the line for being
"asleep on his feet," throwing him down the embankment and kicking him back every time he crawled to
the top again, seventeen times until the guard got bored
with it.

Franz hadn't known how bad things were, when he'd
been in Berlin as a student, an ordinary citizen. Stories
had been passing around, about the concentration
camps, but no one believed them. If he and his friends
had known about this they would have announced it in
the leaflets; but no one would have believed them either.
Somebody, one day, would have to start believing what
was happening to the German nation. Otherwise there'd
be no hope.

They reached the camp in the evening, when the long
day's sun was going down behind the hills, and swallows
dipped and circled across the tall watchtowers and the
barbed wire, hunting for insects on the wing.

They spent the night in cells, though not lying down.
The SS guards bludgeoned them into the narrow cement
confines until they were packed body to body with no
room to fall down; then the doors were forced shut
against them and the ventilators were closed and the
heating system was turned on at full temperature. For
a while they could hear the guards laughing outside, like
schoolboys enjoying a prank. Before morning, several
hundred of the prisoners had fainted, still on their feet
and jammed upright among the rest. The death roll,
duly recorded in the files, was seventy-three.

After morning roll call the survivors were herded into
the SS Political Division for classifying. Among others,
Franz was given a red triangle to wear, as a political
detainee. He was then asked for his personal data.

"What's the name of the drunken bastard that sired you?"

Franz couldn't hear very well. The building was crammed with new arrivals and there were twenty or so SS clerks clattering at their typewriters.

"Come on, answer!"

"I didn't understand the question."

A fist swung and he was pitched across the wooden table. The clerk pushed him back with a curse. "Father's name, you stupid swine!"

Franz shook himself, feeling consciousness slipping. He had been one of those who had fainted during the night.

"General Constantin von Gerlach."

"Ha! Bloody aristocrat, is he?" The clerk began typing. "And what diseased bitch shat you into this unsuspecting world?"

Franz swayed slightly, vaguely aware of what he was being asked. Someone had told him—the man with the beard, who had fallen along the road—that psychological intimidation would be part of the process at the camp.

"Come on, will you!" The guard kicked him in the knees and then, as he doubled over, knocked him upright again. Franz grabbed for support. *"Keep to attention, you sloppy bastard!"*

Consciousness slipped again, and he had to force himself back into reality. The question, yes. His mother's name.

"I will tell you my mother's name. She is Frau Gisela von Gerlach."

"Frau, is it? Airs and bloody graces! You're going to learn a few things here, Franz *von* fuckin' Gerlach. In this place men are men, and *gentlemen* get shoved head down in the latrine by way of a christening." The typewriter clattered again. "Other relatives? Brothers, sisters? Come on!"

The clerk at the typewriter was moving backward

and forward as Franz watched him. His mind kept losing focus, and he began to discover truths about all this, as inner consciousness took over. These people were not, in fact, people at all. They were wild animals, and once you realized this it was more understandable, more acceptable. It was only when you persisted in thinking they were human beings that you felt the stress, the bewilderment. Let them say what they like, let them do what they like, but don't let them make you feel that you are of the same creaturehood. In this way, you can remain whole, and uncontaminated.

". . . *Will you!*"

He reeled against the table as the club struck him; the clerk stood up and shoved him upright.

"*Stand to attention, you lazy sod!*"

From somewhere, from some region of remaining consciousness, he brought the thought forward into words. His voice, he heard, was quite loud this time. "I have a sister. Her name is Fräulein Hedda von Gerlach."

"*Fräulein?* That's quite a fancy title for a syphilitic whore!" His typewriter began tapping again.

It took half an hour. At one stage Franz found himself on the stone floor with his hands clasped around his head as the guard's boot came thudding at him. At another, he regained consciousness with his body slumped across the typewriter, before they dragged him upright and slapped his face till his eyes opened. At intervals he heard the Jewish prisoners being whipped, just outside the door; he had learned enough by this time to know that when you were asked why you were here, and didn't know, you were given a thrashing at once, for not acknowledging your crime. But if you were Jewish you would be thrashed in any case.

At the evening roll call fourteen men were lined up against the wall and shot in the back of the head. Twelve of them had failed to answer their names loudly enough, one had buckled to his knees from exhaustion, and one had dropped his cap.

After roll call certain prisoners were called to the gatehouse over the loudspeakers, and among them was Franz. SS Corporal Trot called his name again and ordered him to stand forward. *"Get that badge off!"* But Franz wasn't quick enough to obey, and the Corporal wrenched the red triangle from his uniform shirt and threw it on to the ground, thrusting a different one at him, a blue disk stamped with a capital *B*.

"Pin it on, come on!" He stood face to face with Franz, his small eyes flickering. Franz could smell drink on his breath. "Know what it's for, do you?"

"No." Franz fumbled with the badge, his fingers numb from blows he'd received on his arms during the day.

"No, *Corporal!*" Trot thrust his face at him. "No, *Corporal!* No, *Corporal!* No, *Corporal!* No, *Corporal!* No, *Corporal!* No, *Corporal!*"

"No, Corporal," Franz said. In the glare of the floodlights his eyes were swimming, and Corporal Trot was only a blur.

"Not interested? Eh?"

"Yes, Corporal."

"Then why don't you ask me what it's for?"

His blurred shaped rocked backward and forward.

"What is it for, Corporal?"

"Don't ask bloody stupid questions!" said Corporal Trot, and threw his head back, laughing in a high shrill cackle. "Get back to your quarters, go on, before I—" He lifted his hand and Franz waited, not trying to dodge, because today he had learned another thing: if you stood still and took the blow, they often left it at that; but if you tried to dodge it you'd get two or three, or maybe a dozen. But the Corporal let his hand drop to his hip. "Go on, then, get back to your bloody pigsty. *Go on—at the double!"*

Franz returned to his quarters in "B" Block, and at

some time during the night decided that he must some-how try to escape, since there was clearly no alterna-tive.

BERLIN, 27 AUGUST 1939

Hedda was just finishing her bath when the telephone rang, and now she was perched on the stool with the towel around her, holding the receiver with one hand and trying to rub herself dry with the other.

It was Lottie, at the hospital.

"It's in the report," Hedda told her, trying not to sound impatient. "You have to do exactly as it says in the report, under 'Postoperative Instructions.'" When-ever the phone rang, these days, it always seemed to be Lottie; she could never get anything right.

"It says hypocalcemia," Lottie said in a puzzled tone.

"Of *course* it says hypocalcemia. It was a massive transfusion of citrated blood. What's the prescription?"

"One gram of calcium gluconate."

"After how many milliliters of blood?" A trickle of bathwater was running down her leg and she mopped at it with the towel.

"Two thousand."

"Well then, you—"

Someone was knocking at the door. "You have to do exactly as prescribed, Lottie!" Why were they knocking, when there was a bell?

"I was afraid of making a mistake," Lottie's plaintive tones came over the line.

The knocking was repeated. "Lottie, is Dr. Vorst in the building?"

"Yes. He's—"

"Then check with him. I've got to answer the door, Lottie. Check with Dr. Vorst, you understand?"

"All right." Lottie didn't sound at all certain; but then she never was.

Hedda said goodbye and rang off, and went quickly to the door as the knocking began again.

"Who is it?"

"Gestapo."

She caught her breath and felt the familiar pain around her heart, crouching over it for a moment and shutting her eyes. When she could manage it she called through the door, "Give me a few seconds—I'm just out of the bath." She dried under her arms and between her thighs and threw the towel on top of the linen basket and took down her dressing gown, wrapping it around her. She couldn't find her mules but there wasn't time to look. Mirror, fingers through her hair, shaking it back, my God I look so frightened. . . .

"I'm coming!"

More questions. They were here to ask more questions. Please God, let me say everything right.

She opened the door.

There were three of them, all in uniform. The one in the middle was an officer; the other two stood rigidly a pace behind him.

"Fräulein von Gerlach?"

"Yes. Yes." He was looking down, and she pulled the dressing gown closer and retied the cord, and remembered her feet were bare.

"Superintendent Vogel, of Gestapo Headquarters." His heels came together. "May I come in for a few minutes?"

"Of course." She stood back for him. The two guards remained outside, turning their backs and standing at ease as she closed the door. "I—I was in my bath."

He moved with small measured steps into the middle of the room, a slight man, but strong-looking, compact and muscular in his black uniform; his eyes were dark in an almost dead-white face. "Who is here with you, Fräulein?"

"No one."

He turned to survey her. "I heard you talking."

"Oh, yes—I was on the telephone."

"Not, then, in your bath?" His gaze remained on her face.

"The—the phone rang when I was drying myself." It sounded intimate, she thought, as if she were revealing something to her doctor. It was because of his stare.

"How inconvenient." He spoke softly, in precise accents. The irises of his eyes were so dark, she noticed, that they were almost black, making it look as if his pupils were unnaturally large. She refused to glance away, even though his intimate stare unnerved her.

"Would you—give me a few moments to get dressed?" she asked him.

His gaze swept her body, down to her bare feet. "That isn't necessary, Fräulein."

She felt her face reddening with anger, and prayed he wouldn't notice. Anger against these people could hurt her brother. She had to be mature, and accept these insulting innuendoes as a compliment to her womanhood.

He took off his cap, looking around uncertainly until she decided to take it from him and put it on the marquetry pier table beside the door.

"Thank you," he said simply, brushing back his thin hair with his fingers.

"Please sit down, Superintendent—excuse me, I missed your exact—"

"Vogel. Superintendent Karl Vogel." His polished black boots creaked slightly as he crossed to the armchair and sat down. He had hardly taken his gaze from her since he'd come into the room, and she felt disturbingly exposed.

"How can I help you, Superintendent?" She perched on the little Italian brocade stool near the bathroom door, feeling its loose joints give slightly. The flat had been furnished out of an antique shop, and most of the pieces, even the worst of them, were her landlady's joy.

"I imagine you have a question for me, Fräulein," the Superintendent said softly. He waited.

Even the silence was intimate, with this man here. The house was in the quietest part of Grünewald, at the edge of the forest.

"Yes," she said, tensing. "I would like to know where my brother is."

He gave a measured nod. "Of course you would. You must have telephoned a dozen times in the past few days." He lifted his pale, dry hands to inspect his nails, and she was aware of immediate relief as his eyes left her face. "I was at Headquarters, Fräulein, when you were interrogated. I passed through the office, and stayed for a moment. Do you remember?" His eyes snapped up to watch her.

"Yes," she said quickly. It was a lie, of course; they all looked the same in their beastly uniform. But he'd be offended if she said no. "Yes, of course."

He nodded again. "I stayed for a moment," he told her softly, "because I noticed how beautiful you were."

She shrank into herself, as if he'd touched her. "Thank you," she said, and tried to smile.

"Unusually beautiful, Fräulein von Gerlach. However, to answer your question: your brother is at present in protective custody, in a camp at Buchenwald, near Weimar."

She tried to calm her breathing. She'd heard Franz was there, but not officially. Now it was official. Buchenwald was one of the major KZs, though ordinary citizens weren't meant to know of its existence.

"I—I see. How—how long will he be there for?"

"You can write him letters, you know. You should do that. They would bring him comfort. Life for him is rather different now from what he was used to. A foolish young man, of course. Extremely foolish."

"Yes, I—know that."

"It's a pity you couldn't advise him, Fräulein, not

to make his objections to National Socialism so evident. He hasn't made things easy for himself. However, you may be pleased to hear that I have used my influence with the camp kommandant. I explained that your brother is too young to appreciate what National Socialism means to the Fatherland, and he has been placed in the *Besonder* category as a special prisoner."

Hedda drew a deep breath. "What does that mean, exactly?"

"It means that the guards are not permitted to treat him harshly."

She almost got up and went over to him in a rush of gratitude, but instinct stopped her. "Thank you, Superintendent Vogel. That means a great deal to me."

She should, of course, feel angry at the very idea of her brother being treated "harshly"; she should be demanding his immediate release. But she'd been through all that earlier in the week, when she'd heard Franz had been arrested. She had almost shouted at the Gestapo men who'd interrogated her—her brother was young, he was still a student, he felt sincerely that personal liberty was being curtailed in Germany by the new leaders, and all they should do was give him political instruction so that he could understand the necessity of discipline, and so on and so on. At one point they had actually laughed at her, and if the desk hadn't been between them she would have slapped their faces. Then it had dawned on her that the more she protested, the worse it would be for Franz. There was no justice anymore: he hadn't even had a trial. The Gestapo was the organ of the state, and the state was the law. If you wanted to complain about something the Gestapo had done, you could only complain to the Gestapo.

"I thought you would be pleased, Fräulein. No one likes to think of such a young person being given . . . the kind of treatment that is routine in such a place. You see, the SS guards can hardly be expected to show much kindness to prisoners who have proved themselves dangerous to Germany. At the moment there are more than three hundred thousand such despicable elements under protective custody, and the task of controlling them is not easy; it calls for rough methods." He got to his feet and moved slowly between the open doorway of the bathroom and the window, his black boots creaking. "Even though your brother has been placed in a special category, he will continue to suffer conditions that you and I would consider unbearable; I've no wish to deceive you on that score, Fräulein. It might be possible for me to have him removed to the special compound reserved for important personages, where the daily life is almost comfortable. The son of a general in the Wehrmacht, a holder of the Knight's Cross, might conceivably qualify. I would have to make quite an effort, however, to accomplish such a thing." He interrupted his pacing to move closer to her, until he was standing over her with his eyes moving deliberately from her face to her body. "Perhaps you can think of a good reason why I should make that effort, Fräulein von Gerlach."

Hedda got up at once, turning away from him and pulling the dressing gown tighter at the waist, her hands shaking and her breath coming fast. She'd expected this proposal from the moment he'd come into the room, but it was still a shock and it left her nerveless. It was a moment before she could speak with any control.

"I'm afraid I can't, Superintendent Vogel, unless it were your natural inclination to generosity."

She heard his boots creaking behind her, and waited with her eyes closed and her thoughts frantic.

"Your own generosity," his soft voice came, "is more to the point. It's all I ask of you—for your brother's sake."

She turned to face him before he tried to touch her.

"No. I refuse." She waited again, furious and afraid, thinking of Franz and his need of her help, then trying not to think of him, clearing her mind so that she could fight this crude brute with his inhuman demands.

"I admire your sense of virtue, Fräulein. However, let me suggest how costly it is—for your brother." He pulled a wallet from his tunic, took out three photographs and dropped them onto the table. "He is not too easy to recognize in these pictures, but I'm sure you'll succeed if you study them closely."

Hedda picked them up, her heart contracting as she looked at them. In all three photographs Franz appeared in the ill-fitting striped uniform of a camp inmate, his head completely shaven and his young face dark with bruises; in one of them, an SS guard was standing over a prisoner in the background, his truncheon raised; in another, a man beside Franz stood holding his face, with blood trickling from beneath his fingers; in the third, Franz was facing the camera, making an attempt to smile—and that was the worst.

"I ask nothing uncivilized of you, Fräulein. Nothing . . . onerous."

She felt tears coming and immediately forced them back, dropping the hideous photographs onto the table and folding her arms.

"No," she heard herself telling him, "I can't be generous to people like you."

I've met a girl, Franz had told her a little while ago, *called Sigrid. She's in Philosophy. She thinks my hair's too long—do you think I ought to have it cut a bit?*

I think you'd look nice either way, she'd told him, *and so should Sigrid.*

He'd always come to her about things like that, trusting her with his confidences.

Superintendent Vogel was picking up the photographs and putting them away, his movements precise and measured. "I haven't actually met your brother—I was absent from Berlin at the time of his arrest—but even in these photographs he seems to be quite a handsome young boy, and once again I've no wish to offer you false reassurances. The unfortunate fact is that the *Besonder* insignia he now wears—thanks to my own goodwill—is not a total guarantee that he won't suffer abuse by older and stronger prisoners. In a crowded camp, such men seek whatever way they can to relieve their sexual tensions. I'm sure you understand."

His soft tones gave way to silence while she stood frozen, her eyes shut and her arms clasped across her body, the blood leaving her face and her mind refusing to combat this horror with logical thought. She wished, instead, that her father was here now, breaking in through the door and seizing this vile creature and hurling him to the floor; she wished her mother was here, gently shaking her awake to tell her she'd been having a nightmare; she wished that in some miraculous way the man in this room with her would vanish from the face of the earth, leaving her to realize she'd been in the throes of hallucination. She had stopped thinking about her brother.

"No," she was saying through her clenched teeth. "No."

There was a faint squeak of leather, and she opened her eyes in case he was coming closer. But he was standing at the window, silhouetted against the sky and the massed green of the linden leaves, his back to her.

"In fairness to General von Gerlach and his wife," he told her deliberately, "I should consider sending those pictures of their son to them by post, so that they'll be fully informed of events and can take whatever action they choose, for what it's worth." He turned to look at her again. "Don't you agree?"

She was shaking all over now and couldn't stop herself. If her mother saw those photographs it would break her heart.

"How vile you are," she said, half-whispering it in the stillness of the room. "How inhuman."

He came a step closer and she watched him, ready to do something if she had to, claw his eyes out if she had to. He was a strong-looking brute and he could tear this flimsy dressing gown off her in a second.

"As for the question you asked me a few minutes ago," he said, his tone hard now, "I'm afraid I can't tell you how long your brother will remain in protective custody. Germany is about to go to war, and enemies of the state must be dealt with ruthlessly for the sake of its loyal and innocent citizens. Unless I can do something, I very much doubt if you will see your brother again."

The sobbing came into her throat and again she blocked it with a physical effort. For three nights after Franz's arrest she had cried herself to sleep, but she would never break down in front of other people, least of all this man.

He turned away suddenly, took out his wallet again and dropped a card on to the table as he passed to the door. "You may telephone me privately, if you wish, at that number. Otherwise you can contact me at Gestapo Headquarters in the Wilhelmstrasse; simply leave your name, it will suffice." He picked up his cap. "But you must do it within the next twenty-four hours. Good day, Fräulein von Gerlach."

7

BERLIN, 28 AUGUST 1939

"Name?"

  "Martin Friedrich Brinkmann."

  "Rank?"

  "SS-Standartenführer."

  "Unit designation?"

  "Totenkopf."

  "Department?"

  "SS-Führungshauptamt."

  "Who is the chief of the Totenkopfverbände?"

  "SS-Obergruppenführer Pohl."

  "Your specific unit?"

  "Concentration Camp Inspectorate."

  "Turn around. Look in the mirror."

Martin obeyed, observing his reflection in the triple-paned tailor's glass. They made him do it every fifteen minutes or so, to familiarize himself with his new image.

  "Turn left."

He looked into the narrower panel.

  "Turn right."

He moved again, seeing himself in profile. At first he'd refused to put on the gray SS uniform with the Death's Head insignia and the colonel's triple-braided emblem at the shoulder; then they had elaborated on their original briefing, developing the scenario until he

74

realized he had to go through with it. They were offering him the chance of carrying his own personal war into the enemy's camp, and one of the conditions was the wearing of this hated uniform.

Already, after only five days, he was getting used to it, and to the endlessly repeated questions at the start of every training session. And he was getting faster with his answers, and more certain of his ground.

"You may take off your cap and sit down, Colonel Brinkmann."

They never called him by any other name.

"Thank you." He took the chair next to Steven Corbett. Withdrawn, watchful and poker-faced, he had sat in at every one of these sessions so far, but no one had told Martin who he was.

The instructor got up from behind the huge and battered desk and stretched his legs. His name was Otto Tempel—or perhaps that was only his cover name. He had not spoken a word in English to Martin, or in any tongue except High German. He was small, brisk and enigmatic. If he didn't wish to answer one of Martin's frequent questions he simply affected not to have heard it. If anyone came into the vast shadowed cellar where the training sessions were held, he ordered them out again, unless they were there to observe and report on progress. Otto Tempel always wore the same neat blue suit and rimless glasses. A hundred times during any working day he would approach his trainee and look him over, shooting rapid questions and noting Martin's reactions. He was not unlike a sculptor, whittling away at a block of stone and gradually revealing the human figure inside.

"Give the Deutschgruss salute," he said now, and watched critically as Martin sprang to his feet and brought together the heels of his black riding-boots.

"*Heil Hitler!*" His voice echoed through the cavernous archways of the cellar.

"Give it more *enthusiasm!*" Tempel said sharply. "I

know you still dislike doing it, but you've got to get over that. I want to report some *progress*. Now look at the Hakenkreuz." Martin swung his left arm up and stared at the swastika. "Now salute again!"

"*Heil Hitler!*" The echoes rang.

"Better. Better. Remember you are *proud* of this uniform. You are *proud* of your sacred duty to the Führer. *Again!*"

"*Heil Hitler!*"

Martin felt the sweat on his face. Every time he made up his mind to tell them he wouldn't go through with it, he remembered what one of them—Haslam, the quiet one—had said. *If you can succeed in doing what you're trained to do, you'll strike Hitler a bigger blow than you could ever possibly imagine. We can't say more, but if we could, you'd be ready to do anything we demanded of you. Remember that, and have faith in it, when the going gets rough.*

This, so far, was the worst; having to spring to attention like a bloody robot and salute that murderous little ex-corporal—and give it *enthusiasm*. . . .

You know, Martin, you really look so wonderfully Aryan. . . . Vanessa's voice, coming and going in his mind. Dear God, if she could see him now. . . .

"Much better that time," Tempel said briskly. "You may sit down again, Colonel Brinkmann." He pressed a button on the wall behind the desk. "It's time for a bit more background. For obvious reasons, the less information we give you the safer it will be for all of us. Incidentally, have they given you the capsule yet?"

"Yes."

"With instructions, I assume."

"Yes. It's insoluble, and will pass right through the body if I swallow it whole. If I bite it, death will occur within one minute."

"Very well. However, we still have to keep information to the minimum, in case something stops you using the capsule. But you have to know that you are working

THE DAMOCLES SWORD 77

in general for the SIS and specifically for one of its Z departments, this one being headquartered in the German Legation at The Hague. This house is owned by Count Gustav von Seisenhorst-Waldenberg, a fervent anti-Nazi. The—"

Someone was coming down the flight of stone steps at the far end of the cellar and Tempel broke off immediately. Martin recognized him as he moved into the light; he was Sadler, one of the men from the office upstairs.

"Did you buzz?" he asked Tempel.

"Yes. Is there anything definite yet?"

"Not really. Troops are still crowding through the city, going east. Germany's told Holland, Belgium and Switzerland she'll respect their neutrality if war breaks out. The Italians are keeping quiet."

Steve Corbett got up from his chair and walked about for a bit, stretching his legs. Martin looked at his watch and saw it was almost midnight. They'd been going since nine this morning, with bouts of physical training and silent-killing techniques in between.

"What news of the British?" Tempel asked.

"Sir Neville Henderson flew in from London at eight-thirty tonight and went into the Chancellory at ten-thirty. As far as we know he's still there talking to Hitler."

Tempel's thin hair gleamed as he paced under the big art deco lamp. "What about the French?"

"We've got a copy of Daladier's letter to Hitler. He says that Poland is a sovereign nation and that France is going to honor her obligations and support Poland if she's attacked. Shall I get the full draft?"

"No. No, thank you. But keep me in close touch." After Sadler had gone he kept pacing for a couple of minutes, hands in the side pockets of his blue jacket, his rimless glasses reflecting the light. "Perhaps there's still a chance," he said absently. "Perhaps they'll listen. But if they go into Poland our task will become rather more difficult." He quickened his step and went behind the enormous mahogany desk and perched on one arm of the chair. "As I was saying, this house belongs to Count Gustav von Seisenhorst-Waldenberg, and for the moment serves your purposes as a trainee agent. As soon as you start your mission you'll be taking leave of it, permanently. I doubt if you'll need the more commonplace facilities associated with an intelligence operation, but you should know that we can furnish you with most of them if necessary: courier lines, escape routes via France, wireless communication, decoding and deciphering teams, microphotographic and mapreading expertise, certain people versed in high explosive and guerrilla warfare techniques and so on. We will give you several secret addresses where you can rely on immediate shelter in an emergency, and you will be reporting periodically through one of several agents-in-place who have been here in Berlin for some years." He folded his thin hands over one knee. "That will probably answer some of the questions I appeared not to have heard. Do you have any others?"

"Yes," Martin said. "When will I be told what the actual mission consists of?"

"At the end of your training, in approximately two months."

"Two *months?*" Martin got to his feet, restless.

"You must surely realize, Colonel Brinkmann, that to impersonate an SS officer and carry out his specialized duties without exposure is difficult, complicated and sensitive in the extreme. Nobody here is confident, yet, that you can do it. In the next two months, we shall see." He hesitated, then added, "You may be reassured to hear that two of your instructors—Klinger and Veidt—were both SS officers until eighteen months ago. They had believed they were serving in an elite organization devoted to the highest human ideals, until the behavior of their masters finally disabused them. They have been, as you can imagine, rather carefully screened.

The point is that you will not embark upon your mission until those two gentlemen are totally convinced of your authenticity as an SS-Standartenführer of the Totenkopfverbände." He came away from the desk and studied Martin more closely, tilting his narrow head and keeping his critical gaze on him. "Look in the mirror, please."

Martin went over to it and turned twice, and noticed that for the first time he immediately identified the gray-uniformed SS officer in the mirror with himself; until now the idea had always flashed through his mind that it was someone else. *How changed was he going to become in the months ahead, how contaminated by his increasing sense of identification with the people whose neurotic ideologies had led Vanessa to her death?*

Turning away from the mirror he said to Otto Tempel, "I hope none of this sticks."

"Sticks?"

"As mud sticks."

"Oh. Don't worry, our psychiatrist gave you a highly satisfactory report. You have what he calls a deeply integrated sense of the persona. Now please repeat the Oath of Kith and Kin."

Martin felt the familiar creeping of the skin as he forced himself to recite the *Sippeneid*, with his cap off, his feet together and his head raised. *"I swear to Thee, Adolf Hitler, as Führer and Chancellor of the German Reich, Loyalty and Bravery. I vow to Thee and to the Superiors whom Thou shalt appoint, Obedience unto Death. So help me God."*

Otto Tempel was pacing impatiently. "Louder, Colonel Brinkmann, *louder!* And with *pride*—great *pride!* You are addressing your master, and your god! Now . . ."

Martin went through it again three times, and was sweating into his uniform by the time he'd satisfied his instructor.

"Very well, then. Now the Catechism. And answer

me with *pride!*" He planted himself directly in front of Martin, his head angled critically. *"Why do we believe in Germany and the Führer?"*

"Because we believe in God, we believe in Germany, which He created in His world, and in the Führer Adolf Hitler, whom He has sent us."

"Louder, please, Colonel Brinkmann! Head high! *Whom must we primarily serve?"*

"Our people, and our Führer Adolf Hitler."

"With *pride,* Colonel Brinkmann! With *conviction!* Now, *Why do we obey?"*

"From inner conviction—"

"Precisely!" snapped Tempel. "Show your *conviction!"*

Martin glanced down at him angrily, then lifted his head again. *"From inner conviction, from belief in Germany, in the Führer, in the Movement, and in the Schutzstaffel, and from loyalty."*

Tempel turned away, pacing briskly with his hands in his jacket pockets. "You are improving, but not fast enough, Colonel Brinkmann, not nearly fast enough. You must get over your absurd diffidence, you know, your distaste for all this. Remember you are not *pretending* to be an SS officer—you are *learning* to be an SS officer. There's a difference." He came to stand in front of Martin with his small feet neatly together and his head cocked. "You didn't *pretend* to be Cyrano de Bergerac—you *were* Cyrano de Bergerac. Surely I don't have to tell you that."

"Cyrano de Bergerac," said Martin evenly, "wasn't a murderous fanatic. That's where the difference is."

"But you are not playing the role of Adolf Hitler himself, but simply that of a German officer. Stop walking about and listen to me, Colonel Brinkmann. *The more successful you are in this role, the more you will help to destroy Hitler.* Now learn that by heart and repeat it, and repeat it, day and night, until it becomes your sacred and undeniable goal. That must be your personal Holy Grail, Colonel Brinkmann. To *succeed, and to destroy.*"

Martin turned away again, wanting movement to get rid of his tension. "All right. I'll try harder. I think it's coming, but every time I have to—"

"Of course—of course! We know this. Your fervent ambition is to help us to destroy Hitler, and yet we ask you to praise his name and swear allegiance to him!"

"Yes. It's just a kind of barrier I've got to get through."

"Precisely. And you must get through it as soon as you can."

Martin turned back to face his instructor, suddenly worried. "Give me a few more days. For God's sake don't take me off this assignment. I couldn't stand that."

"It is up to you," Tempel said sharply, "whether we take you off this assignment. It is up to you." He went back to the desk, making a note. "Tomorrow, Colonel Brinkmann, you will be allowed to go out into the streets for twelve hours, alone in civilian clothes. I want you to observe and memorize everything you see and hear. Talk to people, as a German citizen; you will in future use your German civilian cover, and this will be your first opportunity of working with it. You may well be asked for your papers by the Gestapo or the SS. Be prepared for that. Immerse yourself in German life, German culture and German attitudes. Do you understand?"

"Yes."

"Very well." Tempel looked at his watch. "We have been working for sixteen hours. A good day. Tomorrow, of course, you will be taking a little fresh air. Enjoy it. But remember, Colonel Brinkmann, that if you encounter the Gestapo or the SS or an ordinary Schupo, and fail to safeguard your cover, you may well be arrested and taken for intensive interrogation. It will be up to you to decide at what time you should use your capsule, but you must make absolutely certain that you use it before there is any risk of revealing information that might conceivably endanger this unit. That is sacrosanct."

"I understand."

"Very well. I wish you good night."

Martin nodded to both men and for the first time for sixteen hours allowed himself to loosen his tight-fitting gray tunic as he walked to the flight of steps.

"Colonel Brinkmann!"

Martin swung around and banged his heels together. *"Heil Hitler!"*

8

GERMAN-POLISH FRONTIER, 31 AUGUST 1939

The evening was fine, with a slight breeze blowing.
Earlier in the day there had been clouds over the hills,
threatening rain, but now the sky was clear. Long before
eight o'clock, German Army transports had arrived
quietly on the outskirts of Gleiwitz, Oppeln and Hochlinden, close to the frontier. From most of the transports men had jumped to the ground and moved to
their prescribed assembly points. They had been recruited from concentration camps deep inside Germany, and wore Polish Army uniforms; they were under
the orders of SS officers and men from Standarten 23
and 45, based in Upper Silesia.

The trucks moved slowly through the region, their
lights doused and motorcycle outriders escorting them
to their dispersal points. Several of the men stumbled
as they jumped from the transports; they were grievous-
ly undernourished and their heads had been shaved, so
that their caps often fell off and had to be retrieved in
the half-dark.

From three smaller trucks, dead bodies were un-
loaded at strategic points. They had donned their Polish
uniforms in the concentration camps, where they had
been prisoners, and had been given lethal injections by
the SS doctors. Some of the bodies were already stiff,

which made—as an SS corporal remarked—for easier handling. They had been designated, in General Heydrich's secret orders for this operation, as "Canned Goods."

Under cover of darkness the various units went into action. At eight o'clock precisely the radio station at Gleiwitz was "stormed" by the "Polish" troops, and shots were loosed into the air, ensuring that none of the radio staff was hurt. In the other areas, most of the "Poles" drawn from the concentration camps were mown down by the German "defenders," and in certain places, where SS troops were engaged, the uniformed corpses were dispersed where they could easily be discovered.

Soon after the "attack" was broadcast on the radio station at Gleiwitz, startled citizens heard anti-German announcements in Polish over their wireless sets, mingled with revolver shots. The customs office at Hochlinden was demolished, and shaven-headed corpses were discovered strewn about in the area.

BERLIN, 1 SEPTEMBER 1939

At ten o'clock in the morning Adolf Hitler announced to the Reichstag that German forces had moved into Poland in a counterattack to several armed assaults made the night before in the areas of Gleiwitz, Hochlinden and Oppeln.

In the evening of the same day, Great Britain and France issued an ultimatum to Germany to withdraw her troops from Poland, in failure of which demand their ambassadors would ask for their passports.

As night came, the city was blacked out, and at seven o'clock the air raid sirens sounded. After the all-clear, people came into the streets again, making their way along the whitewashed curbstones to fill the beer halls and the restaurants and the nightclubs until they were doing record business. But nobody was celebrating the new war, and few of them, in the privacy of their own minds, were thanking the Reichschancellor for bringing it into their lives.

BERLIN, 3 SEPTEMBER 1939

At one minute after nine o'clock in the morning a note was delivered to the Foreign Minister by Sir Neville Henderson, stating that, unless German troops were withdrawn from Polish soil by eleven o'clock, Great Britain would declare war.

Soon after that hour he returned to the Foreign Ministry in the Wilhelmstrasse and was given a blunt refusal.

It was a sunny day, and people stood in the streets listening to the amplified radio announcement telling them that Germany was now at war with Great Britain, thanks to the English warmongers and capitalistic Jews.

There was no cheering, and the crowds soon dispersed.

A taxi driver, waiting for the lights to change along the Kaiserdamm, told his passenger indignantly, "Hitler started this war, if you ask me, not them others. He's been thirsting for it ever since he got into power." He'd had a drink or two, or he wouldn't have said such a thing, but that made no difference. He was reported and arrested within fifteen minutes and taken to Gestapo Headquarters.

By late afternoon the staffs of the French and British Embassies had left; the two buildings stood empty, their doors locked and guarded by the city police.

LONDON, 3 SEPTEMBER 1939

The day had been warm, almost sultry, with clouds darkening the sky toward evening. A storm crashed and flickered across London, and an air raid alert electrified the already threatening atmosphere.

Many people mistook the first rolls of thunder for bombs dropping, and went to their shelters and basements, emerging later red-faced but consoled by a BBC commentator in a late-night program in which he said it had in any case been "good practice."

Mr. Winston Churchill, a political outcast, had dinner at the Savoy Grill that night. He had been making himself highly unpopular for years now, claiming that the only way of preventing another world war was to show Hitler that England was ready to fight. But nobody wanted to—life was too pleasant, and so far the German Chancellor had reacted favorably to Mr. Neville Chamberlain's policy of appeasement, and surely Germany had no excuse to invade England.

At the Savoy, the Duke of Westminster—whose admiration for Adolf Hitler was well known in Government circles—chose to make an unpleasant scene, blaming Churchill to his face for having brought about a new war with Germany.

But Churchill was not wholly friendless. A few others were of like mind, and hoped somehow to save England and the rest of the civilized world. Among them were King George VI, President Roosevelt, and the Canadian.

It was the Canadian who telephoned the house in St. James's Street very late that night, and it was the king's equerry who answered.

"Are all your people back from the Embassy?" the Canadian asked. "Back from Berlin?"

"Not all. A few are still waiting for a plane. But we're not worried; the Germans are being quite punctilious."

"And what about *our* people?"

"They're all back." The equerry paused fractionally. "Except of course for those who will be staying."

"Underground."

"Strictly."

"And what about our people for 'Damocles'?"

There was another pause. The equerry was well known for distrusting telephones, but the Canadian didn't have time to worry about that; he was just in by Clipper from Washington and his party there demanded to know everything that was going on. "His party" was the established code reference to President Roosevelt.

"Everything is in order," the equerry said reluctantly. "We've already got a man under intensive training."

"When will he be going in?"

"As soon as he's pronounced ready."

"I'll tell my party," the Canadian said.

"Please do that. Good of you to telephone," the equerry said, and rang off.

9

BUCHENWALD, 20 SEPTEMBER 1939

As the gates of the camp were swung open to let in the work force, the band struck up with a Hungarian folk measure, fast and lively in the evening air. There were a dozen musicians, mostly Hungarian gypsies, with guitars and harmonicas and trumpet and drum, and their music carried to the far corners of the compound. Even the guard dogs pricked up their ears.

A man swung idly from the gallows, his face growing darker by the minute. He had escaped that morning from a work party, and been caught; and now there was a big notice fastened to the front of his shirt: HELLO AGAIN, I'M BACK!

Franz sat with his eyes closed, so that he could listen to the music without seeing anything around him. Over the last few weeks he'd been gradually forgetting the other world he had lived in, not deliberately but because it was more and more difficult to remember it. The images of the past had been in subtle shades and hues, and now they were being painted over with strong brush strokes in black and crimson, until the original was almost lost. But now he saw it again more clearly as the music flowed around and into him, bringing tears that he'd refused to shed until now, even at the very worst of times. In this he was like his sister; in fact

Hedda had taught him the trick, the very first time he'd bumped his knee on their sled: "If you don't cry," she'd said, "you'll be like a grownup!"

But now that he'd grown up he knew different. The old man in Block 13 had been crying all through the night since he'd arrived, not because the guards beat him all the time for being so slow, but because he missed his wife. They had shot his wife in front of him when she'd climbed down from the train and started screaming. It was to stop her screaming, the SS corporal had said with a laugh; very effective, he'd thought. Franz had been there, and remembered how the screaming had suddenly stopped, leaving only the sound of the locomotive's quiet hissing and the call of a bird in the woods, and the old man's thin and desolate crying.

For a while Franz was able to hear the gypsy music and pretend he was in the Tiergarten, lying on the summer grass with his hands behind his head and the sun gold against his closed eyelids; then the other sound grew louder with every minute until the music was half drowned by the tramp of feet as the work force entered the camp.

Then the loudspeakers crackled, as he knew they would, because it happened every day at this hour.

Corpse-carriers to the gatehouse!

He opened his eyes, knowing better than to dawdle. None of the guards had hit him since Corporal Trot had made him pin on the badge, and he hadn't been detailed to any of the work forces; but he was now one of the permanent corpse-carriers and the loudspeakers could bark out the order at any time of the day or night.

He got up and limped to the gate. His shoes were odd—a brown and a black with one sole much thicker than the other—but he was lucky they weren't clogs, which would take the skin off your feet in the first day's wearing. In any case it was his striped shirt that had worried him more than his shoes when they'd thrown it at him in the clothing store: it had been laundered, but there were still rust-red stains near the three bullet holes. He'd told the kapo he wouldn't wear a dead man's shirt, but the man had laughed, showing his yellow gapped teeth, and said the whole consignment had been "graciously bequeathed by the dear departed" and did he expect half the prisoners to run around naked?

Corpse-carriers to the gatehouse!

Franz broke into a run toward the long file of men. Many of them were still walking well enough after breaking stones all day in the quarry, but they were bringing the dead ones with them and couldn't keep up the pace of the gypsy music trying to hurry them along.

Corpse-carriers at the double!

Franz made for the first body, but it came to some sort of life as he held it in his arms, and they performed a strange little dance, staggering about as if each were trying to support the other.

"On the heap!" bellowed Corporal Trot. *"Come on then!"*

"He's not dead!" Franz called.

"Of course he's dead!" shouted the Corporal, and brought his club against the man's neck. Franz heard the spine snap and felt the dead weight on him. "Don't you know I'm always right?" said Trot, and gave his high cackling laugh..

"I have sinned . . . and I have done wrong to my fellow men . . ."

They listened to the Jew intoning his prayers. Franz and Hirzel were sitting together near the open doorway of Block 13, watching the stars glimmering above the peaks of the Harz Mountains to the north. Hirzel wore the red armband of a block senior; he had been at the camp for more than a year and was treated with respect, and not only because of the armband, though it gave him the power of life over death if he chose to use it.

"I have slandered . . . and I have been deceitful . . ."

Hirzel shifted his feet. "Now they're at war," he asked quietly, not to disturb the Jew, "will it be good or bad for us?"

Franz noted that he'd said "they," not "we." His long year here had isolated him from the world outside, and he could not join "them" in the war.

"If they lose," Franz said, "we'll be rescued."

"Yes. But in time?"

They watched the stars above the black peaks.

"I have been proud . . . and I have been disobedient . . ."

There had been no letter, Franz had been thinking all day. It had occurred to him before, but he'd decided it was still too early for one; then this morning he'd known, as soon as he'd woken, that there wouldn't be a letter; and the thought had remained with him all day, through the churning dust and the metallic shouting of the loudspeakers and the thudding of the clubs and the staccato *pock-pock* of the revolver shots in the far corner of the camp. There wouldn't ever be any letter, and he understood that now.

"My God, before I was created I signified nothing . . ."

Hirzel moved again in the starlight. "Letters take time to get here," he said softly, astonishing Franz with his telepathy. "For a lot of reasons."

"I've told you, I don't expect them to write to me." Perhaps Hirzel's telepathy wasn't so astonishing; Franz had talked to him about this several times during the day, it was so much on his mind.

"They're proud of you," Hirzel said.

"No. I thought they would be, one day, when so many people would have read our leaflets that they would have started a revolution and wiped out the Nazis; but I don't think they're proud of me now. There weren't enough leaflets, for a revolution."

"*. . . And now that I am created I am as if I had not been created . . .*"

Someone called out for the Jew to shut up, and Hirzel turned and said with authority, "Let him finish." The Jew had told him, early this morning, that tonight he was going to die. Hirzel hadn't asked him how, or why; that was the Jew's business. He was saying the prayer for the departing.

"Letters take a long time," the block senior told Franz. "And even when they reach here they're searched for money, and then like as not they're simply thrown into the rubbish bin. You ought to know that."

But Franz went on arguing. He'd let them all down, the whole of his family. Even an Army general could lose his status on account of his son's treasonable act. As for Hedda, they would have dragged her along for questioning, or even put her into jail on suspicion of being a party to the act—*his* act. He hadn't eaten for three days when he'd thought of this, even the few scraps that came his way; and Hirzel had found him face down in the mud after a rainstorm, half-drowning. Could he expect the comfort of a letter from his father, demoted in rank because of him, or from his sister, imprisoned because of him? They would never want to hear his name again.

"*I am dust in life, and how much more so in death . . .*"

The Jew was softly beating his chest as he intoned his prayer.

Hirzel lowered his head, staring into the distance until a star that had been poised on the rim of the mountains winked out; then he lifted his head again, and lowered it, creating the star and destroying it, creating it again, playing at God.

"How did you get your badge?" he asked Franz.

"I don't know. They just gave it to me."

"Your father's a general. That'd be it." He said it with pride. His own father had been a sergeant in the

war, and his mother had taught him it wasn't for every-
body to be given command of men, so he'd grown up
with a sense of reverence for those who could lead. Just
to be sitting beside this boy whose father was a *general*
gave him a glow of shared exaltation.

"No," Franz told him. "They knew he was a general
when I was first arrested."

"You must have influence, then."

"No. It was probably some kind of mistake."

"Luck, then," Hirzel said, and created his star again
from the side of the black mountain. "It keeps you out
of trouble, anyway."

Franz hesitated, wanting to take this chance of reminding the big man that he remembered, and was
grateful, yet feeling the embarrassment of putting such
things into words, because of the way it had happened.

"You keep me out of trouble, too. That's even
luckier."

"Don't think any more about it, lad." It had been
that lecherous bastard Kölnich again, the night before
last, finding Franz in the dark and pinning him to the
floor of the latrine. He was a good-looking boy and too
skinny to defend himself and Hirzel had been on the
lookout for that kind of thing. He'd reported Kölnich
to the SS sergeant in charge of the block, for stealing
rations—a major crime—and they'd put him against the
wall this morning, one in the neck and good riddance.
It was one of his little principles; they couldn't stop
the SS from doing whatever they wanted with them, but
let one prisoner take it out on another prisoner and
Hirzel would have his guts for garters, and no mistake.
He'd not told Franz what he'd done about that particular bastard; the boy was sensitive and he was feeling
quite guilty enough as it was about his family.

He lowered his head, obliterating the star, then
brought it to life again.

"... *And I will praise Thee everlastingly, Lord God
everlasting. Amen ... Amen ...*"

"I wish I had his faith," whispered Hirzel to Franz, "but frankly I don't see much of the Lord God everlasting around this place."

The Jew finished, and got painfully to his feet.

"Thank Christ for that," said a voice from the bunks.

"Everyone busy praying," murmured Hirzel, and dug the boy in the ribs, trying to cheer him up.

Franz laughed a little, then grew quiet again, thinking of his sister and remembering the Englishman who'd been a friend of theirs, especially of hers—Martin, tall and confident and a very fast driver. He'd hired a Mercedes sports the last time he'd been in Berlin, three years ago, and taken them for a run in it along the new autobahn at 175 kilometers an hour, Hedda with her hair blowing in the wind and rather frightened, but determined not to let Martin see, because she admired him, the roar of the engine and the needle swinging around on the speedometer and Martin's hands resting calmly on the big trembling wheel. But now there was war, and he'd be in it too. Would he be flying a bomber over Berlin, and would Hedda be found under the rubble one morning?

Hirzel asked him quietly, "How are those plans of yours getting along?"

Franz looked at him. Hirzel meant his escape plans. "I haven't thought any more about them."

"We all think about that, when we first come here. It keeps the mind occupied."

"I suppose so." But he was thinking of the man turning slowly on the gallows out there this evening, his face getting darker because of the flies. No one could escape from this place, except by running against the high-voltage wire. He'd seen some of them do that, suddenly breaking away from the working party or the canteen lines and running as hard as they could with their heads down and their eyes half shut and their hands reaching out, then the flash would come and the puff of smoke and the quivering of the wire as they went down, jerking in silence until the guards started laughing.

That was the only way you could escape.

"I'll keep watch for the mail tomorrow," his big friend said softly. "I'll see if I can stop them chucking it in the rubbish bin."

"Listen," Franz said, "I'm all right now. I've worked it all out for myself. What I couldn't stand was feeling I was being punished by *those* people—by the Nazis. It wouldn't be just. But now I know I'm being punished because of what I did to my family."

"You didn't do—"

"I did, Hirzel. I never told them what I was doing, you see. I never gave them the chance of warning me that sooner or later I'd be caught." Insistently he said, wanting his friend to understand, "I put them in danger, without even thinking about it. The Gestapo will have been to my mother and father, and my sister. Anything might have happened to them. Anything. They always take it out on relatives." He drew a long shivering breath, trying for the hundredth time not think about what might have happened to the only people he loved, because of him. "So it's right that I'm here, in this place. It's just."

And there was a way he could prove to himself that he was ready to accept this. A practical way. He wouldn't tell his friend, though.

Hirzel recreated his private star out of the mountain's oblivion. "When you get a letter," he said, "you'll feel differently. You mustn't go on thinking they've abandoned you. That would be wrong."

In the dark of the early morning a guard came and dragged Franz from his place on the long wooden bunks and marched him to the administration block, sending him down with a blow when he asked where he was being taken.

"You're not here to ask questions," the guard said, and hit him again.

Corporal Trot was waiting for them in the Personal Records room. *"Get to attention!"* he said right away. Franz pulled himself upright, trying to clear the sleep from his head. "Now, then, Gerlach, you're being transferred. You know where?"

"No."

"No, *Corporal!* No, *Corporal!* No, *Corporal!*"

"No, Corporal."

"That's better." He shuffled the papers, not at all pleased. "You're being transferred to the privileged prisoners' section. God knows why, a sniveling little guttersnipe like you. Do *you* know why?"

"No. No, Corporal."

"Must have a fuckin' guardian angel." He shuffled the papers again, perhaps hoping to find it was a mistake.

In a moment Franz said, "I don't want to go."

Trot looked up sharply. *"What was that?"*

"I don't want to be transferred."

The Corporal stared at him, and now his small darting eyes noticed something about the boy. "Where's your *Besonder* badge?"

"I threw it away."

Corporal Trot got to his feet. "Gerlach, have you gone out of your *mind?*"

10

"Break the knee."

Side thrust, leading with the outer edge of the foot.

The knee snapped, angling inward.

"Break the arm."

Twist, clamp and palm thrust, very fast.

The arm snapped at the elbow joint.

"Upward blow to the heart," Jock said. "To kill."

Martin used a reversed rising fist, driving it under the rib area, and the dummy rocked.

"The neck," Jock said. "To kill."

Center knuckle supported by the thumb, below and slightly behind the ear. The head angled over on the spring.

"Nose bone," Jock said, "into the brain. To kill."

Martin brought a heel-palm upward against the nose area, driving it hard.

The head of the dummy jerked backward, even against the tough Mercedes coil-suspension spring buried in the neck.

"Vicious," Jock said, and turned away. "Poor old Adolf."

Adolf was the dummy. Two months ago it had been brand-new, built by the physical training instructor out of hard rubber and wadding and ashwood and springs, and it had looked like a human figure. Now the rubber was split all over and the wadding was mostly gone and the spring of the right elbow had snapped two weeks ago. The head was a mess. Jock had said yesterday, in his grudging way, that he "wasn't dissatisfied."

Martin stood back from the dummy. "Again?"

"No," Jock said, and unzipped his track suit to cool off; there was no real ventilation in this bloody cellar. "Christ, you've been at it for three hours, you know."

Martin went up the stone steps to shower. His hands were still sore but they were improving. Since his training had started their skin had broken and healed and broken again and healed again, leaving scars and calluses. He was limping a little from a tendon strained when Jock had thrown him across the mat too hard a week ago, and the bruise on his shoulder was yellowing, losing its inflammation.

After his shower he put on the gray uniform; except on the four occasions when he'd been allowed out of the house he dressed as an SS colonel. Last week Tempel had had the tailor's mirror taken away—it was no longer necessary.

Martin looked in on Haslam in the room on the mezzanine floor.

"Orders?"

Haslam looked at his watch. It was ten minutes past midnight. "They're ready for you downstairs."

Otto Tempel never considered the time. All the same, to be ordered "downstairs"—that meant the cellar again —after midnight was unusual. Today Martin had worked for seventeen hours without a break.

He went down the stone steps.

"Heil Hitler!"

"Heil Hitler," said Tempel, and looked at him from behind his massive desk. "Come and join us, Colonel Brinkmann."

There were seven of them, including Corbett, Sadler

and the two former SS officers, Klinger and Veidt. They were standing in a rough circle and each man held a clipboard. As Martin walked into the center of the ring he felt a flash of anger against Otto Tempel: after seventeen hours' ceaseless work down here he felt ready for sleep, but this was another Phase 3 test session and it wouldn't stop until Tempel was satisfied—which could be anytime before dawn. But the anger was mostly fatigue. In the past nine weeks the dedicated and humorless Prussian had transformed Martin's outward personality beyond recognition.

"Begin," Tempel said.

Martin tensed, waiting.

"Name three restaurants you would normally frequent as an SS-Standartenführer."

"The Eden Bar, Horcher's, Habel's—"

"What is the magazine of the SS?"

Das Schwarze Korps—"

"Name five major concentration camps."

"Natzweiler, Flossenberg, Buchenwald—"

"Where is Natzweiler?"

"In Alsace—"

"Two more."

"Mauthausen, Gross-Rossen—"

"How far would you say it was from the Potsdammer Bahnhoff to the bridge over the canal?"

"I'd say half a mile."

"What canal is it?"

"The Landwehr."

The questions were rapid and in no sequence as to subject; the interrogators spoke in a prearranged order that was marked on their clipboards. Martin wouldn't begin to recognize it for at least thirty minutes. The next question was always thrown too fast for him to reflect on his answers; he thus had doubts as to how well he was doing, which added to his confusion. There were two goals to a Phase 3 session, Tempel had told him: to assess his knowledge, and to induce mental stress and find out how well or badly he controlled it.

"Address of Gestapo Headquarters?"

"103 Wilhelmstrasse—"

"Julius Streicher's newspaper?"

"Der Stürmer—"

"What is the meat ration?"

"One pound per week—"

"What is the highest secrecy classification?"

" 'Secret Business of the Reich.' "

As his mind darted from one subject to the next, Martin was required to swing around to face each interrogator as he snapped back the answer; after the third or fourth session he had realized it reminded him of bear-baiting. Tonight's session was the fifty-third.

"What section controls records and statistics?"

"The SS Main Economy and Administration Office, Section III, Department D—"

"The sugar ration—?"

"One and—no, three-quarters of a pound."

He turned to his right and answered. He turned to his left and answered. He swung around to face a man behind him and answered. The sweat was springing out again, and he was becoming aware of how bright the light was from the monstrous art deco lamp above his head.

"Who is Himmler's personal physician?"

"Dr. Kers—no. Professor Gebhardt—"

"Are you sure?"

"Yes."

"Where is the air raid shelter at the Adlon Hotel?"

"In the basement, next to the barber's shop—"

"Where are the shelters for the Jews in Berlin?"

"There are no shelters for the Jews."

Tempel made notes at his desk.

Martin turned and answered, turned and answered.

"Are you sure?"

"Yes."

Tempel made his notes.

One o'clock.

"What is the racial heredity certificate required from the fiancée of an SS man intending to marry?"

"The *Ahnenpapiere*—"

"Fats ration—?"

"Three-quarters of a pound—"

"Quicker!" called Tempel from his desk.

"Hitler's birthday—?"

"April the twentieth—"

"Sure?"

"Not—"

"Quicker than that!"

"Yes, I'm sure. Quite sure."

Turn. Turn, under the bright light.

Two o'clock.

"What is the *Sicherheitsdienst?*"

"The Party Security Service—"

"Quicker! You're slowing up. Quicker!"

Making notes.

Heat of the bright light overhead.

"The *Reichssicherheitshauptamt*—?"

"The Reich Main—"

"Speak up!"

"The Reich Main Security Office."

Sweat. No ventilation.

"Who is in charge of Buchenwald Camp?"

"Kommandant Koch—"

"Rank?"

"Colonel—"

"His adjutant?"

"Hackmann—"

"Are you certain?"

"I—yes—"

"Quicker than that!"

"Quite certain."

Turn. Turn. Turn.
Blinding light.
Quicker, yes. Quicker.
Three o'clock.

Seated at his desk in the cavernous cellar, Otto Tempel
noted that in three hours and ten minutes Colonel
Brinkmann had answered three thousand, four hundred
and fifty questions on twenty-three major subjects. Seventeen answers had been incorrect, but these were all
minor and had been given during the final half-hour
when the induced stress had become severe.

Tempel spent a long time reviewing the entire training program, then closed the bulky evaluation file and
sat perfectly still for a moment with his pale hands
spread flat on the desk and his eyes brooding behind
their rimless glasses. Then he reached for the phone.

"Major Haslam, please."

"He went to bed an hour ago."

"I wish to speak to him."

In a moment the Englishman's voice came on the
line.

"Yes?"

"This is Tempel."

"Well?"

"He's ready."

Superintendent Vogel rang the bell at precisely nine
o'clock, and she opened the door for him.

"Good evening, Fräulein von Gerlach." His heels
came together as he kissed her hand.

"Good evening, Superintendent Vogel." Always the
same sickening formality; he insisted on it. This evening
she was wearing a brown day dress, the one she sometimes went to work in, the least attractive in her wardrobe. "I'm afraid I must disappoint you this time," she
said as lightly as she could. "I—I forgot what date it
was."

"Date?" He looked puzzled, standing in front of her with his feet together and his cap in his hand. Then he understood, and put his other hand against her. "Open your legs, if you please."

She drew a breath and hesitated, then obeyed. This was the third time he had come to her flat and she had learned several things about him; one was that she must obey.

"So," he said softly, taking his hand away, "you are trying to deceive me."

She moved away from him, scared by his icy tone. Scared for her brother. "I—I've had a bad day, Superintendent Vogel. We had three accident cases in theater, one of them a child. And I'm not used to the new hours yet. Please try to understand."

"That has nothing to do with me." He hadn't moved.

"I—I always want to be—responsive for you."

She could hear someone singing on one of the floors below—Frau Hartnagel, her landlady, once a soprano in the Dusseldorf Junior Choir. If she ran downstairs and told Frau Hartnagel that this man was—but that was absurd; she must get over these sudden impulses to run to people for help. No one could help her.

"Fräulein von Gerlach." He was putting his cap down on the marquetry table beside the door. "I dislike trickery, and despise it. We have an arrangement, do we not? I have honored my commitment, in having your brother moved to the privileged prisoners' section. I expect you to reciprocate. However"—he was now walking slowly across to the telephone, his boots creaking in the silence—"if you wish to terminate our arrangement, I am ready to take the first step."

She forced herself to wait until he was actually lifting the receiver. "What are you going to do?"

He turned to face her, his black angular frame silhouetted against the brocade curtains—and she realized he was furious with her, and in his own typical way holding it in, refusing to expose his feelings. "I am go-

ing to revoke my request to Kommandant Koch that
your brother should be granted privileges. You will then
be relieved of my obviously unwelcome attentions."
Turning away, he began asking the operator for the
number.

The voice of Frau Hartnagel rose faintly from below,
rich and Wagnerian. She was well over sixty, but she
delighted in treating Hedda like a sister, swapping notes
on lipstick colors and the comparative qualities of
shampoos; but now and then she turned maternal, as
she had yesterday—But you are becoming so thin,
Fräulein von Gerlach, you must have lost three kilos
in the past week! I shall have to smuggle you some of
my fats ration—you are working yourself too hard at
the hospital!

She knew about Franz, but never discussed his arrest.
Discussion would involve opinions, and in the New
Reich an opinion might be overheard, and reported.
She had her own freedom to think about.

"Superintendent Vogel," Hedda said, and he turned,
still holding the telephone. She had slipped off the dull
brown dress and was waiting for him in the black lace
and crêpe de chine that he liked so much, her hands
on her hips and one stockinged leg crooked a little, in
the pose the chorus girls used: it seemed to be attractive to him. She tried to speak calmly, seductively, but
her voice was close to shaking. "I'm sorry I annoyed
you. It's just that I felt rather tired, after such a bad
day."

His eyes seemed to go darker still in his paste-white
face as he looked at her, and in the quietness she heard
a voice at the other end of the line as the connection
was made. She felt certain he hadn't been bluffing when
he'd picked up the phone; there was a seriousness in
his attitude that she could sense, and it ran true to
character: there was only one way for him to relieve
his fury, and that was by simple action. He hated to be
disobeyed or in any way thwarted, and the danger for

Franz at this moment was that Vogel might enjoy
avenging himself more than he'd enjoy using her body.

So she went over to him, smiling, and took his pale
dry hand and held its palm against her, letting him feel
how warm she was under the black crêpe de chine; and
for a moment she believed she'd lost, lost everything
for her brother, because Vogel remained absolutely
wooden with his hand motionless on her body. Then
he slowly put down the receiver, and she closed her
eyes in a mute prayer of thanksgiving.

Spreadeagled naked across the bed, she had nothing
to do. Perhaps this was what had been in his strange
mind when he'd said, that first day, "I ask nothing
uncivilized of you, Fräulein. Nothing . . . onerous."

He'd gone into the bathroom first to wash his hands;
she always left out his own towel. It was just like the
beginning of an operation: Dr. Vorst did the same
thing every time, walking steadily to the handbasin and
running the water.

Superintendent Vogel wasn't naked, as she was. He
always took off his black decorated tunic but never his
trousers nor even his polished boots, either because of
some kind of fetish or because he didn't see any need
to. She was beginning to know how a prostitute felt as
she lay exposed to his mouth and his dry, restless
fingers: she could think, if she tried hard enough, about
something else. When the revulsion became so bad that
she thought she must throw him off her and run screaming out of the flat, she thought about her brother. Sometimes—usually when Vogel telephoned to make an appointment—she found herself wondering bitterly how
Franz could have been so dangerously stupid, exposing
himself and his whole family to unthinkable agonies
for the sake of his adolescent ideals; then she would
shrink in horror at her own thoughts, and get out the
three photographs from the dressing table and make
herself look at them again. She'd asked Vogel to let

her have them, after his first visit under the "arrangement," knowing that if she were to go through with this
she must have the means of reminding herself of the
necessity.

"Turn over, Fräulein. . . . Yes, like that . . ."

She moved for him as if it weren't her own body but
someone else's—a patient's body in the expert hands of
a physiotherapist, a live model scrutinized and manipu-
lated in an anatomy class, anyone but herself—to
escape the reality of what was going on in this over-
furnished flat in the house of Frau Hartnagel, the
widowed ex-chorister from Dusseldorf . . . of what was
truly happening as this vile stranger moved his dry
and busy hands over her defenseless skin, prying open
the privacy she had once thought was sacrosanct in
every woman, his hot mouth savoring her as if she
were some kind of food for which he must come here
every week to satisfy his hunger.

"Up on your knees . . ." his soft voice ordered, still
as precise, still as measured; and as she crouched for
him it was easy, at least when he used his hands, to
pretend he was her gynecologist conducting an examination; but when his mouth made contact she had to think
quickly about the photographs of Franz in his crumpled
prison shirt, with the SS man in the background holding his club aloft over another prisoner.

She had formed the habit of studying that picture
first, and then if her heart didn't break immediately
she'd look at the second picture, the one with the man
whose face was bleeding; and then, this afternoon when
she'd received the reminder at the hospital of "our nine
o'clock appointment," she'd had to look at the third
picture, the minute she'd got home, to remind herself
why she must open the door to the man in black—the
man she hated more than she had believed possible—
and allow him inside, and close and lock the door, and
undress for him and let him rape her slowly and method-
ically, his trousers still on and the black leather belt

creaking slightly like his boots, his dry hands pulling her this way and that while she lay with her eyes closed, thinking about the boy in the photograph whose dark curling hair had been shaved to the scalp, the still handsome boy who was unaccountably, unbelievably smiling.

"On your back, please, Fräulein . . ."

She moved again, aware of him for a moment and reminded of what she'd learned about him: that he looked strong and muscular only in his black tunic, because of the specially tailored padding; that she'd almost frightened him, the first time he'd come here for an "appointment," by starting to unbuckle his belt for him, thinking he would want her to; that his sole interest was in her body, not his; that he was mentally cruel, but not physically: there were no marks on her skin, despite his continuous attention, but she sensed his calculated enjoyment of the power he held over her, and her total defenselessness.

"You have never experienced an orgasm?" he was asking her casually.

Quickly she said, "No. Never."

"Perhaps later," he said.

"Perhaps."

It had happened with Peter, of course, more than once, before he'd joined the SS; and it had happened in her school days, with two of her friends, and alone in her own bed when she'd dreamed of boys; but it would never happen here in this room, with this man. She'd come close to it, the first time, because of the rush of gratitude that had lingered for days, after he'd told her he had arranged for her brother's protection from "harsh treatment"; then the feeling had been chilled into numbness by the idea of this foul creature's satisfaction in knowing he could arouse pleasure in her. Since then she had lain lifeless, whatever he did to her.

Suddenly it was over, and he was in the bathroom again, washing his hands while the relief flooded over her and she lay with warmth coming back into her body as her mind rekindled some kind of hope for the future, for a time when he wouldn't come here any more, and Franz was free.

"I brought a small gift for you, Fräulein."

He was dressed in his tunic again, and reaching into a pocket.

It was a tiny figurine on a brooch, an angel in gold bearing a diminutive harp, his face smiling seraphically and his wings perfectly detailed.

"It's exquisite," she said, making an effort to sound pleased. "Quite exquisite."

"Is it not?"

"Thank you," she said, and smiled for him, detesting him, detesting the exquisite brooch.

He was watching her eyes. "There are many Jewish artisans in the concentration camps, master craftsmen in gold and silver work, sculptors, jewelry makers and so on. The SS ensure they are not idle." His tone was flat and matter-of-fact. "This little piece—it is solid gold, of course—was made from the melted-down dental fillings of prisoners who failed to survive the rather harsh conditions."

Something like a scream was beginning in her mind, a silent, rising scream that only she could hear.

"It was fashioned by a man who tried to escape a few weeks ago, and was beaten to death. In a way, unfortunate—he was a good craftsman."

He picked up his cap from the little table by the door, while the scream rose in silence, filling her head until she had to clench her eyes shut. Perhaps, if the scream became loud enough, it would drown out what he was saying.

"It happened at Buchenwald. I thought you might like to have the brooch, as a reminder of your brother."

She was not sure, afterward, whether he had gone, whether the door had clicked shut before she was run-

ning, still naked, to the bathroom, the little gold angel
flying from her hand to hit the wall as she began
retching and retching over the toilet.

"You mean you don't want the mission?" Haslam asked
in surprise.

They were in the cellar again—Tempel was there,
but not sitting at his desk; Klinger and Veidt too, and
of course Corbett.

"It's not a question," Martin said impatiently, "of
not wanting the mission. It's just that you're being
stupid." Like Haslam, he was speaking in German.

There was a short silence. Corbett looked away.

"Please explain," Haslam said quietly.

"Surely you should have realized that some of this
would stick. I warned that idiot Tempel, but he gave
me a lot of nonsense about an 'integrated persona'—
whatever that means." He moved closer to Haslam,
his hands clenched. "Well, it's stuck, that's all. You
really think I'd do anything against the Führer? My
God, you—"

"Calm down," Haslam said with distaste. "We've
been driving you too hard, that's all." He turned to
Corbett. "Make sure that door's shut, will you? We
don't want anyone else in here." He swung back to face
Martin. "I'm going to give you a few days' rest, under
the psychiatrist, so that you can—"

"You think I need a psychiatrist?" Martin took another step toward Haslam and saw Klinger close in.
"Haven't you heard of a personality change? It's not
that I've gone mad, it's simply that I've become someone else. You mean you didn't think it could happen?
You haven't heard of indoctrination? Psychic persuasion? What do you think that bloody fool's been doing
to me down here, week after week, fifteen or sixteen
hours a day?" His fists were bunched and he moved
again, and again the ex-SS man came closer between
them.

Haslam was keeping his distance, turning away. With an edge on his tone he asked, "Frankly, I refuse to believe any of this, Benedict. You're—"

"Brinkmann! Colonel Brinkmann!"

Haslam exchanged a glance with Tempel. Martin heard Corbett coming down the steps again after locking the door.

Haslam spoke with quiet bewilderment. "Do you mean your sympathies are now with Hitler?"

"My *loyalties!* Yes—to the *Führer!* Who else?" He swung away, moving toward the steps, moving back to face them again. He wanted distance: he knew they were all probably armed. "You've been rather too good," he said scathingly. "Rather too efficient. I didn't realize what it was to have an ideal, the glorious ideal of the New Reich, blazing in my vision like—like the Holy Grail!" He swung to face Tempel. *"Exactly* what that idiot said! *Exactly* as he put it himself, you know that?" He laughed at them, enjoying the irony. "The Holy Grail! Thank you, gentlemen, for showing me the true way of glory! *Heil Hitler!"*

Tempel had turned his back and stood with his hands behind him and his shoulders hunched. Haslam remained staring at Martin, as if he could think of nothing else to say.

Corbett had moved closer. "Benedict—"

"Keep quiet." He backed off, trying to get nearer the stairs, wary of them now, the sweat was running on him under the tunic with the effort of trying to make them understand.

"Colonel Brinkmann," said Haslam, almost soothingly. "This leaves you in an awkward position, as I suppose you realize. If we let you—"

"The awkward position," Martin told him curtly, "is yours." The stone steps were immediately behind him now and slightly to his left. He'd have to be fast, very fast.

"Colonel Brinkmann," called Tempel authoritatively.

"The door has been locked and we have the key. Now, please control yourself."

Corbett was moving one hand inside his jacket, but Martin had the gun out of its holster and was in the aiming position with the center of the man's forehead in the sights. *"Corbett, don't move!"* One of the ex-SS men had dropped to one knee with a gun in his hand. Martin began to fire, three deliberate clicks sounding beneath the archway before Major Haslam nodded and said:

"All right, thank you." He lit a cigarette and looked at the others as Martin put his revolver back into its holster and came across from the steps. "Comments?" asked Haslam.

"Convincing," Klinger said. "Perfectly convincing."

"I agree," Veidt nodded, and borrowed a cigarette from Haslam.

"I would have liked a longer scenario," Tempel said plaintively; but no one expected him to be completely satisfied with anything.

Haslam moved his head again. "Sadler?"

"He took me in completely. No question." Haslam had asked him an hour ago if he'd join them downstairs for a moment, saying, "They're having a bit of trouble with Benedict, some kind of mental trauma."

"Fair enough," Haslam said, and looked at Martin. "Let's go upstairs."

"Sit down," Haslam said, unlocking a drawer in his desk. "How do you feel?"

"Confident."

"Good show. You did rather well last night—only seventeen wrong answers out of more than three thousand. Even Tempel was pleased." He took a thick envelope out of the drawer and broke the seal.

"Did he say so?" Martin remembered it was Haslam's left eye you had to look at; the other side of his face had been remodeled at some time by a surgeon.

"Tempel wouldn't say a thing like that," Haslam smiled gently. "But I know him pretty well. Now, these are your papers." He spread them out on the desk. "Klinger has compared them under magnification with the real thing and he's satisfied. It's identical straw paper and identical ink; the actual wording and numerals are, of course, no problem. As you see, they look appropriately worn: you would have been issued this particular set two years ago when you were promoted to Standartenführer. Questions?"

Martin took the papers and studied them. "No."

"Put them into your wallet, or wherever you decide to keep them." Haslam sat back, tilting his chair and squinting over his cigarette. "Now listen carefully. This is your final briefing, although you'll be here with us for a day or two longer. There are seven men somewhere in Germany who are wanted urgently in London. We are counting on you to get them for us; that is, to rescue them from the concentration camps if that is where they are, to bring them out of hiding, if they've gone underground, and to get them safely to our escape lines for secret escort to England, either through France or the northern territories."

Martin sat perfectly still. This was the first intimation he'd been given of what they wanted him to do.

"As you see from your papers, you are a member of the Concentration Camp Inspectorate, and one of the officers responsible for visiting the camps and reporting on their efficiency, requirements, problems and so on." He dropped another envelope on to the desk. "You can take this with you when you leave here. It's a batch of such reports, duly stolen and copied, so that you'll be perfectly familiar with the job. You'll be joining an officer who has been doing it for the past eighteen months: SS-Sturmbannführer Wolfgang Scheldt. He will be your subordinate officer and will assist you in your duties. Questions so far?"

"How are you getting me in?"

"I'll come to that in good time."

"How much information have you got for me on Scheldt?"

"It's in this envelope." Haslam's patched face took on the hint of a smile. "We haven't managed to get anything on him that you could use against him, if you had to; but that doesn't mean you might not find out something yourself. In fact, you should make it your business, the moment you start work with him; and we'd like to be told of anything useful. Anything else?"

"I'll wait for a bit," Martin said. He'd worked up a sweat down there in the cellar, anxious to give them a convincing performance, and now his skin was growing cold as he listened to Haslam's quiet voice.

"There were originally some fifteen of these people, and we got four of them out during the last five weeks. It wasn't too difficult, and we left the field clear for you; two of them were winkled out of hiding, a man and a woman already on the Gestapo lists as 'missing, believed no longer in Germany.' The other two were in Mauthausen, and are now in the records as 'succumbed to injuries received during recapture.' Their identities were exchanged with two other prisoners. Now that we are at war, things are rather more difficult, and it was decided to place someone right inside the SS. One or two people have said you can't possibly bring it off." He was gazing at Martin with his one real eye. "I think you should know that."

Martin was suddenly aware that for the first time Corbett wasn't sitting in with them. Probably the final briefing was ultrasecret.

"That doesn't worry me," he told Haslam. "In any case, I assume you'll be training others to take over in the event of an accident. Corbett, for instance."

Haslam looked down momentarily. "Did he tell you?"

"No."

Quietly the Major said, "We've only the one training team over here, and only one Otto Tempel. Corbett will be put under instruction right away. When he's ready, there'll be someone else. My orders are to go on training men and sending them in until those seven people are safely on British soil."

"But we'll be going in," Martin asked carefully, "one at a time?"

"One at a time."

"Then you can tell Corbett he's going to be disappointed." Martin's skin was cold, and his awareness of Haslam and this small quiet room, and the ticking of the watch on his wrist was now becoming supersensitive.

"No one," said Haslam gently, "would be happier in his disappointment than Corbett. But I've let you know what the position is, partly in fairness to you and partly to emphasize the extreme importance of this mission. We are not counting the cost, even in lives." He made a small gesture with his cigarette. "But if you're as good as I think you are, we shan't have to worry about that."

Martin got up and paced the small cluttered room, wanting movement and warmth. "Who are these people?"

"These people?"

"The ones I've got to bring in."

"Oh. I can't tell you. I couldn't tell you even if I knew."

"Why not?" Martin asked with slight impatience.

Haslam offered his ghost of a smile. "You used to be in Intelligence, and you are now in Secret Intelligence, and this is one of the little differences you'll have to appreciate. The less we tell you, the less you'll be carrying in your head if something ever goes wrong and you don't have time to reach your capsule." He paused. "Is there anything else you'd better not ask?"

Martin stopped pacing and stood looking down at him.

"Just the way in."

"The way in is going to take a couple of days to arrange. We had to wait until you were ready to go. Tonight there will be two explosions in this city—relatively small ones but sufficient to destroy the appropriate personnel records at present in the files. Tomorrow night a certain Standartenführer Helmut Zimmer of your own SS unit will meet with a fatal accident. You will then take over his duties."

11

My dear Brother,
(She had first written simply *Dear Franz* as usual, and then changed it.) *This is the fourth time I've written to you, but I still haven't had any reply, and I don't even know if my letters are reaching you. I was told on good authority that I should write to you, by which it was obviously meant that you were receiving mail. I know that Mother and Father have written to you too—we phone one another almost every day to talk about you.*

I've nothing to tell you from this end. My life goes on, and the war goes on. But we are so very anxious to hear from you, Franz, and last night when I was trying to get to sleep the idea came to me that if the authorities are withholding your mail from you—for very good reasons, of course—or if your mail is getting lost because of the busy war traffic, you might think we're not writing to you. That would be terrible, Franz. You might feel that your crime against the State was so heinous— which of course it was—that we have no more love for you, and no forgiveness. But the author- ities understand that although your youth and

116

*foolish ideas led you to such an inexcusable act,
your family remains loyal to you, and loving, knowing that you have now realized the great wrong you
committed against your fellow Germans. It is the
right of the State to punish you, as you are now
being punished, but it is the right of your family
to forgive you and go on loving you as deeply as
ever. If you should ever think otherwise, it would
be so very, very wrong, and so very cruel, to yourself and to us. This, above everything else in the
whole world, you must believe.*

> *Please write to us, as soon as you can.*
> *With my fondest love, as always,*
> *Hedda*

The train swayed through the curves, its dim blue in-
terior lights flickering. She had got on at Lehrter Bahnhof, not far from the hospital.

It had been much the same letter as the first three,
for what else was there to say? There was only this
one message for him—*We love you*—and it must be
sent out to him time after time until he received it, and
understood. It was a lifeline they must throw to him
in the dark stormy waters his life had become, and
without it they might not save him. There were many
cases of suicide at the concentration camps, when
prisoners believed nobody cared about them anymore.
That it should happen to Franz was her waking nightmare.

"Have you heard the news, Fräulein?"

The train rocked.

"What news?"

"From Munich!"

"Oh. Yes. Yes, it's terrible."

Everyone was talking about it at the hospital: last
night a bomb had gone off in the Burgerbrau Keller in
Munich, only a few minutes after Hitler and his highest

Party chiefs had left. The British Secret Service was being blamed vociferously in the press.

"We were so lucky," the man said, "not to have lost our Führer. It would have been unthinkable!"

"Unthinkable," said Hedda, "yes." *Oh, God, if only they'd stayed for those few minutes more . . . they would have been wiped out, off the face of the earth. . . .* It occurred to her as the train drew her through the blacked-out city that she had only to say aloud—*I wish to God Hitler had been blown to pieces!*—and she'd be packed off at once to a prison camp, like Franz. These days the margin between life and death, between tolerable living and unbearable suffering, was infinitely narrow. Your own thoughts frightened you.

She'd been on the lookout for people who had friends or relatives in the camps—for anyone who knew anything at all about them, so that she might help Franz in some way, if only by understanding what he was going through. That was how she'd heard about the suicide rate. There was an electrified wire all around the camps, and prisoners ran into it when they couldn't stand it any longer. It was also how she'd learned how to phrase her letters to Franz, though obviously she wouldn't have been so stupid as to say anything *against* the authorities. But it had sickened her to put things like *your crime against the State* and *the great wrong you committed against your fellow Germans. . . .* There'd been those ghastly, treacherous moments— always when she was steeling herself to face another visit from Vogel, or lying sleepless afterward and wanting someone to blame—when she'd wished her brother had used a little more sense before he'd pitched them all into danger, most of all himself. But already she was beginning to applaud him silently for doing what he had; every time these uniformed brutes arrested another Jewish family or took their terrible reprisals against the Polish partisans, she thought with increasing and secret pride, *My brother spoke out against them*

*and accused them publicly, knowing what risks he was
running. . . .*

On the telephone, Mother was always asking, "But
whatever made him do such a thing?" Father had said,
more than once, "He did what he felt he had to do."

Her pride in Franz was the only warmth she knew,
in these desolate days.

"Are you going to Grünewald, Fräulein?"

She half-turned to look at the man beside her; they
were both clinging to the straps in the middle of the
aisle: this was the rush hour ending the day. His face
was simply another in the crowd, ill-defined in the dim
blue light.

"Why do you ask?" These days, she didn't trust
strangers. She couldn't see his eyes; his face was in
shadow.

"Do you remember the Havel, by the little bridge?"
he asked her softly.

"The Havel?"

"Where we swam, not long ago. And the restaurant,
where you insisted on strawberries, remember?" Suddenly he gripped her arm. "Don't say my name."

She drew a quick breath. "You . . ."

"Yes."

"But it's not possible." Her heart was thudding as
she stared into his shadowed face. It must be a trap of
some sort—he was a plainclothes Gestapo man. Martin
had flown back to England weeks ago. "I'm afraid I
don't know you, mein Herr."

In a moment he continued, "There were other people at the restaurant. Someone could have overheard
us talking there. But no one was near us in the water.
When we were swimming, I asked you if you'd kept
the little stuffed monkey I gave you three years ago. I
won it at the fairground. You said you'd lost it, and I
pretended to be deeply hurt. Remember? No one could
know about that. You're safe with me."

She leaned against him in relief, closing her eyes,

and his hand tightened on her arm. "But what are you doing—" and she stopped. Questions were dangerous these days, even in the half dark and with the racketing of the train. "I'm so very sorry," she murmured, "about Vanessa." She'd seen it in the Berlin press, about the accidental death of the young English lady of whom the Führer had said: "charming and intelligent, she was not only a true friend of Germany but also an unofficial ambassador for her own country in her unwavering desire for peace between our brother nations."

"We miss her," Martin said.

The train was slowing, and people began moving along the aisle. During the three-minute stop at Tiergarten Bahnhof neither Martin nor Hedda spoke, but stood close to each other, waiting. There were some vacant seats now but they remained where they were; close like this, they were less easily noticed, less easily recognized. One question was circling in Hedda's thoughts: what was he doing in Berlin? He was an enemy alien now!

"How did you find me?" she asked in a low voice as the train moved off.

"I followed you from the hospital. It wasn't safe to meet you there. I want to know about Franz."

The sound of her brother's name played on her nerves like a sharp pain. "There hasn't been any news."

"You thought he was in Buchenwald."

"Yes, it's been confirmed. They—they say he's now been placed in some kind of special category, and isn't treated so harshly. He—"

"'They' say?"

"A—a friend told me. Someone who knows a little about what goes on. There's even the possibility that he'll be moved to the privileged section of the camp."

"Because of your father's position?"

"I—expect so." She was trying to get that creature's voice out of her mind: *I am going to revoke my request to Kommandant Koch that your brother should be granted privileges,* his dry, pale hand on the telephone. She moved away from Martin a little, feeling unclean. He sensed something wrong at once.

"Is the General all right?"

"Yes."

"And your mother?"

"Oh, yes. They were interrogated, and so was I. But that was all."

"You've tried to get in touch with Franz?" He was drawing her back to him, closer, his strong hand on her arm, and she didn't resist; she closed her eyes against the flickering blue bulbs, feeling his comfort. There was no one she could talk to like this, or be with; at the hospital she had to watch every word—at the hospital or anywhere. It was the same for everyone —you could never be sure who were your friends.

"I've written four letters to him," she said. "But he hasn't answered. He might not be getting them." She turned her head so that she could whisper close to his ear. "I want you to know something. I'm proud of what he did. Very proud."

"Of course. You should be."

"It wasn't just romantic recklessness. He recognized the enemy."

"And said so. Not many did that." The train was slowing again. "Listen to me. We'll meet again, perhaps somewhere we can talk properly. It's just possible that I can help Franz, or at least get news of him for you." They swayed against each other as the train reached the platform and the blue bulbs steadied. "I've got to leave you now. Take care, and have faith."

For an instant his hand pressed her arm and then there were shoulders nudging past, and bobbing heads, and she was alone again among strangers.

It was a half-pound block of nitro-starch and at three minutes after midnight the alarm clock went off and the stab striker impacted and the filing cabinet bellied outward to the shock and hurled the burning contents across the office, smashing three windows and overturning a desk.

On the corner of the street opposite the Schutzstaffel Main Economic and Administrative building a news vendor by the name of Jakob Grimminger, once George Harris of Penge, England, looked up and saw the glow of flames in several of the third-floor windows. He left his pitch, walking comfortably along to the public telephone outside the post office.

"Willi caught the train all right," he said cheerfully.

Just before two in the morning, twenty-three-year-old Fritz Reichhart, duty corporal of the guard at the SS 49th (Friedrichsfelde) Battalion, a satellite unit attached to Berlin Headquarters, was patrolling the Personnel Records Office two floors below ground. Most of the files here dealt with the officers of the SS-Führungshauptamt Department of the Totenkopfverbände.

Reichhart was a conscientious young NCO, but everything seemed in order here and he was thinking about Marthe, his fiancée. Last night at the café she'd alarmed him by saying she'd missed her period—and he knew what *that* meant. Her mother and father were strictly High Church and they'd make sure he smarted for this, all the way to the altar.

It was by chance that Corporal Reichhart was passing near the big green metal cabinet in the corner of the huge room at a few seconds before two o'clock when the two heavy doors blew open and the blast flung him like a scarecrow across one of the tables and then threw the table after him.

A few minutes later a taxi driver named Leopold Janza, a naturalized German born in Kladno, Czechoslovakia, got out of his cab and crossed the pavement to the public telephone box by the railings.

"The engine's running beautifully," he said, "after that overhaul."

Soon after dark the following night, 10 November, a black Mercedes 540-K sports-tourer of the SS Metropolitan Transport Pool was being driven northeast toward Brandenburg, not far from the Mittelland Canal. The passenger occupying the rear seat was SS-Colonel Helmut Zimmer, a hero of the Knight's Cross and something of an amateur painter when he could find the time. A few months ago, soon after his promotion, he had completed a picture of the main entrance to the camp at Gross-Rossen. He painted in the Primitive style, with the bold coloring and the disciplined lines of Henri Rousseau, and the three figures at the gates of the camp stood out sharply: a guard talking with two prisoners, their striped uniforms clean and crisp-looking and their hands correctly at their sides as they listened attentively. The guard had a hand raised as if he were pointing something out to them, as if he were showing them around the camp.

Colonel Zimmer had taken the unprecedented liberty of offering his picture to the Führer, as a gesture of loyalty and homage from the Concentration Camp Inspectorate; and to his deep gratification the gift had been accepted.

The Colonel was admiring the autumnal colors of the trees as the powerful headlights swept across the scene; for that kind of background he would need ocher, burnt sienna and plenty of chrome yellow. As the Mercedes took the last curve before the canal on the outskirts of Brandenburg the bimetal strip of the thermal detonator lodged precisely six inches from the exhaust silencer reached the required temperature and completed the delay-train circuit. The cylinder of straw-colored lead sulphanate alongside was activated, and the young SS driver fought with the wheel as the car shuddered and seemed to lift from the roadway before

it tilted and rolled over in a tumultuous burst of flame
that cast fiery hues among the chrome-yellow leaves
overhead.

In the light commercial van that had been following
the Mercedes for the last fifteen miles sat Ludwig
Androsch, an Austrian-born *Mischling* whose papers
now indicated Aryan descent. He actually felt the
thump of the explosion as the shock wave reached his
van, but he drove past the blazing vehicle in safety
and when he had assured himself that no one could
conceivably survive the blast he drove on to Brandenburg. Stopping at the first *Bierhalle* he came to, he
went inside to use the telephone.

Ludwig had been moon-dropped onto German territory a week ago from an airfield in the Netherlands,
and had witnessed this very event a hundred times—in
the middle of a ping-pong table in a country mansion
in Sussex, and the black Mercedes 540-K sports-tourer
—made by Dinkytoy—had only flicked over against
the green sponge trees when the instructor had prodded
it, without, of course, catching fire.

"I've had a very successful day," he said into the
telephone, "so I thought I'd stop for a nice cold beer."

Three minutes later, in the cluttered office on the mezzanine floor of the house in Charlottenburg, Major
Haslam lifted the receiver on his desk and pushed the
button of the intercom for Martin Benedict's quarters.

"We're sending you in," he said.

12

BUCHENWALD, 12 NOVEMBER 1939

The first snow had come to the region a week ago, its
small hard flecks driven by the wind across the bleak
face of the Ettersberg too fast for much of it to settle;
it had left a semblance of frost on the bare earth in
the encampment.

Today, at four o'clock in the afternoon as arranged,
three black staff cars moved rapidly along Eickestrasse
from the SS Residential Area built for Kommandant
Koch and his senior officers. A few minutes later the
cars arrived at the main gate to the compound, and
nine men climbed out: SS-Colonel Koch; SS-Major
Rödl, First Officer-in-Charge; SS-Captain Weissenborn,
Second Officer-in-Charge; SS-Colonel Brinkmann, a
visitor from the Camp Inspectorate; SS-Major Scheldt,
his assistant; two officer-aides and two noncommissioned officers from Residential SS Troops. They all
wore heavy greatcoats, buttoned securely against the
cutting wind; in addition they had been prudently forti-
fied with schnapps, partaken in Kommandant Koch's
luxurious two-story villa.

A small military band began to play as the visiting
party walked briskly through the gates, and the loud-
speaker system crackled into life, calling the camp to
attention. The bandsmen wore red uniforms with tradi-

tional braid and frogging, but the other prisoners were in the regulation striped cotton shirts and trousers, standing close together in groups against the icy wind.

"The band is mostly Hungarian," the Kommandant told his guests. "They're not too bad with the violin, either, and we sometimes ask them to play for us when there's a party going."

"Typical of the way you run things here," nodded Colonel Brinkmann, "if I may say so, Herr Kommandant. Music is so civilized."

Major Scheldt was having to lengthen his stride in order to keep at the Colonel's side; he wasn't a short man by any means, but Brinkmann was setting a fast pace. Scheldt was still trying to get the measure of him; he seemed likeable enough—he'd charmed Frau Koch with his compliments—but he'd also shown a bit too much fondness for discipline when he and Scheldt were alone. Some of them were like that: they didn't catch on too fast to the idea of "brother officers."

"This is the inner camp," the Kommandant was saying as they moved quickly across the frozen mud of the compound. He indicated the barbed wire enclosure. "We sometimes get a big trainload in and we put the excess number in there for a while. We also house the special prisoners who are waiting for resettlement."

Poor sods, thought Major Scheldt as he hurried along. There but for the grace of God, and so on . . . "Resettlement" meant, of course, extermination. He noticed a pile of dead bodies in the far corner; Koch had either felt it unnecessary to have them removed before the inspection, or he was proud of the way they'd been so neatly stacked. The Major noticed Colonel Brinkmann looking across at them, but he made no comment.

"What's happening over there?" Brinkmann asked the Kommandant, who turned at once to Captain Weissenborn, his Second Officer-in-Charge.

"Those are the open latrines, Herr Standartenführer."
He led the party closer, appreciating the attention. "We
had them dug a week ago to cope with the dysentery
problem."

The group halted, staring across at the prisoners,
fifty or sixty of them, huddling in lines for their turn at
the latrine trenches. Many were fouling themselves
where they stood, and a few of them were squatting
with their heads buried in their arms.

"Get those men up!" the Kommandant shouted suddenly, and a dozen SS guards moved off at the double,
dragging and beating the inmates to a standing position.

"So you have dysentery here?" asked Colonel Brinkmann, looking away from the latrines. Major Scheldt
caught the hardness of his tone and admired him for it;
on the several occasions when the Major had brought
senior officers of the Inspectorate here for the first time,
some of them had stepped aside and thrown up when
they saw these wretches being beaten. One had to be
hard. One had to be above all this.

"The dysentery's no big problem, Herr Standartenführer," said Koch easily. "It's got to work itself out—"
He paused to give a short bellow of laughter, which his
two junior officers echoed immediately. "We're using
ton after ton of disinfectant, which is all that's necessary."

"That's the odor I've been noticing?"

"Calcium chloride, yes. Very effective."

"And those men over there?" asked Brinkmann. He
was pointing to a huddle of prisoners lolling against
the barbed wire on the far side from the entrance gate.
They looked to be skin and bone, their yellow faces
raised like skulls to the darkening sky, their eyes closed.
At this moment the main floodlights came on, but the
prisoners made no movement, nor did they seem to
notice.

"They refuse to eat," said Kommandant Koch.
"They've decided to give up. No character—no sense

of endurance. What else can we do but shift them out there in the open? It makes more room for the others inside the barracks."

"Shall I have the guards get them to attention?" asked Captain Weissenborn.

"No," Koch told him curtly, then his bellowing laugh erupted unexpectedly. "If you stood them up, they'd only fall down again—this isn't a skittle alley!" He glanced at Colonel Brinkmann. "You may feel we treat things too lightly here at Buchenwald, Herr Standartenführer. The fact is that we've had to harden ourselves to the demands of our profession."

"But how accurately you put it, Herr Kommandant." The Colonel inclined his blond head to his companion. "Your profession—in point of fact, *our* profession—is to guard the political enemies of the Third Reich, the Jews, the religious fanatics, the no-goods, the misfits and the human trash that jeopardize the healthy life of Germany and her essential war effort." His tone became almost gentle as he gazed at the Kommandant, his blue eyes narrowed to slits against the wind. "I hope you don't feel that I recommend you should wrap such parasites in cotton wool, Herr Kommandant."

"I see that you understand our situation here completely, Herr Standartenführer. We are going to get along fine, you and I."

In the center of the camp he stopped beneath the enormous tree that the visitors had noticed earlier. "And this," the Kommandant told them proudly, "is the famous Goethe Oak, named after the great poet himself. It's known throughout the region, and of course we took pains to leave it untouched when the camp was built."

They stood in a group to admire the tree, the freezing wind tugging at the skirts of their greatcoats. "Another example of your sense of culture," said Colonel Brinkmann expansively. "Music, and now a monument to poetry! Even under the pressure of your exacting duties, you manage to find time for the humanities. If I may, I'd like to mention it in my report."

He had made his way alone through the camp for an hour, perhaps longer, he didn't know. It was gone midnight by his watch, but he hadn't noted the precise time when he'd told Scheldt he was going to turn in. Scheldt had gone over to the Kommandant's villa again —"for a nightcap," he'd explained.

What were they talking about, in the villa? Were they discussing him?

He stood in the shadows between two of the long brick huts, thinking about Koch and about Scheldt, trying to remember the events of the day, of the last two days, trying to decide whether he'd done or said anything dangerous, even by a gesture or a single word.

"You'll be skating on thin ice," Haslam had told him before he'd left the house in Charlottenburg. "You can become suspect at any minute, on any day. We've done our best, as I think you know; but when you're tired you can make a slip, or forget something vital—or find yourself faced with a situation we didn't anticipate, in spite of all our care. If anything happens, you've got the addresses of our people who can give you temporary refuge; but don't go to ground unless it's the only way you can stay alive."

What were they talking about, over their glasses of schnapps?

He moved through the shadows, startling a man who was on his knees at the edge of the barbed wire. He stared up at Martin, his eyes terrified and his mouth open.

"What are you doing?" Martin asked him. The man was blue with the cold and his hands were bleeding.

"Nothing, Herr Standartenführer. Nothing."

They would all say that, because in this place there was nothing they could admit to doing, without being beaten. Martin bent down and saw something in the dim light; the man was trying to hide it.

"What have you got there?"

The man held it out, knowing he was caught. It was half a human jawbone, with several teeth still present. Near the man's knees, in the frozen earth, was a hole.

"What are you digging for?"

The man bowed his head, forced into a direct admission.

"For roots, Herr Standartenführer."

"Roots?" Martin straightened up and the man flinched, certain he was going to be struck. "Don't be afraid," Martin said with sudden soft anger. He'd first known this feeling as a child, creeping through the bushes and hearing the birds darting away, startled. *Don't be afraid* . . . he'd called out to them; he'd wanted to touch them, and be their friend, and it had made him angry that they didn't understand. "What roots?" he asked the man cringing in front of him.

"They say there are roots here, for eating. There used to be grass here, and weeds."

"For eating . . . I see." They'd lunched on suckling pig today at the Kommandant's villa; he and Scheldt had sent half theirs away, not having Koch's appetite.

"For eating," the man repeated dully, perhaps trying to persuade the tall, greatcoated Standartenführer that such a pursuit was legitimate. Then he flinched again as the SS officer suddenly drew his dagger, its blade making a soft hiss against the scabbard's leather. He knelt down and drove the blade into the freezing earth, prizing it upward in small clods, pushing his dagger harder and harder, grunting with the effort, until the hole was a miniature trench alongside the barbed wire.

At last he sat back on his heels and said emptily, not looking at the man, "No roots." The dagger hung loosely from his gloved hand. "There are no roots here." Then he made himself face the man in the reflected wash of the floodlights. "You were misinformed, my friend."

"I—" But the man could find nothing suitable to say to this strange officer.

Martin wiped his dagger on the back of his glove and straightened. "Don't talk about me to anyone, you understand?"

"Of course, Herr Standartenführer."

"If you talk about me, they won't believe you. They'll punish you for lying, and you don't want that." He turned away quickly.

The prisoner watched the tall figure make its way through the shadows between the huts, until it passed out of sight. Already he was beginning to wonder if the officer had been there at all.

Rage. Rage. Rage . . .

It burned in him as if he'd swallowed fire.

"And these files here?" he asked in level tones.

"They are the inmates in alphabetical order, Herr Standartenführer."

"I see."

This was the Orderly Room, staffed entirely by trustee prisoners and kapos and dealing with camp administration, the roll call roster, assignment to quarters, the rationing system and general routine. There were three of them here with him, standing rigidly to attention behind him as he slid open the big metal drawers of the cabinet.

Rage . . .

Against nothing in particular, against everything in particular, an accumulation of the things he had seen and the things he had heard and touched and silently cried out against, first in disbelief and then in horror and then in anguish . . . and finally in *rage, rage, rage. . . .*

"You won't find it pleasant," Haslam had said in his quiet civilized way, placing his fingers together as he had watched Martin. "We've shown you the films, but they're not reality."

No. The films had been bad enough; they were taken secretly by a political prisoner who had managed to smuggle them out of Mauthausen, hoping to convince the French and British and American governments that something must be done to halt the terror that was loose in Germany. They showed beatings and the shooting of children and the slow hanging of a man who had tried to escape; but they hadn't conveyed the sickening smell of the excrement and the calcium chloride, or the rust-red stains on the wall where the bullets had spattered blood, or the echo of the Kommandant's laughter as he had shown his visitors proudly around his domain.

"You've heard what these place are like, I'm sure," Major Scheldt had told him yesterday, meaning to put him at ease, "but don't worry—we're official visitors and have our report to make, so we'll be seeing things at their best."

Rage . . . Rage . . .

"What order are these entries in?" he asked the dark Czechoslovakian with the lash-mark on his face.

"From left to right, Herr Standartenführer. The green cabinet first."

Martin opened the cabinet and studied the index, pulled open a drawer and ran his thumb along the row of tags, stopping at *Schiendick, Max Julius,* last address Düsseldorf. "These inmates are present in barracks now?"

"Yes, Herr Standartenführer."

Martin pulled open the E to H drawer and thumbed the tabs. There was no Gerlach entered. He tried the W to Z file but there were no "Von" entries. He began to feel cold; Hedda had said it was confirmed that Franz was at Buchenwald.

"What are those other files?"

"Movement and Transfer, Herr Standartenführer. And the deceased."

I want you to know something, Hedda's voice was in his mind. *I'm proud of what he did. Very proud.*

He went to the Movement and Transfer files, pulling the E to H drawer and checking the tabs. *Gerlach, Franz Wilhelm. KO. 11.11.39.*

"What does 'KO' mean, after the name?"

"It is for Kozuchow, Herr Standartenführer. A new camp in Poland, built for the Resettlement Plan."

Martin closed his eyes momentarily. Over his shoulder he said, "You mean it's an extermination camp?"

The Czech hesitated. "A camp for unrepentant political prisoners, Herr Standartenführer."

"I see." By the date, Franz had left yesterday. He slammed the metal drawer shut. "You keep your records in good order. I'll report as much. Heil Hitler!"

Kommandant Koch studied the diamond, turning it to reflect the morning light. "Interesting," he mused.

"Why not send for one of the jewelers?" Martin suggested. "We could ask his expert opinion."

They were standing in the Kommandant's living room. The scent of real coffee was on the air—nothing ersatz for the Kommandant. Koch went to the door and told the guard to fetch Gronowetter, the jeweler, and at the double.

"How did you come by the stone?" he asked.

"By a certain arrangement. I am simply its bearer." Koch glanced at him slyly. "I see."

Haslam had said, *Most of them are totally corrupt, but you'll have to be very careful. Some of them prefer to get a hold over you if they can, to counteract the hold you have over them, as an inspector; they like your reports to be favorable. We don't know much about Koch, so handle him with the utmost care. He could destroy you.*

The door opened and Frau Koch stood there, a

heavy woman with coarse good looks, mannish in her riding breeches. "So here you are!" A big smile for Standartenführer Brinkmann. She wished her husband would learn to turn a compliment like this young officer. "I shall join you for coffee!"

"Not now," Koch told her curtly. "We are discussing official business." The gem was nowhere in sight.

"Oh my God—it's always official business!" She slapped her thigh with her whip. "Then later—and don't keep me waiting too long!"

Martin had seen her riding earlier in the arena built by the first prisoners: the walls were composed of mirrors and the overhead lighting was by chandeliers; the total cost, the Kommandant had told him with pride, was a quarter of a million marks. Thirty prisoners had died from exhaustion during its construction. "But then," Koch had laughed indulgently, "my wife has always been impatient!"

He turned the diamond again to catch the light. "And the 'arrangement' you were speaking of? Or is that not for my ears?"

"But of course it is. We would like to make you a gift of this bauble, if you'd consider accepting it. Perhaps a ring for the charming Frau Koch." Martin laughed gently. Another thing he'd learned about the charming Frau Koch was that every time a new batch of prisoners arrived at the camp and were ordered to strip naked for the showers, she and the wives of the other officers walked down to the barbed wire to watch the fun—and "make comparisons," as she'd told him roguishly after an excellent dinner of caviar, wild boar and crêpes suzette. Martin had been meticulously correct with the woman: as an ally, Koch could be of immeasurable value; as a jealous enemy he could become lethal.

To be a member of the SS, Otto Tempel had warned him, *is not to be invulnerable. At more than one camp*

*there are SS men serving time as prisoners, including
two lieutenants and a captain. They proved too lenient
with the inmates, or they were discovered taking bribes
—nothing very serious, you see, but quite fatal. You
will be, as Major Haslam has said, skating on thin
ice. Remember that.*

"And in return for this 'gift,' " Kommandant Koch
asked casually, "what should I be expected to offer?"

Before Martin could answer they heard the tramping
of boots outside, followed by a knock at the door.

"Who is it?"

"A guard, Herr Kommandant, with Prisoner Gronowetter!"

"Let them in."

The jeweler was out of breath and stood panting, a
small hollow-chested man with rimless glasses, one
lens cracked and an earpiece repaired with adhesive
tape.

"Get to attention!" the guard told him brutally. *"You
call that attention?"* The prisoner gave a jerk and continued to struggle for breath.

"Get out," Koch told the guard. "I want your valua-
tion of this stone," he said to the Jew. "And don't
make any mistakes."

Martin watched the subtle change that came over
the man as he gazed at the stone, turning it in his
sensitive fingers: here was something he understood,
something that offered him the authority of a lifetime's
experience, something he had been taught by his father
and by his father's father to know and to love. From
some inner recess of his ragged uniform he produced
an optical lens, and peered with it.

"It has no flaws, Herr Kommandant. A beautiful
color. Well cut, and in Antwerp, and by one of the
new young artisans." Glancing up, he continued with a
faint smile that transformed his face. "They like to cut
new angles, you know, with the base—"

"I told you to value it, you fucking Jew-pig!" Koch hissed at him, and the man flinched.

"Of course, Herr Kommandant, forgive me." He studied the diamond again, his breath fluttering in the quiet room.

Upward blow to the heart, Jock had said, *to kill.*

Martin remembered.

The neck, Jock had said, *to kill.*

Martin remembered.

Nose bone, he heard Jock telling him again, *into the brain. To kill.*

Yes. Kommandant Koch was a big man, heavy; but his heart and his neck and his brain were as vulnerable as any other man's.

Rage.

Dangerous self-indulgence, even to think about it. The brute would simply be replaced by another brute, and the Jew would die, in reprisal, and take a hundred others with him.

Prisoner Gronowetter looked up from the diamond. "Herr Kommandant, I—I am out of touch with the market at present, you understand, but six months ago, when I . . . six months ago it would have been worth, shall I say, close to a hundred thousand marks."

Martin saw the flicker of surprise in the Kommandant's eyes before he said with a casual nod, "A hundred thousand, yes. About what I would have thought." He took the diamond roughly from the prisoner's fingers, raising his voice. *"Guard!"* The door was opened at once. "Take this pig back to its sty!"

"Herr Kommandant! *Come on, you filthy scum— move!"* He jerked Gronowetter to the door. *"Move!"*

When they were alone again Koch said slowly, "Quite a respectable little 'bauble,' yes. And who suggested I might consider accepting such a gift, Standartenführer Brinkmann?"

The briefing on this had been specific. "I was ordered to offer it to you, Kommandant."

"Ordered?"

"Otherwise," Martin told him in a low voice, "I would never have approached you." He glanced toward the door, and Koch took the point.

"But who—"

"His name is not to be mentioned, Kommandant. But I can say that he is someone very close to the Reichsführer."

"Is that so . . ." He went on turning the diamond, making it reflect the light. Martin remembered a monkey he'd once seen at the zoo, playing with a piece of broken mirror.

Martin took an instant to go over his briefing. The sweat had started pricking at his skin and he was aware of the room's silence as he watched the brutish face close to his own, studying its reactions. *He might not go for it right away,* Haslam had said. *He might decide there's more profit for him in making inquiries. You'll be attempting to bribe him, and if he refuses, he'll be in the clear and you'll be in a trap: he could report you for it and have your scalp—and become a hero, and trade on it. To let him believe this was an order from on high might be enough to scare him. If not, we're counting on the size of that thing to persuade him. We're working on fear and greed. But make no mistake: once you've offered the bribe you're committed, and you can't back out.*

"And what do they want of me?" Koch asked cautiously.

Martin kept his voice low and his tone cool. "They want a certain prisoner."

"A prisoner?"

Martin turned away and began to pace, hands clasped behind him, his tone lighter. "I agree it seems a fair exchange. According to the statistics, a prisoner's body is worth on the average 200 marks, what with the dental gold, and the bones and ashes for use as fertilizer." He deliberately glanced at his watch. "My superiors didn't wish to be thought ungenerous."

"They want him *dead?*"

Martin stopped pacing. "No. But that's how it's going to appear in the records, I imagine." He paused for two seconds. "Of course that's your business, Herr Kommandant, not mine."

Koch went to the window and looked out at the gray frieze of the mountains. Then he turned back and gazed at Martin from under his heavy brows.

"Tell me his name. The man close to the Reichsführer."

"That's impossible. He has my trust."

Koch put his large head on one side. "You seem to be well connected, Standartenführer Brinkmann."

"It may have occurred to you," Martin said pointedly, "that I perhaps look rather young for my rank."

Koch narrowed his eyes, nodding slowly. "I'm beginning to understand the position."

"My superior told me you were a man of keen intelligence, Herr Kommandant." He looked at his watch again. "I don't want to hasten you in making your decision, but time is the essence of the arrangement. The prisoner would have to leave here shortly before I do."

Koch considered again. "I'd have thought someone in that high a position would have simply ordered this man's release through the normal channels."

Martin had been waiting a long time for that; the Kommandant's thought process was sluggish. "You can imagine how long that would take, through official channels. Time, as I say, is the essence." He appeared to reflect for a moment, then took a step closer to Koch and lowered his voice to a murmur. "In your position, just as in mine, you're aware that among the hierarchy of the SS there are certain opposing factions . . . power struggles . . . as in any other massive organization. My superior doesn't want his orders for the release of this man to be countermanded on their way through 'official channels.' That's another reason, and just as urgent." He turned away with a shrug. "In any case, the diamond is a gift to you, and I'm instructed to invite you to keep it and enjoy it, whether you decide to reciprocate or not." He went to the table for his gloves.

Koch studied the stone again. "I suppose it might be considered . . . my duty to cooperate, since you had your orders from a superior. I mean . . . he's my superior too."

In a tone of admiration Martin said quickly, "I knew I could rely on you to grasp the chief essential, Kommandant. Though, for your own sake, I would have made a point of bringing it to your attention; after all, you have an enviable position here at Buchenwald, a fine house with all the comfort the charming Frau Koch can ask of life in wartime, and frankly I'd have felt badly if . . . for some reason . . . you were transferred to a less convenient post. I really mean that."

Koch tossed the diamond into the air and slipped it into his pocket. "As I said before, Herr Standartenführer, we're going to get along fine, you and I."

Twenty minutes later, at 11:35 by the clock on the Kommandant's mantelpiece, Koch telephoned Weissenborn, his second-in-command.

"I want a prisoner taken by van to Weimar station by one o'clock. His name is Max Schiendick. I don't know his number—you'll have to find it. He's to be left on the northbound platform of the station, alone, in civilian clothes. If anyone asks any questions, tell them to shut their mouth, on my orders."

Weissenborn said the matter would be attended to immediately.

Koch rang off and stood, turning the diamond in the light. Then he picked up the receiver again and asked for the Gestapo Political Department.

"I want you to check up on someone's records for me. His name's Standartenführer Martin Brinkmann, of the Concentration Camp Inspectorate. What? No, I'm just interested in him, that's all."

Almost an hour later, at 12:31 by the clock on the wall of the Orderly Room, Corporal Trot came in briskly and slammed the door against the freezing wind outside. He went over to the Movement and Transfer Section and dropped a narrow buff-colored form on to the desk.

"Prisoner 7932 Max Julius Schiendick." He waited for the clerk to produce the relevant file. "Shot while attempting to escape. Got it?"

At 12:55 the two men working on the track a few hundred yards from the railway station at Weimar, not far from the camp, heard a vehicle approaching from that direction. Looking up and leaning for a moment on the long handles of their sledgehammers, they saw it was one of the SS personnel transport vans they had often seen since they'd started work here yesterday afternoon.

The plain black van with its wire mesh at the windows came to a stop outside the station, and two SS men, with a civilian between them, went quickly inside. Almost immediately the SS men came out again, and the men on the track could see the civilian standing alone on the northbound platform.

They watched the van drive back to the camp, then started work again, lifting their hammers high and bringing them down against the burred iron wedges in the sleepers. The ringing of metal sounded as far as the station, where the civilian was waiting uncertainly, staring around him as if he were unused to being in the open, all by himself.

A few minutes passed, then the men heard another vehicle on the road. This time it was a black Mercedes coupé, its hood down and two SS officers sitting in the rear, muffled in their greatcoats and scarves. The car halted outside the station, and one of the officers climbed out and went inside.

The two workmen leaned on their long hammers, looking to the right now, to the other side of the station building. The tall SS officer appeared and walked up to the civilian. The man seemed bewildered, and turned his head a couple of times to look in the direction of the workmen, half-hidden by the curve in the track. Then he seemed to understand, and started walking along the narrow mud pathway that ran beside the track, vanishing now and then among bushes. The two workmen watched him as he made his laborious way toward them, stopping once or twice to get his breath; they could now see he was very tired, or maybe sick.

He came right up to them, lurching clumsily over the rough winter-hard ruts at the edge of the track, and stood there swaying, his long narrow face bewildered, his veined skin blue from the cold. He was in a thin cotton jacket and tweed trousers, and clutched a worn brown bag.

"Schiendick," he said to them, trying to keep his balance on the uneven ground. The wind played with his wispy hair. "Max Schiendick." He stared at them with hollowed eyes, uncertain of what he must do next.

One of the workmen lifted his gaze and looked beyond the civilian, seeing the tall figure of the SS officer still there on the platform in the distance, watching them.

"What else?" he asked.

The man's eyes showed bewilderment. "What else? I don't know what you mean." His voice was cultured, the ganger noticed.

"Max Schiendick," he said stonily, "and what else?" The two of them stood watching him, leaning on their hammers.

The civilian realized he'd forgotten something, and

made an effort to drive away the fatigue from his mind. Then his face cleared and he said, "Oh yes. *Damocles*."

The workmen moved, taking him with them toward the equipment truck at the edge of the road, helping him when he stumbled.

13

LOWESTOFT, ENGLAND, 15 NOVEMBER 1939

Five men waited in the camouflaged hangar, sheltering from the wind. They were all in civilian clothes, their coats buttoned against the cold; one of them was the king's equerry.

They had been there since the early hours, arriving by their several routes from London, Bletchley Park and the RAF satellite airfield twenty miles from the coast. It would be dawn in an hour. From their shelter they could make out the milky glimmer of the sea under the lowering full moon, though the air was hazy.

One of the men said: "They're overdue."

Someone had to say it; they'd all been thinking it more than an hour ago. They felt perversely relieved to hear the bad news voiced.

"Been diverted," someone said, and turned his back on the wind to light his pipe.

They stood huddled in a group, smelling the salt from the sea and watching the east, the direction of the Netherlands. The Lowestoft foghorn was still sounding, and not long ago they'd heard the quick *whoop-whoop-whoop* of a destroyer as it neared the harbor. It was a desolate place, without a light anywhere; there was the impression among the five men, flitting through their heads without the knowledge that they shared it, that they'd been washed up by the sea from a shipwreck, to be standing here in the dark, so isolated and so silent.

The king's equerry, lost in his big overcoat and deerstalker hat, was glumly thinking that in another hour he would have to call the Canadian, and say they'd been out of luck. The Canadian would be mortified; this one was so important to them all.

"Listen," someone said, and they turned their heads and cupped their ears, trying to pick up the sound. The wind fretted at them, making it difficult.

"I can't—"

"Yes. Yes, I've got it."

They all straightened, and found themselves momentarily dazzled as the runway lights came on, spilling their glow across the grass. The men could all hear the aircraft now, and shielded their eyes against the wind, trying to see it. A radio was crackling inside the wooden shed where the windsock jockeyed against the moon. Then suddenly the aircraft was almost down, a single-engined high-wing Lysander, dropping and lifting, dropping again with a nasty slow yawing action that made the waiting men hold their breath as they watched it.

"Bit clumsy, for God's sake."

"He'll make it."

The emergency vehicle was crawling from the end of the hangar, lights off, engine warming up in low gear.

The Lysander hit the runway and bounced and yawed again, left and right, left and right, bouncing badly and starting to pitch, the tires giving a hollow screech each time they hit the ground.

"I wish to Christ he'd—"

"Give him time. That man's an ace."

The aircraft lost speed as the wheels stayed on the ground long enough to give the brakes friction, but the last of the yawing action still carried momentum and the machine slewed around full circle and slid backward, slewed again and rolled forward to a stop within a hundred yards of the hangar.

The men began running toward it through the blinding dark as the runway lights went out.

The pilot dropped to the ground, dragging his parachute after him. The escorting officer followed, catching his foot on the wheel cover and nearly falling; he was white-faced in the light from the cockpit, and stood holding his mouth for a moment, bent over. A third man was in the doorway, looking down at the group of people; he was swaddled inside a fur-lined flying jacket and clutched a small brown bag. The escorting officer managed to straighten up and help the passenger to the ground.

The king's equerry stepped forward and spoke. "You're most welcome, sir." No names were to be exchanged. "I trust you had a good flight?"

They heard the escorting officer give a hollow laugh.

Haltingly the passenger asked with a thick German accent: "This, England?"

"Yes. You'll be all right now."

The pilot was making his lone way to the wooden shed, unsteady with fatigue, his parachute slung across one shoulder. Someone called out to him.

"Many thanks—good show!"

He turned. "What? Oh, pleasure. Tail got shot up a bit—I don't always land like that."

BUCHENWALD, GERMANY, 16 NOVEMBER 1939

Corporal Bockow sat with his feet straddling the black iron stove, a pile of letters on the table beside him.

It is the right of the State to punish you, as you are now being punished, but it is the right of your family to forgive you and go on loving you as deep-

*ly as ever. If you should ever think otherwise, it
would be so very, very wrong, and so very cruel,
to yourself and to us. This, above everything else
in the whole world, you must believe.*

> *Please write to us, as soon as you can.*
> *With my fondest love, as always,*
> *Hedda*

"Shit," muttered Corporal Bockow. This one wasn't
from a girlfriend. He always looked for the ones from
girlfriends, in case there were any randy bits. He
checked the envelope again for money, but there wasn't
any, so he dropped the letter into the stove. If there
was money in a letter, he took the money and gave
the letter to the prisoner: he was a man of conscience.
No money, the letter went into the stove—they
shouldn't be so bloody mean.

He was still going through the mail when Corporal
Trot came in an hour later, puffing against the cold, and
slammed the door.

"I'm up the creek," he said, wiping a drip off his
nose.

"What now?" asked Bockow, sniffing a letter for perfume; he was partial to perfume, real elegance, went
with lace knickers and all that, lovely.

"Right up the fuckin' creek," said Corporal Trot,
warming his hands over the stove. "That stupid prick
Gerlach, remember? All his fault. Look at this." He
pulled out a crumpled blue form. "I got orders to send
the idiot over to the privileged section—"

"What, that clot that refused to go?"

"Him, yes—"

"Clean off his rocker!"

"Thing is," said Trot, "he got transferred out with
that mob from C Block. I've just found out. He's gone
to bloody Kozuchow for mincemeat, and here's—"

"Reprisals, if you ask me, for that bomb attempt on
the Führer. Serves 'em right."

"Thing *is,*" Trot said impatiently, "I should've got him into the privileged block."

"Why didn't you?" Corporal Bockow was only half listening, because here was one from a girlfriend, real hot.

"I chucked him back into barracks for a couple of days to teach him a lesson for refusing. That's when they shipped C Block, him included. Christ, they'll have my fuckin' scalp."

"What?" Bockow looked up, caught by Trot's anxious tone. "Gimme that form." He looked at it and then dropped it into the stove before Trot could snatch it back.

"Christ, what have you—"

"What've I done with that form?" Bockow looked up at him bland-faced. "What form? I didn't see it. Did you ever see it? Course you didn't, for the simple reason you never had it, see. Got lost, see. Happens all the time. They goin' to worry about just one more dead monkey?" He ripped open the next letter. "Take things too seriously, that's your problem."

Kommandant Koch picked up the telephone.

"Yes?"

"Gestapo, Herr Kommandant. You were asking about the records of Standartenführer Martin Brinkmann."

"Well?"

"Everything seems in order. He had new papers issued to him five days ago, November the 11th, along with several hundred other SS officers."

"Why?" Koch was listening carefully.

"A lot of the personnel files got bombed, Herr Kommandant, in Berlin. The work of the Polish Resistance."

"How do they know?"

"There was evidence. One of the bombs didn't go off; it was Polish. And they found Polish cigarette ends lying around. Trying to cause confusion. There's been more bombing since then, one in a Gestapo building."

"That's the official explanation?"

"Yes, Herr Kommandant."

"I see. And you're satisfied with Standartenführer Brinkmann's papers?"

"They're all in order."

"All right. Much obliged for your help."

"It's my honor, Herr Kommandant."

Koch put down the receiver and stared thoughtfully at the hairs on the back of his hand.

BERLIN, 17 DECEMBER 1939

In the peaceful flat in the Grünewald, Hedda lay on her bed with her eyes closed and her hands resting on the coverlet. The curtains were drawn, to black out the glow of the small Venetian lamp that burned on the pier table by the front door: Superintendent Vogel always liked to see what he was doing.

His face rested against her naked stomach, his hot dry mouth playing on her skin as it moved lower and lower; and from a fold in the coverlet she drew out the surgeon's scalpel, moving by slow degrees so as not to alert him, until her hand was level with his neck and she turned the blade upward and pushed it beneath his throat and slashed it back with all her strength, feeling the sudden dead weight of his head pressing down as his tongue ceased its licking and the blood began flowing, flowing in waves across her naked thighs.

"You have used perfume, Fräulein," he murmured softly. "I prefer you not to use perfume. I like to smell your body."

"I'm sorry," she said, "I forgot. I won't do it again."

His tongue went on exploring her, but some of her nausea had disappeared, eased by the terrible delight of her make-believe. She did it every time he came now, taking her revenge on him for what he'd made of her since Franz had been arrested.

It wouldn't be difficult, once she made up her mind. She could bring home a scalpel easily enough from the hospital, exquisitely sharp from its protective package; she was perfectly familiar with the sight of blood and the most hideous wounds; and with a weapon so deadly it would be over before he knew what was happening. But there would be no means of getting rid of the body, from the third floor of a house in a crowded neighborhood; even the blood—and there would be a lot of it, from the carotid artery—would be impossible to deal with: Frau Hartnagel was so often in here for her sister-ly' chats. And with this creature dead, Franz would have no protector.

Vogel began moaning again, like an animal in pain, moaning and snuffling over her body, until her skin crept with disgust. They weren't moans of passion or ecstasy, but of the most intense frustration, she believed. He still wore his trousers and boots, as always.

"Fräulein . . . Fräulein . . ." he murmured, absurd in his bourgeois formality as he plundered her.

Swine . . . she murmured back to him in her mind, *filthy impotent swine* . . .

Through her half-closed eyes she caught the wink of the little gold angel, over there on the table under the lamp. It no longer repulsed her; she was obliged to wear it every time she received this creature, because he'd asked where it was, on his next visit—"You don't care for my gifts, Fräulein?"—his black eyes turning to stones and his mouth drawing tight. Now she was used to the little gold brooch, and thought of it as a shrine to the man who'd created it, holding back the nightmare dark while his hands fashioned beauty in the midst of despair. Had he known her brother, or spoken to him? Had Franz seen him at work on the brooch? Had Franz . . . seen him beaten to death? There was a frightening significance in previously commonplace things, these days, and if you weren't careful it could turn your mind; for instance a routine visit to Dr.

Fischer, her dentist, could be linked with unthink
horrors. *What a beautiful brooch, Fräulein! Yes, isn*
Dr. Fischer? It might be made partly from some
fillings you provided for some of your Jewish patie
aren't the little wings exquisitely worked? It could s
you mad.

He was moaning again, and she quickly tho
about something else—Martin, that bewildering
ment in the S-bahn train when she'd realized he
beside her, an enemy alien, his face in shadow but
voice characteristically Martin Benedict's, gentle, r
suring. . . . *It's just possible that I can help Fr*
or at least get news of him for you. . . . And ther
had vanished in the blackout, leaving her only k
believing that he'd ever been there at all.

He'd telephoned her at the hospital twice since t
for a few snatched moments to ask if she had h
from her brother, and if the Gestapo was worrying
or her parents again. His voice was unmistakably N
tin's, speaking in German as he'd always spoken to
but now it had changed, noticeably: the zest for
had gone out of it and he spoke almost curtly, supp
sing an undertone of bitterness. *We'll meet agair*
soon as we can, he'd told her the last time he'd pho
Keep faith. . . .

But that would be dangerous, she knew now.

This creature was jealous.

"You have no fiancé, Fräulein? No attachmer
That had been last week.

"No, Superintendent Vogel. I had a friend, b
broke it off with him."

"I see. I prefer you not to have men friends, do
understand?"

"Of course. In any case, my work at the hos;
keeps me so busy that—"

"That has nothing to do with it, Fräulein." His
were hardening, his mouth thin. "I *prefer* you nc
have men friends. That is sufficient."

She must tell Martin, if he telephoned again, that they must never meet. Last week, when this brute had left her, she'd put on her coat and gone out into the winter streets, to take deep breaths of cold cleansing air; and she was sure there was someone following her, a man in a trench coat and a soft wide-brimmed hat, the uniform of the plainclothes Gestapo. She'd glimpsed him three times between her flat and Hundekehlen See, and he'd made no attempt to conceal himself.

Vogel was snuffling noisily now, like a dog, and for a moment she felt sick. She was aware also that something else was happening, something strange; his animal snuffling sounded different, rhythmic. His half-clothed body was shaking now, and across her thighs where his face was resting she could feel, in astonishment, the wet droplets of what could only be his tears.

14

"Mama, there's a car!"

"What?"

"A car, pulling up outside!"

Lilli swung around from the curtains, her eyes wide.

"Don't move the curtains, Lilli—I've *told* you." But Gertrud Dresel's voice was not raised; she had expected this for eighteen months, and was ready. "Come away. How many cars have pulled up outside this house every year? Hundreds!" But she turned quietly to the man sitting with her at the table. "Johann—upstairs, just in case."

He left the room at once, making no sound in the felt-soled shoes Gertrud had made specially for him.

"Sit down, Lilli. Finish your meal."

As the girl obeyed, her mother took the man's plate, knife, fork, napkin and glass and pushed them into the narrow cupboard below the sink, swinging the hinged shelf of cleaning materials across and closing the door on it.

"Mama!"

"Shh!" Gertrud saw the fright in her daughter's eyes. Lilli was almost fourteen and very intelligent, doing

152

well at school; but this situation called for more than intelligence. "We have nothing to fear. Nothing. He is safe now, upstairs. We answer the questions politely, the way we've learned it all by heart. Now, be calm."

"Yes, Mama."

They heard the doors of the car slamming, and the tramping of boots across the icy pavement. Gertrud sat down opposite her daughter and broke a piece of bread, listening with her face composed. A hundred such cars, it was true, had pulled up outside this house last year; and each time she had bundled Johann upstairs, just in case. But each time, she'd known the day was coming closer when it wouldn't be "just in case" anymore.

"Is the soup good, Lilli?"

"Yes." She tried to smile, but felt sick, dreadfully sick.

Gertrud had prayed that when they came to find Johann, Lilli would be out of the house, so that her face would give nothing away. For the first few months they had made elaborate plans: if the SS or the Gestapo came, Lilli was to run out of the back door and climb the wall into the alley, so that she wouldn't be here to give anything away; her dinner things were to be pushed into the secret cupboard and she was never to leave her outdoor shoes about, or play the piano, or pass across the curtains in case there was the smallest gap at night. But it had become too onerous, and—they began to think—unnecessary. It wasn't fair to demand of Lilli that she live here in her own home like a hunted animal. Life had to go on, and they'd found what they thought was a better plan: to rehearse Lilli in the proper way to answer questions, calmly and convincingly, doing it every day until she knew it all by heart. But now Gertrud could see there'd been a flaw in their plan. Lilli had always known it was only a rehearsal, until tonight.

"Mama?"

"Why should this car be any different from all thos
others, child?"

Lilli had put down her fork, unable to pretend any
more, and her small hands lay loosely on the table
"Because I know it is," she said very low; and then th
knocking began.

Johann Glauss could hear it from his room upstair
A section of the attic had been screened off with a fals
wall and a sliding panel. They had been built by Emi
Gertrud's son; he was away at the French frontier now
a corporal in the Army. Whenever he came home o
leave he always tinkered with his handiwork, discover
ing imaginary cracks or a stiffness in the sliding run
ners; it was a labor of love, as Johann knew. Johan
was like a father to him, after eighteen months, helpin
him get over the death of his real father, from tuber
culosis.

A search warrant . . . something about a warrant . .
The visitors were noisy, their voices carrying throug
the house. Johann, standing in the freezing dark wit
his hands by his sides, lifted his head as far as the lov
slope of the ceiling would allow, and waited.

The sounds continued: the voices questioning; th
scrape of a chair; Gertrud's voice now, calm and reason
able; the measured thudding of their boots as the
moved into the morning room, and now the garde
room as it was called, because of all the plants (Ger
trud had green fingers); and now Lilli's voice, quicke
and rather shrill, a note of fright in it . . . poor Lilli
growing up in days like these and learning their ter
ror . . . it was hardest of all for the children.

The men came up the stairs, three of them, perhap
four, and the voices were clearer now.

"This room?"

"My daughter's bedroom."

"Open the door."

Johann heard the slight creaking in the sliding panel
it always did that when people moved on the landing

He had never told Emil; the boy would have stripped it all down and rebuilt it.

"This room, Frau Dresel?"

"My son's. He's away at the front. A corporal—a signaler." It was said with pride.

"Open it, please. Hauff—search that cupboard. Fleigmann, check the fire escape. Hurry!"

Someone came into the room next to the attic and began rapping the walls, and Johann Glauss lifted his head again and began silently to pray.

"What are you frightened of, Fräulein?"

The voices were loud now.

"I'm not frightened. I—"

"She's still a child, mein Herr. She doesn't understand—"

"I am questioning her, Frau Dresel, not you."

The rapping went on, reaching the sliding panel. One of them was using his knuckles and, from inside the attic, Johann could hear the sudden difference in the tone. The panel was behind a dressing table and had a picture on it, a forest scene, with a deer drinking from a pool; the wallpaper was the same pattern and the wainscoting was of exactly the same molding. But all of this meant nothing now, because of the sound the man's knuckles were making.

"Fleigmann—check that wardrobe!"

The rapping stopped. Perhaps it had sounded different in the other room. Johann still stood with his hands hanging by his sides, the sweat beginning to drip from his fingertips, though it was freezing in the attic. His head was still lifted in prayer, but he was praying for them, not for himself. He was an old man, almost sixty, with the weight of the last eighteen months added to that; but Gertrud was still a handsome woman, and of great worth, a prize for any man seeking her in marriage; and Lilli . . . Lilli had not begun to live yet, before it was time to die. There'd be no mercy on them;

they were harboring a man on the wanted list, an enemy of the state.

Johann prayed for them.

"And fourteen candles!" laughed Lilli in delight. "Where did you find them?" Candles were scarce; everything was scarce. As for a *birthday* cake, with icing . . . "Uncle Johann, you're not eating any!"

He sat smiling, shaking his head. They were in Emil's room, next to the secret part of the attic; the SS men had been gone more than an hour but Gertrud wouldn't let Johann go downstairs. Lilli's birthday was in two days' time, and Gertrud had asked her if they could have the party now, to celebrate the miracle. The poor child was laughing at everything they said, in her relief from the shock they'd all been through.

Gertrud and Johann looked at each other with steady eyes; Lilli hadn't known it would have meant death for all of them. Only last week a young man was hanged for nothing more than stealing a neighbor's rations.

"Lilli darling, that's your third big slice!" said her mother, laughing.

"And I'm going to have a fourth! It's so delicious!"

Johann's head swung as the knocking came from below, and Gertrud stared at him, a warning in her eyes.

"Quick, Johann."

"Yes."

"Mama! Who do you think—"

"Hush, darling. I'll go and see."

"But they—"

"Be calm. We are having your birthday party, just the two of us, you understand? There's nothing to hide."

She went downstairs as the knocking came again.

It was the SS officer, this time alone.

"You forgot something, Herr Offizier?"

"Yes." He came past her quickly, shutting the door.

"I must talk to Professor Glauss, the man you have upstairs."

"Professor who—?" Her face was blank, but her heart was dying inside her.

"Frau Dresel, we'll sit here at the table a moment." His voice was almost gentle, no longer arrogant as it had been before. He took off his cap, and the lamplight fell on his blond hair. As they sat down opposite each other at the table, he did an extraordinary thing—he put both his hands over hers. "You've nothing to fear, nor has Johann. That sounds strange, but these are strange times. I'm going to take Johann away with me, but to a safe place, much safer than this house." He glanced up as he heard the girl on the stairs, coming down slowly, her young eyes bewildered. "It's all right, Lilli," he told her, smiling, "we're all friends now."

"I don't understand," said the woman evenly. "We don't know any Professor Glauss. There's some mistake."

"I could have arrested him an hour ago." His light blue eyes rested steadily on hers. "It was an official search and I had to report on it. I reported there was no one concealed here. Now I've come back for my own unofficial purposes, which are to take Professor Glauss to permanent safety. Surely you can see now that you can trust me."

"There is no one here," she said.

He pressed her hands. "I can go upstairs and fetch him myself, if you insist. He's behind the wall where the picture is, of the deer in the forest—" He broke off as he heard the girl snatch her breath. "It's all right, Lilli, don't be afraid." To the woman he said, "The paper on that wall is less faded, and the carpet is slightly worn below the picture; the wall is hollow, and when I noticed it I stopped rapping at it at once—do you remember? You wondered why—I saw it in your eyes." He gave her time to think. "I'd rather you fetched him yourself, Frau Dresel, and reassured him."

He waited. If he went up there and spoke through the wall, Glauss wouldn't come out; he'd have to smash his way in and make a lot of noise for the neighbors to hear—including the block warden if he lived close— and it would waste precious time.

"Please hurry," he said. "There are friends waiting for him."

Gertrud watched the young officer, wondering at the strain in his thin face and the urgency in his eyes, feeling the sincerity in the firm hands that enclosed her own. She was close, she knew, to trusting him, but that didn't make any difference: he knew where Johann was hiding, and their lives were in his hands.

"Lilli," she said at last, without looking away from the officer, "go and fetch Uncle Johann. Tell him it's all right."

NEAR SCHWARZHEIDE, 27 FEBRUARY 1940

The train had stopped an hour ago in the middle of nowhere, somewhere between Berlin and Dresden, in flat terrain under a sky bright with winter stars. It was well below zero but there was no wind.

"It'll be there for a couple of hours," Dorfman had told Martin, "maybe longer, but you don't want to waste any time. They're linking another five cattle trucks to the rear before moving on to Grossenhain."

"How do I identify the man we want?"

"You've got his name and description. The rest's up to you."

Three hundred prisoners packed in cattle trucks in the dark, some of them dead, some of them mad, one of them Schroeder. He would have to be found.

Martin had told his driver to halt the Mercedes in the frozen ruts a hundred yards from the track, this side of the level crossing where the road ran to Hoyaswerda and the Polish frontier. His driver was Corporal Kitzel, forty-one years old, a confirmed bachelor with an eye for the girls, a man of enterprise and discretion. Martin had taken more than five weeks to get him, wanting to make sure of the evidence—thirty-four gallons of army petrol in a makeshift tank under the floor of the man's billet, for use in his Adler sports car; two coffee tins of human teeth with the gold fillings still in them, bartered for cigarettes in the camps—so Kitzel had admitted, white to the gills; and a block of blank leave passes stolen from the Orderly Room at the SS 49th (Friedrichsfelde) Battalion satellite unit, for selling discreetly to the troops. God knew what other exotic perfidies the man was engaged in, but any one of those three would have got him stripped of his uniform and thrown into a concentration camp and he knew it.

Martin had been specific. "We're going to make a little arrangement, Kitzel, and it's going to save your neck. I have certain unofficial business of my own to look after from time to time. Start being inquisitive and I'll have you behind the wire."

The night was calm but for the low hissing of steam from the locomotive and the moans of the prisoners. Two or three officers had climbed down from the brake van to stretch their legs and light cigarettes, and Martin went across to them.

"Why has this train stopped?"

They saw the triple braid at his shoulder and dropped their cigarettes, banging their heels to attention. The senior was an SS-Hauptsturmführer. "We're taking on five more trucks, Herr Standartenführer. There's a train coming from Elsterwerda."

"Where are you taking these prisoners?"

"To Grossenhain, Herr Standartenführer."

"Then get them out of those trucks and take a roll call, liven them up! You want corpses for Grossenhain, for God's sake? They've got a quarry to dig! Now get them out and be quick about it!"

"With respect, Herr Standartenführer, don't you think—"

"You want to question my orders? What's your name?"

"Gebel, Herr Stand—"

"You normally question the orders of your superiors, Hauptsturmführer Gebel?"

"No, Herr Standarten—"

"Then get moving!"

It took half an hour, the three officers, twelve NCOs and twenty-five guards working like dogs as the latticed gates of the trucks were swung down and the prisoners brought out to stand in three ranks along the side of the track. There were twenty-seven dead and Martin ordered them to be laid in the knoll of trees below the embankment and left there; if he ordered them to be buried it would kill off as many again with the ground frozen like this. The rage was coming back to him, but after the last three months he could control it without any danger, supported by the philosophy he'd arrived at: these people, these humans suffering their numberless and nameless agonies at the hands of the inhuman on their way to Calvary, were the material he had to work with; from them he must save the few whose importance to the Allies was, as he had been told, "immeasurable." If it helped to bring down Hitler, the suffering of the others would be ended sooner.

Without this as his lodestone, Martin didn't believe he could have stood it, even this long; his rage would have broken through and exposed him, destroying the mission.

"Brackel!"

"Here!"

"Brandt!"

"Here!"

"Buren!"

"Dead, Scharführer!"

They stood freezing under the stars, lacking the

warmth of their close confinement in the trucks. Nine of them fell to the stones and lay there before the roll call sergeant reached the letter *S*. Martin stood close to him, watching the prisoners.

"*Sanger!*"

"*Here!*"

"*Schleiz!*"

"*Here!*"

"*Schroeder!*"

"*Here!*"

Martin's head swung. Schroeder was a big man, standing near the middle of the front rank; he seemed to be supporting the prisoner on his left. While the corporal called out the names Martin made his way slowly along the front rank, choosing ten of the fittest-looking among them, including Schroeder, and ordering them to step forward one pace.

"What's the trouble with this man?"

"He's nearing the end," Schroeder said in a low tone, his eyes steady on Martin's. The choice of phrase was extraordinary, Martin thought, with its formal reverence for the passing of a life in this Godless wilderness where men were dying by numbers.

"You," he ordered the man next in line, "look after your friend here. Schroeder, one pace forward and stay there."

"*Weiner!*"

"*Dead, Scharführer!*"

"*Wöhngrin!*"

"*Here!*"

"*Zimmer!*"

"*Here!*"

Martin walked along to the SS captain. "Now get them moving, Gebel! Get their blood circulating before they freeze to death. And I want those ten men to give my driver a hand—the car's stuck in the ruts over there."

While the orders were passed along and the NCOs

began chivvying the prisoners, Martin walked beside
Schroeder as he and the nine others formed up and
started marching toward the Mercedes.

"What are you doing," Schroeder asked him as they
made their way across the frosted stones, "to Germany?" Once again Martin was struck by the man's
quiet tone. He seemed to have kept part of his
spirit untouched by the horror around him. "You're
tearing down this country's pretensions to civilization,
can't you people see that?"

Martin studied him in the pale light of the stars. The
man's clothes were in rags and stank of excrement:
these prisoners had been packed body to body in the
cattle trucks for three days on end, according to Dorfman. Those who'd died must have died standing, as the
long train crawled from Berlin through the military
rail traffic that took priority. Yet Schroeder had kept his
sanity and some of his strength, and was prepared to
enter into a philosophical debate with an SS colonel
who could have ordered him beaten to death just to
amuse himself.

"Schroeder, listen carefully." He walked close to the
man, his voice not much above a whisper. "When we
reach the car, you'll help the others. But when I send
them back to the train, I want you to stay close to me.
Do you understand that?"

Schroeder's head was turned attentively. Ahead of
them the captain had slowed and was now within ear-
shot unless they spoke quietly.

"No," said Schroeder.

"I intercepted this train," Martin told him, "with the
sole purpose of getting you away."

"Why?"

"There's no time for you to question anything. I
have to get you into the car, without the guards seeing."

Schroeder was still watching him, slowing his pace.
"I'm not leaving my friends. They need me. And I'm
not working for the Nazis."

They were nearing the Mercedes and Martin had to warn his driver what to expect, and what to do. He didn't know what Schroeder meant by "not working for the Nazis." He'd been told to bring these men into the escape network and that was all; he realized they must be important to the Allied war effort, but he'd been given no other information that could be grilled out of him if he was caught.

"You're not being asked," he whispered quickly to the man beside him, "to work for the Nazis." He couldn't say more than that; the situation was desperate and if the SS captain suspected anything it might be impossible to get Schroeder away—and he might later be forced to reveal every word Martin had said to him. "I'm asking for your cooperation, so that I can save your life."

Martin could see Corporal Kitzel standing at ease as the party approached the car. There were less than thirty seconds now in which to persuade Schroeder.

"In any case," the big man said softly, "I can't leave my friends. God knows what kind of treachery you're engaged in, but I'm not helping you."

"*All right,*" the SS captain was shouting, "*form up at the rear of the car!*"

Martin left Schroeder's side and went quickly over to the Mercedes.

"Kitzel, the car's stuck in the ruts and these men are here to help push it clear, got that? *And make it look difficult.*"

The driver didn't stop to answer: he slipped behind the wheel and started the engine. One of the NCOs had come running from the train to work the men.

"*All right,* five at the back and the rest of you along the sides! Come on, get a hold of the running boards and the door handles—*sharp now!*"

Kitzel got into first gear and revved the engine but didn't bring the clutch in yet; the NCO was shouting like a tug-of-war coach and the captain was pulling at the windscreen pillar and, under cover of the noise, Martin moved close to Schroeder. There was only one thing he could say to the man now, even though it was dangerous.

"Schroeder, listen to me. *They want you in London*."

The engine was revving hard and Kitzel began bringing in the clutch now in jerks, letting the car rock backward and forward in the frozen ruts.

"Come on—heave together! Heave! Heave!"

The rear wheels were spinning as Kitzel gave it the gun, and the car was slewing gradually on to firmer ground.

Schroeder's face was turned to look at Martin, his eyes glinting in the starlight. "In *London?*"

Martin spoke in English, close against his ear, "You're wanted by the Allies." If Schroeder didn't understand, he might at least recognize Martin's perfect command of the language; with only a few seconds left he had to try everything. Corporal Kitzel was watching him from the driver's seat, waiting for the signal to move the car clear.

"Come on, you lazy bastards, heave! Heave! Heave!"

Two or three times Kitzel had had to slip into reverse and hold the Mercedes back; the prisoners were weak but with the captain and the NCO lending their weight it was almost clear of the ruts.

Schroeder was still gazing at the SS colonel beside him. "You are an agent?" he murmured.

"Why else would I help you?"

Schroeder kept his hands against the bodywork of the car, his feet slipping on the frost. "Now I understand. Tell me what I must do."

"When I give you the word, drop on to the ground and feign death."

"Come on, then—heave! Heave! Heave!"

Martin went to the side of the car and nodded to Corporal Kitzel, who let the clutch in and jockeyed the car forward.

"One more heave! C'mon, now—heave! All right, that does it!"

Martin hit Schroeder on the shoulder.

"Now."

Schroeder dropped, and Martin bent over him, taking off a glove and feeling for the heartbeat.

Kitzel shoved the gear into neutral and cut the engine, climbing out. The NCO began gathering the prisoners.

"This man's dead," Martin told him. "Heart gave out. Take him over there and throw him into the bushes."

"Come on, then—two of you, sharp now!"

"Get his name and number," the captain called, and the NCO checked the identity tag.

"5893 Schroeder, sir!"

The captain noted it.

Two men picked up Schroeder and started lugging him across to the bushes, but one of them collapsed and had to be relieved. Frost flew off the black winter twigs as Schroeder landed among them and lay still.

Martin turned away and walked back to the train with the captain. "I have a little useful information for you, Hauptsturmführer Gebel," he said coldly. "As a member of the Concentration Camp Inspectorate I've been getting a lot of complaints from the camp kommandants that prisoners are arriving half dead and unfit for work." He paused to watch the horizon as the other train appeared from between the hills, its smoke tinged by the glow from the firebox. "The daily farming-out wage for a prisoner is six marks, so that he is worth approximately 1,600 marks during the average life expectancy of nine months. As a dead body he is worth approximately 200 marks, for use as ash fertilizer. The profits made by the SS, Hauptsturmführer Gebel, are our proud contribution to the war effort, and we are not going to tolerate the gratuitous maltreatment of prisoners by ignorant officers such as yourself. They may be scum, but they are *useful* scum, do you understand?"

"Yes, Herr Standartenführer. I didn't realize—"

"Then you'll be so good as to realize it in future. The less damage you do to these prisoners, the more you'll be helping the war economy, in which I trust you take a dutiful interest."

"But of course, Herr Standartenführer."

The second train was rumbling to a halt along the branch line as they reached the track, and Martin stayed ten minutes to supervise the recoupling of the trucks; then he went down the embankment and across the ice-filled ruts to where Kitzel was waiting with the car.

"Flash your headlights once," Martin told him, and went across to the shadowy line of bushes to find the man who lay there. "All right, Schroeder."

A small plumber's van was nosing its way in from the level crossing, its lights doused; it stopped not far from the Mercedes and the driver got out. Martin took Schroeder across to him.

"This is Dorfman. He'll look after you now."

SACHSENHAUSEN, 3 MARCH 1940

In the small overheated office of the camp's Political Department the Gestapo clerk went through the files again.

"You're sure he's at Sachsenhausen, Herr Standartenführer?"

"According to the form," Martin told him. His tone was confident.

They can put it under a microscope, his contact had told him last night at the rendezvous, *and it'll still stand up.* It was the first time Major Haslam had sent him a forged release form to spring a prisoner; either they were running short of diamonds or they'd decided this method was safer.

"A cup of coffee, Herr Standartenführer?" asked the other Gestapo man from near the stove. "The real thing, of course!"

"Thank you," Martin nodded, and took the proffered mug. "You do yourselves well here." But he was watching the man at the files.

"Lenneberg . . . Lenneberg . . ." the man muttered, sorting the entries. "Not here." He slammed the metal drawer shut.

"There must be some mistake."

The man was scrutinizing the form again. "This came from Gestapo Headquarters Berlin?"

"That's correct." He sipped his coffee, watching the man over the rim of the mug.

"A moment, Herr Standartenführer." He dragged open another file and went through the entries. "Lenneberg . . . Lenneberg . . . *Joseph* Lenneberg, yes, here it is. The other was Heinrich." He pulled out the card, comparing the details with the release form.

Martin let out a slow breath and watched.

"But this prisoner has already been released, Herr Standartenführer. Two days ago."

"You're certain?"

"Oh yes." He showed Martin the card. "On the orders, once again, of Gestapo Headquarters Berlin. Obviously," he said with a shrug, "the orders were duplicated."

"Obviously," said Martin, and finished his coffee.

BERLIN, 3 MARCH 1940

In the cluttered office on the mezzanine floor of the house in Charlottenburg, Major Haslam sat behind his desk, outwardly calm and inwardly shaking.

"What kind of trouble?" asked Otto Tempel.

"Brinkmann has just phoned from Sachsenhausen.

One of our target prisoners—Joseph Lenneberg—has already been released, on official orders from Gestapo HQ Berlin." His fingers had been drumming lightly on the desk, and now they stopped. "I'd say we're done for."

15

Hedda stood sobbing her heart out in Martin's arms. Her whole body shook to the spasms and he was shocked by their violence; sometimes she tried to speak to him but the words were lost in the outpouring of her misery.

He feared for Franz.

There were no lights on in the room; she must have been sitting alone in the half-dark when he'd arrived. Somewhere in the house he could hear, incongruously, a woman singing.

"I'm so ashamed . . ." Hedda managed to say at last.

"Don't talk," he said gently. "Just let go."

"I've never cried before . . . in front of anyone." She lifted her head and looked up at him in the faint light, her eyes red and puffy.

"Then it's about time you started." He gave her the handkerchief from his breast pocket; he'd changed out of his SS uniform at the house in Charlottenburg.

Major Haslam had been very quiet. And very shaken. When Martin had telephoned from Sachsenhausen to say that the prisoner, Lenneberg, had already been officially released, Haslam had told him to report immediately to base if his tour of duty allowed it. There were now signals being made urgently to London via The Hague.

169

At the moment he could think of nothing but Hedda, and her agonizing despair. He crossed to the windows to draw the curtains; the last of the daylight was throwing the spires of the city into black relief along the skyline.

"Don't, Martin."

He stopped and looked back at her.

"Don't go near the windows," she said. "I think the house is being watched."

He came back to her. "By the Gestapo?"

"Yes." And Superintendent Vogel was coming here in less than twenty minutes. . . . "They're still interested in me. They—they think I knew what my brother was doing, and didn't stop him or report him."

"I see." As lightly as he could he asked, "Which particular member of the Gestapo is bothering you?"

"I don't want you involved," she said quickly. "I'm perfectly all right—I've nothing to hide, so there's nothing they can do to me." She was aware of the little ormolu clock ticking away on the mantelpiece. "You must go, Martin. It's dangerous for you here."

Instinctively he began listening to the traffic sounds, and the noises in the house. In the dusk outside, with no street lamps lit, it had been impossible to see whether the house was under surveillance. He might have been observed coming in.

"Hold me again," Hedda told him, and rested her head against him. The fit of sobbing had left her drained and exhausted, but in a strange way purged of the nightmare she'd endured since they'd taken Franz away. "I've been alone for so long, Martin. I'm with people all day, but at the hospital they're all suspicious and frightened of everyone else, trying to win the approval of the party members by giving each other away for the slightest thing they say or do wrong. Last week a nurse was arrested for saying she thought the Führer had made a mistake in going into Poland like that—and you know what? She'd said it in front of her own son, fifteen years old . . . and he reported her to the police."

She was clinging to him in a kind of desperation. "You don't know how I've missed being able to talk to someone about things like that, someone I can trust. I can't bear to think you might not have come."

Outside the house, traffic was stopping at the lights, and moving on again. Martin was listening for the slam of a car door. Or boots on the stairs.

"Have you heard from Franz?" he asked her.

"No."

He felt relief. Franz had been sent to a death camp but without definite news there was still hope. The punctilious Totenkopf made a point of sending notification of a prisoner's death to his next of kin, normally with "heart failure" as the explanation.

"He was moved from Buchenwald," he told her.

She let him release her, looking up at him in the lowering light. "How do you—" But she stopped. In the sleepless hours of her nights she'd realized he could only be an agent of some kind working for England, in Berlin with false papers; some of his last letters to her before the war had been from an Intelligence Corps unit. She must never question him about himself. "When did they move him?"

"Last November."

"Do you know where he was taken?"

"To a camp in Poland. I'll write it down for you."

She got him a pad from the writing desk. "I've sent him two letters every week, to Buchenwald. This must be why he's never answered."

Did Vogel know that Franz had been moved? Would he have told her?

"He's probably found it difficult to write to you," Martin said. "They're kept pretty busy, you know."

"I know what it's like," she said dully, "at the camps."

"Franz is young, and strong. He wouldn't want you to imagine things are worse than they really are."

"I'll write to him again, at Kozuchow."

"If you'd let me know who's harassing you at the Gestapo," he tried again, "I might be able to persuade them to leave you alone. I've got certain . . . friends, in Berlin."

"You could make it worse for me. They're trying to find out if I have any contacts, people who used to know Franz."

You have no fiancé, Fräulein? No attachments? I prefer you not to have men friends, do you understand?

The creature was due here in a few minutes now. If Martin encountered him and realized why he was here, he'd kill him . . . and Franz would lose what little protection he had.

"Martin," she said quietly, "you must go now." She looked at his face for the last time, so that she could remember him. Even in the dim light from the windows she could see he'd changed since that day when they'd swum together in the Havel only a few months ago. His face was gaunt now, and behind his eyes there was an implacability that softened only when he looked at her.

"All right," he said reluctantly. "But I'll see you again, before long."

"Not here."

"No. Somewhere else."

"Yes." For a moment she felt a lifting of the heart as she let herself believe it. But she knew that whatever work he was doing, it must be dangerous.

He held her again and she clung to him with surprising strength. "I'll always be thinking of you, Martin."

"I won't be far away. I'll phone you when I can, at the hospital."

"No. Even that would be dangerous. Everyone's spying on each other, these days."

"Then I'll keep in touch some other way."

At the door she told him in a whisper, "Take care as you leave the house. Goodbye, my darling."

* * *

There was still light in the western sky as Martin went down the steps between the stone balustrades and reached the street. A dark Mercedes was pulling in from Bismarck Allee and stopped not far from the house; a Gestapo officer got out from the passenger's side and climbed the steps, looking neither to right nor left. Martin turned to follow him, then held back. As a colonel of the SS he could talk to most Gestapo officers on equal terms; but there was persistent rivalry between the two organizations, especially where their functions overlapped. He might easily provoke the Gestapo by trying to protect Hedda, and he wouldn't be here in Berlin if they decided to increase their pressure on her.

She'd said it with a note of deep anxiety: *You could make it worse for me.* If she were proved right, he'd never forgive himself.

He turned again and walked below the unlit street lamps toward Hubertusstrasse, and it was then that he heard footsteps behind him. Even in this secluded area it was nothing unusual at the early hour of nine; but he began listening consciously as he lengthened his stride along the pavement. After a minute he was certain the footsteps were keeping pace. He saw nobody in front of him, or on the other side of the street. Shadows were thrown by the massive topiaried shrubs in some of the front gardens, and he risked looking around. The Gestapo Mercedes was now out of sight, but he saw a figure moving close along the railings some fifty yards behind him.

He kept on walking. He might have been seen from close enough, leaving the house, to afford a useful description. Hedda had warned him: *They're trying to find out if I have any contacts.*

This could be dangerous for her.

He slowed, and turned left along one of the alleys that ran between the back gardens; here there were high fences and overhanging acacias. There was no one

ahead of him in the dusk, as far as he could see, ar
the shadows were deep.

The man had turned into the alley; his footsteps we:
hurrying now. Martin stopped.

The worst of the winter's cold had left the city; the:
had been rain recently and the air was damp, but th
evening was almost mild; there was the rich scent (
last year's leaves where they still lay in heaps, waitir
to be burned; and birds called from the trees and high
from the eaves of the old houses hereabouts, their sour
eloquent of spring.

The man was close now, and saw Martin standi
there waiting. Uneasy, he produced his flashlight ar
the beam swept over Martin's face.

"Your papers," the man said curtly.

In the third paragraph of the obituary columns of tl
Völkische Beobachter dated 7 March 1940 there a
peared the following entry:

HOFFMANN, ERICH FALK. A citizen of Berlin,
the deceased was a model student at his school in
the Steglitz district, and later received honors at
Berlin University, where he studied the law. A
loyal and valued member of the Gestapo since the
year 1934, he achieved the rank of Senior Bureau
Detective only last year. Hoffmann leaves a widow,
Frau Brigitte Hoffmann, and a son, Karl Hoffmann. He met his death during the valiant pur-
suance of his duties in the name of the Fatherland
and public order.

On page 6 of Julius Streicher's propaganda newspap
Der Stürmer, there appeared on the same date, 7 Marc
the following item:

*There has been no information forthcoming about
the vicious attack made on Bureau Detective Erich*

*Hoffmann of Gestapo Headquarters, despite the
most diligent inquiries. Hoffmann was brutally murdered in the Grünewald district two days ago at
nine in the evening, following what the police
pathologist has described as "an almost superhuman
blow to the neck." Inquiries continue with great
vigor, following a report that a gang of Jewish
rowdies had been seen in the area at the time in
question. This comes as yet another warning that
we must waste no time in cleansing our fair city
of the last of these Jewish cankers in our midst!*

"Can't you tell London to do something?"

Martin threw another photograph on to the table.

"Can't you inform Geneva?"

And another photograph.

*"Isn't the United States interested in what's going
on?"*

He threw down the rest of the batch and started
pacing the small cluttered room on the mezzanine floor,
while Haslam and Otto Tempel took a cursory glance
at the dozens of photographs and then sat back to wait
for Martin to calm down. Faintly from the next room
there came the measured accents of a BBC newsreader
whose program was being monitored.

Both Haslam and Tempel were surprised at Martin's
vehemence, but not at the physical change in him since
he'd left them at the end of his training five months
ago: they had expected that. They were even pleased
with it. Tempel, with his usual pessimism, had privately
told Haslam that he thought his new creation would
break down under the stress of visiting the camps. (It
was how Tempel always thought of the human material
he turned laboriously into agents: as his own "crea-
tions.")

"I don't think he'll have the patience," he'd told Haslam. "He'll kill one of the guards. Or worse, one of
the kommandants."

Neither Tempel nor Haslam knew how close this prophecy had come to being realized. In the company of men like Kommandant Koch, Martin's secret rage had threatened to break through his control. He was now able to vent it, in the safety of the house in Charlottenburg, and the two men with him acknowledged this, and waited patiently.

"What about the Jewish Defense League?" Martin came back to lean across the table, his eyes burning. "Do *they* know these bastards are murdering people of their own race by the hundred thousand?"

"I'm sure they do," said Haslam quietly.

"Listen, I've seen a boy of fifteen set on fire, with petrol poured over him! I've seen a child thrown into the air like a ball by a gang of SS men till it stopped screaming and died of shock—" The flat of his hand hit the table with a force that split the varnish—"*And I couldn't do anything! I couldn't do anything! Do you know what that means?*"

They sat watching him. His eyes were bloodshot with the tears of his rage and his mouth was drawn back so that his teeth showed like an animal's. Haslam began wondering how the man had got through the mission this far without killing someone and destroying his cover, as Otto had predicted.

"I told you," Haslam said at last, "that it wouldn't be pleasant."

Tempel half rose, thinking Martin was going to attack his chief. Haslam didn't move. He had to get this man back under control by maintaining his own calm. Time pressed and there was a lot to do at this meeting.

"Yes," Martin said between his teeth, "you told me it wouldn't be pleasant. I don't mind the unpleasantness. But by God I mind the fact that London and Washington and Geneva can't be persuaded to do something to stop this murderous rampage the Nazis have started in the name of the master race! Can't the RAF bomb the railheads near the camps, for Christ's sake? Can't the Americans insist on an international investigating team to visit Buchenwald, under the Red Cross? *Don't you see that we've got to stop these bastards?"*

Slowly he stood away from the table, his breath coming painfully, his eyes squeezing shut against the light, his knuckles white.

Haslam said in a moment, almost gently, "We gave you the opportunity to stop them. To help to destroy Hitler. Or have you forgotten that?"

In the silence they heard again the modulated tones of the London newsreader, and in a moment the slow chiming of Big Ben. In the room next door a chair scraped, and someone picked up a telephone.

Martin stood staring down at Haslam, trying to understand what he had just said, in that maddeningly quiet voice of his. An opportunity . . . yes. To help the Allies to destroy Hitler . . . yes. He remembered that. With the back of his hand he wiped the sweat from around his eyes, and got out his handkerchief and mopped at the rest of his face, and in a moment said wearily, "No. I haven't forgotten. But things just . . ." He gave a shrug and turned away from the light, and sat down in the worn Louis Quinze armchair, his head bowed. "Sorry."

The other two men exchanged a glance, and Haslam lit a cigarette, snapping the lighter shut with a definitive click.

"Things just got you down," he said sympathetically. "Of course they did. We expected that. Do you realize you've been in the field almost without a break for five months? It takes a different kind of courage to watch human suffering and deliberately turn your back on it. We thought you had that kind of courage, and you've proved we were right." He gazed critically at the haggard man in the chair. "But we may be missing something. If you want to resign from the mission, you must say so. If you think you're liable to break, it's your duty to tell us. We don't want a disaster."

Martin slowly raised his head.

"Break?"

"A nervous breakdown."

Martin thought about it, taking his time. Ther[e]
been several occasions when he'd believed he'd have
give up the mission before he did something irr[ev]-
ocable; the last time had been when they'd poured
petrol over the boy and set him alight. That had been
Gross-Rossen camp, three weeks ago. He'd stood th[ere]
with the kommandant and three guards, watching. "[An]
example," the kommandant had told him. "The b[oy]
tried to escape, and we can't have that." Martin's
volver had been in its holster, and his hand had be[en]
within inches of it, resting on his hip. A light-head[ed]-
ness had come over him, and he'd thought with ast[on]-
ishing clarity, *I've got eight rounds in the gun. T[he]
kommandant, the three guards, those two guards o[ver]
there, then the boy, then me. And if I don't do it, h[ow]
will I ever keep going?*

The answer had been in something this man Tem[ple]
here had told him, near the end of his training. *T[he]
more successful you are in this role, the more you w[ill]
help to destroy Hitler. Now learn that by heart and [re]-
peat it, and repeat it, day and night, until it becom[es]
your sacred and undeniable goal. That must be yo[ur]
personal Holy Grail, Colonel Brinkmann. To succe[ed]
and to destroy.*

So SS-Colonel Brinkmann of the Concentrati[on]
Camp Inspectorate had stood there with the komma[n]-
dant and watched the boy die, and had experienced [no]
relief from his private agony until three weeks la[ter]
the edge of his hand had struck the neck of the m[an]
in the alley with the superhuman force of his rage a[nd]
sent him spinning against the fence, dead before he [hit]
the ground.

"A nervous breakdown," he said reflectively. "No[, I]
shan't be indulging in any nervous breakdowns. Y[ou]
can take my word for that. I've other things to d[o]

He gazed steadily at Major Haslam, remembering to look into his left eye.

Haslam drew on his cigarette. "That gets us over that part of the program. Incidentally, where did you get those photographs?"

"I took them myself."

"Nobody objected?"

"I outrank most of the kommandants," Martin said, "and as a member of the Inspectorate I'm to be reckoned with. I can give almost any orders I choose . . . except to tell them to behave like humans. That would be suspect." He got out of the worn brocade chair and stretched his legs. "Can I have a workout with Jock while I'm here?"

"A workout? Yes."

"Get rid of the adrenaline. What are you going to do with the photographs?"

"Send them to London. It won't do any harm." Haslam leaned back in his chair, tilting it. "What date do you have to report back by?"

"No specific date. I've got a roving commission. Providing my reports go in from the camps they leave me alone."

"What about your assistant?"

"Major Scheldt? He does what I tell him to do." It had taken him over a month to get his driver, Corporal Kitzel; Major Scheldt had been easier—the man was too confiding. "He's been selling freedom to any Jew he can intercept on his way to the camps, at 50,000 marks a time, cash down. There's the death penalty for that."

"So you could stay absent from your unit for another few days?" Haslam asked him.

"Certainly."

"Fair enough." Haslam glanced at Tempel, who nodded. Intuitively Martin sensed that they hadn't been sure of him since his show of fury a few minutes ago; that Tempel had been watching him closely, trying to decide whether he was still reliable material; and that

Haslam had required his verdict before he went on. want you to know, Brinkmann, that at this mom we're not sure whether the Damocles operation is running."

Martin tensed, but showed nothing.

"Quite simply," Haslam went on, "our job has only been to get these selected people to the esc routes, but to do it before they disappear. This n Lenneberg has, in effect, disappeared. And what it co very well mean is that there's a race on between Nazis and ourselves to get hold of the remaining th men. And if that is so, it's a race we can't possiby wi

Martin was watching him intently. "You mean it' question of time?"

"In a way." Haslam broke a new packet of Th Castles and took out a cigarette with his stained fing "But mostly it's a question of ability. To our kno edge, two of our target people are in the camps. Totenkopf and the Gestapo keep extensive records, with the vast numbers involved, and with corrupt rife among the Totenkopf especially, these two r might have been transferred unofficially, exchan, their identities or purchased their freedom from so one like your Major Scheldt. On the other hand, if Gestapo are able to locate them immediately, they repossess them—if that is the word—and they'll come lost to us, unless we can find out where the gone. As for the other two, we don't know where tl are, but we suspect they're in hiding, like Joh: Glauss. I can assure you we have agents looking them on a twenty-four-hour schedule, nonstop." Fi ing the cigarette in his hand, he lit it. "Questions?"

"We need to liberate *all* these men, I take it. O partial success possible?"

"I don't know," Haslam said with sudden wearin "I really don't know. I assume it's potentially danger information."

"Are certain of these men more important to us than the rest?"

Haslam spread his hands in silence.

"This man Lenneberg. Do you want me to make official inquiries? I can ask the Gestapo where they've put him. I can say I need to straighten out the records."

Quietly Haslam said, "I don't think they'd tell you. And I think it'd be dangerous for you to ask, even officially. These are very special people, you see."

Martin glanced at Tempel, who was sitting blank-faced behind his rimless spectacles. These two, Martin thought, had been sitting here like this ever since he'd telephoned from Sachsenhausen two days ago to tell them the prisoner Lenneberg had been released, sitting here and signaling London and waiting for urgent briefing, waiting to know if Damocles was still running.

"You say these are very special people," Martin said. "Can I know more than that?" If a signal came from London saying that Damocles had in fact come to a halt, he wanted to know how disastrous it would be for the Allies. He saw the need for withholding information from an agent, but he hated working in the dark.

"I can't tell you more about these people," Haslam said, "or why they're so special. But as regards the mission itself, I can tell you that most of the priority signals we send from here to The Hague arrive on the desks of the King of England and the President of the United States. Will that suffice?"

Martin held his breath for an instant. "Yes. That does give me a clearer perspective."

"Let us hope it doesn't give you a clearer perspective on a dead mission." He stubbed out his cigarette.

"You didn't," Martin said cautiously, "order me back to base just to tell me we might be finished. You could have just kept me running until you were certain."

"How right you are." Haslam exchanged another glance with Tempel and seemed satisfied. "If Damocles

has any future, we've got a special job for you. It's a
tricky one, and we want to know if you feel ready for
anything we decide to give you. I expect you know
roughly what I mean by that."

"I'm ready, yes. It was just that I had to yell at someone, about what I'd seen in the camps."

"And we are the only people you could safely yell
at. Understood. And you're feeling physically up to
par?"

"I am."

Haslam regarded him steadily for a moment with his
one pale blue eye; then he nodded and went over to
the map on the wall.

"Within the next two or three days an SS General
named Artur von Fleig will be coming to Berlin by
road from Neustrelitz, here in the north, approximately
100 kilometers distant. With him will be his driver and
one or more aides; we'll have precise details for you
as soon as they come in." He padded back to his desk
and picked up the green and gold packet of Three
Castles. "Have you heard of General von Fleig?"

"Yes. He's in Himmler's entourage."

"That's right. A man with access to a great deal of
confidential information. He'll be carrying certain documents. We want you to get them for us." He took out
a cigarette and tapped the end on his thumbnail.

"You want this done, whether or not Damocles keeps
running?"

"Whether or not Damocles keeps running," Haslam
said evenly as he lit the cigarette, "may depend on how
successful you are in obtaining the documents, which
explains why we are so solicitously concerned with
your morale and your physical condition. I can't tell
you how delighted we are with your reassurance on
both points."

16

BERLIN, 8 MARCH 1940

Martin was lunching at the Kasinogesellschaft, Berlin's exclusive military club, at the invitation of his Brigadier and together with fifty other guests. He had reported to base by telephone and told Major Haslam it was an invitation he should accept, for the sake of his cover. Haslam had told him to turn up at the Kasinogesellschaft, enjoy his lunch, and telephone base at two-hourly intervals to report his whereabouts. The exact departure time of General von Fleig from Neustrelitz was still uncertain, and Martin was told to show himself in the right places so as to establish a bona fide movement pattern, to avoid any later suspicion.

He was leaving the club shortly before three o'clock when a young SS lieutenant carrying a briefcase almost knocked into him on his way in from the street.

"Excuse me, Herr Standartenführer!"

"Don't mention it."

"Er—Herr Standartenführer—could you please point out the Brigadeführer to me? I have despatches for him, and—" His voice trailed off as he stared into Martin's face.

"Is something the matter, Obersturmführer?" Martin's tone was cool and authoritative, but he was being forced to reach an instant decision.

"I . . . didn't expect . . . to see you again in Berlin," the lieutenant said slowly, and the astonishment in his dark eyes was already changing to the glitter of intrigue. "Martin Benedict. Well, well!"

Since the day Martin Benedict had changed his identity to that of SS-Standartenführer Martin Friedrich Brinkmann he had known that sooner or later he'd be recognized by someone from his past life here in Berlin. He had spent so much time in this city, and had met so many people, that it was inevitable. He had been briefed very thoroughly on this potential danger, and was ready to react correctly; but there was no certainty that within a minute he wouldn't find himself under arrest. Within a minute from now, or an hour, or a day or so: it would depend on how skillfully he handled the situation, and on what the young lieutenant decided to do.

It was Rudi Mahler, the newly recruited SS officer who had shared the taxi with him last September, the Rudi who had been falling in love with Vanessa at the 1936 Olympics when Martin and his sister had been in Berlin.

And Rudi hadn't hesitated, or shown the slightest doubt. *Martin Benedict. Well, well!* That was the key, and Martin had made his decision. Had Rudi seemed unsure, he would have brushed him aside and left the club. But Rudi was certain, and for Martin to deny his true identity would be fatal: Rudi would simply call on the nearest SS officers for support, and Martin would be taken away for interrogation.

"Rudi!" he said with sudden pleasure. "I didn't recognize you!" He declined to shake hands; he was ostensibly a colonel and Rudi a subaltern, and they were in formal surroundings. "You're looking well— you've gained some weight!"

"Yes," Rudi said with a secretive smile, "I'm very well, thank you. And very surprised. Very surprised indeed."

"I can well imagine. And I've been expecting to run into you again, Rudi—especially since we're now fellow officers. We must celebrate, as soon as possible! What are your plans for tonight?"

"I've no plans for tonight, Herr Standartenführer. . . ." He said it with studied irony, yet Martin caught a hint of ingrained deference to his superior rank; by ineradicable association, the triple silver braid at Martin's shoulder demanded respect. This, Martin realized, might be all that could save him.

"Splendid!" he said cheerfully. "Then we'll meet again." He gave it the tone of an order. "Tonight at eight o'clock, at the Kabarett Harlekin. You remember it, of course." They had been there before, with Vanessa and Hedda and Peter, in their days of friendship.

"Of course," Rudi smiled his secretive smile. "In Wielandstrasse, just off the Kurfürstendamm."

"Just as it always was. I'll expect you to be punctual, and stone-cold sober—to begin with." A hint of forthcoming revelry. Then he glanced cautiously around. "But I should warn you, officially, that my assignment within the SS is top secret. It would be to your advantage not mention our meeting to anyone at all. Tonight I'll give you my confidence—I owe you that as a friend. And who knows, I might be in a position to help you further your ambitions; my status carries rather more power than that of a regular Standartenführer." He gave Rudi an affectionate slap on the shoulder. "Until eight, my dear fellow!" Standing back, he brought his heels together. "*Heil Hitler!*"

Martin arrived two minutes late at the Kabarett Harlekin, to find Rudi waiting for him in the crowded foyer. He had reached the nightclub fifteen minutes early, to keep watch on the entrance from the far side of the blacked-out street and make sure Rudi came alone.

Both were in mufti, as was correct for SS officers

off duty in public; but both showed their identity cards to the manager, ensuring better service.

Martin had no idea whether his boyhood friend had told anyone of their meeting, and of the fact that an enemy alien had adopted the uniform of an SS-Standartenführer. But he believed not. His boyhood friend would have reported him without any compunction, since he now owed his total loyalty to his country and the Führer; but Rudi had always been fond of intrigue, and particularly if he thought he could profit from it. They'd ragged him about it in the early days, but had tolerated his worst misdeeds because of his flair for leading them into exciting escapades. As Martin sat with him in the small room with its atmosphere of red plush and cigar smoke, he believed that up to this moment he was probably safe.

Their champagne cork popped as the rose-tinted spotlights followed three nude dancers across the tiny stage, and Martin raised his glass. "Your health, my dear Rudi—and our continuing friendship!"

A few minutes later he was asking casually, "You're not still in the Germania Regiment, then?" Rudi had worn the shoulder flash of the 4th Berliner at lunchtime today.

"I decided to transfer," he said, looking down for an instant. "I found the discipline just a bit too much."

Kicked out, Martin thought. Rudi liked the good life, and his pride in belonging to Hitler's elite bodyguard had been compromised by his sensuality. He was already on his fourth glass of champagne and found it difficult to take his eyes off the dancers as their powdered breasts bobbed in the spotlight. Martin noticed again that he'd put on weight, and had the comfortable look of the bon viveur; the SS, after all, had no interest in the general rationing system that had brought near-hunger to the civilian population.

From time to time Martin glanced at the entrance, as more people came in from the foyer; some of them would be SS officers in mufti, and he picked out one or two of them by their arrogant bearing and the immediate attention they received from the staff. But nobody coming in had taken any interest in the table where he and Rudi were sitting, and he felt partly reassured; though there could easily be a whole cadre of SS men formed up in the street outside, at Rudi's instigation.

"I'm dying to know, of course, how it came about . . . Herr Standartenführer," Rudi began when their second bottle had been opened. Martin spoke slowly, taking his time.

"It's quite simple. As you said yourself, the Führer still considers Germany and England as brother nations, in spite of war being declared. You may know that certain peace overtures have been exchanged·in the last few weeks." He shrugged. "I hope they prove effective. For the present we are unfortunately at war, and if the real fighting begins it's going to be my job to look after the English prisoners of high rank, in the hope of getting them to use their influence in London if we send them home. I'm still working on Major Stevens and Captain Best—you remember the Venlo incident on the German-Dutch border last year?" He glanced up as another party came through from the foyer, then lost interest in them. "Hitler doesn't want to have to fight England, Rudi, as I'm sure you know. He told me so on several occasions. He—"

"You've met the Führer?" Rudi tried not to sound impressed, and failed.

"Of course. That's how I got this commission. After Vanessa died, Hitler summoned me to his office two or three times, for private discussions. He was fond of her, you know, and I suppose I provided a living reminder, as her brother. I also provided a means of proving to the British that Hitler has nothing but friendship for them—considering, after all, that the throne has German blood." He leaned nearer Rudi. "You can imagine how effective it would be, if we returned captured prisoners of high rank to England, as a gesture of amity. Could one hope for better ambassadors? Only Hitler, you know, could devise such a brilliant maneuver. It wasn't till I'd talked to him at some length that I saw what my sister found in him—a unique and fascinating talent for the conduct of human affairs. Have you met the Führer?"

"No. I've not had that privilege." Rudi was watching Martin intently, his dark eyes narrowed and the hint of a smile resting on his mouth. "It's an interesting story," he said at last. "Maybe I believe it, and maybe I don't."

Martin stiffened. "I've no wish to stop your checking on my credentials, Rudi, but I'll point out that I wasn't in the least obliged to take you into my confidence, except as a friend. As a fellow officer I must remind you that the difference in our rank demands rather more courtesy from you than you're at present showing."

The smile left Rudi's mouth, and he too straightened in his chair. "I'm sorry," he said. "It just takes a bit of getting used to."

"Of course. Now I suggest we relax for the rest of the evening. We came here to celebrate our reunion, after all." He called a waiter and ordered another bottle of champagne.

Martin turned his attention to the miniature stage as the evening wore on. Whether Rudi believed his story or not was immaterial: the purpose of this meeting was to gain time and give Martin an insight into Rudi's character, so that he could judge how great the danger was, and what action to take. He had now done both.

"You know," Rudi said half an hour later, "that woman is Jewish. The one in the middle, you see? I can tell a Jew a mile away. . . ."

Rudi was flushed and breathing hard. He was holding his drink well enough, sitting perfectly straight, but most of his inhibitions had gone. Martin was watching him carefully. At the end of the number, Rudi told their waiter to fetch the woman.

Suzanne was dark, slight and small-breasted, her smile dazzling but with a spark of fear in it, Martin noticed. The waiter would have told her they were SS officers at this table—otherwise she wouldn't have come.

"You're a Jew," Rudi told her, his narrowed eyes wandering over her body. "Aren't I right?"

"I am French, m'sieur." Her smile was less dazzling, and she glanced at Martin, who said nothing.

"A French Jew," nodded Rudi, his eyes on her breasts. "A foreign Jew. Christ, haven't we got enough German Jews in this place to get rid of, without you bloody foreigners coming here? I suppose you're a whore on the side?"

"I am a cabaret artiste, m'sieur." She was trembling now, her breath coming faster.

"And a Jew. A bloody Jew. Get your papers here, I want to see them."

She turned quickly toward the side of the stage, with the manager talking to her as she edged between the tables.

"They're a bloody nuisance," Rudi told Martin, picking up his glass. "They take our rations, you know that? Take everything and give nothing back, bobbing their tits up and down as if we're expected to cheer or something." He swung his head heavily to look at Martin. "Don't you agree . . . Herr Standartenführer?" He laughed gustily.

"Let the poor little bitch alone," Martin said lazily. "All you want to do is take her to bed, I know you well enough for that."

Rudi laughed again, slapping the table. "You don't think I'm going to arrest her without some amusement first, do you?"

The woman returned, now in a split sequined skirt.

She gave Rudi her papers, turning her head quickly as Martin spoke to her.

"Are you from Paris, mademoiselle?"

"Yes, m'sieur." She gave him a trembling smile.

"A beautiful city." He raised his glass to her.

"You said you were *French*," Rudi said, looking up from the papers. "All you've got is a French mother. A *Jewess*." He dropped the papers on to the table. "Why did you lie to me, you Jewish bitch?"

"I—I tell the customers I am French, m'sieur. The manager says it sounds more . . . exciting, you know?" She was trying to sound coquettish, but it didn't go with her underlying fear, and Martin looked away. The woman was forty, perhaps older, with at least one child, judging by the Caesarean scar he'd seen when she was naked. And her papers were German, though not stamped with the *Juden* franking.

"These papers are false," Rudi said.

Her face went white and the coquettish smile faded.

"You see these?" Rudi asked Martin. "Look. Look here, at these serial numbers. One too many. And the photograph. And the printing—look, this line here."

Martin nodded. The papers were a crude forgery, a replica of her true papers with the *Juden* franking left out. It was probably known to the manager and some of the other people at the club. But she was a good dancer and brought in money; the SS came here in numbers and demanded entertainment, and with so many Jews sent to the camps there was a shortage of good performers. Probably even the SS knew her papers weren't correct—Rudi's behavior was typical enough—but they'd so far turned a blind eye in return for the woman's services.

Rudi threw the papers on to the table again for Suzanne to pick up. "You're a lying Jewish bitch," he told her slowly, his eyes glittering, "and I ought to arrest you. Forged papers, my God! You've heard of the KZs, I suppose? The concentration camps?"

"I—yes, m'sieur—I have heard of them."

She looked as if she might faint, and Martin was ready to stop her falling. The rage was in him, slowly burning into life during the last few minutes; but it would have to wait.

"So you've *heard* of the concentration camps," nodded Rudi, enjoying himself. "And at this rate you're asking for a personal inspection, you know that?"

"No, m'sieur. I—I am only trying to—"

"To do your job here, m'm? Amuse the troops, m'm?" He gave a belch. "Well, I happen to need a little amusement tonight, you lying Jewish whore, and you might find that preferable to the inside of a KZ, m'm? If not, there's always the alternative. Which number's your dressing room?"

"Number one, m'sieur. But—"

"Did you say 'but'?" His voice was a hiss and his eyes had narrowed to slits as he faced her, his hands clenched. *"Did you say 'but'?"*

"No, I—I just meant—"

"One more 'but' out of you, you foreign *yiddische Hure,* and I'll have you into the camps." Then he relaxed suddenly, pleased at the effect on her. "I'll give you one last chance. You be in your dressing room in ten minutes from now, and make sure there's no one else there, you understand? Ten minutes. Now get out of my sight."

She turned away, her face pale.

Rudi got up, taking care not to stumble. "You'll excuse me, I hope, Herr Standartenführer . . . for a few minutes? Some business to attend to, m'm?" He laughed breezily.

"Go right ahead," Martin told him, laughing up at him in bonhomie. "The night is young, after all!"

Rudi slapped his shoulder. "By God, Martin, it's bloody good being with you again, you know that? Just like old times!" He pushed past his chair. "Now 'scuse me while I go and have a nice . . . long . . . leak . . . or it'll interfere with the performance, m'm?" He thought this especially funny.

"Very wise," Martin nodded. "And tell me, my dear fellow, after you've had your fun in the dressing room, are you going to have the woman arrested?"

Rudi frowned at once, his mood changing again. "Certainly. Most certainly. They're vermin, you know —and you remember what Streicher's always telling us? We've got to clean up the fair city of Berlin!" He slapped Martin's shoulder again. "All right with you, Herr Standartenführer?"

"But of course. I absolutely agree."

He watched Rudi making his unsteady way between the tables, toward the *Toiletten.*

One of the other dancers was in the dressing room when Rudi got there, a large wooden-faced blonde.

"Get out," he told her. "I'm an SS officer. Get out."

She almost ran, one stocking on and one off, and his laughter resounded against the mirrors.

The room reeked of cheap scent. Someone had scrawled a lipsticked message across the end mirror: *Phone Hans before twelve.* There was a lace camisole lying on the dressing table, and he used it to wipe out the words, leaving a blood-red smear.

Rudi laughed. Mademoiselle Suzanne wasn't going to phone Hans before twelve or at any other time. He was going to use the phone himself, after he'd made her so bloody sore she couldn't walk, and when the van came he was going to kick her into it and slam the door, and good riddance to another fucking Jew.

He looked at his watch. The ten minutes were nearly up. By God, if she was going to be late, just ten seconds late, she'd never know what hit her!

But then there were footsteps, and the door opened right on time. But it wasn't the woman.

It was Martin.

*   *   *

The following morning, on 9 March, Hedda von Gerlach was drinking a cup of foul ersatz coffee in the senior staff room of the hospital, and turning the pages of the early paper as she tried to relax after surgery.

With her was Lottie, the ward nurse in Postoperative, full of her troubles as usual.

"I told him they were Dr. Vorst's instructions," she said, "but he simply didn't take any notice. He gave the injection just the same and told me to note it." She grimaced as she reached the dregs of the coffee. "Do you think I should tell Dr. Vorst?"

After a moment Hedda murmured, "I wouldn't do that, Lottie." She had stopped turning the paper, and was intent on the left-hand page.

"But supposing we find adverse reactions? Whose fault is it going to be—his or mine?" She put her cup under the tap and rinsed it.

"I wouldn't worry," Hedda said in a moment. A photograph of a young SS officer had caught her eye.

"The thing is," Lottie said, trying to catch her attention, "while I'm thinking of the patient, he's thinking of himself. He's terribly ambitious, you know."

Hedda had stopped listening.

He didn't look any older in the photograph; it was his cap that made him look different, and he was slightly heavier in the face. She knew he'd joined the SS, soon after Peter, but she'd never seen him in his uniform. He looked very proud.

"Hedda, are you listening?"

"Just a minute, Lottie."

He'd been found floating in the Volkspark Jungfernheide, where he was apparently taken after "succumbing to a vicious assault by a person or persons unknown."

Poor Rudi. He'd always been so devil-may-care.

"I think I ought to tell Dr. Vorst," said Lottie, and took Hedda's cup to rinse it. "Don't you?"

Hedda folded the paper and dropped it into the bin. "I wouldn't do that," she said. "Dr. Schmidt won't be here for long, and there's no point in asking for trouble." She looked at the big wall clock. "I'm in theater at nine. See you for lunch?"

17

BERLIN, 9 MARCH 1940

Major Haslam watched Martin as he came into the room. Brinkmann was looking much more relaxed than he'd been two days ago.

"Your little holiday in Berlin has done you good," he told him.

"It's a change from the camps."

"Have a chair?"

"I'm all right."

Brinkmann never sat down for long; he had too much nervous energy.

"Had a workout," asked Haslam casually, "with Jock?"

"Not today."

Haslam lit a cigarette. "Met someone nice?"

"No."

Haslam went on studying the gaunt face that had aged ten years in the last six months. But Brinkmann wasn't looking fatigued—far from it; he'd matured, hardened, weathered. They'd picked the right man for the job, and the job was making the man. But if he'd had a woman he must report it; that was the rule. There were too many informers loose in this city.

"I meant," Haslam said, having to spell it out, "a woman."

"Yes, I know." He met his chief's gaze straight on, and in a moment Haslam looked away. There was an expression behind Brinkmann's eyes today that he'd never seen before. Not quite confidence, not quite defiance; perhaps just the absence of the rage that had been in him before. Haslam liked to know precisely how his agents were ticking at any given moment, and particularly at a moment when they were about to embark on a crucial exercise.

"Feeling in good form?"

"First class."

"Fair enough." He got up and went to the wall map. "General von Fleig is leaving Neustrelitz, here, at six o'clock this evening, with two aides; in other words a party of four, including their driver. They'll be taking this road, crossing the Havel just here and going south through Zehdenick. During the day there's a lot of slow military traffic along this route, but by evening it tends to thin out. Hilly country, bit of forest land, quite a good road." He came away from the map to use the ashtray. "How many people will you need?"

"I'd rather be on my own."

Haslam glanced at him. "The documents are being brought to Berlin for handing over personally to Heydrich, for his eyes only. If you slip up, and Heydrich gets them, we'll never see them again. And people in London, and indeed Washington, want to see them very badly."

"All I've got to do," Brinkmann said evenly, "is stop a car and deal with four men. That won't be difficult. I'll be in uniform, remember."

Haslam considered. Brinkmann hadn't proved to be the cocky type, so far. "I was going to give you Corbett and Jock, in reserve."

"I shan't need them. But you could set up another interception team farther south. Say ten kilometers below Zehdenick, in case I miss the General's car—it gets dark at about seven."

"Good idea." Haslam had planned to do that in any case. He looked at the large-scale survey map on his desk. "We'll put Klinger and Veidt somewhere here, on this 400′ contour line. If all goes well with you, you can make a rendezvous with them afterward, and report. But I'd prefer you to bring us the documents here personally. Any questions?"

"What do I do with the four men, once I've got hold of the documents?"

"All we ask you to do," Haslam said as he folded the survey map, "is to make absolutely certain that none of them will ever report the incident."

ZEHDENICK, 9 MARCH 1940

The evening was growing quiet after the rumbling of the tanks and transports earlier in the day. A few military police patrols were unsnarling a jam of vehicles north of the farm, where a gun-carrier had thrown a track. A red-painted tractor had been trying to leave the meadow on the far side of the road from the farm buildings, and now a laborer was standing in the middle of the road with his hands waving and a dog barking at his heels, and the next troop transport pulled up and gave the tractor the right of way, and the dog nearly got run over in the rush.

Martin was sitting on a low stile near the top of a wooded slope, three kilometers south of the town, his fieldglasses raised to watch the stretch of road below, a kilometer distant. The watery sunlight, already melting into the low cloud, was coming from behind him in the west. The air was perfectly still. The Battalion's transport pool Mercedes was out of sight behind one of the three barns a hundred meters from the road; Corporal Kitzel had signed it out for him and had then been given the evening off, on the understanding that he didn't talk about it.

Martin held the fieldglasses braced on the post of the stile, watching for a staff car to appear on the open stretch a kilometer away. In the past two hours only four staff cars had passed this way from the north, and three from the south.

He had noticed, Martin was thinking: Haslam had noticed something about him. How relaxed he was.

Three army motorcycles moved across his vision from left to right, and he stiffened. But there was no car immediately behind them. Haslam had said that as far as they could find out, General von Fleig wouldn't be using an escort.

Relaxed, yes. Different from two days ago when he'd thrown those photographs on the table and cut up rough. The man in the alley hadn't been enough to relax him. It had needed the man in the dressing room as well, the bright-eyed daredevil boy who had grown out of his innocence in the name of the Führer and become, in his quiet and secretive way, a monster, his mouth hanging open as he saw Martin at the door, his breath catching as he saw the look of death in Martin's eyes, the fear reaching his face in the instant when he suddenly knew everything, too late.

By God, Martin, it's bloody good being with you again, you know that? Just like old times!

No, my dear fellow, not really. Those times are gone.

An open Mercedes appeared in the fieldglasses, a driver and three officers, Army or SS. Army. And no pennant flying.

Rudi had been too dangerous to leave alive. *You'll find the dead body of an SS officer in Number One dressing room,* Martin had told the manager, who had blanched. *You'd better have him taken somewhere less embarrassing for you, if you want to keep your establishment open.*

Suzanne had been in the passage outside, and he'd told her to get some better papers for herself, or try to get across a neutral frontier. *So far you've been lucky, mademoiselle, but your time is running out, and you must save yourself if you can.* She was expecting him to arrest her, and seemed too frightened to take in what he was saying; he'd had to repeat it until she understood.

A glint of light came into the lenses as the lowering sunset was reflected in the polished bodywork of a car—an open 500-K Mercedes with four uniformed men on board and a pennant flying from a front wing. From the time and distance equation he had worked out, this should be General von Fleig and his party. He went down the grassy slope, taking easy leaps over the ridges of chalk, and reached the road in good time, as he'd done more than once this afternoon by way of rehearsal. When the Mercedes came around the curve he stood in the middle of the road, waving his arms urgently.

As his staff car approached the spot, General von Fleig's thoughts were miles away in his family castle near Waren, in Mecklenberg. He had called his group together for a meeting there and it had lasted two days. His colleagues in the proposed venture were of high SS rank and included three generals and a military scientist, and at the conclusion of the meeting it had been agreed that action should be taken without delay.

No approach would be made to the Führer on the matter: at this stage it was far too delicate, and if he flew into one of his rages and ordered the project to be abandoned, they'd be lost. But later, when they were certain of their ground, von Fleig would go to Hitler himself and present what might almost be seen as a *fait accompli*—short of the actual production work involved.

In the meantime the matter would be safe in the hands of Heydrich, who could also expedite the necessary action.

With these thoughts in mind, General von Fleig was in a good mood as the powerful Mercedes rounded the curve between the hills and came upon the tall SS officer blocking the road with his arms waving wildly. Without waiting for the order, the driver pulled up, and the officer—now seen to be a colonel—came to the side of the open car, saluting quickly.

"I'm sorry to delay you, General, but my men are dealing with a group of Polish agents farther along the road. They were planning to throw a bomb at your car."

"Good God!"

"I suggest your driver pulls into that field, through the gateway over there, until it's safe for you to go on."

"Very well."

The tall blond Colonel stepped on to the running board as the Mercedes turned through the gateway and bounced on its big coil springs across the rutted grass. In the fading light the General and his two aides noticed the other staff car parked behind the barn in deep shadow.

"All right, driver, stop just here. Don't put your lights on—we don't want to attract attention."

As the car came to a halt the Colonel drew his service revolver and placed the muzzle against the General's right temple, just below the edge of his braided cap. "General von Fleig, you will order your companions to throw their revolvers into the weeds over there, beside the barn. If you hesitate, or if anyone disobeys, your brains will be blown out. I'll give you three seconds. One . . . Two . . ."

Von Fleig gave the order, and the Colonel standing beside him on the running board noticed his voice was distinctly shaky. Three revolvers sailed into the grass, one of them clattering against the side of the barn. The Colonel pulled von Fleig's gun from its holster and tossed it after the others.

The evening was quiet, save for the distant murmur of traffic along the road.

All we ask you to do is to make absolutely certain that none of them will ever report the incident.

But there was also rage, and it contracted the muscles in the Colonel's trigger finger as General von Fleig began speaking, his tone cautiously indignant.

"I'm not sure what this means, Standartenführer, but you run the risk of—"

Rage, and the shock wave spattered some of von Fleig's brains against the Colonel's tunic.

For the boy. The boy they poured petrol over.

The air reeked of blood and cordite.

Rage. SS-Hauptsturmführer Emil Horst's right arm came up to protect him but the bullet tore through the muscle and smashed into the cranium.

For the child they were throwing into the air.

The driver had started whimpering.

Rage. SS-Obersturmführer Wilhelm Messinger had wrenched the door open on the other side of the Mercedes and threw himself out, perhaps in the hope of running for cover or finding one of the revolvers among the weeds. The bullet shattered his spine, its force pitching him flat on the ground and producing a strange belching noise as the last breath was pushed out of his lungs.

For the man hanging from the gallows at Buchenwald.

Birds flew up from the elms at the edge of the field, alarmed by the shots.

Rage. SS-Unterscharführer Anton Mohr had twisted around in the driver's seat and was trying to reach the Colonel's gun hand in time to deflect the next shot, which he knew would be for him. This brought his face close to the gun when it was fired, so that it was obliterated, the eyes and nose and mouth suddenly becoming a black and red area with no particular shape or feature.

For Franz von Gerlach, wherever he may be.

The evening was quiet again, and after a while the birds flew back to the elms and settled.

Within six days the entire population of Zehdenick— 7,323 citizens—had been interrogated by a special unit of the SS, assisted by the local Gestapo force. A detailed questionnaire had been drawn up and copied by nine o'clock on the morning following the shooting.

Have you noticed any strangers in town recently?

Where were you on the evening of 9 March?

Do you suspect that friends or neighbors are hiding someone?

Were you traveling on the road south of the town at dusk on the evening of 9 March? If so, did you notice anything or anyone unusual?

There were seventy-three questions in all.

Within the same six days every building, every house, cottage, shop, office and apartment block was invaded by Gestapo and SS men and searched so thoroughly that wallpaper was left hanging in strips, the space beneath staircases broken into, roof tiles removed to gain access to attics from the outside.

A guard platoon of the SS had been drawn around the barn in the field three kilometers south of the town, and a detachment of the Berlin Homicide Squad worked for two days searching for clues to the identity of the assassin or assassins. They drew a blank, though there would be a forensic laboratory report later, after microscopic and chemical examination of the Mercedes and the surface of the surrounding grassland. It was known almost immediately that three briefcases had been taken from the car.

Three Jewish intellectuals with outdated papers were dragged out of hiding, one from a friend's house, one from the signalbox at Zehdenick station where bricks had been removed from a walled-in area below the control room, and one from a pigsty only a kilometer from the scene of the assassination. The Jewish intellectuals were shot in the graveyard of the Lutheran church, together with the railway signalman and a farm laborer.

Apart from this, the enormous amount of work carried out by the small army of investigators during those six days was unrewarding. But four people reported having seen, in the afternoon or evening of 9 March, an SS colonel moving alone in the vicinity of the barn and using fieldglasses. They all assumed he had been watching the road to supervise the military traffic. This was noted and reported to the authorities directing the investigation, who sent copies of the summary to the relevant departments, including Gestapo Headquarters Berlin.

18

BERLIN, 10 MARCH 1940

The envelope was creased and filthy, with ocher stains on it that looked like dried blood. The single sheet of paper inside was not much better, and the writing was shaky, though she recognized it as her brother's.

Dear Hedda,
I am well. Things aren't too bad here, now I've got used to them. After all, I committed a crime against the State. I can quite understand your not writing to me. I exposed you and Father and Mother to suspicion and interrogation, but I pray to God nothing worse. I was ordered to write to you, by the camp Gestapo. I don't know why. But it's a good opportunity to tell you I understand your silence. One day, if we all survive, I'll see you again, and try making up for what I did. Look after each other. I can't very well put "with love" at the end of this letter, after all the trouble I caused. But I still love you. After all, you never did anything to me, it was the other way around.
Keep well.
Your brother, Franz

Before she had finished reading it, the sheet of soiled paper was shaking in her fingers and her heart was

breaking. So *none* of her letters had reached him . . .
not one. And she had sent forty-nine, their number
carefully recorded in her diary, two every week since
his arrest in August last year; she had never given up,
even when she felt sure that by now he could no longer
be alive to receive them. And now she was being torn
apart by the relief that he was still alive somewhere,
and the torment of knowing that in his loneliness he
believed she refused even to write to him. . . . She'd
thought there was nothing more for her to suffer, until
now.

"So you see, Fräulein, I have kept my word," Superintendent Vogel told her softly. "Your brother is still
alive and well."

His voice shocked her out of her reverie. He'd given
her the letter as soon as he'd come in, presenting the
stained and ravaged envelope with the studied courtesy
that made everything else he did seem infinitely worse.

"Where is he?" she asked dully. The postmark was
too smudged to read.

"He is in transit." Vogel was standing by the window
with his back to it, a favorite place. "I shall tell you the
moment I learn where he's been sent. By earlier reports
it was to Kozuchow, in Poland."

She had dared to ask him, that evening last week
after Martin had been, if he were certain Franz was
still at Buchenwald, because she had still received no
letters from him. Martin had told her Franz had left
Buchenwald, but she couldn't tell this creature that she
knew.

"I hope his letter is cheerful, Fräulein?"

"Cheerful?" She turned to look at him, trying to fit
a meaning to the word. "Oh, yes. Quite cheerful." She
wasn't going to reveal a single thought of her brother's
to this foul brute—the letter was private; creased,
soiled, perhaps bloodstained, but private.

"A mistake was made," he told her primly. "With so
many in the concentration camps, mistakes are in-

evitably made. Your brother should have been transferred to the privileged section at Buchenwald, as I'd requested; instead he was sent to Kozuchow with a group of prisoners selected for punishment, following the monstrous attempt on our Führer's life last November."

"Punishment?" She felt she was going to fall, and had to put out a hand to the edge of the table.

"Yes. But I was in time to sort things out, as soon as I received the list of prisoner movements. You mustn't worry, Fräulein. I have appointed myself your brother's guardian, as we agreed in the beginning." He came closer to her, his black boots creaking in the quiet room. "Now that you are reassured, we can proceed to other things. You have never looked more beautiful, you know, than tonight." His voice was very soft now. "I think losing a little weight has made you even more attractive, if that were possible . . . your eyes seem larger, in the hollows of your face . . . I would like to write a poem for you, or paint a picture of you, just as you are now, or even better, as you'll be in a few minutes, in all your exquisite nakedness . . ."

She supposed, as she always supposed when he approached her like this, with his clumsy attempts at tenderness, that her stillness and her closed eyes could be interpreted as a kind of surrender, even as pleasurable anticipation; he must certainly see it like that, because if he suspected what she was thinking of him he'd kill her, and Franz too. In any case, the tenderness was only the prelude to his habitual little show of caveman ferocity.

"Take off your clothes," he commanded abruptly, "or do you want me to tear them off?"

His mouth caressed her body.

Every time he came here it was more difficult for him, more painful, more tormenting.

The heat was flowing into his groin as it always did,

tantalizing him, making him think that something at last was happening, that he was becoming a man; but nothing was happening, nothing.

Long ago, with other women, he had given up trying to imagine he was doing what other men did; it made the torment worse. He would have been spared, if only he could look at women, even women as beautiful as this one, without any feeling, any desire for them. But the desire was always there, as strong as with other men, until he was forced to go with whatever woman he chose from among the many at his disposal —and then there was this torment, this nothingness as his hands and his mouth did all they wanted, touching everywhere, savoring her body and making it entirely his, a slave, a toy to play with, while the heat burned enticingly and nothing happened, nothing happened, until he moaned in his frustration, once shedding actual tears on her while she must have laughed silently at him, lying helpless under him but laughing . . . laughing . . . until he had jerked himself away from her as if suddenly she had become a corpse.

But she daren't laugh at him openly. She daren't taunt him with being only half a man, a freak. None of them dared to make fun of him, because they knew his power.

Let this one smile incautiously, even for a second in the glow of the lamplight, and her beloved brother would be strung up from a gallows and left for the flies. She knew that.

"Fräulein . . ." he murmured, the scent of her moist body maddening him, the feel of her skin kindling the heat in his groin. "Fräulein . . ." as his hands moved, as his tongue delighted in her.

But he knew that one day it would become too much for him, and he would have to kill her. This one was so beautiful that he couldn't bear to think of another man with her, giving her what was utterly beyond him to give. She must remain his forever, and he could make it so.

Until then she must be taught how much he hated her for being what she was, the exquisite incarnation of the unattainable, his whole life's torment.

"A perfect example of gold inlay work," he said, "as I think you'll agree."

Fully dressed now, he had presented the diamond and amethyst ring to her as a parting gift.

"It's quite lovely," she said, her heart shrinking.

"I think so, yes. It was made by a man named Grono-wetter, at Buchenwald. He had a shop, you know, on the Kurfürstendamm, until last year—Gronowetter and Kader, they were partners. It was quite a famous place, I'm sure you were acquainted with it."

"I think I've heard of it," she said. She was in her blue flowered dressing gown, her feet still bare, her body aching for the cool cleansing water of the shower, where she would soap and soap herself until her skin was raw. She had never got used to it; since the first time this creature had come into this room she had never felt clean.

"Gronowetter was an expert on diamonds," Vogel told her conversationally. "He was an official appraiser to the Berlin Chamber of Commerce." Watching her face he went on. "Unfortunately there was an accident, soon after he made this piece. He was running toward the main gate one day in answer to an announcement on the public address system, and one of the guard dogs thought he was trying to escape, and slipped its handler. They keep the guard dogs short of food, you see, so that they don't become lazy. It took four men with whips to get the dog away from Gronowetter—the beast was maddened with blood lust, once he'd broken the skin."

She had learned, by now, to shut her mind to what

this creature was saying, just as she'd learned to think of other things while he raped her with his hands and his mouth. She knew what he was telling her, but she was able to go on listening as if his voice came from a long way off, on the far side of reality.

"How unfortunate," she said, staring at the delicate inlay of the ring. "But accidents will happen, won't they?" And she looked up at him with her eyes dead, giving him nothing, seeing his disappointment. "It's a magnificent gift, Herr Vogel, and I'll wear it with great pleasure."

He turned away brusquely, picking up his gloves from the marquetry table by the door. "Next week, Fräulein, perhaps you'd care to accompany me for dinner somewhere?"

It was intended to shock, as she knew; until now her shame had always been private, in the seclusion of her own home. But she kept her control, and even smiled for him.

"I'd be delighted, of course."

Superintendent Vogel climbed into the black saloon and slammed the door.

"Is this as close as you could bring the car?" he asked his driver curtly.

"There was someone parked right outside, Herr Superintendent."

"Why didn't you take his place?"

"I was just about to do that, Herr Superintendent."

"You'll have to be a little quicker the next time. I prefer not to have to walk the streets in the blackout, do you understand?"

"Of course, Herr Superintendent."

The driver looked at the pale face in the mirror and glanced away quickly, pulling out from the curb and changing gear. The Chief was in a filthy mood, as was to be expected, after seeing a woman. It had been the same pattern for three years now, since Fritz had been his personal driver.

"Go to the Wilhelmstrasse."

"The Wilhelmstrasse, Herr Superintendent."

The pattern never varied. He'd pick a new woman, visit her once a week and every time come away like a bear with a sore arse, worse than before; they seemed to get his rag out instead of calming him down, as if they wouldn't let him have it or something—though Fritz very much doubted *that*. This one, the von Gerlach woman, had lasted longer than the others, but the signs were there, the signs were there all right—the Chief was thinking in terms of a change to someone new.

"What is that crowd?"

"I don't know, Herr Super—"

"Pull up here."

Fifteen or twenty people were watching four or five Gestapo officers struggling with two civilians.

"They're making an arrest, Herr Superintendent."

"Quite so. Well, get on, man."

"Yes, Herr Superintendent."

One of the civilians managed to break away and lunge for a gap in the crowd but a man tripped him and he went down, one arm hitting the wing of the black saloon. Then the officers were on him, and a club swung and he stopped yelling.

It used not to be like that. They used not to make a fuss when their turn came. But everyone was getting to hear of the KZs by now, and no one wanted to go there.

Fritz made a left turn and headed through Wilmersdorf, going as fast as he dared behind the cowled headlamps in the pitch-dark street.

"Is this as fast as you can go?"

"I'm thinking of the Superintendent's personal safety, Herr Super—"

"You can still go faster than this."

"Yes, Herr Superintendent."

Bite your bloody head off, and just had a woman. Two hours he'd been in that house, and much good it had done him. The signs were there, and no mistake. Next thing he'd be taking her out somewhere, dinner or a nightclub or maybe both, let everyone see what a catch he'd got—they were always absolute smashers, you had to admit that much—then it'd be curtains, and there'd be a new address to go to every week, a new woman. He'd seen five of them disappear, one after another, in the last three years. Ravensbruck, of course. A shocking waste of good crumpet, when you came to think of it, with the brothels so short of fancy material —but that was the Superintendent's game, all along; once he'd finished with them he didn't like anyone else taking over. Exclusive, that was the Chief.

Fritz checked his mirror again and found the eyes of Superintendent Vogel watching him steadily, forcing him to look quickly back at the road, a chill running down his spine; his eyes were like a reptile's, and he'd never got used to it.

'Faster!" the cold voice came. "Have you forgotten how to obey an order?"

"No, Herr Superintendent!" Fritz put his foot down and sent the car through the darkened street with one hand on the horn, and God help anyone trying to cross the road.

Watery sunlight was filtering through the windows of the American Embassy.

"I am charged by the President," said the Ambassador slowly, "to make the situation clear to you, and also to offer his warm personal congratulations to you on your success with this project to date. No one can say whether the United States will find herself at war with Germany in the near or distant future. You may already know that the sympathies of our President lie with England and her allies, not only because of the hereditary bonds still joining our peoples in continuing friendship, but also because we realize that if Europe should fall to Hitler's armies, the British colonies—whose strategic location is of vital interest to the United States, especially in time of war—would also fall under the German yoke. The way would be open for the conquest of South America, and subsequently our own country just across the border."

Pausing for a moment to look from the windows across the wide boulevard, he turned suddenly to face his audience. "Until recently we believed it would take a long hard war to carry the Germans to world conquest. Today we must face the terrifying fact that it will happen much sooner than that, if Hitler develops this new and unimaginably powerful superweapon that we call the atomic bomb."

The tension in the room increased. They had all read the von Fleig documents and understood their significance, but this was the first time the threat to world peace in the future had been put into words.

"You've studied the papers that were taken from General von Fleig," the Ambassador continued, "and you know what I'm talking about. Until the Nazis assumed power here in Germany it was easy for all of us, in the rest of Europe and in the United States, to scoff at scaremongers and keep our faith in a bright future. Today we know that the most frightful horror stories have become reality, and even commonplace. And what is happening in this country will begin happening all over the world, on the day that Adolf Hitler has the atomic bomb. From the information the heads of government have received from the nuclear physicists in Britain and the United States and other countries, it is not too much to say that with the atomic bomb in Hitler's possession we would witness the end of the civilized world as we now know it. Hitler would become a global potentate, and his Thousand Year Reich would cover the earth."

Major Haslam hadn't moved since he'd come into the room; he hadn't even exchanged so much as a glance with Martin or Otto Tempel. In these surroundings and in the presence of the Ambassador he looked exactly what in fact he was: the blank-faced, enigmatic chief of an enemy intelligence network, for the moment on neutral ground. Martin felt now that Haslam must have known the true objective behind the Damocles operation: in direct terms, the rescue of certain physicists and their safe conduct to England; in indirect terms, the destruction of any chance Hitler might have of possessing the atomic bomb, and beyond that, world conquest.

"I'm permitted to tell you," the Ambassador said in his level tones, "that whether or not the United States is brought into the conflict, plans have already been made to develop the atomic weapon as speedily as possible, in the hope that one day we might stop the war simply by demonstrating its awesome power. And to develop the bomb we shall need the help of those eminent physicists who are already safe in England on their way to the States and the nuclear laboratories there—thanks to the work you have done."

With something like a smile he added quickly, "We'd like to help you do it. We have quite a few trained men who'd give a great deal to pitch in with you, here in the field where the action is." Then the smile was gone. "But I don't need to remind you that at present America is a neutral power, and that even if only one of her agents were caught in a clandestine operation here on German soil, she could be pitched into a war she's not prepared for, either in terms of armaments or public opinion." The smile came again, fleetingly. "It doesn't look, in any case, like you need any help at the moment."

Before he ushered them to the door he made a final statement. "The crux of the message I was charged by my president to convey to you, gentlemen, is that we want you to know that the work you're doing behind the scenes here in Germany *cannot* be overstated in its importance to the civilized world; and we hope this thought will inspire you to even greater courage and even greater determination as you proceed with your mission."

Haslam lit his fourth cigarette from the butt of the third, his right eye narrowing against the smoke.

"We've seen the documents," he said quietly, "and we know what we've got to do."

They were assembled in the enormous cellar of the house in Charlottenburg, Haslam occupying the dilapidated baroque chair behind the desk, the others seated or perched around it. Tempel had come straight here from the American Embassy; Klinger, Veidt and Sadler had come down soon after them, their footsteps echoing from the bare stone walls as they descended the stairs. So far, no one except Haslam had spoken. It was known throughout the network that Damocles had suddenly swung into a new dimension, but this had nothing to do with the fact that the true objective had now been revealed—and revealed to be momentously important; it was because a reading of the documents showed that the von Fleig faction was at this moment on a collision course with their own operation.

"There's a race on," Haslam said, "to reach the last three physicists, particularly a key man named Ernst Kramer. The death of General von Fleig won't change the situation significantly; these other characters are going to press on and persuade Hitler to start work on developing the atomic bomb. They've got a handful of what they're pleased to call 'Aryan' scientists lined up, but they've lost a critical number of Jews, including the two who actually did the original work on uranium fission, Otto Hahn and Fritz Strassman. The one thing in our favor is that the Nazis don't know precisely where the last three people have got to."

Martin was alerted. As a matter of principle he'd been kept in the dark as to his chief's facilities and the background of his network; but from his last remark it was clear that he must have at least one agent working inside the SS or the Gestapo administration, or both.

"Nor do we," Haslam said, and blew out a slow plume of smoke. "The Nazis keep meticulous records, as you know, but they're not foolproof by any means. The actual camp records are serviced by low-ranking SS NCOs—who can be inefficient, unintelligent and always bribable—and the prisoners themselves, who'll alter a man's records for a packet of cigarettes or a lump of bread. There's also an immense amount of shuttling around going on, mostly because these camps are filling up so fast that whole trainloads have to be sent somewhere else—chiefly to Poland, where the death camps are being built."

He looked at Martin. "Colonel Brinkmann, is that an accurate picture, from your own experience?"

"In general. In particular, where people like these scientists are concerned, there's a lot of protection, especially where a prisoner's well known—a musician, writer, surgeon, anyone with something to offer if they can be helped to survive. If someone like that is marked down for transfer to a death camp, the kapos with influence will smuggle him on to the sick list and get him into the camp hospital. I've found a dozen cases of a prisoner ostensibly 'dying' in the wards but in fact living on in the name of someone actually dead."

"Does that go for the death camps in Poland too?" asked Haslam.

"Not really." There was an edge to Martin's tone, and the others were aware of it. "In a death camp there's no hospital. The only way a man can survive there is by volunteering to work. They can also be selected to work—usually the physically big men, strong enough to push the 'material' into the gassing room and carry it out for cremation. That's what they call it, you see. The 'material.' ' "

For a moment there was silence in the big room, and Haslam was quick to break it. He and Tempel had exchanged opinions after Brinkmann had thrown those photographs on the table upstairs. Tempel said he was starting to break, and ought to be called in and replaced by Corbett. Haslam felt that Brinkmann was simply getting rid of the pressure. But neither could know; neither was sure. The civilized young intelligence officer who had been sent out here to learn ruthlessness in the atmosphere of a ruthless enemy was no longer the same man. His family and his friends in England would hardly recognize him now, after only six months in the field; he had aged and his eyes were hard, his voice cutting, his temper dangerous but kept under an iron control. He was a casualty of war, Haslam thought, still alive and still strong, able and useful to his masters, but a casualty.

"One day," the calculating, observant Tempel had told his chief, "he's going to break out. You should call him in before he does, because that would wreck our operation."

"You think he's that bad?"

"Not yet," Tempel had answered. "But one day. In the meantime, you have to lower the pressure in the man, and I know how to do that."

Tempel had been a military psychologist before he'd gone to ground to combat the new rulers of the Reich; and he'd forgotten nothing. Haslam had taken note of what he'd advised, and it was in his mind as he watched Colonel Brinkmann in the silence that had come to the room.

"You say they choose the physically big men?" he asked quickly. "But two of—"

"They choose anyone who's got the strength and the stomach to do the job." Martin was on his feet, his chair scraping on the bare stones, his boots sending echoes from the walls as he paced restlessly. "They choose anyone who's capable of pushing a screaming man or a screaming woman into the gas chamber and slamming the door on them." His voice cracked but he controlled it instantly. "They've got to be strong enough to throw small children into—"

"Colonel Brinkmann," said Haslam sharply.

"I said children!" Martin found himself standing against the desk, staring down at Haslam with his eyes bright. *"I've seen a pile of dolls, just inside the barbed wire at Kozuchow. Children's dolls. And teddy bears, and golliwogs, you know the sort of thing I mean, that children play with?"*

From the other side of the desk Haslam looked up at the blond, blue-eyed man who towered over him, the whole of his lean body galvanized, his knuckles white, the sweat bright on his face under the SS officer's cap with its skull and cross-bones insignia; and Haslam knew he was looking at the angel of death.

"Colonel Brinkmann," he said with more force, "sit down."

Otto Tempel tensed in his chair, ready to do something, though he wasn't sure what. Even with the four of them here, this man would become a tiger the instant he was touched, and he wouldn't remember they were friends.

"When the children are pushed into the compound, don't you see, they're told to drop their dolls on to the pile. *You know why? I said do you know why? Because if they take them into the death chamber, the prisoners at the entrance doors might lose their reason at last and run berserk—and that's inconvenient, don't you see, it holds up the work. Jesus Christ, don't you understand what I'm—"*

"Brinkmann, sit down!" Haslam was on his feet, but Tempel was faster, signaling that he was taking over.

"Martin," he said quietly. "Martin Benedict. Yes, we know what you're saying." He looked straight into the bright staring eyes. "It's terrible. We know it's terrible. We understand, Martin."

It was the first time he had ever called this man by his real name, and he hoped it wasn't too late. He should have seen this before. Over the months, Martin Benedict had been losing his identity. He wasn't the English ex-actor, ex-Intelligence Corps captain any more; and he wasn't the SS Colonel of the Death's Head division he pretended to be; he was somewhere in between. And he no longer thought very kindly, Tempel know, of anyone here. They were forcing him into almost daily contact with the blackest barbarism, yet refusing to let him act against it, except indirectly. The orders he longed for were never given. *Go in there with a machine gun and massacre them to a man—the Kommandant and his senior staff and every stinking bastard you see in the SS uniform. Then let the prisoners free.*

Up to now, Martin Benedict had held on to the rational thought that in keeping control, in quietly releasing these vitally important scientists, he was helping to bring down Hitler and his dreams of world domination, thus opening the way to peace terms and the eventual dissolution of the camps. But that idea was abstract, and this man's constant exposure to human suffering was driving him to the now desperate need to do something concrete—to free those prisoners with his own hands. That wasn't possible, but Otto Tempel knew there was a compromise, and he'd told Haslam, and Haslam had listened.

"Martin," said Tempel now, "you mustn't think we're not aware of what's going on in the camps, or that we don't care. Have you ever wondered why I gave up a successful career in military medicine, to live underground and go in fear of my life? It was because I had a brother. Hans Gerhart Tempel." His unblinking eyes fixed on Martin's under the big lamp. "He gave shelter, for a few hours, to a Jew who was on the wanted list of the Gestapo. And when it was discovered, my brother went with the Jew to Buchenwald, and died with him there. I loved my brother, and I understand how you feel about the camps."

Martin stared at him in silence, while Major Haslam waited, keeping absolutely still. Tempel continued to hold Martin's gaze, knowing from his professional experience how easy it is for the eyes and the voice to invoke light hypnosis. Suddenly Martin drew a deep breath and looked down, his whole body relaxing.

"Sorry," he said, "about your brother."

"We all have a brother," said Tempel slowly, "in the camps. Many brothers." He turned away and Haslam sat down again behind the desk; Sadler coughed and Klinger asked for a cigarette.

"As I said before," Haslam told them briskly, "we know what we've got to do. Find Joseph Lenneberg, free him and get him to the escape lines. Make sure exactly what has happened to the last three psysicists, before the opposition can get at them if they're still alive. And deal with the von Fleig faction in whatever way we can, to obstruct their efforts." He looked neither at Tempel nor Martin, but at the smoke curling from his cigarette. "Has Colonel Brinkmann any ideas on that?"

Carefully Martin asked him, "On dealing with the faction particularly?"

"Particularly." Haslam still didn't look at him.

"Yes," Martin said softly. "All I need are their names."

"Very well." Haslam turned to the documents. *We can use our other people,* Otto Tempel had told him earlier, *for the work of elimination. But Brinkmann's SS rank gives him an entrée, and besides, it's urgent that we let him vent his rage. He must draw blood, with his own hands, in the name of the prisoners. I don't see, otherwise, how he's going to keep his sanity.*

"These are the names," he told Martin, "of the other

members of the von Fleig faction." As he read them, Otto Tempel listened to the characteristically toneless voice that for these few moments had become the voice of the executioner. "SS-General Egon von Kassel . . . SS-General Walther Maihof . . . and SS-General Bruno Heidel."

He read them again twice, then closed the file.

19

DEBNO, POLAND, 12 MARCH 1940

It had been a peaceful day at the camp, partly because the wind had dropped at last, leaving the air still, and partly because today there had been no train from the railhead at Kostrzyn on the German border. There had been three trains in the last five days, creating a severe pressure of work for the SS officers and men; but tonight the place was calm, though there were three blocks still crowded with newcomers awaiting dispatch.

This was a new camp, experimental, and not yet completed. Four months ago its kommandant, SS-Hauptsturmführer Karl Axen, had been summoned with other Totenkopfverbände officers to a confidential meeting with Reichsführer Himmler, during which it had been mentioned in passing that "sooner or later, something would have to be done to settle the problem of all these Jews." It was rumored that Göring himself was to announce some kind of official program on this subject.

Kommandant Axen, a young and energetic officer of captain's rank, had received personal orders to build this small and special camp near Debno and to set it in operation as soon as possible. He had worked without sparing himself, from the moment the electrified wire was erected and the first prisoners arrived; and now, on this peaceful evening, the young Kommandant surveyed with pride the miracle he had achieved in four short months: a habitable, workable acreage of flat land containing ten metal-and-concrete permanent buildings for his staff and inmates, plus a large all-concrete edifice at the opposite side from the main gate to which every new arrival was finally ushered. With its fifteen-strand electrified barbed wire fence, four watchtowers and machine-gun posts and battery of arc lamps, the camp already had the appearance of what it was designed to be: a model for other and larger camps to come.

Sixty-seven laborers had succumbed to fatigue during the intensive work that had been necessary to perform the miracle, but the labor supply had been unlimited and the work had proceeded on schedule. Two weeks after Kommandant Axen and his pretty young wife Ilse had arrived here to take up their residence, the lady had drowned in her bath, leaving a note to the effect that she no longer wished to live in what she described as "the suburbs of Hell" or with the "inhuman fiend" her once-loved husband had become. It was his own fault, really, as one of his personal staff had remarked; the young Kommandant had, after all, allowed his wife to believe that the "Resettlement Program" was just that: a resettling of the Polish labor force into work for the Fatherland. The note was never actually seen by the grieving husband, since his staff felt he had suffered enough in the loss of the pretty Ilse, and had destroyed her farewell message. Fortunately the work of creating the new camp at such a speed had taken Karl Axen's mind off the tragedy, to the point where, only ten days later, he selected a teenage Polish girl of stunning good looks from the line of new arrivals and installed her in his private quarters.

This afternoon, despite the tremendous pressure of work due to the recent shipments, the camp was running to perfection, and a little before nine in the eve-

ning the young Kommandant was standing at the head
of the line of men, women and children outside the
large concrete building, known as the Chamber. It had
no windows, and only two doors—one at the front and
one at the back, where an engine could be heard
throbbing. The shadows of the prisoners made a black
frieze against the wall, thrown by the brilliant floodlights, and the silhouette of Kommandant Axen was
there beside them on the wall, his slim figure swaying
gracefully as the bow of his violin passed across the
strings, producing a slow and haunting melody from
the folk music of Poland.

Axen, in appearance and to a certain extent in character, was not unlike Obergruppenführer Reinhard Heydrich, chief of the SS Security, with his sharp, ratlike
features and slender body, with his pale blue eyes and
fair hair. Karl Axen was not unaware of this resem-
blance, and took discreet pride in it. Heydrich's prowess
with the violin was well known throughout the organization, and so the young officer had developed his own
skill with the instrument, and enjoyed playing to the
long lines of people waiting outside the Chamber.

"They shall have music, wherever they go," he had
once said to his staff. A lieutenant, seeing the funny
side, laughed raucously at this, stopping only when he
saw his commander's face watching him in silence.
"That was not a joke," he was told curtly, and by the
morning had been stripped of his uniform and beaten
to a pulp before joining the new arrivals as a prisoner
on his way to the Chamber. The point was—as the
rest of his staff at once realized—that Kommandant
Axen sincerely wished to grace the departure of the
prisoners with the sweetness of his playing; and it was
an absolute fact that most of them, as they stood listening to the music of their native land, were quite unable
to believe that anything bad could possibly be going
to happen.

This evening, as the slender young officer played for them, six trustee prisoners of the permanent staff—known as kapos—were moving down the lines with small canvas bags, asking the new arrivals to deposit any personal medicines or drugs into them for safekeeping at the hospital. A second team was also working its way along the lines, requesting that any jewelry should be handed over for looking after in the camp strongroom, in exchange for formal receipts. (The loss of such property, the kapos assured them, was a severe problem for the guards, especially while the showers were being taken and everyone's belongings were in the waiting room.) In the small building on the left, watching from the windows, a team of nine skilled dental surgeons drawn from the permanent prisoner staff was awaiting the moment when the huge door of the Chamber would be opened again and the mouths of the emerging cadavers could be searched for gold fillings. Meanwhile, tresses of long silky hair cut from the heads of the women in the previous batches were spread evenly across the floor of a nearby building to dry.

The entire operation was running without a hitch this evening, and the enterprising young Kommandant celebrated his success by conjuring from his violin the wistful folk tunes that went drifting across the heads of the waiting people and high over the barbed wire fence, to fade at last among the spring grasses of the meadow beyond, sleeping peacefully beneath the moon.

* * *

Dear Frau _____

Your husband, _____, *died in the Camp Hospital on* _____. *Allow me to express my sincere sympathy on your sad bereavement.*

_____ *was admitted to the Hospital on* _____ *with symptoms of exhaustion, and complained of pains in the chest. Despite competent*

and devoted medical attention it proved impossible,
unfortunately, to maintain life in the patient.
The deceased voiced no final requests.
The Camp Kommandant _____

Franz von Gerlach filled in the blank spaces of the
ninety-seventh form he had taken today from the card-
board box on the desk. Three other prisoners were
helping him with the work, among them Kurt Wolff
and Willi Helm. Kurt wore the red armband of a block
senior, and both he and Willi had the red triangle of a
"political" on their prison shirts, like Franz. Most of the
men here in the Orderly Room wore the same badge,
since articulate political protest was usually made by
those with a clerical background. There were only
three green triangles of the "criminal" designation in
the bleak concrete office at the moment, though that
could change at any time—the slightest misbehavior or
technical fault discovered in a clerk would put him
immediately on the list for the Chamber.

Franz bent under the worn trestle desk and blew his
nose again on the scrap of newspaper he'd filched from
the rubbish bin outside, though each of these trivial
actions brought him close to death. For any kind of
stealing, even from a rubbish bin, a man would be put
straight on the list for the Chamber; the same thing
applied if he showed signs of disease, even a cold—the
Kommandant prided himself on the excellent health
record of his model camp. But then, for any one of
seventy-five infractions—carefully enumerated on the
board in each barrack block—a man would find himself on the list, and Franz wasn't overly concerned. On
the other hand, you didn't just ask for trouble, and he
had no faith in this "guardian angel" of his. It could
only be a coincidence that the phrase used by Corporal Trot at Buchenwald had been repeated a few weeks
after Franz had arrived here at Debno. He'd been on
the list for taking a pair of shoes from a corpse, but

half an hour before he was due to report outside the Chamber he'd been called to the gatehouse to see Sergeant Steiger.

"I see you're down for light duties, Gerlach."

Franz waited in silence. Sergeant Steiger had made a statement, not asked a question. He spoke very softly, his thick lips moving carefully in his plump face, as if he were tasting something. You had to listen as hard as you could, and even lean toward him without letting it show, because in speaking softly his aim was to make you ask him what he'd said, and then he'd look up with his bland colorless eyes and tell you that if you didn't care to listen to what he said, you'd better go on the list.

You could die, at Debno, by taking a scrap of newspaper, or blowing your nose, or not understanding Sergeant Steiger.

"Why didn't you tell me you were on light duties, Gerlach, when you were put on the list?"

"Because I didn't know, Sergeant."

The fleshy lips made their little rings. "You didn't know."

Statement. Don't say anything.

The initial terror that Franz had felt when he first met this NCO hadn't diminished; it had become a means of defense. He had learned to regard Sergeant Steiger as a venomous snake that would strike at the slightest movement. Provoking Sergeant Steiger was not one of the seventy-five infractions on the board, but it was just as fatal.

"Since you are officially on light duties, Gerlach, I shall remove you from the list for the Chamber."

Don't say anything.

From outside in the main compound they both heard a man scream, and Franz watched the Sergeant's round pink face take on a hint of a smile. Then there was the sharp crack of a gun and the screaming stopped, and in a moment Sergeant Steiger looked back at his papers.

"You must have a guardian angel, Gerlach, to have been put on permanent light duties."

Statement. Don't speak.

"Have you a guardian angel, Gerlach?" So softly that an SS clerk typing at the far end of the room almost obliterated his voice. But Franz had heard. He had learned to listen.

"I don't think so, Sergeant." He spoke without thinking.

Mistake. A dangerous mistake.

The small colorless eyes came to rest on him, taking on a glitter. "Just a moment ago, Gerlach, I told you that you *must* have a guardian angel. You now say that you don't think so. Am I, therefore, wrong?"

"No, Sergeant."

"Then," silkily, "you do indeed have a guardian angel?"

"Yes, Sergeant."

"Who is it?"

"I don't know, Sergeant."

As the clerk at the far end of the room stopped typing there was a moment's silence, and in that silence there came another scream from outside. Sergeant Steiger turned his head again to listen, and Franz later realized the dying man had probably saved him, by distracting the Sergeant's attention. In a few seconds there was another shot, and the screaming stopped. Sergeant Steiger looked down, and made a mark with his pencil.

"I'm glad, Gerlach, that you don't consider I was wrong, after all. I might have put you on fatigues, to correct your thinking. You wouldn't like that, would you?"

"No, Sergeant."

Normal fatigues meant hard physical work, helping to extend the buildings in the camp, or break stones for the road to the railhead. Sergeant Steiger's fatigues were more refined: as his personal concession to Kommandant Axen's pride in a healthy camp, he picked three men each day and had them perform exercises for the improvement of fitness—press-ups, running on the spot and so on. They knew that once they stopped they'd be shot for disobeying orders, so most of them tried to survive, and finally fell exhausted with their lungs gasping and sweat running on them, and were shot for being unfit, and therefore diseased. "Sergeant Steiger's fatigues" had gone into the camp language, and it meant the same as "going on the list."

"You will know in future, then, Gerlach, that until otherwise ordered, you are on light duties." He folded his plump hands and gazed up at Franz with a glitter coming again to his eyes. "And by whose bounteous providence, would you imagine, is this privilege granted?"

Listen carefully. Think.

"My guardian angel's, Sergeant."

"Very good, Gerlach. I'm glad you agree. You are now dismissed."

Heels smartly together, the right arm shooting up. *"Dismissed, Sergeant! Heil Hitler!"* And about turn, with his heart still pounding, as if reminding him that thanks to a miracle he was still in the land of the living.

"One day," Kurt Wolff had told him, "I'll go on the list, like we all shall, and just before I report outside the Chamber I'll go along to the gatehouse and spit in the face of Sergeant Steiger, right here, see, right here between his fucking eyes."

They all said they'd do something like that, when their name went on to the list. But they didn't mean it. In the Chamber you'd die in a matter of ten minutes or so, quietly saying your prayers to the throbbing of the big engine that was feeding you the gas; but if you touched an SS man they'd make sure you took days over it, fingernail after fingernail, until the madness killed you. And they took great care that you knew what would happen; otherwise there was always the danger that a man with nothing to lose would take someone with him. It was all part of the functional efficiency of a model camp.

"You sound," Kurt Wolff told Franz as they worked at the letters of condolence, "as if you've got a cold." He turned his intense olive-brown eyes on his friend.

"Thanks," said Franz. It was a strange answer but Kurt understood that here at Debno it meant: *Thanks for reminding me. I don't want to die.*

Later, when they'd eaten their supper at the crowded canteen table, they sat on their bunks in B Block, as the sweet strains of the violin floated across the compound. They had eaten well, each of them taking a whole slice of stale bread and a small bowl of cooked beans, with scraps of meat in them; not many could eat like that, but Kurt was not only the block senior— he also enjoyed respect as a veteran, with a low Buchenwald number tattooed on his wrist. He'd already survived over two years' detention, and was experienced; within a month of his arrival at Debno he had taken over control of the crude but effective intelligence network that was a feature in every camp.

He had sought out Franz and Willi for his lieutenants after watching them for a time and finding out from the Orderly Room what it was that had brought them to Debno. Franz, despite his youth, had shown not only an iron sense of justice in what he'd done, but a lot of guts. Willi, the quiet ex-tennis champion, had been in love with a Jewess, and had killed the Gestapo man who'd found them together one night in Dresden, where her father had owned a small porcelain factory. He needed men like these.

"We might begin," he told them quietly, "by starting three fires, one here in our own block, one in the Orderly Room, and one in the Kommandant's quarters."

They listened intently, watching the shadows for movement; the SS guards were always on the prowl. At first they'd had no real faith in Kurt Wolff's plans, simply because they seemed impossible; but Kurt was a forty-year-old Rhinelander, a farmer, short, strong, built like a bull, with a brand of countryman's wisdom they responded to, in this place where insanity was the norm.

"Once the fire's going," his low voice came again, "we take advantage of the confusion and jump the guards, taking their guns. Each of us, you understand, going for one guard, and one gun."

They listened to every word, committing it to memory, as he'd told them they must. As he talked on in the shadowed hut, the notes of the violin outside died away, and the heavy metal door of the Chamber slammed shut. Then there came the strange sound, itself not unlike music, that they'd never got used to. It was a chorus, faint and discordant, like a huge kettle singing. After ten or fifteen minutes it faded away, and there was only the throbbing of the big engine, while here in the long open-ended building three or four Jews began chanting the Viddui.

Kurt stopped talking for a moment, sitting on the edge of the bunk with his blunt head lowered as he fretted with the calluses on his thick square hands. Willi, a lithe and quietly moving Berliner not much older than Franz, went to the doorway, not making a sound. He stood with his shaven head lifted, but his friends couldn't tell whether he was praying or just looking up at the stars; his head was outlined faintly in reddish gold as the fine hairs on his scalp caught the light from the distant arc lamps outside: he'd arrived here sporting a thick ginger mop, before the camp barbers got at him. (Kommandant Axen had stopped for a moment on his rounds of inspection to tell Willi that he'd watched him winning on the courts in the national amateur championships, and to congratulate him.) Willi differed from Kurt and Franz in that he now wore the green triangle of the *Befristete Vorbeugung-*

shäftlinge, as a prisoner in limited-term protective custody.

Franz sat listening with his friends to the familiar sounds of the night, waiting, as they were, for the business to be finished. After a while they heard the big iron door of the Chamber swinging open and slamming back against the wall with the clang of a gigantic bell; then immediately there came the tramping of feet as the nine dental surgeons left the building next door at a run, heading for the scene of their work.

Willi moved back from the doorway and crouched on the concrete floor, his body bouncing lightly to keep his thigh muscles exercised, a habit of his. As Kurt began talking again, adding to his plan the changes that had occurred to him during the day, the faint smell of exhaust gas came drifting across from the Chamber.

"The timing is very important, you understand. At three in the morning there would only be twelve guards at the night stations and two on patrol. We would wait for them to come around first, and then go for the others. We would take their uniforms and put them on, and slide their bodies under the latrine hut."

It was impossible for Franz not to feel excitement, even though he didn't expect to leave this place alive. But in listening to the confident tones of the farmer he also felt strengthened, remembering that in the history of the world nothing had proved stronger than men's dreams. At Buchenwald Franz had lost touch with reality for a time, drowning in the black despair of knowing what he had done to his family. They were never out of his thoughts. Through the days and the nights, while the guards shouted and the clubs lifted and fell, he had loved his family, longing for a letter from them, just one, in the hope that they might have by now forgiven him; and then, as the whips cracked and the train rumbled beneath his frozen limbs and the gates of Debno swung open for him, he had hated them, his family, for not writing to him, not even one letter, and for not forgiving him; then he'd realized how wrong that was, and that he could go on loving them, even if they'd stopped loving him. Here at Debno, where death was so close that every day he saw it come to the people around him, he'd finally arrived at a true perspective, in the way that people, dying, could accept truths they'd always been afraid to live with, because there was a future to get through. That made it easier for him, and he realized that in the hardest of schools he'd now reached maturity before his time, as if in compensation for the fact that whatever manhood he might have had was already on the block.

Yet, listening to the deep voice of his friend Kurt Wolff, it was impossible for him not to feel the excitement flickering through his body, because his body was still young in spite of his solemn philosophizing; and his spirit, still not bludgeoned to the point of apathy, was also listening.

"Wearing SS uniform," Kurt told them, his voice so low that it was no more than a resonance, "we would approach the watchtower on the left of the gate, and say we had a written message from Sergeant Steiger that must be read at once. If the guard decided not to break the rules and come down, that would be all right. One of us would go up to him, taking the message." He paused, and when he spoke again they both heard the rising energy in his voice, the force that was driving his thoughts day and night to the moment when his dream would break its chains and become a storm, a hurricane. "I would be the one," he said, "to go up to the tower. A minute later, we would have a machine gun in our possession. This, you understand, would be the end of the first phase of the action. And remember, we are not alone. In A Block, and C Block, the others will be working with us, just as I've instructed them."

As Franz and Willi listened to him they became aware of a faraway sound, among the hills beyond the camp, the heavy rolling of metal in the night. For a few minutes Kurt went on talking, then stopped to listen with them.

"They didn't tell us," Franz said.

The rumbling grew louder, slowing at last toward the railhead. There came the hissing of steam, then the piercing sound of brakes.

"It must be from Kozuchow," said Willi, his head turned to the doorway. "They're full up again, at Kozuchow."

They listened to the distant sounds, the banging of the cattle ramps as they were swung down from the trucks, and the barking of the guard dogs.

"We'll get no sleep," Kurt said, "tonight."

They went outside to look at the train, a distant frieze of light and dark along the skyline with the lamps of the SS guards swinging their beams across the crowded trucks. The voices of children could be heard, calling out in their bewilderment, and once again the Rhineland farmer had to force his strong body to stillness and silence, holding back the terrible urge to rush the watchtower there and then, and pump death out of that machine gun wherever he saw an SS uniform. But that would do no good: it would be an act of self-indulgence. The most difficult part of his master plan was not in the recruiting of fearless and resolute men, nor in designing its complex strategies, but in having to wait, while night after night the cries of the children kept him from sleep.

Franz took another card from the box.

"Name?"

"Jungerman."

"I want your full name."

"Hans Jungerman."

"Age?"

"Fifty-two."

Franz went on with his questions, his head hot and dizzy with the temperature he was running. The new arrivals had already been through the Gestapo office, but these details were for the Orderly Room files of the SS.

"Stand over there, please."

None of these people showed any bruises. Things were different here from the way most of the camps were run. *We have a job to do,* Kommandant Axen had told them, *and it must be carried out smoothly, quietly and efficiently. The new arrivals will proceed more willingly to the Chamber if they are not alarmed. You must use your intelligence. We have a heavy quota to deal with: seven hundred and fifty people must receive treatment every day, even more on the occasions when Kozuchow reaches temporary saturation point. I expect you, the members of the prisoner staff, to work with efficiency, cheerfulness and a good heart, and show the Reichsführer that in Debno Camp we have created a model of its kind.*

Franz took another card.

"Name?"

"Rosen."

"Other name?"

"Rita."

Franz felt the mucus blocking his nose again, and tilted back his head, closing his bloodshot eyes against the glare of the light bulb, snuffling hard.

"Have you a cold?" the woman asked him.

"No. Age?"

"Thirty-two."

A small boy was beside her, his hands on the edge of the desk, his large eyes watching Franz.

"Is this your son, Frau Rosen?"

"Yes."

Franz took another card.

It was four in the morning.

Just before half past five the last of them were coming through, among them a tall, graying man who held himself well considering he had spent six hours in a jammed cattle truck.

"Name?"

"Professor Ernst Kramer."

Franz wrote it down. The yellow card kept blurring as his eyes watered from fatigue and the throbbing of his sinuses.

"Age?"

"Forty-six."

"Occupation?"

"I am a physicist."

20

BERLIN, 12 MARCH 1940

While Professor Ernst Kramer was walking through the gates of Debno death camp, on the other side of the Polish border, a man rocked and moaned in a chair in a basement room of Gestapo Headquarters in Berlin. This was the second upright wooden chair they had given him, lashing him to it with one-inch straps; the first had broken, half an hour ago, the back legs buckling under the man's weight as the blow from the truncheon had sent him against the wall.

Soon after eleven o'clock, Superintendent Vogel came down to inquire as to progress. Stepping across the shining pool of blood on the floor, he stood in front of the prisoner and thumbed open his eyelids.

"Don't go too far," he ordered the two men. They had taken off their tunics, and their singlets were soaked with sweat. The man in charge of the detail was Sergeant Grossfeldt, a heavyweight boxer who had brought honors to his unit in the last three intercity tournaments.

"I think we're winning, Herr Superintendent. Just now, he spoke in English, or it sounded like that."

"In *English?*" Vogel looked again at the man in the chair. "How very interesting. What did he say?"

"It sounded like 'Go and get fucked,' if you'll excuse me, Herr Superintendent."

The other man gave a coarse laugh, but it died in his throat as he caught the Superintendent's glance.

"He spoke in *English,* you say . . ."

Vogel turned back to study the bruised and lacerated face of the man on the chair. It could only be that he had relapsed into his mother tongue as the pain had overwhelmed his control. From the reports, he'd been picked up this evening in the Tiergarten, after a routine check on his papers; the officer wasn't satisfied, and had booked him on suspicion. Within ten minutes of his arrival at Headquarters, the credentials analyst had declared his papers a forgery, and he was brought downstairs for interrogation in depth. It was one of those cases, Vogel thought, that began with a routine check and sometimes finished in the headlines.

"Be careful with him," he told Grossfeldt. "He sounds like an enemy alien, and could be important to us. I shall send a clerk down to take notes."

He went back upstairs, humming a tune.

In the main reception office, the six equally spaced electric light bulbs with their white china shades cast an acid brilliance on the desk, sparking a highlight from the officer's pen and casting deep shadow below his face.

The man in the overcoat stood before him, ashen with fear, his hands working ceaselessly at the brim of the hat he was holding, his eyes watching the movement of the officer's pen.

Beside him the girl stood silently, her face also white, the shadowed folds of her sweater deepening and straightening to the hurried rhythm of her breathing.

"Do you admit to listening to the foreign radio, Herr Mühler?"

The man hesitated. "No. I need my lawyer here."

The officer looked up at him expressionlessly. "This is not a case for a lawyer, Herr Mühler. There were two witnesses, the required number, and their status is un-

impeachable—one is the block warden." His eyes
strayed to the daughter, but his expression was un-
changed. "I am asking you if you admit to the charge,"
he said to the man.

Mühler hesitated again, his eyes frantic with indecision. In the silence, Superintendent Vogel spoke.

"Were you listening to the BBC news broadcasts,
Herr Mühler?" But as he put the question his dark eyes
were on the girl.

"No," Mühler said, and swallowed.

Superintendent Vogel was passing through, nothing
more. It was his habit, especially in the long winter
evenings when the main work of the day was over and
he felt the need for relaxation. In this room, every hour
of the day and night, the totally defenseless were
brought face to face with total power, and Karl Vogel
found the spectacle fascinating. One might almost say
that Fate itself was enthroned here, an invisible and
implacable presence under the bright and all-revealing
lights.

The girl had turned her head slightly, and was looking at Superintendent Vogel across the desk. The terror
in her eyes moved him strongly, seeming to burrow
deep into his body until the familiar tingling began in
his groin, the sensation that never grew to fever heat,
as he knew it did with other men, but gave him at
least a certain pleasure.

"What is your name, Fräulein?" he asked her softly.

"Magdelene." Her voice was hushed with fright.

"How old are you?"

"Nineteen."

He held her eyes until she looked away. "Continue,"
he told the lieutenant, and waited until the interrogation
was finished.

"Wait in the next room," the lieutenant told Mühler
and his daughter. When the door had closed, he looked
up at Vogel. "Your instructions, Herr Superintendent?"

"Send the man to Buchenwald, and put him in the

Besonder category. I want him treated leniently—for the time being. The girl can go home, but she must report here every week, without fail."

The lieutenant made a note on the report. "Very good, Herr Superintendent."

When Vogel went back to his office he found a visitor waiting for him—Deputy Commissioner Konrad Luftig of the Greater Berlin Police Department.

"We've been asked to assist the inquiries," he told Vogel when the courtesies had been exchanged. The two men were old acquaintances, and recognized the value of unofficial contact at frequent intervals; it could produce much faster results than official channels allowed.

"I'm not surprised," Vogel told him. "An SS general, after all . . ."

"I know you're interested in the other case yourself. The SS lieutenant found in the Volkspark Jungfernheide."

"Only because he was killed in the same way as my man in the Grünewald," Vogel said. "An unusual way." The report had mentioned "a single blow with superhuman force." "Have you made any progress at the Kabarett Harlekin?"

Luftig's hands, folded on his lap, opened and closed again. "All we've established is that the Lieutenant was at the nightclub on the evening of his death. He was seen in mufti by three other SS officers, but they can't identify the man he was with. He could have been a civilian, but from his general bearing they think he was an SS officer like themselves, in mufti. He is described as tall, and 'very Aryan.' " He said this with a slight tone of contempt; being himself on the short side, with brown eyes and hair, he resented the official description of the perfect German type as being taller than five feet ten inches, blond and blue-eyed. He thought his good friend Vogel didn't care much for it either. "From the man's bearing," he went on with less distaste, "the wit-

nesses think he could have been an SS-Sturmbannführer or higher."

"Possibly a Standartenführer?"

"Possibly."

They paused in their conversation as a scream
sounded, faintly at first, from the depths of the building. The Deputy Commissioner studied his hands while
Vogel picked up a telephone and pressed a button.
"Haven't you got a gramophone down there?" he demanded, his mouth tight.

"Yes, Herr Superin—"

"Then use it!" He slammed the receiver down, embarrassed. "How many times do I have to tell them we
get distinguished visitors here, such as yourself?"

"I always find the sounds of honest work," Luftig
told him graciously, "quite acceptable." Through the
parquet floor they could now hear the healthy rhythm
of a Tannhauser march.

"So there are certain links," Vogel said in a moment.
"Certain similarities."

"Or coincidences." Deputy Commissioner Luftig
hadn't reached his position by indulging in flights of
optimism. "We have a Gestapo man killed in the same
way as a junior SS officer, who was murdered in cold
blood. We have three senior SS officers also murdered in
cold blood, the very next day. I think we can leave out
the driver, as far as the motive's concerned." He opened
his hands again. "Links and similarities, yes. But tenuous. Tenuous."

"Plus the fact," said Superintendent Vogel reflectively, "that the lieutenant was last seen in the company of
a man who might have been an SS Colonel, which
compares with the reports from Zehdenick that an SS
Colonel—also of Aryan appearance—was seen in the
field where the general and his aides were killed."

Luftig considered this. "Tenuous," he said cautiously,
"because we're not at all sure the lieutenant's com-

panion at the nightclub *was* an SS colonel. But *less* tenuous, I fully agree. We should bear it in mind."

Half an hour later Superintendent Vogel was standing in the small basement room staring at Sergeant Grossfeldt with venomous eyes.

"You are a fool!"

"I'm sorry, Herr Superin—"

"I don't want to hear your apologies!"

The room smelled of sweat, blood and leather. The gramophone, an old black portable, stood on the table by the door, silent now. Grossfeldt and his assistant were at attention, both with sweat blotching their singlets. The doctor was still examining the man on the upright chair. The clerk was also at attention, gazing at the wall and thanking God he was not Sergeant Grossfeldt.

Vogel picked up the clerk's pad and studied the notes again. "These phrases you've underlined—are they English? Idiomatic English?"

"Yes, Herr Superintendent."

"You're fluent, I believe?"

"Yes, Herr—"

"You would say this man is English?"

"I would say his natural tongue is English, Herr Superintendent, but he might be American, Australian, Irish—I'm not familiar with the accents."

Vogel nodded and picked up the telephone, staring again at Grossfeldt as he waited. "I want a raid organized. Two vehicles and twenty men, at once. I shall take charge of it myself."

By the time he had given the instructions the doctor had straightened up from the man on the chair, and was putting away his stethoscope.

"Yes, he's certainly dead. From cardiac arrest, due to prolonged stress. I'll send you my report, Herr Superintendent."

"Thank you, Doctor Meyer." Vogel turned to the

Sergeant, his black eyes narrowing. "Sergeant Gross-feldt, it has not, clearly, occurred to you that a dead man can give no further information. We believe this man was an enemy alien, possibly an intelligence agent. Thanks to your flagrant show of incompetence we may have missed the most vital information. What have you to say?"

"Perhaps he had a weak heart, Herr——"

"You're seeking excuses!" Vogel cut in sharply. He took a step and faced the man, his eyes flickering with anger. "I'm not interested in excuses. You'll report to Personnel Administration on a charge of gross incompetence, do you hear me!"

He strode out of the room without a glance at the body on the chair. It hung against one leather strap, its head down and its tongue forever stilled.

At two minutes past ten the following morning a close-knit, tousle-haired civilian named Paul Gantz was sitting hunched over one of the round iron tables in a bar halfway along the east side of the Nordhausenplatz in the Plötzensee district. His stubbled face was gray and his eyes bloodshot from lack of sleep. He had looked at his watch three times in the last two minutes, his gaze returning always to the entrance door. A glass of schnapps was on the table—his third; the trembling of his hands, noticeable when he had arrived, had stopped.

At three minutes past ten a uniformed SS colonel entered from the street and looked around him. At the corner table the untidy-looking civilian lit a cigarette and immediately stubbed it out. The Colonel went up to the bar, ordered a schnapps, and took it across to the corner where Gantz was sitting. The voice of Marlene Dietrich was coming from the big horn of the gramophone behind the bar, and it was possible to speak quietly without being overheard.

"Colonel Brinkmann," the officer said.

"Paul Gantz."

Martin watched him, steeling himself. The message had said *very urgent*.

Gantz was hunched over the table again, raising his dull, bloodshot eyes to look into Martin's. "There was a Gestapo raid," he said, "last night. They were wiped out. Major Haslam, Sadler, Klinger, Veidt and the two signals crew." He watched the color draining from the face of the man in uniform. "Jock got away. We don't know, yet, about Otto Tempel. The Major used his capsule, so did Sadler and Klinger. The others were shot dead, trying to get clear. Steve Corbett wasn't there. We think they must have picked him up, sometime earlier, and put him under the screw." He looked down at the table. "We think he broke. Understandable. Always a risk of that." Raising his eyes again he said, "There's a chance we can get you to an escape line. One in a thousand, but a chance." He drained his glass. "We'll have to be quick."

21

BERLIN, 14 MARCH 1940

Hedda von Gerlach clung to the strap above her head as the S-bahn train jerked around a corner. She was half asleep, not having slept at all last night after her evening with Karl Vogel; and today there had been three emergency operations at the hospital. One of them—a street accident case with a ruptured spleen—had died after the first two hours in Postoperative, the reason being, according to a rumor Lottie had heard, that it had been discovered that the patient was a Jew, and couldn't expect to receive the same attention as an Aryan. Dear God, Hedda thought as she hung on to the strap, the world had finally gone mad. . . .

The train was packed, and people's faces were blue-lit and flickering under the blackout pilot lamps, like faces in a ghost train. Hedda let her eyes close as the numbness of fatigue crept from her body into her brain, where the evil presence of Vogel shadowed every thought. She was never free of him now; her knowledge of him had permeated her very soul, like a stain.

You may call me Karl, he had told her with Victorian formality over dinner at the Eden, *and I shall call you Hedda.* In the strangest way, this new familiarity seemed worse than anything he'd demanded of her, because it suggested they were now friends. . . .

The train swung into the long left curve after Belle-vue, and the standing passengers were sent lurching in the opposite direction, tightening their grip on the straps.

"Get off," a man's voice said softly, "at the Tier-garten, and go into the station café."

The voice had been close to her ear and she caught her breath, certain it was Martin; but when she struggled to look around she could only see the back of a man in uniform, as he made his way through the jam of people at the doors. She tried to keep the certainty in her mind, but her longing to see Martin again could be playing tricks on her, and deliberately she let the excitement die and the numbness creep back into her mind as the train rumbled on toward Tiergarten Bahn-hof.

At the station she went straight into the café, but took care not to look around for anyone; Vogel had his brutes watching the house where she lived, and she might even be under their eyes when she left the hospital. *I prefer you not to have any men friends, Fräulein . . .*

A tall SS officer was coming toward her, and the next moment she found herself slumped on one of the upright chairs with an arm supporting her and Martin's quiet voice telling her it was all right, everything was all right. It was just a dizzy spell, she knew, from lack of sleep, and from the shock of seeing him in SS uniform. Her head felt light and floating, with strange thoughts drifting through it . . . the world, yes, had finally gone mad, and they were letting Jews die in the hospitals, and Englishmen were joining the SS. . . .

When Martin thought it was safe to leave her, he went to fetch tea from the counter, receiving a salute from two SS subalterns. Every few moments he glanced toward the blackout screen in front of the big glass doors, and at the civilian who'd come in just after him and was now sitting at a corner table alone, reading a newspaper. At every hour, since Paul Gantz had told him what had happened, he had expected sudden arrest; and each time the telephone in his office had rung, or General Holst had sent for him to discuss a routine matter at the barracks, his fingers had closed over the capsule in his pocket. Damocles was wiped out, but there was still vital information in his head that he must die with if he had to.

Hedda was still pale when he went back to the table, her large eyes shadowed in the dim light. "It's really you?" she asked him.

"There's no time," he said, "to explain. You must be home soon."

"Yes." So he knew the Gestapo were watching the house in the Grünewald.

"Tell them, if they ask, that the first train was too crowded."

"All right." She was still trying to relate his face with the cap and its Death's Head insignia.

"We mustn't waste time," he said, glancing again at the screened doors. "Hedda, how well do you know Superintendent Vogel of Gestapo Headquarters?"

She thought she was going to faint. Her work at the hospital strained her nerves, day after day, and in the last few months there'd been so much on top of that— Martin suddenly here in Berlin as an enemy alien, his sister dead by suicide; Franz in torment, his face in those photographs almost unrecognizable; and Vogel, her living nightmare—and the one humiliating secret she must keep from Martin. *Or did he already know?*

Shakily she asked him, "Superintendent Vogel?" She needed time to think.

"Of the Gestapo." Watching her anguish, he sensed the truth. Waiting for her outside the hospital last night he'd seen the Gestapo staff car pick her up, the driver handing her in with ceremony. Later, at the Eden Bar, where he'd followed in a taxi, he had ordered the reservations clerk to show him the book. Yes, the clerk had told him, that is Superintendent Vogel sitting over there with the young lady.

Martin knew she was there on sufferance—the Gestapo could send her to a camp whenever they chose, on a charge of complicity in her brother's acts; meanwhile, she was something to play with. He felt the rage beginning in his head, the controlled fury that made an undertone to everything he experienced in the brave New Germany.

"Vogel is the man who questioned me," Hedda told him haltingly, "at Gestapo Headquarters, after Franz was arrested."

"And now you are in his hands?"

She flinched, and he put one hand over hers on the table, but she drew hers quickly away. "Don't touch me. I'm not—" But she couldn't finish. He must never know.

The rage hammered in him now, pulsing in his blood. He'd tried to talk to her last night when she left the hospital, to tell her he was going home to England, though he knew it was more likely he'd stay on German soil, a dead man with blue cyanosed skin, their jackboots kicking him in frustration. But first he must deal with Vogel.

"How did you know about him?" Hedda asked him in almost a whisper.

"In the SS, we have access to information." The image came to him, of Vogel forcing himself on her whenever he chose; and his rage reached the point where he longed to kill. "I'll see he doesn't trouble you anymore."

"How?" she asked quickly, frightened.

"All you need to know is that you won't be seeing him again."

"Martin, listen to me." She leaned over the table, her voice low and the words coming fast. "He's protecting Franz. That's why my brother's still alive, and that's why you mustn't do anything about Vogel, anything at all, even to see him or talk to him. I want you to promise me, Martin."

Franz, he thought, of course. It was the way they always worked, through fear.

"You can't ask me that much," he said thinly. "To stay away from Vogel." But as he said it he knew he was wrong.

"Yes," she said, "I can. I'm asking you to let my brother go on living."

Her hands were on the small stained table, knotted together with their knuckles white. He put his own over them, and this time wouldn't let her pull away. "Where is Franz now?" he asked her.

Her eyes were still on his. "I want you to promise, first."

"Not to see Vogel?"

"Yes."

He didn't believe he could do it. Killing Vogel was the only way he could keep his sanity. With the others it had been impersonal: the man in the alley, the three generals, Rudi Mahler. For the first time, with Vogel, it was personal, and very close to him. But there was Franz.

He tightened his hands on hers. "I promise," he said. "I have to."

He felt the tension go out of her hands. "Yes. You have to."

The blackout screen shook slightly as the door opened and two Gestapo men came in. His nerves quickened, as they had so many times since he'd left Paul Gantz sitting alone in the bar in the Nordhausen-platz yesterday. *I'm not going to the escape lines,* he'd told Gantz, *until I'm certain I've been exposed.* He watched the two Gestapo men, noting the look of recognition as they passed the man in the corner, the one with the newspaper.

"Where is Franz now," he asked Hedda. "Do you know?"

"No."

"Have you asked Vogel?" The Gestapo men were checking everyone in the café, but not asking to see their papers.

"He says he doesn't know where Franz is. He says he's in transit, and that he'll let me know when he can."

"Do you think that's true?"

"No." There was a tremor in her voice. "He just wants to keep me guessing."

"I'll find Franz." Before, he hadn't been able to change his schedules to make a thorough search. Now he would have to. Once Franz was freed, he could go for Vogel.

The two Gestapo men were close now, checking the civilians at the next table.

"Martin." Her fingers moved under his. "Don't think about me anymore. Think of me as I was."

He only just caught what she said, her voice was so small.

"You haven't changed." His hands tightened again. "I'll go on thinking of you just as you are now, courageous and beautiful and inviolate. I'll think of you, as I always have, in admiration and with love."

She shut her eyes quickly to stop the tears, and in a moment whispered something that Martin didn't catch. The two Gestapo men were looking down at him as they approached the table.

If Corbett had been broken, as Gantz believed, he must have died or got to his capsule before he could expose Martin; otherwise the Gestapo would have gone straight to the Führungshauptamt Department of the Totenkopfverbände, asking to see Standartenführer Martin Brinkmann. Jock and Tempel had got clear of the house in Charlottenburg, but could be caught at any time, with or without a chance to use their capsules, and again the Gestapo could be on their way to interview Standartenführer Brinkmann, or its street patrols could be looking for a tall, Aryan SS officer at large.

Martin waited, not looking up, his hands around Hedda's on the table.

"Heil Hitler, Herr Standartenführer!"

Martin glanced up now. "Heil Hitler!"

They exchanged the Deutschgruss salute.

When they had gone, Martin said, "You must be on the next train through. I'll make sure you're given a place."

A quarter of a minute after the SS Colonel and the young lady had gone through the blackout screen, the man in the corner folded his newspaper and followed them out to the westbound platform.

His name was Fraenkel, Detective Werner Fraenkel of Gestapo Headquarters. He had followed his subject, Fräulein von Gerlach, home from the hospital every day for three weeks now with nothing to report, but here at last was something of interest for Superintendent Vogel.

22

LONDON, 14 MARCH 1940

The two men walked along St. James's Street through the pouring rain, their black umbrellas bumping together as they dodged the puddles.

"Easier going," the stout and rather shabby man said, "when we used to have street lamps."

"Nothing, these days," the king's equerry said, "is easy going." It sounded, by his tone, more than a light remark, and his companion glanced at him, but could see nothing of his face in the near darkness.

They had met by appointment ten minutes ago, under Admiralty Arch, when the stout man had been looking forward to a spot of dinner at his club. His daughter Daphne was in town and he'd wanted to show her off on Ladies' Night, damned pretty girl.

"Let's park ourselves in this doorway," the equerry said, "till it lets up a bit. My feet are soaking—what about yours?"

They sloped their umbrellas, folded them, and shook them out. They were alone in the doorway of the tobacconist's, and could stop talking if anyone went by.

"Someone broke," the king's equerry said, "in Berlin. We've lost most of our people, including Haslam. Quite a massacre."

His companion stared at the rain slanting across the

hooded lights of a passing taxi, seeing nothing. In
hushed voice he said at last, "When?"

"We're not absolutely sure. The Hague found mo
of the lines jammed—everyone went straight to ground
But we think it was something like forty-eight hour
ago."

"Who was it who broke?"

"Does it matter?"

The stout man stared at the puddles. "No."

"Tempel got clear," the king's equerry said. "Th
Hague is in touch with him again."

"Tempel? Oh." It required courage to ask the next
question. Everything had been going splendidly up t
now. "What about the agent?"

"He's still operational. He wasn't at base, when
happened."

"Oh. So we've still got Tempel and the agent."

"Yes."

They watched a young man and a girl getting out o
a Bentley that had just pulled up across the road. The
ran hand-in-hand through the rain to a doorway farthe
along, the girl giving little screams as her party shoe
got soaked.

Stupid bitch, thought the king's equerry abstractedl
He was waiting for his companion to make his decisio
It wasn't going to be easy.

A door slammed in the distance, and the girl's squea
were cut off.

"Could Tempel still run the agent," the stout ma
asked, "if we told him to?"

"Yes."

A moment passed in silence, but for the great hissir
of the rain.

"For how long?"

"For as long as their luck would last."

"I want more than that," the stout man said wit
a sudden show of anger. It was because he was afrai
as many of them were afraid these days, in the Cabine

in the House, at the Palace, afraid that England was going to miss the boat again, with these bloody appeasers playing into Hitler's hands. There was talk of kicking Chamberlain out and getting someone else, perhaps Churchill, though he was already an old man. "I want something more specific," he told the king's equerry.

"I can't give it to you. Tempel can run his agent for just as long as they can get away with it out there, with almost no support. As I say, it's simply a question of luck. The agent is going to expose himself more and more, as a result of his own hostile acts, until finally—" He shrugged, and shifted, the water squelching in his polished shoes. "It's a question of time."

"How much damage," asked the stout man, "can he still do?"

The equerry considered. "Judging from his record, I'd say quite a bit. Quite a bit."

"It might be worth, you mean, keeping him running." His voice didn't lift at the end, but it was a question, and the equerry knew it, and wasn't going to answer it.

"This is your show. And your decision."

The stout man was silent for a while, then stepped out of the doorway and put up his umbrella, and they set off again through the downpour. In ten minutes they found themselves in Piccadilly Circus; it was almost deserted, because of the rain and the blackout, with all the advertisements dark and the figure of Eros buried under sandbags.

"He has the option," the king's equerry said at last, "of getting out of Germany—if he can—or staying there. Judging from his record, he'd probably choose to stay." He was trying to make it easier for his companion.

"No doubt." The rain was drumming on their umbrellas, and he had to raise his voice. "All things considered, I'm going to ask him to continue his operations, for as long as Tempel can keep him going."

The equerry drew a slow breath. "Very well." It was for him to tell the Canadian, and indirectly the party in Washington, what had happened to Damocles, and what had been decided for the future.

"You know Sir Thomas Benedict, I believe, rather well."

"Yes," the equerry said.

"I wonder if it might not be a kindness, you know, for someone to—to have a word with him. I mean, to give him fair warning that although the agent is at present in no immediate danger, we can't really—" He was hesitating badly now—"I mean we can't offer much hope that—"

"I'll talk to Sir Thomas," the equerry said in a dull voice. "I'll make a point of it. And I'll see the Canadian."

23

BAVARIA, 15 MARCH 1940

The spring showers that had inundated the streets of
London were widespread across Northern Europe, and
in the Bohemian Forest, not far from the Czechoslovakian frontier, it had been raining throughout the
night. The forecast for the Regensburg area suggested
"clearing slowly, with sunny intervals," but from the
windows of the hunting lodge at the edge of the forest
nothing could be seen but the rain haze across the
dripping pines.

"I would, if necessary, kill myself," said Gisela von
Gerlach quietly, and the General's hand reached out for
hers, as he closed his eyes.

"We're not committed yet," he told his wife.

"I know." She watched him with her calm eyes, her
hand still in his and aware of its strength, without
which she would be lost in this new and terrifying Germany. "But you've got to be committed, both of you.
This thing has got to be done."

A distant sound came, perhaps one of the doors
closing in the main hall; but neither the General nor
his beautiful wife took any notice. The three servants
here were utterly loyal, and utterly opposed to the Nazi
rule.

"We've got Hedda to think of, too," the General said. "And Franz, unless . . ."

"Franz is still alive, Constantin. I know it. I keep telling you." She spoke with quiet conviction.

"Yes," he said patiently, but he still had his private doubts. Gisela was extraordinarily intuitive; on the very night when Franz had been arrested she complained of deep depression, saying she knew that "something horrible" had happened; and that was almost twenty-four hours before they got the news. But there was no certainty that he was still alive.

Watching her husband as they sat together on the settle seat beside the hearth, Gisela grieved for him. Constantin was one of the younger group of the Wehrmacht, promoted to the rank of full general at the age of forty-three; his brilliant theories on strategy, together with his magnificent record as a subaltern in the war, had caught Hitler's attention, and for a while Constantin had enjoyed the Führer's highest approval—until his frankness during discussions on military planning, and finally his open criticism of Hitler's own policies, precipitated his fall from grace, to the point where he was at present suspended from active duty. Like a caged lion, he spent his time here at the lodge, keeping in touch with events through his loyal friends but powerless to take any part in them.

It was this bitter resentment, week after week, that had brought forth his plan to save Germany, if it wasn't already too late, by cutting down the dangerous megalomaniac at its head and seeking an honorable peace with the Allies.

With him in the plot was Major General Gunther von Reitlinger, a cool, dedicated technician in the 4th Tactical Field Weaponry, who had privately declared that "he was damned if he was going to see this country brought to its knees by a short-arsed Austrian baboon."

Constantin and Gunther were not alone in their opposition to the Reichschancellor. Hitler had antagonized the High Command since the conference he had held immediately prior to the invasion of Poland. "Things will occur," he had told them, "that will not be to the taste of German generals. But you must not interfere with such matters. You will simply restrict yourselves to your military duties." He was speaking, as they discovered soon afterward, of the wholesale slaughter of Polish Jews, intelligentsia, clergymen and nobility in the wake of the Army's advance. Shock and disgust had become widespread among its ranks from that day onward.

"I'd like to wait," Constantin said now, "until we can be absolutely certain of bringing it off."

"But you're certain now, my darling. And you can't wait any longer. You know that." He feared for his family, that was all, if anything went wrong.

He went to stand by the windows, brooding, his feet apart and hands on hips, a man of action consigned to the boredom of enforced retirement until the Führer chose to release him. He knew that Hitler planned to push his armies into Denmark, Norway and the Low Countries within a month, and that he stood a good chance of success. From there, the war would spread throughout Europe, with England—undermanned and underequipped and with Chamberlain's crowd of pacifists in command—unable and unwilling to save her neighbors from destruction. If Hitler were to be stopped, he must be stopped soon, within a week, two weeks at the most, before he could unleash the carnage.

"If I could get you and Hedda to Switzerland," he said, "or Spain, I wouldn't hesitate any longer."

"You're thinking of failure, Constantin. Only if you fail shall we all be in trouble. If you succeed, as I'm sure you will, nothing will happen to us, and Franz will be freed as soon as the new government takes over."

"If we succeed . . ." he said, staring out at the rain. He'd never had doubts about success, until recently. He would have thought it impossible for the son of a

Wehrmacht general to be thrown into a prison camp without trial and left there, cut off from his family and all who loved him. But it had happened, and the blackest doubts had begun to undermine his faith in himself and in Germany. Gisela wrote to Franz every day, every single day, and there was no reply. He himself had flown to Berlin week after week, storming into Gestapo Headquarters and demanding to know his son's whereabouts. But it was widely known that he was out of favor with the Führer and suspended from active duty, and his protests were brushed aside. It was no longer possible to rely on any kind of justice in the land, and he and Gunther had·decided there was only one thing to do. The attempt on Hitler's life at the Burgerbrau Keller last November had been bungled, and there had been merciless reprisals taken against the Jews. If he and Gunther also bungled it, they would both die—as they were perfectly ready to do; but Gisela would also die, and Hedda, and Franz. . . . "If we succeed," he told his wife, "yes, everything will be all right. If we succeed . . ."

"You've always succeeded, Constantin, in everything you've set out to do. This won't be any exception." She heard the confidence in her voice, and marveled at it. He was her confidence, and her strength, and it seemed that in giving it to her he'd lost it for himself. She must somehow give it back. "You've always taken risks, my darling, and always come through. Now you must take another, and it will be the same. You'll come through. We all will." Did he know why she was risking all their lives, by urging him to act? It wasn't for Germany. If he could save Germany it would be a fine thing, but if, in saving Germany, he could save her son . . .

"If I could get you and Hedda to Switzerland," he said, "I'd go straight at it."

It was one of his characteristic phrases: as a former cavalryman he often said the only way to take a horse over a jump was to "go straight at it." She left the fireside and stood with him at the window, and in a moment his strong hand closed over hers, as she knew it would. "I don't want to go to Switzerland," she said, "and neither would Hedda, if she knew. The moment you tell me you're ready, you and Gunther, I'll send for her, so that we'll all be together."

"You've asked her to join us here before, but she says she can't leave Berlin."

"Her work's important, that's all. She's dedicated. But I can persuade her."

He was tempted. The thought of success was heady: he and Gunther planned to smuggle the bomb into the Chancellory itself, when Hitler and his chief henchmen were together at the meeting in three weeks' time, before the invasion of the west was launched. One gigantic explosion . . . and Hitler, Göring, Himmler, Goebbels, Heydrich and the rest obliterated, gone from the face of the earth. . . . Yes, he was very tempted. But in the small hours of each night he lost courage, and could see only the Gestapo staff car on its way here through the trees, with Gisela and Hedda waiting for it, helpless to save themselves. . . .

He had never before known indecision, or known that it could tear a man apart.

BERLIN, 15 MARCH 1940

Superintendent Vogel picked up the telephone at Gestapo Headquarters and asked for the connection. It was not yet eight o'clock in the morning, but as usual he was already at his desk.

"Deputy Commisioner Luftig," came the voice on the line.

"Good morning—Karl Vogel here." The courtesies were exchanged. "This man who was killed last night at the Tiergarten Bahnhof, Detective Werner Fraenkel—you've had reports about him?"

He waited impatiently. *That deceitful bitch,* he thought. *I'll have her sent to Ravensbruck. And I'll have her brother shot.*

"Refresh my memory," Luftig asked him ponderously. Vogel could hear the clink of a coffee cup in the background.

"Fraenkel—one of my men—fell in front of a train at the Tiergarten Bahnhof at 6:43 last night. The platform was crowded, and in the blackout no one saw how it happened. The point is this, Konrad. This is the *second* man to have been killed while keeping surveillance on that woman Hedda von Gerlach."

"You're not suggesting she did it?"

"Of course not. But it could be someone she's meeting."

He had to wait again. Luftig was so damnably *slow* in the morning.

"Someone who wants to keep his identity secret."

"Exactly. The same man, possibly, who also killed SS-Lieutenant Mahler at the nightclub, and General von Fleig and his aides out at Zehdenick."

He thought of the "tall, very Aryan" civilian who was seen in Mahler's company, "possibly an SS major or colonel in mufti." Had that been the description in Detective Fraenkel's head when he was pushed under the train?

"So you're going to put the thumbscrews on this Hedda von Gerlach," rumbled the voice of Luftig on the line.

"Immediately." He would supervise the interrogation personally. She would be shown what happened to people who deceived him.

"That's typical of you." There came the clink of a teaspoon. "But slow down a bit. She might not even know this man. Or, if she knows him—which I agree seems more likely—she might not know that he's killing off your surveillance men, either to protect her or himself, or both. He wouldn't do it in front of her. He'd do it soon after leaving her. So you can turn your thumb-screws until she goes insane, and still end up none the wiser."

Impatiently Vogel said, "We shall simply ask her to name this man she's been meeting. She must have been there at the Tiergarten Bahnhof, or Detective Fraenkel wouldn't have been there. And she had no legitimate reason for being there. She doesn't normally break her journey home on the S-bahn. It was a secret rendez-vous." The words stuck in his throat. *A secret rendez-vous with another man.* Who was he? And what did they do, perhaps somewhere at the hospital behind the locked door of an unused room, or even in her flat in Grünewald, where the surveillance men couldn't see them? *Did they laugh about him? Did she tell him she knew a high official in the Gestapo who wasn't . . . who couldn't . . .* His whole body was growing hot at the thought, *his cursed, useless child's body that sent them all into fits of silent laughter when he tried to play with them . . . By God in Heaven, when she was brought to the interrogation room in the basement here for him to play with, she wouldn't laugh then . . . she wouldn't laugh then . . .*

He could hear someone's voice, a long way off, and became aware of the receiver gripped in his hand, slippery with sweat. Luftig's voice, yes of course.

"What did you say?" he asked him, releasing his breath.

"Is there something wrong?"

"No. No. I was thinking. I missed what you said."

"I was saying," Luftig told him in a tone of measured rebuke, "that you can offer this young woman extreme duress at Gestapo Headquarters, but still risk losing your objective—indeed, *our* objective, since I'm offi-cially involved." There was a friendly warning here, which Vogel didn't miss. "Some women are extra-ordinarily loyal, you know, and this one might hold out to the death. It's happened before, if memory serves, and not only with women."

Vogel knew he was referring to the Englishman, and that idiot Sergeant Grossfeldt. If Deputy Commissioner Konrad Luftig had been officially involved in the case of the Englishman, he would have come down on Vogel like a ton of bricks for letting him die.

"But if we don't put Hedda von Gerlach under interrogation?" Vogel asked cautiously.

"You can do better than merely ask who the man is. Even if she told you, we might never find him. You'll do best to trap him. Double the number of your surveillance men. Treble it. He can't kill them all. Then you'll have him, in the flesh."

"But that could take time," Vogel protested. "It's been ten days since Detective Hoffmann was murdered in the Grünewald district." He wanted to see Hedda von Gerlach in that room downstairs. He wanted to hear her screaming, instead of laughing. But then, he could do that any time. He could do what he wanted.

"Be patient," Luftig told him easily. "Give him another ten days. This is an important criminal we're after. He's wiped out seven men, five of them in the elite and sacrosanct SS, including a general, and two of them in the Gestapo. To knock off a couple of men who are bothering his girlfriend is one thing, but why should he take pains to ambush and slaughter an SS general and his aides? Why General von Fleig, specifically? The Homicide Department has no answer to that. Will our man select another general, specifically, and leave him with his head blown off? We have to stop him."

Vogel was wiping the receiver with his handkerchief. Under his uniform his skin was beginning to prickle with sweat. "I'll do as you say, Konrad. Your point's well taken."

The Deputy Commissioner could now afford to take the heat off. "Simply a suggestion, my dear fellow. When we put our heads together we usually come up with the answer. It won't be long now. Use your best men. Deploy them with discretion. Have them stand well off, and issue fieldglasses. Then the next time this man makes contact with Hedda von Gerlach, he's yours."

NEAR SCHONEBECK, 15 MARCH 1940

Twelve hours later, and a hundred and thirty kilometers southwest of Berlin, a black Mercedes staff car swung the beams of its hooded headlights across the moonlit waters of the Elbe and turned southwest, in the direction of the bridge. The small Opel cabriolet was already there, parked in the shadows below the trees.

Martin got out and walked over to it.

"What held you up?" Tempel asked him.

"Troops on the move north."

"I've been here an hour."

Martin couldn't see Tempel's face clearly, but he heard the bared nerves in his voice. "Where were you," he asked him, "when it happened?"

"Not far away."

So he'd seen it all, or most of it.

"What happened to Jock?"

"We don't know. He remains a potential danger. Please bear that in mind."

"Noted." If they'd managed to subdue the man before he could reach for his capsule, they'd work on him for days, weeks, and even Jock wouldn't be able to do anything.

"You have never," Tempel said thinly, "been very secure. You must now take every conceivable precaution. At the same time"—something like disbelief came into his voice—"you must proceed with your operation. Those are the instructions from The Hague."

They listened to the distant rushing of the river,

where a bough had drifted against one of the pylons of the bridge and got caught.

"Will you be running me now?" Martin asked.

"Yes."

"Who with?"

Again he heard a kind of disbelief in Tempel's voice. "They will send us a contact."

One director, Martin thought, one agent and a contact. The network must be under a great deal of pressure. He'd been held up by the massive troop movements that had been going on for days now, and there were rumors of the Netherlands and Denmark going next. That would knock out The Hague.

"When I'm finally caught," he said to Tempel, "will you still have someone to take over?" They'd been training Corbett, but he'd gone now. And there was no point in pretending he could finish Damocles alone, with so little support and no base.

"When you are finally caught," Tempel told him, "we shall bring our operation to a stop." His voice was toneless now, as if he were reading from notes. "We successfully infiltrated you into the SS, and it's as a spurious SS officer that you'll be caught. That is inevitable. If you're to go on at all, it must be in your present role. But we can't do it twice, obviously. The others we were training were to go in clandestinely, Corbett leading them in a last-ditch operation. Perhaps The Hague will try to do that, with a new cell; but it won't involve the SS, nor will it involve us. When you are finished, Damocles will be finished."

Standing close to him in the shadows, Martin could feel Tempel's tension, as if the air itself was vibrating with it. Even so, he was unprepared.

"I warned them about Corbett! I warned them!" It was no longer Tempel's voice, but a soft screech in the night. *"He was too confident! Too heroic! I told them!"* Then he was suddenly bending over with his hands clasping his stomach and his breath coming in spasms,

his rimless spectacles catching the reflection of the moonlit river as he crouched motionless, struggling for breath. After a while he began talking again, but very quietly now, with a soft rush of words that he seemed to want to get out before anything could stop him. "I told them we didn't want any heroes. I said heroes were dangerous. All Corbett could think about was you being caught, or killed, or both, and getting his orders to go in. I told Haslam, but it was no good. It was no good."

He tried to stand straight, but the pain wouldn't let him.

"What did Corbett do?" Martin asked him. He was beginning to understand this man's fury.

"He tried to steal some files from a Gestapo office."

Martin drew a quick breath. "On his own?"

"On his own. *Without instructions.*" He was slowly straightening up, but still holding his stomach. "Without instructions. He wanted to be a hero, you see. A hero." He was silent for a long time, recovering his breath, and when he spoke again his voice was quite normal. "So here are the remains of Damocles. Two men standing under a tree, one of them crippled with stomach pains. Before I brief you, I should tell you that The Hague is perfectly ready to receive you through the escape lines and get you to England, if you feel you've done enough."

"I don't."

"Or you would have let Gantz try to take you out." The glasses flashed again to the river's reflection as he turned his head to look directly at Martin. "The implications of Damocles are too far-reaching to allow personal considerations the slightest importance. But we are alone, and there will come a time, as we both realize, when we shall no longer be able to make contact. So I would like you to know, Colonel Brinkmann, that I am grateful for what you have done so far, on behalf of my brother."

Hans Gerhart Tempel, Martin remembered, who had died in the camps. But it meant nothing to him.

"What I've done so far, I've done for myself. And what I'm going to do, I'm going to do for myself. I want their blood."

24

FURSTENWALDE, 17 MARCH 1940

General Egon von Kassel was dining late. It was almost eleven o'clock. But this didn't trouble him in the slightest. The others—Heidel and Maihof—had wanted to hold the meeting over dinner, but he had dissuaded them. He was a man of some sensitivity—many called him capricious, and he graciously conceded that they might be right; indeed he was pleased with the word, for only those with power and authority could afford caprice and expect other mortals to tolerate it.

He preferred, for instance, to eat alone—or more precisely, to *dine* alone. Luncheon was a necessity, a means of replacing energy and meeting with his fellow officers in the course of duty; but to dine was to celebrate, and to celebrate so many things: the ending of the day, the simple fact that he was here to enjoy it—unlike poor von Fleig, for example—and of course the excellence of the pheasant and the nobility of the Côtes de Beaune '35 and the artistry of the heavy silver and the cut glass that reflected the glitter of the chandelier above the table. It would be correct to say that when SS-General Egon von Kassel dined, he made a meal of it; and he preferred to do it alone, without the social demands of distracting conversation.

Tonight's meeting had gone well. They had all of

them been concerned over the appalling murder of Artur von Fleig only eight days ago; you could call it an assassination, considering the importance of the man. And not only that. The documents had been seized. (There was no file on those ultrasecret papers. They did not even come under the classification of *Geheime Reichssache*—Secret Business of the Reich—since any business of the Reich had to have the tacit approval of the Führer himself, through official channels and proper delegation. If the Führer were to see the documents before the time was ripe, Generals von Kassel, Heidel and Maihof could well find themselves thrown out of their commands, or worse. The means of global domination, the so-called atomic bomb, must be presented to the Führer as a practical, feasible proposition, supported by the physicists—Ayran and non-Aryan—whose work could produce the miracle.)

The seizing of the documents had concerned them as much as the shocking death of their comrade. But after due discussion it was felt that there was no risk of those vital papers being brought to Hitler's personal attention. On the contrary. It was more likely that some other faction was out to beat them to the goal of presenting the Führer with the means of world mastery. The ranks of the SS, unfortunately, were plagued with intrigue, power-seeking and betrayal, and this shocking tragedy could well be an example.

It had been decided at the meeting tonight that (1) they should bide their time and eschew panic, (2) they should wait a while before handing a copy of the documents to Heydrich, who was to have received the originals from the hand of von Fleig on that fatal night, and (3) they should go into intense action as soon as the coast seemed clear again, and present the atomic feasibility study to the Führer as soon as possible, before another attempt was made to stop them.

The dream, thought Egon von Kassel, was still intact. A dream as dazzling as theirs would not be realized

without travail, and they must be prepared for a few
setbacks, however temporary. As to the matter of finding out who had killed von Fleig—which they would
dearly like to know—they need do absolutely nothing.
Investigation was still in progress, and on a massive
scale, involving Schellenberg's Security Service of the
SS, the Greater Berlin Police Department and the Gestapo. It wouldn't be long before they found the culprit.

Egon von Kassel was thus able to enjoy his dinner as
usual. The Rhine salmon had been poached—in the
culinary sense—to perfection; the venison from the
Black Forest was proving both succulent and rich in
flavor; and his young manservant Alexis had roguishly
hinted at the possibility of crêpes suzette to grace the
conclusion of the festivities. There was but one flaw to
spoil the mood, and that was easily attended to.

"Alexis."

"Herr General?"

The boy left his post beside the door to the kitchen,
behind the General's chair. This arrangement was precise; to dine alone was to dine alone, and he preferred
not to be watched by his servant.

"The music is a little too loud," he told Alexis. He
watched the boy, slim-hipped in his short white jacket,
cross to the radiogram and turn down the volume little
by little, watching his master.

"Just there," the General nodded.

Alexis went back to his post without a word and
without a further glance; he knew his master's wish for
privacy at the table. The General listened to the brooding intonations of Bax's Fifth Symphony, savoring its
dark intensity and allowing his mind to luxuriate in the
rich succession of its cadences; in its theme, he fancied,
he could detect the power and the purpose of the
Führer's own magnificent struggle to take his country
and his countrymen out of the shadows of past humiliation and into the golden light of their true and glorious
destiny.

And he would be there, in the forefront of affairs and by his Führer's side. To the men who had offered him the keys to world conquest, their leader could grant no less than everlasting honor and acclaim.

The venison finished, hs knife and fork were at rest on the gold-rimmed Dresden plate no more than fifteen seconds before Alexis, soft-footed and attentive, came to remove them and to change the wine and napkin.

"My compliments, if you will, Alexis, on the venison."

"I'll tell François at once, Herr General."

Herr General . . . Herr General . . . The boy was punctilious in the extreme, all the time he was on duty. But later, in the privacy of the black silk sheets, he would call him Egon, of course.

There followed the prescribed interval of ten minutes or so, before the presentation of the dessert. There must be time to allow the palate to rest and prepare for change, for the monocle to be polished and reset against the clear blue eye, and for the somber moods of Arnold Bax to beguile the spirit and bear it onward to the day of triumph awaiting the New Germany and the New German World. . . .

Tonight the interval before the dessert was rather longer than usual, but the General charitably decided he would make no comment when Alexis returned. Crêpes suzette, too, had its caprices, and should not be hurried.

He was not to know that the boy was already dead, or that the figure approaching him from behind his chair was not that of Alexis. He may have caught the sound of an indrawn breath, or felt the soft rushing of the air on his right side; but there was no time to turn. The force of the blow sent him sprawling across the table with one of the chair legs buckling and the tall-stemmed glass of Moselle spinning against the crystal fruit bowl before it shattered, its fragments scintillating in the light of the chandelier as General von Kassel's monocle flew from its cord and the bright blue eye began clouding. . . .

BERLIN, 18 MARCH 1940

SS-General Bruno Heidel, commanding officer of the Third Training Division, Prison Administration, had been called by his batman at six o'clock and was now shaving in his bathroom. His suite of three rooms—sleeping quarters, office and reception room—were on the fourth floor of the Staff Residential Building. The barracks were in darkness at this hour, save for the sparsely deployed pilot lamps permitted by the blackout regulations for military and paramilitary establishments.

General Heidel had already cut his face twice with the razor, the result of his thoughts being elsewhere. With part of his mind he was rehearsing certain changes in the credo he had composed six months ago for general distribution to all SS training camps. Since that time, war had been declared, and a patriotic note was called for in certain passages, to remind the trainees of their increased responsibilities. Also, the Jewish question was now being handled along much firmer lines, and he could dispense with a few of the euphemisms.

You will bear it in mind, at all times, that a concentration camp is not a correction facility for those who have misbehaved themselves. It is a prison for those who have dared to challenge the sacred authority of our Führer and the supreme authority, under him, of the Third Reich. By their political, subversive and rebellious acts they have shown—

He cut himself again, and cursed under his breath. This was to be a big day, because of the breathtaking decision he had made in the hour of sleeplessness that usually came to him between three and four in the morning. Using the shaving brush, he got on with the business more slowly, relathering under his chin and watching with slight distaste the pinkish coloration of the foam as the new cut bled freely.

The war, yes. *In time of peace, their defiance would be intolerable. In time of war, in which we now find ourselves, they have lost the right to be treated as Germans, and you must treat them with the same hatred and the same ruthlessness you would show a foreign enemy in our midst.*

He picked up the razor again and began drawing swathes through the foam. The Jews, yes. *As for the Jews, you will remember that they have now been officially declared to be subhuman. Their very existence in our complex of clean, orderly and well-run camps is an insult to our endeavors. You will not treat them as dogs. True Germans are always kind to dogs. You will treat them as vermin. You will—*

That was going a bit far, perhaps. The business of the Totenkopfverbände was one of discretion, and if a printed version of the credo was picked up by the general public it might arouse comment. On the other hand, Reichsführer Himmler himself had referred to the Jewish race as a "virulent disease," and in a public broadcast. And what about that loudmouth Julius Streicher and his Jew-baiting rag *Der Stürmer?* He was being too soft, dammit!

You will treat them as a virulent disease, that must be contained, controlled and finally stamped out.

But part of his mind was occupied with quite another matter. At the meeting last night at that precious von Kassel's villa—he ought to keep that bloody houseboy out of sight when visitors were there, for God's sake!—they'd all agreed on what to do next, following von Fleig's murder. Nothing. At least for a time. Nothing. But during the night he'd changed his mind. They ought to keep going, and with renewed vigor. If some rival faction was trying to beat them to it, they ought to go faster, not slower. But one thing was certain: he'd

never convince von Kassel of that, nor Maihof. Von
Kassel had that startling intuition of his, almost an
ability to see into Hitler's mind, and of course he'd
started the whole plan in the first place. But he was
too "sensitive." Too "subtle." And he wore too much
bloody eau de cologne! And if that sounded irrelevant,
one must remember that the Führer was thoroughly
masculine in his tastes, and almost a monk in his way
of life—hardly ever a drop of alcohol, simple food, not
a womanizer like Heydrich (now *that* man ought to
take his daily bath in kitchen disinfectant!) and certainly not a man to wear eau de cologne. It might sound
ridiculous, but their whole plan for world dominion
could easily founder, simply because that poof von Kassel stood a bit too close to the Führer while they were
trying to put it across.

He went cold just thinking about it. And Maihof. A
good man, clever, persuasive—and Hitler would want
persuading, above all—but distinctly lacking in guts.
He'd opted for stopping the whole plan dead in its
tracks, the moment he'd got the news about von Fleig's
assassination. And it was going to take guts to go to
the Führer and tell him face to face that they'd worked
out a feasibility study on a project he'd already abandoned.

So he would go to see Hitler alone.

The blade slipped again on the thought of it, and he
rinsed off the reddening lather and got the antiseptic
stick from the cabinet. Go it alone, yes. Cut out von
Kassel—Hitler was dead against homosexuals—and cut
out that gutless Maihof. And when the day came when
Hitler stood before the world and gave it his ultimatum,
he—Bruno Heidel—would be there, ready for the
honors. What reward would be considered too lavish for
the one man who had offered his Führer the world?
None. He'd remain by Hitler's side, the second most
important man in the entire New German World!

Grandiose? Yes. Possible? Certainly. He'd spent

hours talking to that Jew Lenneberg at the physics laboratory where they'd now got him under close guard. He had a little girl, Hildi, nine years old, now being cared for by his sister, his wife having been run over in the blackout. Did he want to see little Hildi again? Then he knew what he'd got to do. Give them the facts, the figures, the equations, the physical requirements, the estimated cost, and put it in the kind of language the Führer and his advisers could understand. The man was working well, practically around the clock, and it was already clear that his word alone might be enough to convince Hitler that the super-weapon could be his for the asking. Professor Joseph Lenneberg had been nominated for the Nobel Prize before the Nazis had come into power.

The General splashed hot water onto his razor and shook it dry, using the antiseptic stick again as the blood still oozed from two of the cuts. A sign of his nerves, of his excitement this morning; a sign, if you like, of eventual success, even glory, if he took the bull by the horns and let nothing stop him.

Today he would request a formal but private interview with the Führer. Subject: the national interest and the future of Germany.

Someone was knocking on the door. It could only be one of his batmen, probably Ulich.

"What do you want?" he called loudly. They had orders never to disturb him at his ablutions. A General couldn't look the part with shaving soap all over his face.

Ulich called something about an urgent message, so Heidel bellowed for him to come in. If the message didn't sound urgent enough, he'd scalp him.

"A message by bearer," the batman told him, and handed him a card, keeping his distance and a correct stance.

An SS-Standartenführer, according to the card. And much decorated. "Tell him I'll see him in half an hour."

But Ulich was back in two minutes.

"What the hell is it now?" shouted General Heidel.

The message was urgent in the extreme, his batman told him. It concerned the death of General von Kassel.

"The what?"

Ulich repeated the message, and stood watching the color leaving the General's face and the three blood clots darken in contrast.

He looked at the card again, and in a moment, much more quietly, said, "I'll see him now." He went thoughtfully through his sleeping quarters into the slightly smaller reception room, with its dark furniture and the framed photograph of the Führer.

The visitor came in quickly and offered a smart salute, his briefcase tucked firmly under his left arm.

"Heil Hitler, Herr Obergruppenführer!"

"Heil Hitler. Now what the devil's this about General von Kassel? And who are you?"

The SS Colonel stood at ease, pulling at the zip of his briefcase and producing an envelope. As Heidel watched him, his mind was buzzing with questions and worries. First von Fleig and now von Kassel . . . dead within nine days of each other. Not just dead. Murdered. If it were true, about von Kassel.

"Am I to understand General von Kassel is *dead?*"

"Regrettably, Herr Obergruppenführer."

There was something else nagging for attention in the General's mind as he looked at the tall blond Colonel. Hadn't there been something about an SS Colonel's having been seen in the Zehdenick area at the time of von Fleig's assassination?

"This letter, Herr Obergruppenführer, will explain everything." The visitor took another step toward him, holding out the envelope. As the General closed his fingers on it his eyes were still on the other man's, and in that instant he knew without any doubt that he was looking into the face of death.

Bruno Heidel was a big man, and strong. He had

received, in a flash of intuition, a warning of what was to come, and was thus prepared for it, and prepared to fight to the death. But he lacked one element. Rage.

Rage, and the authority of relentless training.

Half-fist to the throat. To kill.

Heidel reeled and his arm came up to block the strike as the envelope fluttered to the maroon Bavarian carpet beneath his feet and for an instant the face of the other man was close to his, staring, unfamiliar and inhuman and almost unconcerned as the second blow came to spin his wide-shouldered, heavy body the other way, one boot catching against the end of the sofa and sending him off balance, his hands flung out to save himself, because his animal instinct told him that once he was down he was finished. The dark brocade of the fabric swirled across the field of his vision and then he steadied, the sofa supporting him so that he could halt the momentum the blow had set up in his frame and react to it, kicking forward and going for the groin, his right boot lifting and altering his balance, altering it dangerously.

Sword hand to the jugular. To kill.

At some time Bruno Heidel was aware of glass smashing, perhaps the Lalique figurine of the girl with the borzoi that stood on the coffee table, a gift from the Mayor of Berlin. Later, perhaps one hundredth of a second later, he was aware of pain shooting along the muscles of his forearm on the left side as it struck against an object, conceivably the service revolver in the other man's holster as their bodies spun together. But always he was aware of the force that was here in the room with him, invincible and inescapable, as if, when the door had opened, a whirlwind had found its way in here and was destroying everything it touched.

But Bruno Heidel was difficult to kill. His brute strength was an element that could function almost by itself, a vehicle for the conditioned reflex that had been triggered a few seconds ago when the other man's fist had reached for his throat. He struggled as an animal struggles against the steel of the trap or the jaws of the predator, and for almost a minute was able to keep his balance and spin and turn and react, backing and recovering and going in against the adversary with blows that would have felled him if their aim had been good. The coffee table was tipped on end and sent hurtling against the wall with two of its mahogany legs breaking off and fluting through the air, drawing blood from Heidel's temple; one of the dark upholstered chairs went over backward with the fabric ripping as a boot caught its heel in the leather. But he was prolonging the agony of his death by force alone; there was no subtlety in him, no science.

Heel-palm. The nose bone upward into the brain. To kill.

And something screamed and the world burst into a kind of fire, before the dark came down.

Silence remained, save for the breathing of the man who still lived. The door opened, and one of the batmen came in, drawing his revolver. But he was a small man, and too slow, because of his astonishment. The second one was bigger and had his gun in the low aim as he came in at a run, but he was off balance and uncertain of the target, distracted by the sight of the General's face as it lay on the bloodied carpet, one eye staring. They had no chance.

The door was still half open, and the man who was left alive stood listening, fighting to quiet the breath that was heaving in and out of his lungs. He waited fully a minute, but no one came. Then he walked out of the room, and away.

SACHSENHAUSEN, 20 MARCH 1940

"We've made great progress," said Himmler, smiling as he held the bright yellow wildflower between his

finger and thumb. "Great progress, in such a sh(
time."

The men around him looked pleased. They we
standing in the neat, brick-pathed and beautifully ke
herb garden adjoining the main compound of the cam
Kommandant Voess, following the example of t
Reichsführer, was himself becoming a veritable expe
on the healing properties of herbs and their prop
cultivation. It had only been in January of last ye
when the Reichsführer had inaugurated the Deutsc
Versuchsanstalt für Ernährung und Verpflegung as
official institute for experimental nutrition and prov
sioning, but already most of the concentration cam
boasted an herb garden and a horticultural staff, ma
of them drawn from prisoners with degrees in bota
or related subjects.

"We know," Reichsführer Himmler told his listene
"that this rather common-looking little flower—saffro
or the *Carthamus tinctorius*—has powerful properti
as a laxative, a diuretic, a carminative and a sudorif
We know that its seed has also some of these propertie
The plant, suitably cultivated, processed and applie
has proved extremely useful in cases of influenza, col
and general fevers. In women, it regulates the menstru
flow."

From where SS-General Maihof was standing, t
little yellow flower was reflected in the Reichsführe
round, rimless spectacles, and outlined boldly agai
his black uniform with its broad gold band at the c
of the left arm, almost the same color as the flow
The General was listening to every word, in case t
Reichsführer asked a question; but there was more
his mind than the therapeutic properties of the *Cc
thamus tinctorius*. He was a very frightened man.

"But this is the first time," said Heinrich Himml
with deep solemnity, "that the saffron flower has be
seen to bloom in this area so early in the year—than
to Kommandant Voess's experiments with cultivati

under glass." His mild, contemplative eyes came to rest on the Kommandant. "I sincerely congratulate you. We have made great progress, since the beginning of last year, with our studies, thanks to people like yourself."

"It's been my privilege to follow your example, Herr Reichsführer."

It was a blithe spring day, a little cool, perhaps, but with a hint of coming warmth on the fragrant breeze. The birdsong from the nearby woods was sweet.

"We are beginning to know—" The Reichsführer started again in his quiet, melodious voice, but was interrupted as a sound came from the other side of the wall; it was something like a scream, but rather too low, too guttural; it was difficult even to tell whether it was a man or a dog. Other sounds began, of men laughing, and then, quite unmistakably, the deep-chested barking of a guard dog as it went for a target; then there was a clear, high scream, and the dog's muted growling as its jaws closed on something; then finally there was the sound of a shot, and the scream was silenced, and in a moment the growling of the dog died away. In the walled herb garden, no one looked anywhere but at the Reichsführer's face. "We are beginning to know," he continued in his measured, schoolmaster's tones, "our good friends of the earth—the Lily of the Valley, which strengthens the brain; the Milkweed, an emetic, a purgative and splendid for women's complaints; the Valerian plant, with its excellent tonic properties for the nerves, and so on."

General Maihof appeared to be listening attentively, though his thoughts were elsewhere. In the last eleven days von Fleig, von Kassel and Bruno Heidel had been murdered, and he was now the last of the secret faction left alive. To be a marked man, he had discovered, was to suffer the waking nightmare of not knowing: of not knowing when he might be drawing his last breath; of not knowing if the footsteps behind him were simply those of an aide; of not knowing how it would come, when it came—with a bullet, a blow, or a blade.

"We should explore this treasure chest of Nature with delight, reverence and the wish to learn. These simple wild plants will gradually replace the harsh chemical medicaments stacked on the shelves of the chemists' shops—and accumulating in our own bodies. . . ."

From the edge of the group, some fifteen feet or so immediately behind General Maihof, the tall blond Standartenführer listened without expression, watching the bland face of the Reichsführer as he pursued his discourse, and occasionally glancing slightly to the left at the pale bare neck of SS-General Maihof.

The evening light was deepening among the soft hills north of the Elster, and a few vehicles moving along the road between Elsterwerda and Kirchain had their sidelights on. Traffic was light, and most of it was military.

A camouflaged tanker, carrying 15,000 liters of high-octane aviation fuel for the provisioning of fighter stations along the Czechoslovakian frontier, had passed through the town of Kirchain some ten minutes ago, and was proceeding south. Every so often, lighter traffic would pile up behind it and then overtake it along the straight stretches of road.

Southward, half a dozen SS staff cars had left Sachsenhausen Concentration Camp an hour ago, with little distance between them; but by now they had spread out along the road and only two of them were still within half a mile of each other as they drove through the town of Elsterwerda, heading north toward Berlin.

In the leading 540-K Mercedes sat General Walther Maihof, an aide beside him on his left and a second aide in the front seat next to the driver. He'd spoken hardly a word since leaving the camp, and his aides summed up his mood and left him alone. For the past two days he had been trying to make a decision between two alternatives, both of them desperate: to get himself and his family across the Swiss frontier with the help of his influential connections in Basel, or go straight to Hitler and ask for physical protection as part of his reward for presenting his atomic bomb feasibility study. If he didn't do one or the other, he was going to follow his late colleagues to a violent death. Whatever rival faction was systematically wiping out his own, it wasn't going to stop now.

Von Kassel had been all for taking their plan to Heydrich, in the first place. Heydrich would know precisely when to approach the Führer, and how to do it without the risk of a costly rebuff. They had all agreed to this: the logic of it was undeniable. But now Maihof was alone, cut off from the support of his colleagues and with some rival faction hounding him to the grave. Every reason, then, for going to Heydrich, and sooner than ever. But he didn't trust the man. He was a fox: Reinhard the Fox, as everyone called him (out of his hearing, if they valued their life). *It could even be Heydrich who was the* éminence grise *behind these ghastly assassinations, making a bid to seize the kudos for himself when Hitler bestrode the world like a Colossus.* To go to Heydrich might be to go to his executioner. Go, then, to Himmler. He outranked the Fox, and had no ambitions. He was a civil servant, plodding, loyal, predictable. He would lead his legions of secret policemen over the brink of a cliff at a moment's notice, if his beloved Führer told him it was for the good of Germany. He was a robot, and as such could be trusted not to get any ideas—such as taking over the atomic feasibility study from General Maihof.

"Report to my office at General Headquarters," the Reichsführer-SS had told him amiably as they were leaving the herb garden. "I shall be interested to hear your plans for a New German World."

So the decision was made. It wasn't to get out of

Germany by the skin of his teeth, and it wasn't to beard the lion in the Chancellory. Himmler was a man he could work with, and also the man to give him a dozen devoted bodyguards if he asked for them. Which he would. As the big open Mercedes purred through the hills of Sachsen-Anhalt he began feeling better, and took deep breaths of the evening air, like a man reprieved.

"Magnificent countryside," he told the aide on his left.

SS-Captain Howitz looked across the monotonous hills half lost in the lowering light. "Magnificent, Herr Obergruppenführer," he answered in slight surprise.

Behind them, the other staff car had now closed the distance to fifty yards, having overtaken an armored reconnaissance vehicle a few minutes ago, so that there was now nothing between the two open Mercedes. General Maihof's driver, SS-Sergeant Bockman, was keeping an eye on the mirror, as he always did, and noticed that the staff car following them was still gaining ground and might wish to overtake. He was mildly surprised to see that it was being driven by an SS officer whose rank he couldn't discern. A Mercedes 500 was normally the transport of a staff colonel or upward, and he would normally have his personal driver. An officer below that rank didn't rate a driver, and would be at the wheel alone, or with passengers; but he didn't rate a Mercedes 500 either. But then, a colonel or upward could break quite a few of the rules, and this chap might have put his driver down at a railway station and gone off to meet a girl; strictly forbidden, of course, but a lot would depend on how many oak-leaves he had on his tunic, and how many crossed swords. There were some wild ones in the SS, no doubt about it. It wasn't the Army.

Sergeant Bockman maintained his speed at 85 kph and kept circumspectly to the right side of the road. If the car behind him wanted to overtake it could do so; there was only light traffic coming the other way from the north. He drove instinctively, with the precision of long habit, and part of his mind was occupied with the problem that had come into his life, hitting him right between the eyes only a week ago. He still couldn't believe it.

He'd been wiping the rainspots off the Mercedes at the Transport Pool garage when a clerk from the Rasse und Siedlungshauptamt office had come to find him. "Before you were married, did you submit the required *Ahnenpapiere* certificates?"

"Of course." The clerk hadn't addressed him by his title, and he didn't like that. He was proud of it. When you were an SS-Unterscharführer, you were on your way up.

"You believed your prospective wife was a pure Aryan?"

"Certainly. And she still is," he said sharply.

The clerk shook his head slowly, looking down at the papers he'd brought with him. "We've been checking. It looks as if she was lying. She's a *Mischling,* second degree. There's Jewish blood. Look." He thrust the papers at Sergeant Bockman. "A Jewish grandmother. Didn't she ever tell you?"

After a long time Bockman said, "No." He turned away from the papers. "Are you sure of your facts?"

"Certainly." His glance of surprise was downright insolent. "You'd better present yourself at our office, Unterscharführer Bockman, at the earliest opportunity."

And that was that. Right between the eyes.

He'd said nothing to Rita, when he got home off duty. He'd wanted to think about it. After all, she was a good wife, a good little woman, kept the place shining, always made sure there was a hot meal for him at any time of the day or night—in this job you worked odd hours. And she was pretty. Well, attractive, say. But he couldn't keep his mind off it, her being partly a Jewess. All they'd told him at the Race and Resettle-

ment office was that he'd have to make up his mind
about what he'd do. That was all they'd said. He supposed they meant he'd have to divorce her, if he didn't
want to be thrown out of the SS. And him a full sergeant! But he knew how strict they were. Even an
officer had to get his fiancée's family background
checked over before he could marry. Any sign of
Jewish blood, and out. She could be a cripple, a for-
eigner, anything you like. But not Jew, or even part
Jew, even a tenth. This was the SS, an elite organization and the Führer's greatest pride. You could see their
point of view.

For a whole week now, he'd turned over and gone
to sleep the minute he put out the bedroom light.
Couldn't fancy her, somehow. She'd always been very
good, Rita, let him do anything he felt like, anytime,
never complained. She'd always been able to stir him
up whenever she wanted, just by the way she undressed
for bed, a bit more slowly than usual, standing nearer
the light. But not now. It was disgusting to think about.
Jewish blood. She didn't know what was happening,
of course. "Don't you love me anymore?" she'd been
asking for days now. Putting on different lipsticks, doing her hair twice a day, getting out her black under-
wear. Pathetic, really. A *Jewess.*

So there it was. He'd have to choose between the SS
and Rita. And tomorrow, when he was off duty for
the weekend, he'd get it over with. Tell her straight.
She'd been a good wife to him, but if she and her
family thought they could bring dirty blood into the
SS, they'd have to think again.

The staff car behind him was going to overtake now.
He kept well in and maintained a steady speed, hearing the rush of its engine merging with his own.

No, it had been a shock all right. But there was this
about it: there was no question of what he must do.
He wasn't, as you might say, on the horns of a dilemma.
A *Mischling.* Even the very word felt dirty in his mouth.

No wonder she was always talking about money, telling him how she wanted to help him save the good money he earned, save for a baby, save for their first little house where they could be on their own, save for this, save for that, never buying a new dress, always making them herself—money, money, money, it was all she could think about. By God, you could always tell a Jew, if you listened long enough!

He'd tell her tomorrow. Mince no words. She'd got to go.

The revolver bullet entered his brain on the left side and its force pitched him against the Lieutenant sitting in the passenger's seat as the bloodburst spattered against the windscreen, the slipstream whipping some of it back to leave crimson flecks on the faces and uniform of General Maihof and his aide. Sergeant Bockman's death had been instantaneous and without warning, so that his gloved hands had simply dropped away from the steering wheel as his torso had rocked from the hips in the direction of the bullet's travel. The bullet itself, fired at very close range, passed through the skull on both sides and smashed the nose of the Lieutenant as Sergeant Bockman's body lurched against him. The car kept to its course for a few seconds, the road being straight and smooth at this point, but it was now accelerating, since the dead driver's boot had been thrust against the throttle pedal as the weight of his body slumped downward, its muscles inert.

In the rear seat, General Maihof was unable to make out exactly what was happening. At the sound of the shot—very loud at such short range—his fear of assassination, recently lulled by his decision to see Himmler and seek his protection, had returned in an instant and with overwhelming force, to the point where he half believed the shot had gone into his own body and produced some kind of paralysis, so that he could feel nothing. But Captain Howitz, sitting beside him, kept his head in the first few seconds, and saw that the open staff car that had been overtaking them was now dropping quickly behind again as the driver applied the brakes. The Captain wasn't quite sure what had happened. He'd seen the driver of the other car—an SS-Colonel, by his insignia—aim his revolver straight at Sergeant Bockman and fire. And Bockman was now lying against the aide in front, with blood flying all over the place. But the scene was so appalling, so terrifying, that the mind of Captain Howitz was trying to rationalize the whole incident as a hallucination. But this degree of shock lasted only for a few seconds, and he was now perfectly conscious of what was happening.

The car was veering slowly across to the wrong side of the road, and coming from the opposite direction was some kind of fuel tanker, with its powerful horns blaring and its headlights flashing in warning. Captain Howitz stared for another half second, then his mind went blank again as he realized there was nothing, absolutely nothing, that he could do.

The driver of the fuel tanker attempted at the last instant to swerve away from the oncoming Mercedes into the ditch at the roadside, where the first of the wildflowers were coming into bloom, orange and yellow and amethyst. But his attempt was too late, and the two vehicles met head-on at a combined speed of approximately 155 kph. The immense weight of the tanker was hardly checked at all as the much lighter vehicle impacted against it; but its degree of deceleration, however slight, was enough to bring the 15,000 liters of high-octane aviation fuel surging against the baffles. The baffles held, because the tanker was full, but the heavy steel lugs holding the tank to the chassis broke away, and a split appeared in the forward end as the tank shifted under the momentum and smashed through the driver's cab.

SS-General Walther Maihof, his face and tunic spattered with the blood of Sergeant Bockman, was hurled against the front of the tanker at approximately 100 kilometers per hour—the speed at which the Mercedes had been traveling after the dead Sergeant's boot had been thrust against the accelerator pedal. His uniform, in the instant before his body struck the tanker's radiator, was suddenly darkened by the spray of aviation fuel that was escaping from the split in the tank itself. In the climactic impact of metal against metal, more than one spark was produced.

It was reported later that the light of the ensuing conflagration was seen against the low clouds from the streets of Luckenwalde, seventy-five kilometers away.

25

BERLIN, 21 MARCH 1940

Dr. Joseph Lenneberg took his slide rule and checked the figures on the graph, noting the results and entering them with the comparative study of Lise Meitner's work on the initial phase of the reaction, involving bombardment of the uranium nucleus with slow-speed neutrons. The two studies were in perfect agreement. He had already told them that, General Heidel and the others. What did they want him to do? Disagree with people like Meitner and Otto Hahn?

No. They wanted to be sure.

It wasn't cold in here anymore. He had pressed the electric bell and one of the guards had come. He had said he was cold, and they had turned on the radiators, and now he was warm again. It was unbelievable. He wanted to laugh. In Sachsenhausen he had been cold, but there was no electric bell to press, nor any radiators. He had nearly died of pneumonia, there. All winter, people had been dying of the cold. Max, Amos, Lajos the Hungarian and all the others, so many others, while the snow had come whistling and whirling through the barbed wire, driven by the wind and heaped against the huts along the east side of the camp.

Shoveling parties! Double up, there! Shoveling parties!

It was the only time they had been warm, when they had been shoveling the snow, their thin cotton shirts soaked with sweat until the wind froze it into ice, despite its salt content. Many of them had been warm when they had died, swinging their shovel for the last time before their hearts gave out and they dropped into the snow. They had died so fast, and the snow had drifted so fast, that they were buried within a few minutes, only to be dug up again by the men moving behind them.

Shoveling parties!

When his friends heard he was on the list for extermination they had pushed him under the end hut, near the garbage dump, coming to feed him every day and to bring rags, old newspapers, anything they could find that would help to keep him warm, even at the risk of their own lives, because to pick up a rag was stealing, and the penalty for stealing was death. There had been only three inches of space between his chest and the planks at the bottom of the hut, so that he couldn't turn over, or turn on his side; he had lain flat on his back for six days, letting the drips of melting ice trickle into his mouth, moving his hand from the place where they left the food for him to his mouth, as a crab did with its pincers, fouling himself where he lay, and sometimes sleeping, though never knowing the time, because the winter day was so dark and he could see nothing but the planks only a few inches in front of his eyes; only when the searchlights swept the main compound did he know it was night.

Now he pressed the electric bell, and said he was cold; and they turned the radiators on, to warm him.

"Work well," the SS General had told him, "and you'll live in comfort, and your child will be safe."

Hildi safe.

That was all that meant anything to him now. And of course they knew that. So he worked well, and lived comfortably, and listened to Hildi's voice over the telephone every day, as they'd arranged for him to do.

"When are you coming home, Daddy?"

"Soon. Soon now, my darling."

Hildi safe.

He had gone through all that business with his conscience, of course. Days ago. Nights ago, more accurately, when there was time to think. He knew what they were asking him to do. Help them make an atomic weapon, so that they could conquer the world with it. Thousands would die. Perhaps millions. The fallout of partially decayed radioactive products would be lethal. It would rise high into the atmosphere and then drift on the winds, covering vast areas of land and spreading death. Lise had warned people of this; so had Fritz Strassman. And the Germans were asking him to help them create this kind of world, the end of the world, or certainly of civilization, so that they could rake among the ashes for the survivors, and make them slaves, and commit them to the camps, to the crematoria, where they would become ashes themselves, joining the ashes that were spreading across the surface of the earth. The Ice Age, now the Ash Age. It had driven him half out of his mind, trying to encompass the enormity of what they were going to do. With his help.

Then he had at last decided to admit the obvious: that the Germans had gone mad, that the world would soon be mad, if they were in command of it, and that a man, any man, must think of himself and whatever he valued, or cherished; himself first, and the things dear to him, and the madness afterward.

Hildi safe. It would be his watchword.

He peeled the graph from the block and began on the next, following Otto Hahn's equations this time and preparing the figures for comparison. He knew perfectly well what the result would be. Hahn and Strassman had made the discovery; Meitner and Frisch had elaborated

on it and explained it in their papers. Was he expected
to discover something new, or find mistakes? No. He
was expected to reassure these power-mad fanatics that
the figures were correct, that this doomsday weapon
could be made, and that Adolf Hitler could possess it.

So, Joseph Lenneberg, you have decided to risk
the safety of the entire civilized world, for the safety
of your child.

Yes.

Then you must be mad too.

If you care to think so, yes. I am mad too. Lying
under the hut with my eyes against the darkness for
all those hours, all those days, I went mad. So be it.
But I will tell you this. I have worked out a few equations of my own, a few graphs; and the results are
these, my friend: a man must think first of himself, in
these mad times, and of the things he values. That is my
watchword now.

Hildi safe.

He peeled the sheet off the block and began on the
next graph, and was still working on it when the night
guard opened the door and came in. Joseph went on
with his work, his thin blue-veined hands moving under
the angled reading lamp. "What do you want?" he
asked in a moment, without looking up.

"Dr. Joseph Lenneberg?"

It wasn't the guard's voice.

He looked up in surprise. His eyes had been con-
centrating on his work in the glare of the lamp for
hours on end, and all he could see was a tall figure in
uniform looking down at him.

"Yes?"

"Come with me."

Joseph got up from the stool, his thin body cramped
and aching. He could see the man better now, and was
uneasy about him. He was an SS Colonel, which was
nothing remarkable in this place; the laboratory had
been taken over by these people. But his face was

deathly pale, and his eyes looked haunted, set deeply in their sockets and ringed with fatigue. Even the shaded light seemed to worry him, as if he had not slept for a long time. Joseph had seen faces like this in the camps but not under a cap with the Death's Head insignia.

"Who are you?" he asked the Colonel.

"Never mind. You will come with me." He took a few paces, looking down at the sheets of equations and the three worn files. "Bring this with you. All of it."

"But I—"

"And hurry." The Colonel swung around on him with his eyes bright for an instant. *"Hurry. You understand?"*

The small SS Mercedes turned the corner of Reinhardbrunnerstrasse in the Lichtenberg district of East Berlin, moving slowly along the blacked-out street.

"Where is the house?"

"Halfway along," said Joseph. "Just this side of the fifth lamp standard on the right." He knew where the house was, without any question. It was where they were looking after Hildi, keeping her safe.

The haggard-faced SS Colonel had barely spoken a word on the way from the physics laboratory. "I will tell you later what is to happen," was all he had said in explanation. He had seemed almost too weary to say more. When they had left the laboratory there had been two SS men lying on the floor not far from the room where Joseph had been working. A third man had been near the main entrance to the building, one leg lying doubled under him and his right hand near the revolver he'd been trying to use. Joseph had realized they were not men, in actual fact, but bodies; he had seen the stillness of death too many times to mistake it. When they had driven through the gates the two guards there had saluted the Colonel; as soon as they were outside, he had stopped the car and got out. Joseph had heard two shots in quick succession; one of the guards had raised a shout but it was cut off; the other had fallen against the iron bars of the gate, rattling them. The Colonel had got back into the car and driven away.

Who was he?

The Mercedes came to a stop, just this side of the fifth lamp standard on the right-hand side.

"Is this the house?"

"Yes," Joseph said.

26

LOWESTOFT, ENGLAND, 24 MARCH 1940

The first light of the day was seeping eastward from the cloudbanks, delineating the squat radio hut and the curved roof of the hangar. The wind had increased since midnight, and now the windsock was blowing horizontally, shifting and fretting in the glow of its mast lamp. The sea began reflecting the dawn light, its surface broken with light and dark as the wind whipped at it. The three men sheltering in the lee of the hut could hear the crash of the waves along the undercliff.

Ten minutes ago the radio had come to life inside the hut; then there was silence again. The king's equerry had gone inside to find out what was happening; it had been a routine signal from the observer ship in the North Sea herring fleet. The equerry had come back, the tails of his plaid raglan flapping in the wind.

"We'll have to switch routes," he said, "after this one's down." He'd been wondering how to tell them.

"Are we rumbled?"

"No. But they're going to close down The Hague."

"What on earth for? It's been working splendidly for—" Then the civilian with the deerstalker fell silent, hearing in retrospect the equerry's tone.

The third man asked quietly, "Are those bastards going into Holland?"

"That's right."

"When?"

"Any time now."

None of them spoke again until they saw the small dark shape drifting closer against the silvered wastes of the sea. It was coming in very low, and for a while it looked as if it might not clear the cliffs. The radio was crackling again inside the hut, and in a moment the airstrip lights came on and the single emergency vehicle started its engine.

It was always at this moment when the waiting men felt their hearts trying to lift, as the small shape took on size from the distance and the voices from inside the hut grew more animated in their exchange; but the Lysander was not yet down. In the past four months, three of these machines had crashed on landing, one of them flying straight into the cliff face and exploding; a fourth had simply flopped into the sea, its controls riddled with bullets. There had been fighter-interceptor sorties by the Luftwaffe from the north German coast, and a leak was suspected. The death roll stood at nine, with four agents, three pilots and two escorting officers losing their lives.

The Lysander was banking low against the north, to make its approach from the west against the wind. There was a lot of turbulence here, with dead pockets caused by the updraft over the cliff; the windsock lifted and fell as the gusts shook it, bending the thin mast.

None of the waiting men spoke. In the early days they had let their anxiety show, expressing it in short phrases that had varied from a prayer to a curse as the frail aircraft had come dropping out of the dawn. Now they stood silent, keeping their fears to themselves, in case in some mystic way they might hinder the pilot as he struggled to bring himself and his passengers to the waiting earth, safe and alive.

At the last moment the Lysander slipped sideways, yawing to a dead pocket of air and dropping fast, and the three men on the ground stood with their fists clenched in their coat pockets, holding their breath. Then another gust came, slapping the windsock level and lifting the high-wing monoplane and providing resistance for the controls. It staggered again, then righted, settling between the runway markers and bouncing three or four times before the brakes came on and it started slowing, its single airscrew hazing with light against the eastern sky.

The three men began trotting across the grass as the runway lights went out. Somewhere to their left, the ground crew were running toward the aircraft.

The escorting officer was already on the ground when the king's equerry and his companions reached the plane. The passenger, a thin and starved-looking man with the nerves twitching in his face, caught his foot on the metal step and flung out an arm as the escorting officer grabbed him in time, moving to the step again to help down the child. She was bundled in a big plaid rug, with only her face showing.

"Who the devil's that?" someone asked the equerry.

"His daughter. He wouldn't come without her, so we had to make the necessary arrangements."

27

"Twenty-eight men," said Superintendent Vogel, his tone shrill with exasperation. "Twenty-eight!"

Deputy Commissioner Luftig sat cleaning his nails. He had given his good friend Vogel five whole minutes to let off steam, but now they ought to get down to an actual conversation. The Minister was breathing hard down Konrad Luftig's neck, as hard as the Reichsführer was breathing down Karl Vogel's.

"Is it twenty-eight?" he asked blandly. "We've counted only five."

Vogel stared at him from behind his desk. *"Five?"*

"Or perhaps you're just concerned with the grand total. That doesn't interest us."

Vogel tried to relax, to counter Luftig's calm with a calm of his own. But he wasn't like that. When he was faced with a problem he went at it hard, pounding at it until it gave him rest. Luftig wasn't of the same nature; he preferred to study the problem from all sides, and then attack it from underneath, or from the rear, or even from inside, if he could get there—and he very often could. "You'll never fill a saucer," he'd once told Vogel, "with a high-pressure hose."

"The grand total doesn't interest you?" Vogel demanded in frustration. "Then it interests Reichsführer

297

Heinrich Himmler—of whom you may have heard. This man Der Jäger—which is what everyone's calling him for some absurd reason—"

"We might as well call him something," reflected Luftig equably.

"I'd call him a homicidal maniac. I also prefer to think that *we* are the hunters—not him, The point is that he's managed to kill twenty-eight—"

"Karl, allow me to point out that most of those deaths were purely incidental. We believe his *intended* victims were SS-Lieutenant Mahler, in the nightclub, and SS-Generals von Fleig, von Kassel, Heidel and Maihof. Their various aides, servants and chauffeurs were either killed by the blast, so to speak, or permanently and effectively silenced—like the five men who were guarding Dr. Lenneberg."

"Oh, very well then. I take your point, but you must admit that our man doesn't hesitate to kill when he makes up his mind."

The Deputy Commissioner of Police for Greater Berlin worked carefully at his cuticles. "What does it matter," he asked reasonably, "that seven men were accidentally killed when the fuel tanker went up? You're not seriously suggesting we should look for motives there. Nor in many of the other cases. Let me break this thing down for you as regards the *motives*. We think he killed your two men—one in Grünewald and one at the Tiergarten Bahnhof—because of Fräulein von Gerlach, either to protect her in some way or—which is much more likely—to protect himself from recognition later. We tend to think that those killings have nothing to do with the rest. They touch upon an affair of the heart. Nor do the many *incidental* deaths amount to much—the servants, drivers, guards and so on. What I'm really interested in is the motive for killing the five SS officers, four of them with high rank." He looked up for a moment to gaze at the man behind the desk. "Because there could be a *hell* of a lot going on, you see, behind the scenes. Behind those deaths. If we could find the motive for *those* killings, my friend . . ." He went on with his manicure. "But there's no connection, it seems. We've been in constant touch with the SS, from Heydrich downward—Himmler doesn't really know what's going on at any particular time, if you'll pardon my saying so, but Heydrich assuredly does. They can find no connection between those four generals—apart from their having been friends and in some instances colleagues—to offer the slightest clue. As for the young Lieutenant, I'm inclined to think his was another 'incidental' death. The *motive* is what interests my department. The motive in the murder of four high-ranking SS officers. And I think we shall find it easier to trap Der Jäger than to find his motive. The trap is, of course, already set."

"I could break this case for you in twelve hours!" Vogel got to his feet, restless. "Give me Hedda von Gerlach, for twelve hours."

"My department couldn't permit that. She is our bait. Our lure. You could stick pins into her all day long and she wouldn't necessarily name our man, as we've already agreed, if you remember. Even if she named him, and told us his address, would we find him there? Waiting for us? We could lose him forever. I realize it's tempting—" But he broke off. This case rattled him far more than he was going to admit to Vogel—or anyone else—and when he was rattled he tended—like other mortals—to speak his mind. He had been about to say that he realized it was tempting for Vogel to take that girl slowly to pieces down there in the basement, but self-indulgence wouldn't get anyone anywhere. "It's tempting to press matters," he said instead, "and try to force a solution. But my department feels we should simply leave the trap open, with the bait inside." He felt a word of warning might not come amiss. "The Gestapo is involved in these killings because two of your officers were victims and because your organization has the most voluminous repository of information, which is valuable to us. The SS is involved because most of the other victims were SS officers and lower ranks. But murder, particularly in the area of Greater Berlin and generally in outlying areas where our help is often requested, is my department's very specific pigeon. I'm therefore asking you, officially, to leave Fräulein von Gerlach alone, apart from our joint surveillance coverage on her movements, day and night." As a concession he added, "Once we have Der Jäger, you can have his girlfriend, and do what you like with her."

He was preparing to leave when a report was handed to Vogel by one of his staff. It was a summary of the evidence of all available witnesses to the "accident" that had killed SS-General Maihof and his aides four days ago. After glancing through the five typed sheets, Vogel thrust them at the Deputy Commissioner, his dark eyes glittering.

"Page three," he said, "paragraphs two and four."

Luftig read more slowly. A lance-sergeant of the Wehrmacht, one of the survivors from the reconnaissance vehicle which had crashed off the road in avoiding the conflagration, had recovered consciousness last night in Kirchain Muncipal Hospital without any trace of retrogressive amnesia—unlike several of the other witnesses. He corroborated earlier evidence that the sound of a shot had been heard shortly before the crash.

We were some distance behind the staff car, but near enough to see it was trying to overtake the one in front. The tanker was not in sight at this time. One of my men (Private Hans Flöcken: see relevant report under this name) said: "There's someone shooting," or a remark of that nature. I thought I observed a flash ahead of our vehicle, but at the time believed it was some kind of light flickering on, such as the rearlight of one of the SS staff cars.

The Deputy Commissioner skipped paragraph 3 and went on to the next. *Shortly before the accident, I*

*noticed the overtaking staff car dropping back suddenly,
leaving tire marks because of its brakes coming on. We
came right up close, as a result, and I saw the car making a quick U-turn and going back past us in the opposite direction. The driver was an SS officer, with a
Colonel's insignia on his greatcoat. I noticed him particularly, because we were all wondering what he was
playing at. (See corroborating reports under relevant
headings.) His appearance was definitely Aryan, and
even with him sitting down, I could see he must be quite
tall. I could not see any other details. At this time one
of my men gave a shout, as the other staff car began
edging to the wrong side of the road, into the path of
the tanker.*

The Deputy Commissioner pushed out his underlip
reflectively for a moment, then dropped the report on
to Vogel's desk. "So. Our friend the SS Colonel again."

Vogel was on his feet, his tone shrill with excitement.
"Exactly! *This* is how he can kill so easily. He has his
victims' confidence. His authority gives him immediate
access—to General von Kassel's house, to General
Heidel's quarters, to the Landsberger Physics Laboratory. *This* is how he comes and goes as he chooses.
This is how he gets so close to them—close enough to
kill. I shall order an immediate check on every colonel
in the entire SS organization, tall, and of Aryan appearance." He paused. "With Himmler's approval."

Luftig folded the nail file against the clippers and
lumbered to his feet. "And Heydrich's," he said blandly.

"And Heydrich's, of course."

"I commend your sense of determination," Luftig
told him heavily. "Of the several hundred colonels in
the SS, most are of Aryan appearance and above medi-
um height, according to Professor Schultz's decree concerning 'correct racial type.' It's going to take you
months."

"You suggest we do *nothing?*"

Luftig sighed gently. "We have set the trap, my dear

fellow. All I'm suggesting, in the light of this corroborating evidence, is that when Der Jäger walks into that trap he's liable to be wearing an SS colonel's uniform. All that has happened, I think, is that our earlier suspicions—*your* earlier suspicions particularly—have been supported by this new evidence. This colonel has killed two men, in order to see the von Gerlach woman. When he wants to see her, he lets nothing stop him. I feel confident he'll try to see her again—not in a matter of months, which your massive operation would take, but in a matter of days." He reached for his round, wide-brimmed hat.

As usual, his plodding logic served only to exasperate Vogel the more. "So we just go on sitting still, is that it?"

"One of nature's most efficient beasts of prey," the Deputy Commissioner told him patiently, "is the spider. Yet it spends ninety percent of its entire life sitting absolutely still. I think I might say that the modest success I've achieved in my long career is due to the fact that I've always followed the example of the true professional."

DEBNO, POLAND, 24 MARCH 1940

Kurt Wolff and Willi Helm were working side by side, swinging their long-handled ladles into the boiling fat and pouring it across the top of the conflagration. The handles of the ladles were three meters long, and they worked them in unison, like oarsmen; otherwise they might collide and spill the oil. Their faces were red in the light of the flames, and blistered by their heat. They had wrapped rags around the ends of the metal handles, and over their hands; but at night they slept only an hour or two, because of the burning pain.

The new cremation pits had presented a problem at first. The bodies from the Chamber had been thrown in layers across the iron grating and sandwiched with pine branches, rags and waste paper soaked with alcohol; and for a time they burned well; but gradually they became a solid mass, and no air could get in, so that the fires burned low and finally went out. The supplies of wood alcohol were limited, and Kommandant Axen had called his technical staff together, urging them to find a solution. But the result was disappointing: a mixture of impractical ideas that depended on some kind of fuel—and all fuel was in short supply. It was the Kommandant himself who had produced the brain-wave, as so often happened here at Debno. There was an ample supply of fuel available, he pointed out, and it was absolutely free. A very large but shallow pan had been made, and placed below the iron grille to catch the fat that trickled constantly from the corpses as they burned.

As Kurt, Willi and the ten others on the crematorium labor force swung their ladles in unison, the flames leaped higher above the massed bodies, with a constant sizzling. During the six-hour period allotted to each new batch, the heat engendered became so fierce that the flames became bluish white, and the cadavers themselves became their own fuel. Today the Kommandant had come down here to watch from a comfortable distance, pointing out to some visiting officers the efficacy of his invention.

In the evening, when the pit was filled with glowing ash and cobbled with incandescent skulls, Kurt Wolff hooked his ladle on the rack beside the pit and murmured, "Two days."

Willi Helm, the ex-tennis champion, stood with his eyes burning, and his hands burning, and his soul burning, and braced his feet to keep himself from falling over. "What?"

"Two more days," Wolff told him. His mouth was a husk, and he could barely move his tongue in it; but he wanted his friend to know what he'd been thinking about, all day, and what he'd decided. He'd seen that Willi, though young and strong and as near physically fit as any prisoner could be in this place, was beginning to die, in his mind. It would rally him, perhaps, if he knew that there would be only two more days of this. He moved his tongue again, scraping it against his scorched and shriveled palate and producing the semblance of words. "We do it in two more days."

They had told Franz.

He had been able to think of nothing else all day. They had told him last night, when they'd lain along their bunks swinging their arms slowly to make a draft for their blistered hands. Now it was evening, with only one day left.

"Inspection," said Stefan beside him.

Franz glanced up quickly from the files. Speech was important here; a single word had the power of life over death, if you were quick enough to take its meaning and act at once.

"When?" he asked Stefan.

"I don't know. Officers going by."

Franz turned his head toward the windows but saw nothing but the distant roof of the Chamber. Stefan, the short, quick-moving Pole who had replaced Kurt at the "reception desk," often knew what was going on before anyone else had read the signs.

They straightened their wooden box files, and shuffled the pending forms together, reclipping them neatly. A broken pencil, a paper clip at the wrong angle, and you could go straight onto the death list for "slovenly work."

"One more day," murmured Franz, as he had done throughout the morning, unable to contain the strange slow feeling that had been rising within him since last night, when Kurt had told them, a feeling his bruised spirit was hardly able to remember, a feeling of hope.

"*Freiheit . . .*" murmured Stefan in reply, as he always did. Freedom . . .

Then they both stiffened to attention.

The SS Colonel had entered alone, and was standing in front of them, looking around, his hands behind his back. Franz and Stefan threw him the Deutschgruss salute, which he returned perfunctorily.

"The main files," he said with a strange weariness.

"Over here, Herr Standartenführer!" Stefan told him, and opened the low wooden gate separating the office from the waiting area. Franz watched the officer from the corner of his eye, thinking it odd that he'd come in here alone; he outranked Captain Axen substantially, and the Kommandant and at least one aide should have accompanied him. His whole manner was odd; as he went through the files he said nothing, asked nothing, as he pushed each drawer shut with an impatient little bang, his movements almost like those of a sleepwalker. Maybe that was it: he'd been missing his sleep for some reason, the pressures of duty.

"Ernst Kramer," he said at last, turning to face them. "He's reported in your files as deceased. Is that correct?"

Franz and Stefan each waited for the other to speak. A wrong answer would be fatal, yet if they let their silence go on for another half second, the Colonel would suspect something.

"Yes, Herr Standartenführer!" Franz said with emphasis. "If the file reports him as deceased, he is deceased." It was a lie. As soon as it was known that Ernst Kramer had been an important man, a professor of physics, Kurt Wolff had taken the usual vote and they'd put the new prisoner into the labor force, entering him in the files as "deceased." This tallied with the Gestapo files in the Political Department, since the man should have gone straight to the Chamber for extermination. The Labor Force files were never checked: they were run by the kapos themselves, and served purely to provide clerks, roadmakers, corpse-carriers and the Chamber and crematoria staffs. The kapos saved the lives of anyone they could, but chose prisoners who could help the rebuilding of Germany if the Nazis were ever thrown out.

"So Ernst Kramer is deceased," said the tall, hollow-eyed SS Colonel, "according to your files. You know, of course, what will happen to you if your files are found to be incorrect."

So he knew the system. But then most of them did; it was common practice in all the camps, and they hardly ever objected. They weren't in the least interested in who lived and who died.

"Yes, Herr Standartenführer." It was Stefan who answered this time, wanting to share the responsibility. "It would be a very serious matter for us."

"Very serious," the Colonel nodded abstractedly. He came across to the long trestle desk where they worked, looking at the neatly shuffled pending forms and the open box files. "And Franz Gerlach is also reported as deceased. Is that also correct?"

Franz looked down at once, and heard Stefan's lips part as he drew a quick breath. "Yes, Herr Standartenführer."

The Colonel looked steadily from one to the other. "If you know that either of these men is in fact alive, you may say so now. I would overlook the fact that the files were acknowledged to be incorrect." He waited.

They kept silent, simply because nothing good could come of their doing otherwise. No SS man could be trusted to keep his word; it was extremely unusual for the SS to check the Labor Service files; and if this Colonel were trying to find a certain prisoner, it wouldn't be for his good.

"Very well." He turned away, not even acknowledging their salute as he reached the door. Then he paused for a moment and came slowly back, to stand facing Franz with a pensive stare. "Where have I seen you before?"

*   *   *

Listening to the haunting notes of Kommandant Axen's violin as twilight descended, SS-Major Scheldt reached a decision. It was nothing to do with the violin; he had found himself occupied with this problem for weeks now, and his thoughts had accumulated gradually to the point where he was sure of what he must do.

He began pacing again, avoiding the eyes of the prisoners as they stood waiting for the huge door of the Chamber to be opened for them. He'd been aide and first assistant to Colonel Brinkmann since last November, and had found it easy enough at first to mind his own business and keep to the bargain the Colonel had spelled out for him. But the man had been behaving more and more strangely of late. He was seldom in his office at the Inspectorate, so often asking Scheldt to "take over and keep things running," then vanishing for days on end. On every single visit to a camp he left Scheldt to pass the time talking to the resident officers while he went off on his own, on more than one occasion—as Scheldt had found out later—going through the files in the Orderly Room, for some obscure reason. They'd kept to their schedule for the most part, but lately Brinkmann had started making "snap" visits, turning up at a camp without warning and putting it through an impromptu inspection—often to the Kommandant's barely concealed disapproval. There were even occasions when he'd told Scheldt simply to stay at the Inspectorate, while he took a car and went off to God knew where.

What the hell was his game? Women, dispersed all over the map? A black market trade in valuables made by the prisoners? This kind of thing was almost the norm, as Scheldt knew only too well; but he didn't think Brinkman was in that kind of game.

The heavy metal door of the Chamber swung open, and the guards and kapos began moving the two lines of prisoners inside, while the Kommandant played for them. Scheldt turned away as one of the children dropped her doll and began to cry. There were some things he'd never managed to get used to.

No, Brinkmann was on to something much bigger than graft or the black market. He'd got some kind of job to do, and nothing was going to stop him. Sometimes he'd be so tense, so wrapped up in this thing he was doing, that he'd snap your head off for no reason. And sometimes he'd calm down suddenly, and share a joke or two, take you out to a slap-up dinner in Berlin. *He'd been like that just after General von Fleig had been assassinated, and just after General von Kassel was found dead at his villa. And General Heidel. And Maihof.*

Major Scheldt believed he would never have suspected the connection, if it hadn't been for the rumor going around: that an SS colonel had gone out of his mind and had started a blood-letting vendetta.

Der Jäger.

A shiver went down his spine as he thought of it. Ever since the twentieth, four days ago, when General Maihof and his aides had died in that appalling smash on the road to Berlin, Major Scheldt had climbed into the Mercedes beside Brinkmann with his right hand close to his revolver, sitting with him mile after mile and trying to make some kind of civilized conversation to break those almost mystic silences of his, until by the end of the journey Scheldt was a bag of nerves. *Der Jäger.* It didn't bear thinking about.

So he'd reached his decision. Tomorrow they were due back in Berlin, and he would quietly lift a telephone and make an anonymous call to Gestapo Headquarters. *Why don't you ask Colonel Brinkmann along for a few questions? SS-Colonel Martin Brinkmann, of the Concentration Camp Inspectorate. I think he's Der Jäger. No, my name isn't important.*

"I can't leave here," Franz said.

Martin stared at him in the glow from the reflected

floodlights, wondering if the boy's mind had been turned by his experiences in the camps. "You can't leave here?"

"Not yet."

"Why not?"

In a moment Franz said, "There's something I've got to do."

Martin went on watching him. It was nearly midnight, and most of the camp was asleep. He had told Franz to meet him here, on the far side of the big concrete building where the engine had been throbbing all day. There were guards on the move, patrolling outside the wire fence with leashed dogs, and the four machine-gun posts were manned, high in the watchtowers; all else was quiet.

"What is it," Martin asked slowly, "that you've got to do?"

"I can't tell you." Franz wouldn't look at him.

Martin knew that the boy didn't fully trust him yet. They hadn't recognized each other immediately in the Orderly Room simply because both had changed so much since their last meeting, and Martin had had to work on Franz with gentle persuasion, reminding him of things that only Martin Benedict the Englishman could know about Franz and his family in the days before the war. The boy had finally come to believe what he was saying, but it was Martin's SS uniform that was unacceptable. For months now, every time Franz had seen cruelty, bestiality, inhumanity in its most vicious form, it had been personified by the uniform of the SS. Martin understood this; in these past months he had seen what Franz had seen, and could imagine only too well what the uniform he was wearing looked like to a prisoner.

"I came here to find you," he told the boy gently. "I've been trying to find you for a long time. I came to free you."

Franz was silent for a while. At last he said, "I ought to be shouting for joy. It's a kind of miracle. But I've got to stay here for one more day."

Martin knew there was no point in asking him why, a second time. Franz would tell him when he was ready, if at all. He must make him see, instead, why he had to leave here, though he'd never thought it would be necessary.

"Franz, I've told you that your sister has been writing to you every week, even twice a week sometimes. And I've told you that she's well. I didn't tell you that she is helpless in the hands of a Gestapo officer, and that only you can free her."

Franz looked at him now, trying to see his eyes in the half-light. Then his head went down. *"Oh, my God. So that's why I'm still alive. . . ."* It was a long time before he raised his head, and spoke so softly that Martin missed some of the words. "There was some kind of guardian angel they talked about, at Buchenwald . . . and here, too. Someone who was protecting me . . ."

"You can leave here with me, in the morning." There would be no trouble from Kommandant Axen, Martin knew. He outranked him and could make it an order; and if Axen decided to report the incident to higher authority, nothing would come of it: there was no time left. As it was, he didn't believe he could save himself unless he made for the rescue lines, and he wasn't going to do that without orders. There were thousands on the watch for him now, on the watch for Der Jäger. But he could get Franz to the lines, if they hurried.

"Your guardian angel," he said quietly, "is Hedda. But she's having to pay a price."

A sob came out of the boy, but he stifled it with his hands. Martin waited. One of the guards was passing close to them, on the other side of the fence, his dog loping with its head held low, scenting. From the meadow on the far side of the big building came the reek of burned flesh, and Martin breathed lightly, sickened by it and by what it meant. What kind of courage was in this seventeen-year-old boy, that he could refuse to leave here? What kind of reason could he have?

"One day," Franz said, the words muffled by his hands. "All I ask is one more day." He was shivering, though the night was not cold.

"I'll be gone before then. And I can't come back."

"Then I've got to take my chance."

With sudden anger Martin said, "For Hedda, too?"

A sound came from Franz as if he'd been hit. "I can't stand—" But his hands were against his face again and his thin body was rocking. Martin put his arm around him, feeling nothing but bones.

"Let me help, Franz."

"Yes. Yes. Listen—tomorrow night we're launching a mass escape. Some friends, and myself. We've got it all—"

"An escape? To where, for God's sake?"

"Just to be free. We're going to—"

"Free for how long?" He shook the thin shoulders gently. "You won't get half a mile, any of you. Even if you could, where would you go in these rags, without food, across hostile terrain under German occupation? You—"

"Listen to me, Martin. This is what we're going to do."

He talked for a long time, and when he'd finished, Martin sat thinking, his back against the cold concrete of the extermination chamber, his eyes resting on the skeins of electrified wire that shone silver under the distant floodlights.

"I don't think you've got a chance," he said finally.

"We do." It was said with confidence.

"A chance of getting out of the camp, maybe, with half your number dead. But no chance after that, of getting to safety. Even the Poles would turn you in, for the sake of their own lives."

"There are partisans, out there."

"The partisans out there are being driven into the camps by the hundred, every day, and you know that. And you'll come back with them."

"No. If we've got to, we'll die out there. But we'll die free."

So that was it. A clean death out there to a bullet, if it had to be, rather than the filth and the humiliation and the servitude here behind the wire.

And if this boy died, freedom for Hedda too. Franz must have thought of that.

"I could take you out of here tomorrow," Martin told him. "I mean by force, and under restraint. I could take you to meet your sister, who's breaking her heart over you. I could take you home, where all they can think about and all they pray for is a chance of seeing you again. It's not easy for you, I know, to realize that apart from Franz von Gerlach you're also somebody's son, and somebody's brother." He was managing to keep the anger out of his voice, the deep and bitter frustration.

"And somebody's friend."

Martin nodded wearily. "I know. The friends who've kept you alive here, as you've kept them alive."

"I won't leave them." His voice was strong, but in the next second the defiance broke and his hands flew to his face again as he whispered, "But it's not an easy choice."

Martin held him again. "No. But I think it's the choice they'd want you to make, if they knew. Not your mother, perhaps, but certainly the General. And, I believe, Hedda. So in their name I'm going to leave you here. But in their name there's a condition, Franz."

"I don't have to agree to conditions." The bones in the thin rags moved under Martin's arm, shivering, and Martin felt awed by the strength in the boy's voice.

"Yes, you do. If you get clear of the camp, tomorrow night, I want you to make for the barn on the road into the village, alongside the railway. It's half a mile from here on the other side. I'll be there with a car."

"We don't know how things are going to turn out. I—"

"Give me your word, now, that you'll keep the rendezvous if you get clear. Or I'm taking you out of here in the morning." He waited.

"All right. I'll meet you there. If I can."

Martin got to his feet. "You're starting the attempt at three in the morning, you told me. I'll be there from that time onward." Franz stood up and Martin added, "This man I was asking about, in the Orderly Room—Ernst Kramer. Is he, in fact, dead?"

"No. We decided to save him if we could."

"Do you know where he is now?"

"Yes."

"Tell him to report to the gatehouse at first light tomorrow. I'm ordering his immediate release."

"He's pretty weak. We did our best, but—"

"I'll take care of him." He looked at the boy for the last time in the reflected light, memorizing the shaven head, the narrow bruised face, the skeletal body. They'd never manage it, tomorrow night, a half-starved rag-and-bone army running straight into the guns. But he knew they had to try. "Franz, if you change your mind before morning, be there at the gatehouse with Kramer."

"Look after him for us," Franz said, and Martin watched his thin lurching figure as it became lost in the shadows among the huts.

"You look quite smart, Herr Kramer. Quite smart."

Sergeant Steiger's small colorless eyes surveyed the crumpled, ill-fitting suit the stores had found for the man; the shirt had blood spots on the collar, faded to a rusty brown; the shoes were split, each of a different size.

Professor Kramer said nothing. The Sergeant had simply made a statement, requiring no answer. Kramer's mind was still trying to accept the idea that he was being released, but he had come far enough to believing it for terror to begin all over again, the terror of being told there was some kind of mistake, or of Sergeant Steiger's pouncing on an incorrect word or gesture and sending him back to his hut for later punishment. It was difficult, Kramer found, to stand perfectly still at attention; there seemed no strength left in his legs; but to relax his stance would be to show flagrant insubordination. . . .

"Down in the files as deceased, one day," Sergeant Steiger said softly through his fleshy lips, "and down for release, the next. Quite a busy time for you, Herr Kramer. But then, the Orderly Room files are never really reliable, are they?"

"No," Kramer said quickly, knowing he must agree.

The Sergeant raised his round pink face, widening his eyes. "No? Did you say No, *Herr* Kramer?"

"No, *Sergeant*." It came out on a breath.

"You didn't say *no*, Herr Kramer?" He put his round head on one side in elaborate puzzlement. "I could have sworn you said *no*, Herr Kramer."

Ernst Kramer closed his eyes as the terror mounted in him. The Sergeant had brought him here to play with him, that was all; he'd told them to fit him out with some old clothes, pretending he was to be released; it was just one of Sergeant Steiger's little jokes.

"Didn't you, in fact, say *no*, Herr Kramer?"

The prisoner tried to fathom out what he must say. "Yes, Sergeant, I did say no."

The small eyes glittered with amusement. "I thought you did. I thought I wasn't mistaken." Suddenly tired of the game he tapped the papers on his desk. "You are being released by order of Standartenführer Brinkmann of the Concentration Camp Inspectorate, with the approval, needless to say, of Kommandant Axen. That is most unusual, Herr Kramer. Most. The Gestapo has been informed, you see. In normal circumstances the Gestapo would decide whether a prisoner should be released or not. The SS are simply the custodians of those persons and sundry pigs whom the Gestapo wish incarcerated. Don't you find all this rather interesting, Herr Kramer?"

"Yes, Sergeant." His legs were so weak now that he felt himself swaying, and wondered if fainting in front of an SS noncommissioned officer would amount to insubordination. His head was beginning to swim. Perhaps none of this mattered; they were going to kill him anyway.

"I shall make immediate inquiries into this most unusual situation, Herr Kramer. I believe that Gestapo Headquarters in Berlin should be informed that a prisoner's release has been effected without, presumably, their orders." He tore off the top sheet of a pro forma and handed it to the prisoner. "Here is your release, Herr Kramer. I hope that in the few days of your liberty you'll speak well of this model institution we have here at Debno, where you have been treated with both consideration and clemency, as I'm sure you agree. Do you agree, Herr Kramer?"

"Yes, Sergeant."

"But of course you do." His fleshy lips moved appreciatively, tasting each word as he uttered it. "I'm quite sure, however, that when the Gestapo in Berlin have been informed of this patent error in the administration, they'll rectify it speedily, so that we can all look forward to seeing you back with us in a day or two."

28

"The name again?"

"Hedda von Gerlach."

"Nurse von Gerlach, do you mean?" The staff matron was frowning at the telephone. Personal calls for staff below matron's rank were strictly forbidden.

"Yes. Nurse von Gerlach."

"Who wishes to speak with her?"

"The SS Office of Security, Berlin."

"This is official business?"

"Of course. And our time, madam, is as valuable as yours."

"I will get her at once."

The Matron found Hedda in the staff room, sitting alone with a cup of half-cold ersatz coffee. She was a woman, the Matron had noted before, who kept herself to herself.

When Hedda went to the telephone she saw the red lamps winking in the ceiling again, the whole length of the corridor. That would be the fifth accident case for major surgery since she'd come on duty four hours ago. Everyone on the streets seemed to be going crazy, the way they drove. Or perhaps it was a domicile incident.

"Hello?"

"Hedda. Do you recognize my voice?"

316

She caught her breath. "Yes."

"Franz is alive and well. I saw him last night."

Her heart was thudding. "Where is—"

"Hedda, there's more to tell you. We must meet, as soon as possible."

"But—" She longed to say his name, to hear herself say it; but he'd warned her about that so often. "But I think they're—I mean, wherever I go, I think there's—"

"Yes. I know. But I can deal with that. Are you off duty this evening?"

In a moment she said, "No, there's a staff meeting." She must always leave her evenings free, in case Vogel telephoned, saying he was coming to see her. "But I'll be free after ten o'clock." He was always gone by nine.

"Ten o'clock, then, tonight. In the park between the Halen See and Trabenerstrasse. Opposite the island."

"Yes." It was a few minutes' walk from where she lived, which was obviously why he'd chosen it. "Yes. I'll be there." Her heart was thudding, thudding. "But be careful. Be very careful. Please."

"I will."

In the stuffy bar of the Gasthaus at Eberswalde, not far from the Polish frontier, Martin put down the receiver. It had taken him until noon to get Kramer to the airfield: Tempel had called for the rendezvous on the north side of the river, and the two nearest bridges had been clogged with military traffic moving north to the Danish frontier. The team at the rendezvous had started giving Kramer intravenous protein injections the minute they saw him; the man could hardly stand up. He was being flown direct to The Hague in a civilian plane, and should reach England tonight.

Tempel had been very quiet, shrunk into himself.

"Eckstein and Schütz are dead," Martin had told him.

"You are certain?"

"I've seen Gestapo files, one at Buchenwald, one at Sachsenhausen."

"So." Otto Tempel's voice was infinitely weary. "They were the last two. We have been lucky. Only two, out of our reach. With the death rate in the camps—" He shrugged. "And Kramer was the key man. You know that." His rimless glasses caught the light as he turned his head, watching the stream of amored cars along the road. "And finally, I have no further orders for you, Colonel Brinkmann."

They were sitting in Tempel's Adler coupé, at the edge of the freight yard at Eberswalde Bahnhof, with the March sky dark above the bridge. Tempel, thought Martin, must be older than he looked; or he had known Major Haslam and the others for longer than it seemed. The massacre at the house in Charlottenburg had shaken him, shaken his faith. His Teutonic sense of order hadn't prepared him for disaster.

"You've done what we asked you to do," he said in a tone bordering on disbelief. "I have signaled The Hague. I have asked them for your immediate withdrawal from the field, if possible through the lines here, though time looks short." He watched the military convoy that was approaching the bridge, its field-gray crews sitting high on the vehicles gazing ahead. Last evening the Führer had made a broadcast, speaking of "the coming challenge."

"I'll remain in contact," Martin told him.

"At the same number." His head went down again. "For as long as I am there. If we can't get you out through the lines here, we shall get you out through Switzerland." He looked at Martin with narrowed eyes. "You were a success, Colonel Brinkmann. I told Haslam you would fail. I said you hated these people too much, that you would lose your control. I was wrong."

Martin had left him soon afterward, driving through the town to clear the worst of the traffic and head south for Berlin. It was then he'd decided to telephone Hedda in advance. She had to be told that Franz was alive. That he was likely to die within twelve hours from now couldn't be said over a telephone: he must see her and try to explain the unacceptable—that he'd decided to leave her brother at Debno, for his own sake. When Franz von Gerlach had started to put up anti-Nazi posters all over Berlin, it hadn't been a student's prank or a pocket crusader's cry for recognition; it had been a statement made in the name of justice and made at the risk of his life. In the few months since then, Franz had matured into the kind of man whose suffering had tempered the spirit inside that bruised and emaciated body to the point where rage had taken slow fire. The knowledge had come to this boy-turned-man that if he were ever going to live with himself, if life were granted him, he would have to wipe out the humiliation of all they had done to him in the camps, of all they had done to the men who were now his friends, and to Germany, which was his country and which he loved. *What are you doing,* Schroeder the physicist had asked Martin, *to Germany?* They had walked together from the cattle train across the frosted stones last February, beneath the winter stars. *You're tearing down this country's pretensions to civilization, can't you people see that?* Schroeder, a grown man, had kept his spirit untouched by the horror that had become his daily life, and had been ready to challenge an officer in SS uniform, to accuse him of high treason.

Franz von Gerlach was such another, already a grown man with his father's courage burning in him, adding to the fierce heat of the rage that was keeping his flesh and bones alive inside their prisoner's rags. He wasn't in a mood to let a savior take him from his friends and lead him by the hand to safety; he was in a mood to seize his own deliverance, in hot blood and in their faithful company, pitting the last of his strength against the brute savages who thought they could subject him. For him there was no other way to live, and no other way to die.

Would Hedda understand? Perhaps. *I want you to*

know something, she had told him as they had stood close together on the S-bahn train. *I'm proud of what he did. Very proud.*

There was another reason why Martin had to see her. The news of the mass escape from Debno camp would reach Gestapo Headquarters within the hour, and the ringleaders would be named. Whether Franz lived or died, the man tormenting Hedda von Gerlach would have no mercy on her. Before the escape was launched at Debno tomorrow morning, Martin would have to get her out of Berlin and into hiding.

Touching her nipples with rouge, she thought of marriage.

The three photographs were propped up against the bottom edge of the mirror in the bathroom, where she sat now. The one of Franz with the SS guard standing over a prisoner in the background, his club raised. The one of Franz with the prisoner standing next to him, holding his face while the blood trickled from his fingers. And the one—the worst one—of Franz facing the camera and trying to smile. To smile.

She used more foundation cream, to hide the lines that had started to form in her face, weeks ago, months ago. Her skin was loosening; at twenty-eight she was losing her looks. Frau Hartnagel never left the subject alone. *But Hedda, my dear, my darling, you are working too hard! And you are not eating enough!* Wringing her plump operatic hands, rounding her heavy-lidded eyes, their lashes caked with mascara. *Your gentleman must take you out more often, my dear.* He *has no problem with the rationing, in the restaurants* he *goes to!* Her rich voice vibrating with roguish intrigue. No other house in the whole of Grünewald, surely, was honored with regular visits from a high-ranking officer of the Gestapo!

Hedda studied her face in the mirror, deciding to add a hint of silver-blue to her lids. Tonight she must play the whore, the most beautiful, the most practiced whore in all Berlin. She must writhe in ecstasy, she must moan for him, assuring him that he was the greatest lover in the world.

Then there might be a chance, when she proposed.

It was Frau Hartnagel who had put the idea into her mind.

And will there be wedding bells, my dear, when the gentleman is ready? A peal of operatic laughter, her palate glistening. She would be invited, of course, as little Hedda's most devoted friend and patroness (the rent for this particular apartment was reduced). A splendid and glittering wedding, with a Gestapo guard of honor and banners flying!

Hedda varnished her nails, glancing at the little ormolu clock. He was coming at eight, in fifteen minutes. She felt the familiar creeping of her skin as she waited, the increase of saliva prompted by her disgust. He liked the black lace negligée, and no perfume; she would oblige him. Tonight, if she could, she would save her brother.

It was a week ago when she had caught sight of her face in a mirror at the hospital and realized that her brother's safety was being gradually compromised. Her looks were going, as the stress and nervous fatigue mounted; and the moment she lost her attraction for Superintendent Vogel, Franz would lose his protector. She was sleeping only a few hours each night, spending the rest of the time walking to and fro in the cage of the apartment, trying to think, trying to think, trying to think how to bring this horror to an end. Whatever she did, however courageous, however desperate, Franz would suffer. If she fled the city and found a refuge somewhere, if she defied the Creature—even if she killed him with the bright-honed scalpel she used on him so often in her mind—Franz would suffer. But if she did nothing, if she simply continued to make her

body available to this immature monster, Franz would
suffer before long, when the day came for Vogel to
look at her critically and note the circles under her
eyes, the droop of the mouth, the ravages of stress and
fatigue.

There was still time to do something, if she were
ready to face it. She must persuade him to marry her.
It would be dangerous to make conditions, to demand
her brother's liberty in return: Vogel must believe she
wanted this marriage for its own sake. Then he would
order Franz's release: his pride wouldn't let it be known
that he had a young brother-in-law languishing in the
camps. Later, when this war was over, or even sooner,
if the war went on, she and Franz could leave Berlin
and go into hiding somewhere, and the long nightmare
would be over.

But how did one propose to an impotent sadist?

*We've known each other a long time now, Karl.
I'm—I'm beginning to miss you, in between your visits.*
Her skin crawled. *I think we've come to understand
each other by now, don't you? If you'd care to think
about it, Karl, I'd like to—to grace your household,
officially.* Oh God, how stilted, how arch! *To share
your life, officially. I realize a young woman isn't
supposed to do the proposing, but . . .* Her mouth was
turning sour with self-disgust. She must keep the photographs in the forefront of her mind, every minute.
Franz, in the photographs, in the one where he was
trying to smile. Was he at this moment falling under the
blow of a club, while she was making such a fuss about
offering her precious body to a man she found unattractive, to a man who, in fact, had never hurt it?

Five minutes to eight.

She slipped the gold and amethyst ring on to her
finger. He liked her to wear it. The work of Herr
Gronowetter of Buchenwald, and quite exquisite. *They
keep the guard dogs short of food, you see, so that*

they don't become lazy. It took four men with whips to keep the dog away.

For a while she'd hoped that Martin would somehow be able to free her brother, in his role of an SS Colonel. But this afternoon when he'd telephoned, that hope had died. *Franz is alive,* he had told her. But his voice had been sober, premonitory. The rest he would tell when they met, in only two hours from now. But it wouldn't be good news.

So tonight she must save Franz herself.

She was half naked, the little slut, posing for him under the light. *Did she think he needed a whore?*

He closed the door carefully behind him, and dropped his gloves on to the pier table. He didn't remove his cap.

"Put something on," he said curtly. "Cover yourself."

Surprised, she reached for the rose patterned dressing gown.

Did she think she was irresistible? He'd change her mind about that.

His dark eyes were perfectly expressionless, while the cold fury consumed him. He'd kept it under control, at first; then gradually he had come to realize what she had done to him.

"It was good of you to receive me, Fräulein, considering how busy you are with other visitors."

Hedda stood frozen. So she'd left it too late, and Franz was lost.

"Visitors?" She was able to say it almost calmly. Martin had been here only once, and for a few minutes.

"I think I told you, Fräulein, that I preferred you not to have men friends." His black leather boots creaked as he took a step toward her.

"Of course you did. And I haven't any. You are all I—"

"You have been meeting a man. A Colonel of the

SS. You have been seen with him on more than one occasion. And I notice, Fräulein, that your face is losing its color."

He was taking a risk, he knew.

Luftig had told him: *I'm therefore asking you, officially, to leave Fräulein von Gerlach alone.*

"You have disobeyed me, Fräulein. You have deceived me and betrayed me." He took another step closer, gratified by the shock in her eyes. "Before I inform you what will now happen to your brother, do you wish to say anything?"

He took another step toward her, then his black-uniformed body tilted and the whole room spun, and she was aware of the smell of carpeting. At some time—she did not know when—there was a cold shock against her face, and the light in the room seemed to splinter against her closed eyes. Then slowly she opened them, and looked straight into the dark reptilian eyes of the man in the Italian brocade chair. As the memory of what he had said rushed back into her mind, she almost passed out again. *Before I inform you what will now happen to your brother, do you wish to say anything?*

She got slowly to her knees, and felt water trickling against her neck; he must have splashed her face with it; there was a glass from the bathroom on the stool beside her.

"I'm glad you have recovered your senses, Fräulein. I have no time to waste this evening. I had asked you, if you recall, whether you wished to say anything."

She felt so cold. So cold.

He was waiting, the fingers of one pale hand drumming on the other. The silence in the room was broken only by the ticking of the little clock.

"Yes." She found it difficult to put her thoughts into the right words, in the right order. All she could see was the face of Franz, in the photographs. "Yes." Still on her knees in front of Vogel, in the unconscious attitude of prayer, she asked him, "Is there anything, anything in the world, that I can do to save my brother?"

The drumming of his fingers stopped, as he appeared to consider. It was a long time before he spoke.

"Perhaps. We are trying to find this Colonel friend of yours. If you chose to help us, I would order your brother's immediate release."

29

LOWESTOFT, ENGLAND, 25 MARCH 1940

It was blowing a gale across the North Sea by nightfall
and the East Coast lifeboat services had been called
out three times in the last three hours, one boat taking
the crew off a seagoing barge under sail before she went
down.

Four of the reception committee had reached the
clifftop landing strip an hour ago, alerted by an emergency signal from Bletchley. One of them—the king's
equerry—knew that this must be Kramer coming across:
they hadn't expected to receive anyone else from The
Hague before it shut down. Kramer was a key man,
and the last.

"They'll have diverted this one, surely."

They stood huddled against the wind, watching the
east.

"Bletchley said he was coming down here."

One of them tried to relight his pipe, but gave up.

"Bletchley can't know what it's like."

"The pilot had to divert in any case. A pack of MEs
had started hunting for him."

They listened to the windsock tugging at its cleat.

"All I hope is that he doesn't hit the hangar."

No one spoke further. Later, in between the wind
gusts, they thought they heard the sound of an engine,

326

and strained their eyes to to look for the Lysander, one or two of them believing they could see its shape above the cliffs. But the sound faded out, and soon afterward the door of the radio hut banged open and a man came trotting across to them, his head lowered against the wind.

"No luck this time," he told them. "He's down in the sea."

The night editor of the Lowestoft *Evening Herald* looked at the piece of paper.

"What's this?" He'd thought everyone had gone home.

"I just got it myself." The cub reporter stood panting, his cheeks flushed from the night air. "Got a chum, down at the coastguard station." He dared all. "Can I have a byline, chief?" It would be his first.

The editor ignored that as he read the story. *Reports have been confirmed that late this evening an unidentified aircraft went down in the sea not far from the coast. Boat 3 of the Lowestoft Lifeboat Service, called out by the Coastguards, was successful in taking the occupants off the plane before it sank.*

The editor picked up a telephone, asking for the special extension number. He read the story, nodded a couple of times and rang off.

"We can't print it," he told the cub. "You'd get shot as a spy. Listen, there's a story about old Mrs. Fawcett-Jones, the lady who hit an air raid warden over the head with an umbrella tonight, thinking he was a German parachutist. You want a byline on that?"

30

BERLIN, 25 MARCH 1940

The night was clear overhead, but a light mist was creeping from the surface of the lake across the parkland, moving between the few trees and masking their outlines. Here and there, starlight still penetrated where the mist was less dense, and from the northwest edge of the lake the little island could be seen. It was approaching ten o'clock.

The silence in the park was accentuated by the sound of the traffic along the Kurfürsten Allee, as the citizens of Berlin sought comfort and distraction among the restaurants and nightclubs that were still doing good business. Germany was officially at war, but nothing had happened since its declaration, except the invasion of Poland. Berliners, having prepared themselves for the onslaught of air bombardment, felt in a strange way cheated. Doomsday was to be delayed for a while, and the city passed its days and nights in a worsening state of nerves.

Most of the vehicles streaming along the Kurfürsten Allee were taxis, but earlier, just before nine o'clock, a succession of dark official cars and black vans with small barred windows had begun closing in on the park surrounding the Halen See. Other vehicles had arrived along Trabenerstrasse, northwest of the lake, and from its neighboring streets: Halenseestrasse to the northeast and Erbacherstrasse to the southwest. By half past nine, some thirty such vechicles had taken up station in unobtrusive locations around the park, and one hundred and twelve armed Gestapo officers had infiltrated the park itself, using the mist and the trees for cover and deploying themselves among the shrubs at the periphery.

The decoy had not yet appeared.

Superintendent Vogel was standing on a grassy mound not far from the water's edge, southwest of the neck of the Halen See, where the sparse trees gave cover but permitted observation. Until thirty minutes ago, the Superintendent had not known that a decoy would in fact be necessary. He kept his fieldglasses raised to his eyes most of the time, to study the terrain between the water of the lake and Trabenerstrasse, opposite the little island. Even with his night lenses he failed to see more than two or three of the one hundred and twelve men who were now in or around the park, so effectively were they using their cover and the advantageous creeping of the mist. He was very pleased with them. An officer of sound training and long experience, he knew that it was now impossible for anyone to enter the park and leave it again of their own free will.

Once again he checked his luminous wristwatch, noting the time at five minutes before ten. He raised the fieldglasses again.

Martin had come into the park from the southeast, driving through Bismarkplatz and leaving the car halfway along Schinklestrasse, then crossing the Kurfürsten Allee on foot and rounding the lake at the north end. He was now standing beneath a linden tree a hundred yards from the rendezvous point.

He'd seen four Gestapo vehicles on his way here from Bismarckplatz on foot, but that wasn't unusual at this hour, when the streets were crowded and people were leaving the restaurants for the cabarets and the night-clubs; it was a good time for impromptu raids.

Hedda would almost certainly be followed, as before. If there were one man, he would deal with him after Hedda had gone. If there were two, he'd keep his distance and use caution. He must be absolutely sure that their meeting would leave Hedda in no danger from the Gestapo.

She was coming now, walking quickly from the edge of the park alongside Trabenerstrasse, her dark hair flying out as she hurried toward the rendezvous point. A man in plain clothes came fifty yards behind, his figure emerging from the mist. When she stopped walking, and stood uncertainly by the water's edge, he moved toward cover and waited.

She was looking around her, but Martin waited two minutes to watch for a second man to appear. None came.

It was three minutes past ten when he left his cover and went down to the lake's edge, calling Hedda's name softly as he neared, so as not to startle her. She swung around and stared at him, and he saw she was not Hedda, but someone like her.

Beyond her he saw a man in uniform, and then another. Turning, he saw three more, then five. They came from the mist, from the trees, from everywhere, twenty of them, fifty of them, more, their revolvers drawn as they closed in on him.

Soon after 10:30 the same evening, a nurse came into the waiting room at the Accident and Emergency Care Clinic in the Schmargendorf district, adjacent to the Grünewald.

"She will be all right now, Frau Hartnagel."

"She will be all right?" The thick-bodied woman was out of the chair in an instant, despite her weight. "How do you know she will be all right?" She stared at the nurse, her heavy makeup smudged and tear-streaked.

She had been here since nine o'clock, when the patient had been brought in by ambulance.

"Because I know what I am saying," the young nurse told her evenly. "We induced vomiting immediately, and she's been on forced liquids until now. She is out of danger."

"She is out of danger?" The tears welled anew from the encrusted eyes. "I must see her, then!"

"I'm sorry, Frau Hartnagel. You are not a relative, I believe. You may return in a few hours, if you wish. Meanwhile we shall need a corroborative statement from you in writing, for the police. It seems there's no question that she attempted suicide."

"My poor lamb! My poor child! It was lucky I found her like that, so lucky! There was no answer, you see, to my knocking, yet I knew she was in. I knocked and knocked, and then I used my key—I am her landlady, you see, her patroness—"

"It was lucky, Frau Hartnagel, yes. You should go home, as soon as the desk clerk has your statement, and rest yourself. It was a shock for you."

"Such a shock, I cannot tell you! I am like a mother to her! She—"

"The desk clerk is along the corridor and down one flight of stairs. I'll repeat that the patient is out of danger, officially. Good night, Frau Hartnagel."

31

BERLIN, 25 MARCH 1940

There were five men in Superintendent Vogel's office at Gestapo Headquarters: Vogel, the SS Colonel, a stenographer and two armed guards with drawn revolvers. Two more armed guards were stationed in the corridor outside. The clock on the wall showed 10:17. The arrested officer had been brought straight here from the Halen See.

"Do you wish to smoke?"

"What?"

Vogel repeated his invitation, in the same silky tones. The man hardly seemed to know what he was talking about. He looked like death, his face drawn and his eyes, unnaturally bright, in great hollows.

"No."

They had taken away his revolver and ceremonial dagger. Four armed guards were sufficient, even for Der Jäger. And an SS-Standartenführer was, after all, an SS-Standartenführer, and for the moment would be treated as such. Luftig would have insisted on that.

"You may sit down, if you wish." Vogel moved behind his desk, taking off his cap and smoothing his thin dark hair. Luftig, yes. But he was not going to telephone his good friend Luftig with this news until the morning. Tonight the prisoner was his.

"I'll stand." The Colonel was restless, his bright eyes everywhere except on the armed guards—they didn't appear to worry him. "What is your name?" he asked Vogel suddenly, in a tone of impatience.

"I introduced myself, if you remember." The tone was still silky, but hardening.

"I have a great deal on my mind."

"Superintendent Vogel." The flat of his hand came down on the desk. "Please be good enough to remember my name in future, Colonel Brinkmann."

The prisoner frowned abstractedly. "Vogel, yes. I'll give you one hour." He looked at his wristwatch, comparing it with the clock on the wall. "Your clock here is two minutes slow."

Vogel leaned back, watching the man. "You will give me one hour?"

"It's all I can spare."

Vogel glanced at the stenographer, wondering whether to have this statement noted. It probably wasn't worth it. First he would shake this bastard out of his skin; then his statements would be more relevant.

"Do you know how we found you?"

"What? Yes. You used a decoy."

"Ah. And do you know why we had to use a decoy?"

"No." The Colonel was pacing again, watching the floor.

"We had to use a decoy, Colonel Brinkmann, because Fräulein von Gerlach, your mistress, was unavailable at the time. She had just committed suicide."

The Colonel's step faltered slightly as he turned at the wall to pace back past the desk, but he didn't raise his head. "Poor woman. Did you witness this, Herr Vogel?" He was looking suddenly, at the Superintendent, his eyes oddly bright.

"Do you think I'm trying to deceive you?"

"You might be. I'm not unconversant with the workings of the Gestapo mind."

It was how they'd described him, Vogel thought. Tall,

Aryan, and arrogant. A typical fucking SS autocrat. And he was trying to provoke him, that was obvious, even to the workings of the Gestapo mind. But he .wouldn't succeed. Der Jäger had lost, and he, Vogel, had won. This was the ferocious assassin the whole of the SS had begun to fear; and he was in Vogel's hands. This was the mysterious lover who had flitted in and out of Fräulein von Gerlach's tawdry little life, while she'd been the protégée of a Superintendent of the Gestapo; and he was in *his* hands. And it was going to be very difficult to provoke him. Vogel felt something approaching tolerance tonight, as he often did when speaking with a man who was shortly to die.

"I'm not trying to deceive you," he said evenly. "The report I received was that Fräulein von Gerlach had swallowed a bottle of aspirins. A bottle of a hundred, if I recall. That would be the standard size, I assume."

"A hundred?" The bright blue stare considered. "Yes, I suppose that's the standard size. Poor woman. Was she found in time?" The tone was indifferent, as if he felt he was expected to take an interest.

"Whether or not Fräulein von Gerlach is dead or alive," Vogel told him equably, "hardly matters. If she ever recovers, I shall be committing her to Ravensbruck Concentration Camp in any case."

The Colonel glanced at his watch again. "We are wasting time. You can hardly expect me—"

"Don't you realize she betrayed you?"

The stenographer looked up. He was a thin man with a small moustache, his uniform slightly too big for him. His heart had begun beating faster. He had attended many interrogations with Superintendent Vogel, and lived in abject fear of his eyes and his voice and his very name. He had seen the Superintendent intending to keep his patience with someone, and then failing. The stenographer, whose name was Fassbender, didn't know which tone of voice filled him with more terror: the silky one, or this one with the ring of menace.

"I gave her a choice," Vogel said. "Your life, or her brother's. She chose her brother's."

"Hardly surprising." The Colonel's tone was cool.

The Superintendent put both his hands flat on the desk in front of him, a habit he had learned long ago when he realized he was losing control; Luftig had taught him to do it, unknowingly. Luftig had the same infuriating calm that this autocratic bastard was showing. More than calm; a strange kind of indifference. There was something wrong.

"Colonel Brinkmann, how well do you know—did you know this woman?"

"Woman? Oh, I met her on the S-bahn one night, a few months ago. We—"

"How often have you seen her?"

"A few times. Once at the Tiergarten Bahnhof. I went to her apartment for a few minutes, to take her a little gift—she's rather a lonely soul."

The pale hands on the desk remained still. "You haven't enjoyed carnal relations with Fräulein von Gerlach?"

The Colonel swung around and his eyes flickered. "You'll confine your questions to the matter in hand, Herr Vogel." Then at once he relaxed, smiling vaguely. "No, there was nothing of that sort in our brief relationship. She's got a young brother in the camps, you know. She wanted me to get him released, but I explained it was a matter for the Gestapo, not the SS."

"It is indeed. For your information, Standartenführer Brinkmann, I personally ordered that her brother should be placed in the *Besonder* category, so that he should come to no harm." Watching the man, he thought he saw a flicker come into his eyes again, but wasn't sure. It was difficult to know what the devil he was thinking.

"She must have been very grateful to you." He was

turning again, this time pacing away from the desk, and Vogel could no longer see his expression. "No one expects that kind of consideration from the gentlemen of the Gestapo."

"Nor from the gentlemen of the SS-Tottenkopfverbände," said Vogel sharply, nettled.

Touché, my friend."

The Superintendent said carefully, "Since your relationship with Fräulein von Gerlach was so . . . inconsequential, why did you feel it necessary to murder two of my officers?"

The Colonel swung around, astonished. "Your officers? But that's absurd!"

"One in an alley in the Grünewald district three weeks ago on March the fifth, and one at Tiergarten Bahnhof eleven days ago on March the fourteenth."

"They were Gestapo men?"

"They were."

"How was I to know? They looked such a couple of shady characters I thought they were after Fräulein von Gerlach. She was a damned pretty girl." He resumed his pacing, and came to a halt face to face with one of the guards, who brought up his gun into the aiming position, while Fassbender watched in frozen consternation. The muzzle was two inches from the SS Colonel's chest, and three inches from his heart, and the guard's finger was crooked on the trigger.

The room had become very quiet. The other guard had taken a step forward, also bringing up his gun. He glanced toward Superintendent Vogel for instructions. Vogel sat motionless, trying to work out what was happening. Was the Colonel deliberately provoking the guard? Was he thinking of attacking him, for some lunatic reason? He mustn't be allowed to do that. He was Vogel's prize pigeon, ready for presentation to Deputy Commissioner Luftig, an example of how effective the Gestapo could be—and Superintendent Vogel particularly—when it set out to capture a wanted man.

This would teach Luftig that spiders weren't all that clever, when it came to the push.

"Colonel Brinkmann," Vogel said softly, "you will cease provoking my officers in that fashion. They are very dangerous."

The guard was holding the bright stare of the Colonel, the sweat starting to trickle from under his arms. There was something unnerving about this bastard, and he wasn't sure what to do. He couldn't look at the Superintendent for any kind of signal, and if the Colonel came another inch closer he'd blow his chest out of his uniform; otherwise he might try grabbing the gun and using it against the Superintendent. This was Der Jäger, the man who'd slaughtered all those generals. The sweat from his right hand began moistening his trigger finger; he wished to Christ the man would go away before something happened. His eyes weren't human, they were like a beast's deep in a jungle, unblinking. The guard could smell his own sweat: he knew it was the smell of fear. Standing here with a loaded Mauser in his fist he was afraid of the man standing in front of him, unarmed and at point-blank range.

"What is your name?" The Colonel's voice broke the silence so abruptly that the guard felt his finger tighten on the trigger. He relaxed it, letting out a breath.

"Streck."

The eyes of the Colonel narrowed slightly. "Streck," he nodded. "What are you holding that thing for, Streck? It's hardly civilized." Suddenly he turned away, and the upright wooden chair on which Fassbender was perched gave a creak as his body flinched.

As Superintendent Vogel drew his hands from the surface of his desk they left sweat prints. "Colonel Brinkmann," he said with an edge of uneasiness, "did you kill SS-General von Fleig?"

The Colonel swung around so fast that each of the guards brought his gun up into the aim again. *"Yes!"*

Vogel got to his feet.

"And SS-General von Kassel?"

"Yes! And Heidel! And Maihof!" He took three rapid paces and reached the desk, halting within arm's length of the Superintendent. *"And I shall kill more! I shall kill more of those traitorous hounds, do you understand? Do you understand, Vogel?"* His stare was bright, and the sweat was springing on his face. His voice reached the pitch of frenzy as he brought his right fist down on the desk with a force that shook the inkwell. *"Do you understand that I shall go on killing every treacherous enemy of the Führer until he's safe again?"*

Vogel watched him with his eyes narrowed, seeing the naked rage on the man's face. He signaled to the stenographer to start taking notes.

"The Führer?"

"The Führer." The Colonel drew himself up suddenly, his heels coming together, his eyes flashing. "His life is in danger. *Now do you understand?"*

In the brief silence, Fassbender's pencil raced over the notepad.

"These men were conspirators?"

"Of course!"

"What evidence have you that—"

"Evidence?" The feverish stare remained for a moment; then a slow, cunning smile came to his face, and Vogel felt a sudden chill touching his nerves. "You think I'm going to hand you the *evidence,* so that you can start interfering? A *Gestapo* man? Don't you realize this is the Führer I'm talking about—*my* Führer? The Father of the New Germany? The Creator of the Third Reich?" His voice rang stridently against the walls. "Do you know the sacred creed of the SS, Vogel?" His heels snapped together again and he threw the Deutschgruss salute. *"I swear to Thee, Adolf Hitler, as Führer and Chancellor of the Third Reich, Loyalty and Bravery! I vow to Thee and to the Superiors whom*

Thou shalt appoint, Obedience unto Death! So help me God!" His stare was fixed on the wall above Vogel's head, on something no one else in the room could see. Then he looked sharply down at Vogel. *"Heil Hitler!"* The salute was thrown again, his whole body galvanic. "Do you not say *Heil Hitler? Do you just stand* there, Vogel, while I'm saluting our Führer? *Heil Hitler! Heil Hitler! Heil Hitler!"*

Vogel had moved back until his shoulders were touching the wall. He'd glanced at the guards and they were ready to shoot this maniac if he tried to attack. This was Der Jäger, and he'd already killed twenty-eight men, some of them with his bare hands.

"Fassbender," he said as levelly as he could. "Bring in the other two guards."

"You want more guards?" Brinkmann's voice was shrill in the confines of the room. *"More guards, damn you? It's the Führer you should be guarding—the Führer!"* He took one step toward Vogel past the side of the desk and the guards squinted along the sights of their revolvers, their fingers tensing against the triggers. Then Brinkmann's face went into a spasm of agony and he doubled up, his hands against his stomach. His eyes were squeezed shut and his mouth was open. "Vogel . . ." he whispered through the spittle on his lips, "get Heydrich . . . on the telephone. Get Heydrich, for God's sake . . . I must tell him who the others are . . . the others . . ."

Vogel released a slow breath in the silence, looking at the guards. "Two of you keep your guns drawn and shoot this man instantly if he looks like getting out of control. The other two make ready to take him to the cells." Brinkmann was straightening up, using the corner of the desk for support, his eyes coming open painfully.

"Heydrich," he said in soft desperation. "Get Heydrich."

"Colonel Brinkmann, I am going to bring you a

doctor. Meanwhile, will you make your full confession in writing, to murdering SS-Generals von Fleig, von Kassel, Heidel and Maihof, and others?"

"Confession . . . ?" The man's eyes were glazed, trying to focus. "Confession? Yes. Yes. They were— they were going to kill the Führer . . . my Führer . . . so I killed them first . . . you see . . ." His eyes closed wearily and his head went down.

"Take him now," Vogel said quietly. "Be careful with him. He could still be dangerous." He watched Brinkmann go through the doorway like a man dead on his feet, with two of the guards supporting him. "Fassbender, get hold of Dr. Toller immediately. Give him my respects and ask him to check the prisoner for signs of a weak heart."

"At once, Herr Superintendent!"

Vogel sat down and telephoned the night office of Deputy Commissioner Luftig at Greater Berlin Police Headquarters, leaving a message for delivery to him the moment he arrived in the morning.

Greetings! I have Der Jäger in custody for you. He is, as I surmised, a homicidal maniac. Karl Vogel.

The eye glittered for a moment at the small square peephole, then vanished.

Martin watched the line of light below the steel door of the cell, and the shadow of the guard's feet as he passed. The light in his cell was too bright, but there was no way of switching it off from inside. The guard had been passing at fifteen-minute intervals, and it was now midnight.

A state of physical and mental exhaustion, Dr. Toller had written on his report, putting away his stethoscope and blood-pressure kit. He had prescribed rest and a sedative. Martin had drunk the half-glass of water, but spat out the pill two minutes later when the doctor had gone. The writing of the confession had taken longer, almost half an hour; then he had lain on the narrow bed and begun thinking, alone in the cell.

Physical and mental exhaustion, yes. That was partly because the role of Cyrano de Bergerac was far easier than the role he'd assumed tonight: his life had depended on the performance. At the least it had prevented interrogation; if Vogel had put him under the bright light and the rubber truncheons he wouldn't have held out. In the last ten days he'd slept only a few hours, and the psychological strain of the repeated killings had worked on his nerves to the point where in all truth he thought he was going mad. Inside Martin Brinkmann's SS uniform with its Death Head insignia was Martin Benedict, an ordinary man increasingly exposed to extraordinary stress. Of late he'd begun doubting his true identity.

A voice came into the silence, but from nowhere close. Tonight the basement of Gestapo Headquarters was quiet, except for the footsteps of the guards. An hour ago a man had been screaming, three cells away on the other side of the corridor, screaming obscenities at first, then defiance, and finally the names of those who might perhaps help him in the last minutes: Jesus Christ, Almighty God, until it had ended in gibberish and whimpering. But since then it had been quiet.

There were two guards in the corridor. He'd listened to them talking. One had a cold, and blew his nose every few minutes. The other had a rather high voice, and was fond of complaining that he was on duty tonight because "Erich hadn't turned up." They both wore holstered police revolvers.

Vogel. So this was the Gestapo officer Hedda had told him about. *I personally ordered that her brother should be put in the Besonder category.* Martin had known then.

Hedda. Was she alive?

Don't you realize she betrayed you?

Of course. He had realized it when the girl in the park had turned her head and shown him the face of a stranger. Betrayed? Not really. She'd chosen between someone she hardly knew and the brother she loved. But perhaps she'd found it difficult to help to trap him in the park. A hundred aspirins had been her only escape.

Had anyone found her?

She lived alone.

And even if she recovered, Vogel would send her to Ravensbruck.

The slow footsteps paused again outside the door, and the eye glittered in the small square peephole, and in a moment vanished.

Martin checked his watch and saw 12:15. It was morning, and in less than three hours Franz von Gerlach and his friends would storm the gates at Debno, a hundred kilometers from Berlin across the Polish frontier, and die summarily in freedom outside the wire, instead of slowly in captivity. And if Franz managed, by sheer chance, to run as far as the barn halfway to the village, Martin would not be there to help him. And no one would ever know that in trying to save her brother's life, Hedda had cost him his last chance.

At 12:30 one of the guards put his eye to the peephole in the door of Cell 9 and saw the SS Colonel lying across the narrow bed with his eyes and mouth wide open and blood oozing from his slashed wrists. The guard shouted to his colleague and went in.

32

DEBNO, POLAND, 26 MARCH 1940

Just before 12:30 A.M. Prisoner 937 Heinrich Schmidt
left his portion of the communal bunks in B Block,
making no sound, and passed through the wide doorway at the north end and into the open air.

Since the order to retire at nine o'clock last evening,
Schmidt had not slept. The decision he had had to
make was a difficult one, and it had tormented him
as he had lain awake, hour after hour. Finally he had
decided that it was any man's first duty to survive, at
whatever cost to his fellow men, since it was a natural
law. Whether or not he was right about this was of
no practical consequence. Once his decision was made,
he acted on it.

The starlight was bright above the dried mud of the
main compound, and for a minute or two his shadow
followed him, then swung alongside as he turned between the barrack block and the extermination chamber,
moving at a steady pace toward the nearest guard
house. The bittersweet smell of charred flesh was on
the air, and for a moment Prisoner Schmidt forgot
where he was, and could smell only meat cooking; he
began salivating and the image of roast beef came to
his mind, surrounded by succulent vegetables; then
the hallucination faded, and he remembered where the

smell was coming from, and had to stop, leaning against the corner of a hut to vomit bile, which was all that was in his stomach. When he felt better he straightened up and lurched on, his decision unaltered. On the contrary, the incident had proved to him that if he stayed in this camp any longer he'd lose his reason.

SS-Corporal Hoepner was in Guardroom No. 7, near the rear gates of the compound leading to the crema-tion pits in the meadow. He was writing a letter to his brother Viktor, to tell him he should join the SS and become a real man, as he had. The life in the camps, he said, was cushy; you wanted for nothing, there was a chance of very good pickings every day from the new arrivals—who would give you a gold bracelet or a watch for a mug of water, after the long train journey —and you could sometimes get at some of the nice-looking Polish girls, the night before they "listened to the violin," and take them into the meadow for an hour. The Corporal went on to explain what he meant by "listening to the violin," saying how beautifully the Kommandant played.

He was on the third page of the letter when there was a tapping at the door. Puzzled, he looked up. An SS man would open the door without knocking, while no prisoner would ever approach a guardroom, for fear of being beaten.

"Come in!" he called brusquely.

And there was Prisoner Schmidt, standing in front of him in his torn rag of a shirt, bracing himself to say something. The Corporal eyed him with distaste.

"What the fuckin' hell are you doin' here, you shitty old swine?"

"Corporal," the man said, shutting his red-rimmed eyes for a moment as if something were giving him pain, "I've come to tell you that some of the prisoners are going to try breaking out of the camp at three o'clock." He paused to get his breath. "I can give you their names."

Corporal Hoepner tilted his chair, eyeing the old scarecrow with interest. "Break out of the camp? That sounds rather ambitious. You sure you're not drunk, you stinking pig, or out of your stinking mind?"

Prisoner Schmidt cupped his hands in front of his face, trying to stop the coughing that had been shaking his bones for the last few days. "I can give you the details, Corporal. You'll find I'm right. But please tell the Kommandant I warned you in time. Put in a good word for me, Corporal. I want to ask for my release, for good conduct."

Hoepner straightened his chair and took a pencil. "Might even get it," he said with a grunt. "Right, gimme the names of the ringleaders."

"Kurt Wolff, Willi Helm and Franz Gerlach."

33

BERLIN, 26 MARCH 1940

In Gestapo Headquarters the guard bent over the limp form of the prisoner in Cell 9, putting his hand inside the tunic to feel for the heartbeat. The last he saw were the two bloodied hands flashing upward toward his throat, and the murderous eyes of Der Jäger.

His colleague, the one with the cold, came along the corridor at a run, alerted by the first guard's shout. Sliding to a halt in the doorway of Cell 9, he saw his colleague sprawled on the floor with blood on his throat and his eyeballs protruding in a fishlike stare, and the SS Colonel standing there with a police-model revolver in his hand.

"Don't move."

The guard had never seen such a look in a man's eyes, and a shiver went through him. He stood perfectly still as the officer reached with his free hand and pulled the gun from its holster.

"Where are Superintendent Vogel's quarters?"

The guard moistened his lips, then found his breath. "On the fourth floor, east wing."

"Turn around."

As the guard obeyed, one of the revolvers was rammed into his spine with such force that blue light

346

burst inside his head and he almost fainted with the pain.

"Take me there."

Superintendent Vogel was not yet asleep, though he had retired to his quarters an hour ago. He found it impossible to stop thinking about tomorrow, when Deputy Commissioner Luftig would enter his office and find that message waiting for him; when it would become known throughout the Gestapo, throughout the SS and the Greater Berlin Police Department that he, Superintendent Karl Vogel, had personally tracked down the infamous Der Jäger and arrested him.

There would be special dispatches sent to SS-General Heydrich, to Reichsführer Himmler, perhaps even to the Führer himself. The SS had lived in terror of the man since the bloody assassination of von Fleig, and much amusement had arisen among the ranks of the despised Gestapo following reports that at least a dozen SS generals had requested bodyguards in addition to their aides.

Tomorrow was to be a most notable day.

The last thing he had done before retiring was to sign an order for the release of Prisoner 383 Gerlach from Debno Camp. A few minutes beforehand, he had received a report from his patrols in the Grünewald district that Fräulein von Gerlach had been discharged from the Accident and Emergency Care Clinic in Schmargendorf shortly after eleven o'clock, in the safekeeping of Frau Hartnagel. This meant that Vogel could pursue his original plan, which he had decided on when he'd realized the woman was deceiving him. He would have her brother released and allow their sentimental reunion, after which he would have the boy sent back to Debno for immediate extermination and his sister to Ravensbruck, where the robust female guards would amuse themselves with her in their own inimitable fashion. Hedda had begun looking so tired of late, so unattractive, just like the ones before her.

The Mühler girl was another matter. Magdelene, the nineteen-year-old. She had been reporting to the main office regularly once a week, as ordered, and he had talked to her more than once in private. She appeared to be very fond of her father, the aging clerk who had been blatantly tuning in to the English radio, and had pleaded rather touchingly for his release from Buchenwald, on one occasion sinking to her knees in front of Vogel and clinging to his legs, crying uncontrollably. He had felt deeply moved, for she was a pretty child with large green eyes and a tender mouth. He had assured her that provided she did nothing to arouse the disapproval of the Gestapo, he would keep an eye on her father and see that he came to no harm.

Her apartment, from the reports given him by Fritz, his personal driver, was rather seedy, and in the Siemenstadt district, inconveniently distant from Headquarters. He had decided to install her in a pleasant little suite in Charlottenburg, once the property of a Jewish composer who was now at Sachsenhausen Camp. It was cozy there, and had its own private entrance from the street. The time was getting close when he would visit her there and see her for the first time in all her exquisite nakedness. He had already ordered a gold bracelet for her, from Buchenwald.

Below his window, along the Wilhelmstrasse, the late traffic was quiet, punctuated occasionally by the slam of a taxi door. It was his city down there, he often fancied, a place where the people went about their lives according to their own lawful decisions, until he reached down with his hand and moved them like pieces on a chessboard. Here he wielded enormous power, and could bring terror into the eyes of anyone he chose.

Magdelene. He remembered the terror in her eyes when he had first noticed her in the main office. It always moved him greatly, to see it in a young and pretty woman.

His thoughts were merging with the first scenes of a dream when the knocking on the door aroused him.

"What is it?"

A man was calling through the closed door, but he didn't catch all the words. It was something about a prisoner. He was out of bed at once: it sounded important.

He switched on the lamp, went to the door and unlocked it.

During the rest of his lifetime, which lasted another five seconds, his conscious impressions were confused. He had expected to see a black uniform on the man outside his door, but this man's uniform was light gray. A second man, in black uniform, was lying on the parquet floor with his head at an awkward angle and one hand flung out. The man who had knocked was Der Jäger, and for an instant Vogel saw him as a ghost— as someone who could not possibly be here at this or any other time of the night; then he remembered that Der Jäger was not dead, but a prisoner. These impressions were crowding in upon one another with the speed and complexity of a kaleidoscope, but one memory leapt into dazzling clarity: Der Jäger was insane, a homicidal maniac. This was how he looked now, in the light of the bedside lamp. The pale, cadaverous face was rage incarnate, the eyes ablaze and narrowed like those of a predator in the instant of the kill.

Karl Vogel, for the first and last time in his life, discovered for himself the meaning of terror as he faced the man who was here to bring him his death. His final impression was of Der Jäger's open hand rising against his face, the heel of the palm driving the nose bone with tremendous force into the brain and giving his distorted features the look of a clown with crimson make-up as he crashed backward to the floor.

*   *   *

It was at 1:06 a.m. when Unterscharführer Bittrich, on night duty in the 49th Battalion Transport Pool, saw the Standartenführer approaching him from the main gates. As soon as he seemed appropriately close, the Sergeant saluted. As the salute was returned, he noticed that the Colonel's right wrist was covered in blood. He of course made no comment: there had been an accident of some sort and if the Colonel wanted to ask for first aid, he would do that.

"Get me a car, Unterscharführer."

"At once, Herr Standartenführer! May I file the requisition form?"

"There's no form. I am on urgent business of the Reich."

"Yes, Herr Standartenführer. But I'll need your—"

"Get me a car, at the double, before I slam you on a charge!"

The threat was serious, coming from a Colonel, but Sergeant Bittrich might have still held out, knowing the strictness of the regulations on the requisitioning of a vehicle; but it was the expression on the officer's face that got him moving. He looked, as the Sergeant told the Kommandant of Transport later, "like someone straight from Hell."

34

DEBNO, POLAND, 26 MARCH

The prisoner staff at Debno Camp were not men of
property. Some of them who had been sent here for
extermination, but who had been selected to work as
slaves for as long as their work was satisfactory and
their conduct impeccable, had recently owned busi-
nesses, offices, town and country houses and all the
appurtenances of men of affairs; but on the day after
their arrival at the camp they owned nothing. They
possessed not a pencil, a handkerchief, a coin or a
comb; their nakedness was covered by borrowed rags,
and that was all. For a prisoner to have worn a wristwatch would have meant instant death, for he could
only have stolen it.

Yet tonight there were four wristwatches ticking off
the seconds in their secret hiding places among the four
barrack blocks where the prisoners slept. Three of them
had been taken from new arrivals on their way to the
extermination chamber, on promise of return. The
fourth had been taken, more recently, from a dead man,
and brought to Kurt Wolff. An hour ago the four
watches had been synchronized.

It was now ten minutes to three, and Kurt Wolff, the
block senior of B Block, was standing just inside the
open end of the barrack, eyeing the night. The Ingersol

watch that had been brought to him by Georg Todt, the second-in-command of his operation, was now strapped to his wrist. Fifty yards away, across the dried mud floor of the compound, Franz von Gerlach was waiting inside the entrance of A Block. Each breath he took was heady to him, like the aroma of wine. At right angles, near the extermination chamber, Willi Helm was squatting in the north doorway of C Block, bouncing gently on his heels to keep his leg muscles exercised. The feeling in him was not unfamiliar; he had felt this tingling tension in his nerves when he'd waited in the dressing room before going on to the courts in a major tournament. In D Block, closer to the main gates, Georg Todt was waiting. An ex-policeman, his mood was steadier; he privately estimated that even if the outbreak succeeded, only a handful of prisoners would ever see permanent freedom. A watch ticked on his left wrist, below the sleeve of his SS uniform; a service revolver was holstered at his waist.

"Where did you find these?" Kurt had whispered, earlier.

"They're Corporal Hoepner's."

Kurt had gripped his arm. "Is he dead?"

"I saw that sniveling bastard Schmidt on the prowl, and followed him. I heard him talking to Hoepner through the open door of the guardroom. He was giving the game away."

Kurt had gone pale. *"It was as close as that?"*

"He's gone to Jesus now," Georg grunted.

"How did you get Hoepner?"

"I went in there fast, don't worry. Thing is, they never think you're going to do anything to them. They're like sitting pigeons."

"That's why it's going to be easy, tonight."

"No," Georg had said quietly, "it's not going to be easy."

At five minutes to three, one of the perimeter guards was patrolling with his dog between the cremation pits and the Chamber; the other was passing the main gates, almost opposite on the far side. One of the four watch-tower guards had just lit a cigarette, shielding the match because for this he could be stripped of his rank. There was no movement from the other three, but their steel-helmeted figures could be seen from the main compound, silhouetted against the clear night sky.

In the meadow, the heaped ashes in the big crema-tion pits were still glowing, and the cobbled skulls of the six hundred Poles who had arrived that morning shone white in the starlight. From somewhere near the Chamber the infant was still crying.

They had tried to find it. The sound had begun about midnight, long after the prisoners were in their com-munal bunks. A mother, realizing what was to become of her and her family, must have managed to hide her child beneath a hut—there was no other shelter here—in the hope that it might somehow be saved. None of the guards had heard its crying, or by now it would have been butchered on a bayonet. Kurt Wolff had or-ganized units of his fellow prisoners to locate the sound, but in vain. The infant must have crawled underneath the wire, escaping electric shock by a miracle and moving out of reach of the prisoners who might have saved it.

Its plaintive voice had been driving some of them mad as they stood helplessly. The perimeter guards must be deaf tonight—or they simply couldn't be bothered to find the brat and finish it off.

The prisoners were scared, most of them, of what they were planning to do. Many of them realized that the chances were thin of getting out of here alive, even with three hundred and forty of them against only fifty SS officers and men. But they were risking all, because they were desperate, and their desperation would lend them strength. Until tonight there had been no anger in them, of the kind that will lend one man the strength of ten; but tonight as they stood silently waiting they heard the thin crying of the infant beyond the wire, and were moved to a fury they had never known before. It was a favor from the gods that they should be moved by this much anger, and armed by this much strength as the minutes ran out toward their testing time.

At two minutes past three by the watch on Kurt Wolff's wrist he was into the night quarters guardroom and at the throat of the SS corporal who sat there playing patience. He had no time to cry out.

Within the next five minutes the five guardrooms between the extermination chamber and the main gates had been invaded, and there had been no sound but that of the opening and closing of doors. Kurt had drilled the teams on this, time and again: *Too much noise in the first phase and we're done for.*

By fifteen minutes past three o'clock there were twelve prisoners fitted out in SS uniforms, each with a gun at his hip and a makeshift yellow armband on the left sleeve to distinguish him later as a friend. The guardroom lights had been left burning, with the bodies of the guards pushed out of immediate sight.

At this stage Willi Helm had the urge to go berserk and yell his way to the attack on the gates, but was aware of the critical danger. It was simply that his blood was up and the initial success was driving him to action that must wait, and take its time. He was young and could feel the sense of freedom surging through his body.

Franz von Gerlach had killed for the first time in his life, and found it unremarkable, an anticlimax after the death he'd seen dealt out to thousands since he'd been here. One dead SS guard was nothing; now there was a man, now there was a doll with its neck broken. But with the dead man's gun in his hand, Franz felt closer to freedom than he had ever believed possible.

It was the word they had been murmuring, all of

them, during the past weeks of clandestine preparation: *Freiheit.*

A moment before 3:20 one of the guard dogs started barking. No one knew why. Had it at last heard the infant crying? Or was it puzzled by the unusual sounds of movement among the huts? Whatever the reason it was a signal for Kurt Wolff to make a sudden change of plan and postpone an attack-by-stealth on the workshop area for the cutting tools they needed for the wire. He sent Georg Todt, his second-in-command, to hold the attack while he made his way past D Block on the north-side to appear from the front of the gatehouse, where the watchtower guards could see him in the starlight. In the uniform of an Unterscharführer he walked briskly to the base of the main-gate tower and called up to the guard.

"Message from Sergeant Steiger!"

He climbed the rungs of the broad wooden ladder, a piece of paper in one hand.

"What's all that noise down there?" asked the helmeted guard as Kurt neared the platform.

"What noise?"

"Doors slamming. Have they got a party on?"

The SS NCOs would often hold a party in one of the guardrooms, for a birthday or to celebrate a promotion; the schnapps would flow and they'd go to their bunks sick-drunk after rousting out a prisoner or two and baiting them to death.

"Yes, Scharführer Berger's been promoted," Kurt told the guard. "Didn't you know?" He had four steps to go. The guard was looking down at him, the machine gun beside him.

"Berger went on leave two days ago. Who are you?"

"You giving lip to an Unterscharführer, are you? What's your name?"

Three steps.

"Sturmann Wehner."

"Sturmann Wehner what? You forgotten how to address a noncommissioned officer?"

Two steps.

Kurt Wolff had told Georg: *If anything goes wrong at the watchtower, you take over and launch the assault.*

The sweat was breaking out on him and his heart was banging in his ribs.

"What's your name, then, Unterscharführer?"

"Fichte. I got here yesterday."

One step more to the platform. He could already see the man's eyes as he stared down at him, his hand on his gun, the big steel helmet outlined against the stars. Kurt had rehearsed this phase a hundred times, using one of the ladders to the upper bunks in B Block. He'd decided not to climb to the watchtower with his own gun concealed behind him and ready to use, because his one-handed ascent would look awkward from above and cause suspicion. There was a killing drop of thirty feet, if the guard chose to put a boot on his hand.

"Fichte?" came the voice from above him. "I've never heard of you." Panic came into his tone and he went for his gun. *"Halt and be recognized!"*

Kurt reached up and hooked a hand over the man's belt and dragged downward, clinging to the ladder and bringing his weight low, flexing his legs and feeling the guard begin to topple. The man's helmet struck the roof post as he lost his balance and fell, one boot catching the top of the ladder and then clearing it as his body turned over head first. He screamed once and Kurt heard him bounce against the ladder and fall clear again and then hit the ground thirty feet below, his steel helmet rattling against the hard packed mud.

The man's scream had set the two dogs barking but Kurt was on the platform now and crouched against the machine gun, releasing the safety catch and sending the first fusillade crashing into the silence with the long ribbed muzzle aimed at the nearest watchtower.

My job's to knock out the tower guards, he'd told his

teams. *As soon as I stop firing I want the towers manned.*

As the cordite fumes clouded from the gun he watched the dull red tracer bullets stitching through the gloom. The daytime standard ammunition belts were changed every evening to tracers, but the starlight was bright enough to reveal the tall shapes of the other three watchtowers and he now altered his aim to the second. The first guard was dead: Kurt had seen the tracers smashing into the roof posts and bringing white splinters away as they traversed the platform and caught the guard in the line of fire. A scream was coming from the second tower now, shrilling above the baying of the dogs below, and something clanged to the ground, maybe the man's helmet. Kurt swung his machine gun to the left and brought his aim on to the third tower as a dull red chain of tracer bullets began streaming toward him: the guard had caught on to what was happening and was exchanging his fire.

Tracers curved in to Kurt's platform and he dropped low as they crashed into the roof posts with a force that shook the tower. Splinters flew against his face and a bullet struck the machine gun, deflecting and plowing upward into the wooden canopy. Kurt kept low but locked his finger against the trigger, pumping out the shot as he traversed and retraversed the source of the enemy fire. A tracer caught his shoulder and spun him around, half-pitching him off the platform as his hands flew out for something to hold on to; the gun swung its long muzzle skyward but his finger was off the trigger and there was no sound but the barking of the dogs and voices calling from over by the SS Residential quarters outside the camp.

Kurt got to his knees, pain flaring in his left shoulder and blood streaming from it. But the third tower was silent and he could hear Georg Todt using the whistle he'd taken from a guard. It was the signal for manning the towers.

Below him, Franz was sprinting across the compound with his team of five, one of them wielding the crowbar that had lain in hiding for three weeks under a plank in the floor of B Block. They reached the door of the workshop, sprang its hinges and found what they wanted: the five long-handled wire-cutters with insulated grips.

Willi Helm had not moved since he and his team had taken up their positions, ten of them dispersed throughout the barrack blocks with rags soaked in wood alcohol and ready to fire.

Phase One, Kurt had ordered them, *has got to be dead quiet. Phase Two, when I start using the tower gun, is going to alert the SS in the Residential Block. Make as much noise as you like after that—it's flat out and every man to his job. But wait till the signal for Phase Three: it'll be short blasts on the whistles, from near the gates. After that, hell's going to break loose.*

Georg Todt and his team were running for the towers and climbing to the platforms, kicking aside the bodies of the guards and manning the guns, bringing their aim to bear on the main gates. Lights were on in the Residential buildings half a mile from the main camp, and headlight beams were swinging down the curving track and probing the dust.

They won't have a target, at first, Kurt had said. *They won't know what's happening. But when you hear the armored car start up, or see it on the track, give the Phase Three signal.*

Voices were still calling out from the higher ground, asking questions and getting no answers. A handler had opened the doors of the kennels and a group of dogs began racing alongside the vehicles, barking in excitement. Like their masters, they didn't understand what was happening; but they'd been trained to attack, hold or kill any man in striped uniform and that was what they would do when they got inside the wire. Kurt had ordered: *The man in Tower 4 is to get the dogs before the pack breaks up. A dog can scent and outrun a man and the guards can't. Once we're clear of the camp we don't want those brutes after us.*

The man in Tower 4 was already sending his tracers into the body of the pack, but one or two of them were darting to the side, where they were hidden by the vehicles. The gun shifted aim and the windscreens shattered and a man screamed somewhere as the withering fire swept across the track; two of the scout cars hit and went swerving off course, their drivers dead.

Kurt Wolff hadn't moved. He was hanging from the top rung of the ladder to Tower 1, trying with one hand to haul himself up to the platform. One of his team found him there, as soon as it was realized that the gun was silent. Three others brought Kurt down the ladder, the blood from his bullet-torn arm smothering them. A fifth man went up to the gun and swung the long muzzle to cover the track from the Residential quarters as whistles began blowing from below. It was the signal for Phase Three: someone had heard the heavy throbbing of the armored car starting up, and the position was suddenly critical. *Once they bring the armored car into action we'll lose the towers,* Kurt had warned them. *It can pick off the gun crews in safety. When the whistles blow for Phase Three, you're to abandon the towers, fire the barracks and go for the break in the wire. After that, it's every man for himself.*

Flamelight was already flickering in the open doorways of the barrack blocks as Willi Helm and his team lit their flares under the heaped straw paliasses, and smoke began pouring across the compound. One of the team had raced to the main guardroom and set off the alarm bells and sirens, and the night was filled with their sound. *In the last phase,* Kurt had said, *we create confusion. Fire and smoke, bells, sirens, the whole lot.*

*It'll give us the cover we need for the break through
the wire.*

Two minutes ago Georg Todt had smashed the main
junction box for the camp floodlights, and now the
compound was dark with rolling smoke as the barracks
took fire and the flames began spreading. The SS contingent approaching from the Residential quarters was
going into a choking, blinding inferno.

On the far side from the gates a breach fifty feet wide
had been made in the electrified wire as Franz and his
team worked with the cutters. A dozen men were
through and running and the main mass of prisoners
was surging toward the gap.

"Where's Kurt?" Franz called.

"He got hit!"

Franz swung around and stared through the pall of
orange smoke that covered the compound.

"They're bringing him through!" a man shouted.
"Anton's got him, and Hans!"

Franz cursed and moved clear as the prisoners
swarmed for the gap in the wire. Others, he saw, were
holding back, though there was room enough.

"What's wrong?" he yelled at them above the roar
of the burning huts. They didn't answer, but stood
huddled in the smoke, coughing and groping blindly
for clear air; and Franz realized they were afraid of
leaving the camp, of going into the unknown.

"Make a run for it!" he shouted to them, waving them
to the gap. But they still held back, and he left them.

The guns in the towers were silent now as the crews
abandoned them. The armored car was through the
main gates with its lights swinging across the smoke-
screen. A prisoner ran forward and clung for a moment
against the armored panels, thrusting his revolver inside and firing wild; then he reeled back as a shot hit
him and threw him to the ground. Kommandant Axen
was leading a group of his SS guards on foot, trying
to find the site of the main action as two of the

battle-trained Alsatians went racing past, one of them downing a prisoner and tearing at his face. The fire bells and the main alarm siren were still ringing, and men standing close to each other had to yell to be heard.

"How many down that way, Franz?"

"Twenty or thirty. They're bringing some wounded."

"There won't be time for the wounded . . ."

After that, Kurt had told them, *it's every man for himself.*

But Kurt was no longer with them. He lay at the base of a watchtower, his legs doubled under him and a bullet in his brain, a stray shot from one of the SS guards.

The armored car was rolling across the main compound, its driver half-blinded by the smoke but moving on, looking for the break in the wire that he knew he would find. Already its front wheels were bumping over the prone bodies of men in prison stripes who had tripped or been shot down by the Kommandant's guards. The action was concentrated to the north, toward the cremation pits in the meadow, and the vehicle made its way past the extermination chamber, past the hut where the dental surgeons kept their vigil, past the low wooden platform where the Kommandant played his violin through the mild spring evenings; and at twenty to four, forty minutes after Kurt Wolff had led his teams into action, the lights of the armored car picked out the mass of prisoners still clambering for the break in the wire, and the two gunners opened fire.

Six blazing cans of wood alcohol came swinging through the smoke at the vehicle and a man fired wild, trying to hit the crew through the vision slits in the armor, but the guns worked on, traversing patiently across the mass of prisoners, taking their time.

"Where's Kurt?" a man yelled.

"Dead. Got hit!"

A dozen men were through the gap and running, but

the two guard dogs were at their heels, their jaws white
in the starlight as they reached the meadow and downed
a man.

"Where's Franz?"

No one answered.

"Paul, are you hit?"

"Leave me, for God's sake! Run!"

The staccato beat of the two machine guns kept on
unhurriedly, its rhythmic percussion sharper than the
roaring of the flames; the voices of men and dogs rose
more faintly as the first of the prisoners through the
wire spread out and ran through the night.

There were not many.

"Freiheit!" a man screamed, but no one was listening
as he pitched forward with his skeleton hands clawing
at the new spring grass, a bullet in his neck.

If we've got to, Franz had said, we'll die out there.
But we'll die free.

The two guns puckered at the night.

Among the dead leaves of winter, below the elm
trees that formed a knoll of spring green near the
meadow, a stray bullet from the armored car hit the
small shape that had crawled there hours ago, and its
crying was stilled.

Martin climbed on to the boot of the Mercedes again
and watched the skyline to the east. The conflagration
was dying, and the shooting had stopped. He had
reached the barn an hour ago, soon after the first machine gun had barked into life from one of the camp
watchtowers.

Smoke was on the air, drifting on the soft night wind.

Franz had not come.

From this distance it was difficult to make out
whether any of the prisoners had got clear. The sounds
had been confusing: shooting, shouting, sometimes the
movement of vehicles. The last long fusillade had

THE DAMOCLES SWORD 363

ended suddenly, as if it had been decisive, with nothing more to be done.

There had been no vehicles along the road here, beside the railway. If anyone in the village had heard the noise, they hadn't inquired.

Two or three times Martin had left the car and walked a short way toward the camp, looking for Franz; but it was risky. The boy might come from any direction, making a detour in the faint light, to find a deserted car and keep on moving, hoping to make distance before dawn.

Martin stood watching the glow of the smoldering huts. White smoke had begun rising a few minutes ago; or perhaps it was steam from the fire hoses; Kommandant Axen was a man to restore order as soon as possible. Rooks were still calling from the elms, awakened by the false dawn of the fire. They would find carrion tomorrow.

Before going through the frontier post into Poland, Martin had torn his handkerchief in half and bandaged his wrists, so as not to attract further attention. The bleeding had stopped soon after he'd left Gestapo Headquarters: he had chafed at the veins with the knurled winder of his wristwatch, leaving the arteries untouched. If the guard had used his head he'd have seen there was no great loss of blood; but he'd panicked, because this was their star prisoner.

The taxi driver had noticed the blood on Martin's wrists when he'd paid the fare at the gates of the SS barracks. So had the transport sergeant. They'd remember. The moment the dead guard was found in Cell 9 there'd be a hue and cry; it would have started already. It was possible that at some time during the night the SS number plate of this Mercedes had been reported throughout the police networks.

The longer he waited here, the greater his chances of being caught. But he would wait till first light, in three hours from now.

One of the dogs was still barking excitedly, and men's voices called. They were still hunting stragglers in the fields and woods.

He had been mad to listen to Franz. He should have got him out of the camp two days ago: there'd never been a chance for him.

By five o'clock the glow of the fire had died away to darkness, and the barking had stopped. Soon afterward the floodlights suddenly came on: they would have been put out of action when the escape was launched, and now the damage had been repaired. Smoke still drifted from the camp, blotting out some of the stars overhead, even at this distance. The rooks began calling again, confused by the light.

It was nearly six o'clock when Martin heard a sound in the undergrowth, and moved cautiously toward it. He found the boy in striped rags crawling on his stomach toward the barn, his left leg dark with blood.

Martin lifted him, and carried him to the car.

35

BERLIN, 26 MARCH 1940

The telephone rang soon after eight o'clock, in the house in the Grünewald.

Frau Hartnagel answered it, red-eyed from lack of sleep.

"Who is it?"

For a moment there was silence, save for the faint crackling on the line. Then a man's voice came tonelessly.

"I would like to know if—" He broke off. Frau Hartnagel was puzzled. He began again. "I would like any news of Fräulein von Gerlach."

A sound came from the stairs, and she glanced over her shoulder; but it wasn't Hedda. The old house was creaking as the morning sunshine warmed it. Hedda would still be sleeping.

"She is better now," Frau Hartnagel said into the telephone. "Much better."

Again the man was silent, until she had to ask, "Hello?"

"I'm still here," he said in a moment. "Don't ring off." There was more life in his voice now. "You say she is *better*?"

"Yes. Yes. I got her to take a little broth, when we

came back. Now she is stronger, but still sleeping. Who is this, please?"

"I'm talking of Fräulein von Gerlach, you understand. And you say she is better?"

"But yes! She will be all right now! Who are you, please?"

"My name is Martin. Would it be possible to speak to her?"

"No, mein Herr. I could not allow that. She must have her sleep out. But you may telephone again in an hour or two, if you wish."

"Listen, please, *gnädige* Frau. Listen carefully. My name is Martin. Have you got that?"

"Yes. Yes. Herr Martin."

"Tell Fräulein von Gerlach that as soon as she is well enough she must go to her parents, in Regensburg. Tell her that her brother will be there tonight, or perhaps by tomorrow morning. Her brother Franz. Do you understand, *gnädige* Frau?"

"Yes. Of course. Her brother Franz." They must have released him, then. He had been sent to a prison camp somewhere. "I will give her your message, Herr Martin."

"Tell her to get a train to Regensburg as soon as she can. And please listen: you must not tell anyone else. For her sake. That's understood?"

"But, yes. I love her. I will tell her all you say, and no one else. She'll be so joyful, to hear about her brother."

36

REGENSBURG, BAVARIA, 26 MARCH 1940

General von Gerlach paced the room, from the hearth
to the windows and back, without stopping. Martin
had never seen so much restlessness, so much energy
locked inside a man.

"I remember you, of course, very well."

"I'd prefer you to forget me," Martin told him
quietly.

"I understand." For the first time he stopped by the
great stone hearth, hands on his hips. "I need hardly
say that I shall keep silence. My son has told me almost
nothing, but I suspect I owe you—we owe you, his
mother and I—our very deep gratitude." He looked up
at Martin.

"No, sir. Franz is his own man. He took his own
chances, and made his own escape."

The General's head came up. "Ah. Went straight at
it, did he? I'm glad." He turned for a moment as a
woman's laughter sounded faintly from another room,
then looked at Martin again in quiet disbelief. "Do
you know," he said slowly, "that it's the first time I've
heard my dear wife laughing since the day they arrested
him?"

"I can believe it."

"Yes. It's always harder for the women. For

mothers." He looked away. "Not that it was easy for me."

Martin thought he could hear Hedda's voice now. She'd reached here before him, two hours ago; it was now almost midnight. She and her brother had held on to each other for minutes, not speaking, while the tears had made their way down her face in silence, until Franz had released her, embarrassed, and begun to laugh in relief. Martin had left them, asking if he could use the telephone.

Otto Tempel had answered. *I shall always be here, at this number,* he'd told Martin at their last rendezvous by the bridge. *If I don't answer, you'll know I'm dead. Then you should take care. You'll be alone.*

He told Martin he would do what he could. The Hague was shut down now: the invasion of the Netherlands was imminent, according to intelligence reports. But he would try Switzerland, via London.

Later, Martin had tried to exchange a few words with Hedda, when for a moment they'd been alone in the dining room after the meal. But she would barely look at him, and refused to come close.

"You know what it means," was all she'd said, "for me to see my brother again." Her face was pale and she wouldn't meet his eyes. "All day, I've felt my life coming back."

"I'm happy for you."

She'd looked at him, then, fleetingly. "I don't understand how you can talk to me, or be in the same room with me. All I—all I want you to know is that I'd rather have died than do what I did to you, and that's—that's why I tried. But first I had to save my brother."

She'd gone quickly from the room, before he could stop her.

General von Gerlach was pacing again. "I need to know what the position is. Only you can tell me, of course."

"The position is that Franz and Hedda are still in immediate danger from the Gestapo. They'll find Franz is an escapee from the camp and they'll want him back, and the penalty for escaping is always death. They're liable to arrest Hedda as a reprisal. They might even come here."

"How soon?"

"As soon as tomorrow."

"What about you, Colonel Brinkmann? You prefer me to call you by that name, I assume."

"Just for tonight, I think I prefer to be called Martin Benedict. It's a long time since I've been among friends."

The General eyed him obliquely, trying to remember the tall young Englishman who had been his guest for a few days in 1936, only four years ago. He was now looking at a man who seemed to have aged ten years or more, his eyes haunted by what he had seen, his mouth set in an implacable line.

"Martin, then. What are your plans?"

"I've got to get out of Germany, if I can."

The older man considered, pacing more slowly. "I must tell you that I and certain friends will shortly be involved in a desperate enterprise. If we succeed, there will be great changes in Germany. If we fail, my life will be forfeit, and probably my wife's also. We are prepared to face the consequences. But we are not prepared deliberately to expose our children to danger. The fact that their lives are already at risk is none of my doing, but I'm not going to jeopardize them further. And yet, if I were free to carry out this enterprise, it could bring an end to the war." He came to a halt in front of Martin. "So you know what I'm asking of you. Asking you to consider."

"Franz won't leave Germany."

"What?"

"He wants to join the Allied escape teams. We talked about it on the way here in the car."

"I see. Would they have him—a German?"

"He's an anti-Nazi. They need them, on this side of the frontier." He looked at the General with compassion. "I don't think you'll dissuade him, sir." Franz had started to talk about it as soon as they'd left the country doctor's surgery in Furstenwalde, where his leg wound had been dressed. He'd had to strip Franz of his prison rags, telling the doctor he was an SS man who'd been left for dead after a skirmish with Polish partisans. The doctor had found some slacks and a sweater for him, much too big. "Now that I'm free," the boy had said with the same restless intensity as his father, "I want to work against them. I don't care how."

"I don't think I want to dissuade him," the General said, "from anything he's keen on doing. He's a man now, God knows."

"I've mentioned it to my network. They'll take him, if that's the decision. But whatever he does, he can't stay here long."

Von Gerlach turned away, hiding his pain. He'd watched his wife's suffering, all these months; now he'd have to tell her that by the morning, Franz would be gone again.

"I understand that," he nodded soberly. "But that leg of his won't mend for a while. He—"

"The bone wasn't touched, sir. And he'll be given medical attention. There are several doctors working with the escape lines, helping to get wounded men across."

The General stopped pacing again to face Martin. "Very well. That leaves my daughter." A quiet agony was in his voice. "I hardly recognized her."

"She's been worried sick about Franz." Martin looked away. "And there's been the stress of her work. The demands of an operating theater are pretty exacting." Intuitively he knew that Hedda would never tell her parents how close she'd been to death last night, or how much she'd suffered at the hands of Vogel for her brother's sake.

General von Gerlach turned away for a moment while he considered how to put his next question. There was too much pride, he thought, in his family; too much independence. In a moment he looked up at Martin. "I'm not a man for asking favors. Perhaps that's wrong. Perhaps in this war we're all going to need friends more than we realize. You say you must get out of Germany, if you can. To take someone else with you would hamper you, perhaps critically. But would you consider taking my daughter to safety?"

"I'd count it a privilege. But the risk is high."

37

WURTTEMBERG, SOUTH GERMANY,
27 MARCH 1940

It was midafternoon when the military patrol vehicle
began gaining ground on the SS staff car through the
low hills south of Ulm along the Donau River, and
Martin saw it closing on him in the driving mirror,
even though the needle on the speedometer of the big
Mercedes was showing 150 kph.

The rising note of a siren came thinly in the roar of
the slipstream and Martin slowed a little, waiting for
the military patrol to overtake him.

"Do they want us to stop?" Hedda called above the
noise. She was watching him anxiously; it was the first
time she'd spoken since they'd left Regensburg just before noon.

Martin didn't answer. He was watching the patrol
vehicle as it drew alongside, with its gray-uniformed
passenger waving for him to slow down.

Until this moment it had seemed that no reports
could have gone out concerning the Mercedes staff car
requisitioned from the SS barracks in Berlin yesterday
morning. Martin had considered taking General von
Gerlach's offer of one of the cars at the lodge; but it
could well be that his rank and uniform in an official
staff car might get them through the traffic faster, espe-

cially in the towns. Changing the number plate had also been considered; but it must carry the SS insignia, or it would attract immediate attention. To use the Mercedes for the two-hundred-kilometer run to the Swiss frontier south of Singen was a gamble, but there'd been no choice. The risk, as he'd warned the General, was high.

The military policeman in the other car was still gesturing to him to pull over. There was no traffic coming the other way, but the half-kilometer stretch of straight road gave way to mountain bends in the distance, and Martin put his foot down hard and drew ahead by half a length before he brought the big wheel over to the right, crowding the patrol car to the edge of the road. The driver reacted at once and the two cars touched, the wing of the patrol grating against the scuttle of the Mercedes with a scream of metal. Martin braked hard and changed down and gunned up again, getting control of the rear wheels and bringing the Mercedes across the bows of the patrol car again until its driver lost the steering as a front stub-axle sheared and sent the vehicle spinning as the wheel buckled with its hub gouging into the road surface. The patrol was totally out of control now and Martin gunned up again to drive clear, watching in the mirror as the other vehicle spun once more and then turned over, rolling across the edge of the road and smashing through the guard fence, dropping to the lower ground beyond.

Martin pulled the big Mercedes to a halt and jumped out, walking back to the wreckage of the patrol. Two of its crew were dead, but a man was crawling across the grass and trying to get up, reaching for his revolver; another was moving feebly in the wreckage, calling for help.

From the Mercedes, Hedda heard two shots; then Martin came back, his mouth in a hard line.

"We're still three hours from the frontier," he told her as he got behind the wheel, "and they're now on the lookout for us. I'm going to hide up somewhere till nightfall."

She had slept for an hour, curled up on the back seat of the Mercedes with Martin's greatcoat over her. The effects of the overdose were still lingering in her nerves, and the wrecking of the patrol car and the sound of the two shots had sickened her, though she'd said nothing; she knew it had been necessary.

Now she was awake, stretching her legs outside the car, watching the pale sunshine fading behind the clouds across the mountain range as the day began to die. Below, through the gap in the hills where the sheep-track ran, she could see occasional vehicles moving along the road. Martin had driven fast for an hour after leaving the wreck of the patrol, putting distance between them before it was found and the alert went out.

"When did you know?" she asked him at last.

"When she turned her head, and I saw she was some-one else."

"And what did you think?"

He came close to her, but she moved away, standing alone to stare into the dying light of the sky.

"You should get it off your mind, Hedda."

"Just forget?" Her smile was bitter.

"It's not worth remembering. We're still alive, both of us."

"No thanks to me," she said with sudden soft anger. "They would have shot you, if you hadn't escaped."

He saw there was no point in arguing.

"I love you," he said.

She turned to face him now, and spoke so softly that her voice barely carried on the mountain wind. "What did you say?"

"I love you. And I want you to forget everything else."

She didn't understand. Angry again now, she said, "You wanted to meet me, in the park by the lake, to tell me my brother was alive, and that you'd seen him. And I led you into a trap, knowing they'd probably kill you." Her voice broke on a note of anguish as she finished. "And you say you love me?"

He came close to her again and this time she didn't move, because this time she couldn't. "You're putting things the wrong way," he said, "that's all. You had the choice of saving your brother, a boy still in his teens being systematically brutalized in a prison camp, or saving me, almost a stranger, a grown man trained to look after himself in any situation. I would have done what you did. Anyone would."

Her sobs came so suddenly that he thought she was going to fall, and caught her and held her while she shook in his arms, minute after minute, until he had to begin talking quietly to her, his mouth against her dark hair, her tears on his face; and in the end she said in despair, her voice muffled against him, "I'll never feel clean again, Martin, don't you understand? I'll never feel whole."

"You fought harder for Franz than anyone will ever know. And now Vogel is dead. I killed him. And Franz is alive. And so am I. And I love you, for being what you are and for doing what you did."

She cried again, and he waited, stroking her hair.

"I don't understand," she said at last.

"One day you will, if we get through. It was your innocence and courage that gave me a kind of spiritual refuge in the midst of so much evil. I thought of you so often, as you were when we walked by the river before the war, and you'll never know how much it helped me."

She was quiet against him at last, drained of the guilt and self-disgust, making herself believe him; and he lifted her face and kissed it, and as the last of the day's light left the sky he drew her down and they lay together and made love, while the grasses moved beside them under the dark mountain wind, and he

tried to keep from his mind the fear that this was to
be the first time and the last.

The black Mercedes moved through the night.

South from the town of Singen the mountains rose
higher, and the hairpin bends became tighter as the
road plunged through the hills. There had been snow
here, and the black pines stood against the skyline as
the stars appeared.

Martin drove in silence, with the cold slipstream
whipping past his head. In Singen, where they had
stopped for refueling, he had telephoned the number
in Berlin. Tempel had said, "The Hague was shut down
three hours ago, but I called on diplomatic channels
through Paris. London has been in contact with Zurich,
and the Swiss frontier between Singen and the canton of
Thurgau will be open to you. Of course we could do
nothing about the German side."

A civil police patrol had driven into the service
station while Martin had been at the telephone; he'd
watched as a gendarme had strolled across to the Mercedes and spoken to Hedda. Martin's hand had rested
lightly on his holstered revolver until the patrol car had
refueled and driven off. The man had said it was a cold
night, for this time of the year, Hedda had told him
afterward.

"You must not try to cross the border on foot,"
Tempel had warned him. "There are many tracks
through the mountain passes, but none without snow.
Jews and others on the wanted lists have been trying
to cross into Switzerland every night since last September, but the SS have deployed ski patrols along the
border with orders to shoot on sight. The ground snow
presents good targets. Your only hope is the frontier
post on the road."

It was three miles ahead of them now, hidden from
sight by the snow-covered curves through the foothills.
The road itself was clear, with sand on its surface, but

the Mercedes began to slide through the worst of the hairpins and Martin had shifted gears. The roar of the slipstream was muted now and the engine throbbed in the quiet of the snows.

"I suggest you halt at the barrier," Tempel had said, "and use your authority. Tell them you have to survey the neutral zone as far as the Swiss checkpoint, something of that sort. I leave it to you."

Lights came fitfully through the pines as the Mercedes cleared the last curve and joined the straight section. He could make out a huddle of dark buildings with snow on their roofs; the lights came only from the lamps on the barrier: two red and two white, all that were permitted by the blackout regulations.

"If you succeed," Tempel had told him in his characteristic monotone, "I would be obliged if you would let me know by telephone, from Switzerland. This number has been kept open expressly for you, and for my own safety I'm anxious to close it down. Good luck."

The red and white lamps grew brighter.

"Is that the frontier post?" asked Hedda.

"Yes."

In a moment she asked, "Will it be all right?"

"I don't see why not." Unseen by her, his right hand was unclipping the flap of his holster.

The throbbing of the big engine died as he slowed toward the buildings. They were no more than large huts, he saw now. The barrier was a single length of timber, a pine trunk, stripped of its bark and painted. The thick end was hinged on a cement block; the other rested across a red-and-white painted oil drum, secured by an iron fork.

There were three guards. Two of them came slowly forward, shining their torches at the front of the Mercedes, then at the driver and passenger.

They were courteous, respectful, and adamant.

"We have our orders, you understand, Herr Standartenführer. We can do nothing."

"Tell the guard commander I want to see him."

The man came, sweeping the beam of his torch across the car, noting the number plate and insignia.

"I have to inspect the road through the neutral zone," Martin told him. "We're looking for a group of Jewish activists, as I'm sure you've been informed."

The guard commander had not been informed. His breath steamed in the frosty air as he looked from the SS-Standartenführer to the lady and back.

"I have not been informed. Who is this lady?"

"She's one of them. Her husband's attempting to cross on foot."

Earlier he'd considered hiding her in the boot of the car, but it was too risky. If he were asked to open it he couldn't refuse without causing suspicion, and if they had to try breaking their way through he wanted her to leave the car and make a run for it in the confusion.

"I have no orders to let anyone through, Herr Standartenführer. I regret."

Martin argued, but not too emphatically. This man was a stolid Bavarian and would harden at any attempt to bully him.

"I regret, Herr Standartenführer. You must turn back."

"Very well."

He climbed back into the car and turned it slowly, the tires grating across the loose sand, the headlights swinging past the two half-track vehicles and the scout car parked by the buildings.

He drove back into the hills.

At the border post the acrid smell from the exhaust faded, and the guard commander went back into the building.

"The SS," he told the two men, "think they own the whole of Germany."

"Too true," one of the men said. "But the girl was pretty."

"Yes, the girl was pretty."

The men went over to the brazier they'd set up, holding their gloved hands to its heat. They were there ten minutes later when the headlights of a car brightened from the distant curve in the foothills.

"Busy tonight," one of them said. "It's getting like the Kurfürstendamm." They got to their feet.

"He's going fast."

"Too fast."

They began waving their lamps.

The headlights grew bright, throwing their shadows against the barrier. They could hear the roar of the engine echoing from the hills.

When they realized the car was going too fast to pull up in time they ran to the side and drew their revolvers, one of them calling to the guard commander. Then the Mercedes was on them.

There was no room for a vehicle to pass on either side of the barrier, and Martin aimed the star mascot on the radiator at the thinner end of the pole, keeping his speed at the 100 kph mark and the headlights full on. Bursts of orange flame were coming from the guns on the left side of the barrier and a shot hit the wind screen and sent a blizzard of glass fragments into the slipstream as it shattered. Martin shielded his face with one arm, driving blind and feeling the rear wheels lose their grip on the sand as he swerved involuntarily, correcting and straightening and then sliding again as the road's camber pulled the weight of the car to one side.

Two more shots came, then a third as the guard commander came from the buildings, firing as he ran. Bullets were drumming on the metal of the long black bonnet and Martin felt a sudden burst of pain in his shoulder as he fought to pull the Mercedes out of the slewing action set up by the loose surface; then they hit the barrier and the car was slowed and he sensed Hedda pitching against the dashboard with her arm

crooked across her face as he'd told her to do w'
the impact came. The sand-filled oil drum bounced
the big car's momentum wrenched the pole from
fork and snapped it in the middle, the splinters flu
through the buckled windscreen frame as the air-r
caught them and whirled them back as another s
came and then another, one of them tearing the gl
from the back of Martin's hand and glancing off
windscreen pillar.

One of the headlamps was smashed and the ot
canted over, its single beam stabbing at an angle acr
the roadway as three more shots came and Martin
the gear lever, racing the engine into second and k'
ing the throttle down to thrust power to the rear wh
and send the car straight. Something had caught
tween a front wheel and the wing, and its scream
filled the night. The radiator had been pushed back
an angle, buckling the bonnet and wrenching one s
clear of the hinge; steam was blowing back from a b
pipe.

When the speed was high enough he changed i
top and kept his foot down until he saw the lamps
the Swiss checkpoint winking across the snows.

38

ZURICH, 28 MARCH 1940

They stood on the balcony of the hotel, looking down at a scene they'd almost forgotten: a city filled with light.

"What will you do?" Martin asked.

"I'm joining the Red Cross. I went for an interview this morning, while you were at the surgery. Does it still hurt?" They'd extracted the bullet and put his arm in a sling.

"They said three weeks, before I can use it again. That hurts."

"When you're better, what will you do?"

"Go home to London, and see my parents." He watched the pigeons curving and dipping through the light from the street. London wouldn't be like this; it would be dark.

"And then?" She moved closer against him, afraid of the question; but she wanted to be sure.

"Then I'm going back."

"Into Germany?"

"Yes."

"Will they make you go?"

"I'll ask them to send me. There's more to do there. Much more."

A shiver passed through her in the night air. "When will you go home, to London?"

"Soon." He held her closer. "But not for a day or two. They're flying someone out here to the Consulate first, to debrief me."

He'd tried to phone Tempel, late last night to tell him they'd got across safely; but the phone had gone on ringing and finally he'd put it down. *I'll always be here at this number,* Tempel had told him. *If there's no answer, you'll know I'm dead.*

The pigeons dipped and wheeled through the brightness.

"So we have a few more days," Hedda said. A slow breath was coming into her. "That's almost a lifetime."

ABOUT THE AUTHOR

Elleston Trevor is a rarity among novelists of the first rank. He has reached fame not only as Elleston Trevor, author of *Squadron Airborne* and *Flight of the Phoenix,* but also under the name Adam Hall as the creator of the supremely successful Quiller novels.

Having lived for many years in the South of France, Elleston Trevor now resides in Arizona.